CW00557841

ISBN: 9798393000585
Independently published

Cover design: Ian Feeney
Cover image: Sergey Nivens / Shutterstock

philip-parrish.com

By the same author

Game of Life

The Bleeding Horizon

Philip Parrish

To Sofia, for those younger times
when we would hold hands
and stare up together at the stars

O for a muse of fire, that would ascend
The brightest heaven of invention.

*William Shakespeare, somewhere on
an ellipsoid orbiting a minor star in the
Orion arm of the Milky Way galaxy*

To fall is to yield to a force beyond your control
ie. from height (gravity), under a spell (magic)
or in love (wow).

*Handwritten notes from an anonymous exercise
book found in the Gallagher School for Orphans*

I

The edge of the universe wasn't all it was cracked up to be. The temperature was a hundred clicks below the Hadesian line, dust devil winds burned bare flesh and a tumult of spicy smog shrouded heaven's outermost stars in a sickly, copper-coloured haze.

High in the mountains of Cys, the Tantalus Arms emptied its inebriated patrons into the desert night with a gaseous belch. Only one suction cup in the solar system's solitary cephalopod skybar remained open. Inside, a geriatric Andavarian tenor serenaded two dewy-eyed, terminally ill aphromorphs at the VIP table. Near the reptile-wrestling pit, a trio of cyclopic scavengers lay lashed on maroon pod bays, mumbling excavation yarns into the gambling portals.

The last goddam tune I'll ever hear, thought Lucius as he downed his final shot of M86 Throatwarmer. Waiting was the two-hearted bounty hunter's only play now. Waiting for his two Ogressian captors, sitting slab-faced either side of him, to drag his lacerated ass to the lava gulag. Waiting to accept his sentence from the odorous overlord of Omega-69. Waiting to have his soul sucked out by the singing spidergirls of Lestrygonia, who loved to lather their victims in Kublan honeydew before drawing the terminal bleed.

Wuuupppppaaahsssssshhaaajjjuuddeeeeerjuddderr cluckercluckaphssst. The sleeping doorslith, three hundred calcics of wobbly green flesh, rocketed across the vacated gyration zone and splattered into the optics of designer toxins above the bar. An inferno of XX chromosome swept into its space. Lucius recognised her from his datacast. *Electra Medici*. The Syphillian galaxy's most wanted. A hot blizzard of voluptuousness from the planet Norkus, rumoured to store the Fleece of Dragus under her scarlet spacesuit. She drew her Querff Company assault rifle and fired two plutonium parcels into the bloated bellies of his custodians. As their green guts seeped onto the sticky, sand-swept floor, osmotic tentacles twitching in tune, Lucius smirked.

Everything they said about Electra was true. The she-wolf fragrance. The crystalline eyes. The rolling, flame-coloured hair. She had journeyed fifteen celestial blocks to encircle his soul. Lucius's eyes locked onto her Arcadian amulet, a cut of pure eroticinium. The universe's most sacred gem. The jewel gave its owner second sight and lay like sunken treasure between a gravity distorting pair of-

"Adam!"

Outdoors on the unkept lawn, the other side of the dusty classroom window, The Pretty Girl In The Year Above with the big red backpack was glistening in the late afternoon sunshine. She was supposed to be painting a picture of the sea. Her easel was set apart from the other classmates. While they splashed their canvases with murky blues, the collage she crafted orbited a different sphere. Elegant, precise and suffused with reddish fragments torn from paper. Adam could see a grand flaming tower floating beacon-like above the waves, under which swirled lovely mermaids and lavishly detailed leviathans. A strange interpretation of the pale vista which formed the circumference of the orphanage's world. In the make-believe sky at the top of the picture was a white disc with swirling red at its centre. Sunset on a liquid Mars, seen through the eyes of an angelic aesthete from Venus.

"Stop daydreaming!"

A shrill sound from across the cosmos. The dragon had stirred, breathing fire from its dank pit. Adam sensed Miss Guffrey's squinting, slate-grey eyes zero in. He pictured the saliva drooling from her mouth, falling to the floor, melting the classroom tiles and seeping downwards to poison the earth's core.

"Pay attention and look at the board!"

The Pretty Girl In The Year Above was caressing the last scraps of paper onto the canvas. Despite the sea breeze, none blew away. Her red backpack, big enough to hold a Querff gun and both of Lucius's hearts, lay tucked under her stool. *Please turn round.* Adam wanted to see her immaculate face in the post-meridian light. Savour that constellation of incorruptible beauty no one else noticed. *Weirdo. Freak. Alien.* The vixens would shout these names as she swished serenely down the corridors. Lance said he'd once seen her alone in the woods on the other side of the island, sitting cross-legged and staring into a makeshift fire. Happy in her solitude.

"Are you listening to a word I'm saying?"

The reptile was advancing, dragging her gammy leg.

"Sorry Miss Guffrey, I thought I saw something out the window."

"Yes Adam. Your life passing you by."

Claws clasped on hips. Venom stewing behind the eyes. Slapped-on lavender lipstick. The bobbles on her fossil-grey cardigan reminded Adam of lunar craters. Below her yellowy-white matronly blouse was a long skirt the colour of graphite, which she probably ironed religiously every evening while spawning visions of geometric cruelty in her soul. Grey in dress. Grey in face. A creature who'd emerged fully formed from the leaden walls of the staff room. Her breath stank too, as if she'd just lowered twitching vermin by the tail into her slobbering chops. The whole school was like that. Bland, inconspicuous monsters lurked in every corner. *What a crazy idea. To turn an old prison for funny people into a place for lonely children.*

"Now you're back on planet Earth, please answer the question every other member of the class has managed."

"Sorry Miss can you –"

"*Whaaat* will you be when you grow up?"

3

The rest of the art class had headed to the dormitories, but The Pretty Girl In The Year Above wasn't finished. She'd seen them off one by one, like Electra. Maybe she would read Adam's story with second sight too. Softly prise him apart, sensitively tuning into the space-age symphonies stirring in his head, then leading him out of boredom's abyss on the blaze of a million mystical torches.

"The answer's on the board, Adam. Not on the bleedin' horizon."

Bleedin' was Miss Guffrey's favourite swear word. She was very tetchy. Adam suspected if pushed too far, she would run out the classroom and through the iron school gates howling like a coyote. Lance said he'd seen her one day in the science lab, shaking and alone, drinking the funny stuff and listening to *Message in a Bottle* by The Police. She liked to dress up as a man too. That's what Bill the caretaker told him, and Bill knew about people. Bill said she wanted to be mayor of the island one day.

"Explain to the whole class how you're going to help build a better world."

Adam never understood vocations hour. Terrifying kids for no good reason. On the whiteboard was A Great Big List of Ways to Spend the Rest of Your Life. He liked that so many began with A. An idea for a new comic-book heartthrob percolated in his mind. *Adam the Alliterative Argonaut. The aquatic assassin armed only with his alphabet.*

"I'd like to be an architect during the day," he said. "An astronaut at night. An artist at weekends. An author during my lunch break. And an archaeologist if I get the time. Then go on adventures with arctic explorers. 'Twould be ace."

"Did you know the chance of having a human life is like being picked up as one grain of sand out of all the grains on the beach?" Miss Guffrey replied, slivers of ice sliding from each word. "You just want to waste yours, don't you? Slip down the plughole into the sewer of emptiness. Away from the real world."

Adam looked down at his exercise book. A chirpy green mono-eyed extra-terrestrial in a UFO hurtled across a galaxy of A4 ruled paper towards the margins. He'd drawn it at the start of the lesson, inspired by an escapade in the Dyonisian Delta, where his alter-ego Lucius had stayed too long, won too big and made too many enemies at the crellenium tables.

"I don't like the real world, Miss."

"The real world doesn't like you either, DeBreeze. It doesn't like anyone who doesn't have a purpose."

"I *do* have a purpose." Adam rose from his chair in mock-indignation, painting a pretend sphere in the air with his hands. "I want to read a book that's written by an alien. To explore strange new worlds. To seek out new life and new civilizations. To boldly go where no man has gone bef-"

"Detention," spat Miss Guffrey, specks of saliva tapping him on the teeth. "In the tower. Two hours after school. Every day for the rest of the week. Starting today. Until then, you're in the corridor. When the rest of us go higher, you always go lower. What a limited little boy you are. There's nothing up there at all, is there? Ugly on the outside. Ugly on the inside. Your punishment will be to write an essay on what you want to do with your life. Tell us how you can make our world a better place."

There was nothing worth looking at in the corridor except closed doors. Uncommunicative rectangular blocks tamping toxic fumes. The medical room. The headteacher's room. The staff room. Lance said the teachers assembled there at weekends to drink petrol, steal another pupil's soul and perform Satanic rituals wearing costumes from the drama cupboard. Further down was the Dark Room, where the Bald Man Whose Name Nobody Knew made pictures come alive.

It was fortunate the school smelled of bleach because everybody dumped their garbage here. Nobody seemed in control of themselves. Especially the people in charge. They were all collateral damage in some invisible wizard's evil puppet show.

Adam's eyes wandered to the fire exit at the end of the corridor. There was a television-sized square of yellow sunshine, bottle green bushes and a hazy blue horizon. He imagined a magic remote control which could turn all the school's windows into screens, broadcasting *Star Trek* when it was pissing it down. All the computers in the building would come to life, finish his geography homework and take over the school in the name of enterprise.

"I am here."

A warm whisper from behind. A fluid visual breeze of rolling red hair that almost lifted Adam from the floor. The red backpack was over her left shoulder, the art folder tucked under her right arm. Fire flew with her. The Pretty Girl In The Year Above looked back once and grinned. Pale stardust danced around her supernova smile. Adam worried she might trigger the alarms. Petal by petal, red collage pieces slipped out the bottom of her folder. Like fluttering butterflies struggling to be airborne, they ascended and descended on the tempests of her languid motion, falling to the floor and forming a mosaic of roses on the bland ash-grey tiles. More flowed, until she was drenched in a fountain of scarlet, crimson and candy blush confetti, each a separate love song let loose. Then she was gone. Embers dipped and dissolved in the trembling space left behind.

"Take notice of what's around you for once," said Miss Guffrey twenty minutes later in the detention room, before slinking off down the spiral stairwell. "See if you can find some inspiration. *Put some heart into it.*"

The detention room in the tower was about six metres by six metres. The high ceilings were cracked, and the dusty floors were made with timber torn from Noah's ark. Lance said it was where the prison guards used to shut up the worst of the nutters. Supposedly it was infested with beetles, but Adam hadn't seen any yet. On the grey wall someone had unimaginatively scratched *I woz ere*. He looked out the window. In the distance was Gallers Cove. Access to the smugglers' portal was restricted to the padlocked gate in the safety fence, which led to narrow stone steps down the cliff face. Bill the caretaker kept the key up his ass, Lance reckoned.

Above and to the right was the staff entrance to the school. For the next ten minutes, Adam watched the lights of the teachers' cars exit under the huge iron 'G', turning right along the coast road to the real world. Lance said that sometimes, when she wasn't sacrificing stray cats, Miss Guffrey enjoyed a ride with the headteacher in his big black saloon car which came with satellite navigation. But that had stopped. No one saw much of Mr Droning around school anyway. Apparently, he owned an impressive set of golf clubs which he liked to show female teachers on his many days off.

Nothing had changed since Adam's last visit to the tower, the consequence of drawing an intergalactic battle in his science book instead of decoding the periodic table. Against one wall was a huge wooden bookcase with six shelves. In it were shoved volumes of every conceivable kind. Atlases, encyclopaedias, reference guides, dictionaries, children's fiction, serious fiction. Books with unpronounceable titles. Thick books, thin books, battered books.

On the opposite wall was the picture board, renamed The Picture Me Bored by Lance. The theme this week was Famous Italians. Julius Caesar being set upon by his classmates. Marco Polo asking for directions. Dante descending into the nine circles of hell. Galileo pointing at the sun. Christopher Columbus floating above three ships sailing into the sunset. Some guy called Machiavelli. A sexy lady in the buff on the beach at a place named Botticelli. DJ Marconi wearing headphones and tinkering on the decks. Adam's favourite Michelangelo, alongside a naked man trying to touch the fingertips of an old fogey. A real-life beetle scurried across space behind them. Not everything about this place was bullshit after all.

Through the window and from this elevated vantage point, he may even glimpse The Pretty Girl in the Year Above in her dormitory, which extended into the far right of frame towards the road. He imagined reaching across space. Their fingers intertwining to melt them both into another dimension. She would show him a red sky full of things no one else could see. He would watch the sun rise and set with every wave of her hair and turn of her hip.

After a few minutes gazing, Adam opened his art book to a blank page. A sketch of a defiant Amazonian queen soon materialised, a spear in each hand and his name tattooed on her exposed midriff. With enough time and patience, she would descend through the cracks in the ceiling to nurse his imaginary wounds, like a maiden caring for an injured knight by convent candlelight. Vows would be made, before they retired to a mountain castle for moonlight mythmaking.

The next evening, after two tedious hours listening to the science of coastal erosion, Adam saw The Pretty Girl in the Year Above again. Alone as always, sitting cross-legged on the beach of the cove. The sea wetted her pointy black leather shoes, buckles decorated with ancient romantic runes. Nobody else had a big red backpack like that. Nobody's hair lift and lilted peacefully in the sea breeze like deep sea coral. And nobody but her would be so brave as to go there alone. She must have climbed over the gate somehow or swooped down from her window like the serenest of swans.

"Don't bother your silly little head about her," said Miss Guffrey at the end of detention the next day when Adam recounted his vision. "She'll be leaving us next week. Sick in the brain. Seeing things apparently."

Adam didn't think Miss Guffrey should be saying things like that. She was always saying strange things and he didn't like any of them. Miss Guffrey wouldn't be mayor if she kept talking like that.

"Seeing things, Miss?"

"Yes. Lights, flashes. Patterns. She plays with matches that one. So they're going to cut her head open to see what's in there. Just empty space I imagine."

"I think they'll find she's the cleverest person in the world."

"Yeah right," said Miss Guffrey, folding her arms and squinting through the window at a big black car pulling out the school gates. "More like the oddest."

"We're all odd, Miss. Just one big family of odd. None of us are meant to be alone. We're meant to be connected. At one."

Miss Guffrey didn't respond. She was already gone, dissolving through the fog-grey walls of the detention tower in pursuit of the fleeing love-mobile.

The following night, The Pretty Girl in the Year Above returned to the cove. She wore a calypso-coloured swimsuit. The red backpack was nowhere to be seen. Hands confidently on hips, she was standing about ten metres out to sea, looking to the horizon. The surface of the unsettled water lolled and lapped around her knees. Adam imagined the hairs on her exposed flesh rising to the occasion, her sweet soul singeing away the frostiness of the sea.

She was going to make a break for it. To the mainland. Or some other place faraway. So they couldn't get into her mind.

Pressing his nose against the window, Adam tapped excitedly on the glass. She was too far away to hear. Balancing himself on a chair and holding the bookcase for support, he climbed until both feet were on the windowsill. The upper sash was jammed, so he couldn't even stretch his fingers into the chilly evening air.

"I am here," he shouted, banging the pane with his palm. "I am here. Why can't you see me? Take me with you. We'll go together!"

The Pretty Girl in the Year Above turned, looked up and smiled. Thunderclouds smashed and parted, leaving a dreamy space through which slid an avalanche of sunlight evaporating all the coldness of the mature world. She blew a kiss and waved, then breast-stroked merrily into the twilight before diving down below. A flicker of light, a spectral spark. A ball of white with a red flame at its centre hovered over the settling water. The orb exploded, particles of light travelling through the glass, into the detention room and illuminating the pictures on the board. Then it disappeared. The only sensation Adam could feel was his pounding heart. Thud. Thud. Thud.

When Miss Guffrey came by, Adam didn't say anything. He wanted his muse to have a head start. She wouldn't drown. She knew how to breathe in the deepest spaces, gliding unsurpassed through water throned by rings of protective fire. Adam spent the following night and day in disguised delirium. Mr Joyce warbled on about Greek myths. Lance jabbered on about *Star Trek: The Next Generation*. Both seemed like atomic vibrations on a distant star. Adam would close his eyes and slide silently into another world, emerging underwater alongside her. Together they would dive deeper into the dark, search for shipwrecks and see glowing red where everyone else saw blue. Then rise hand-in-hand into purified air on the surface of a magical shell, just like Miss Botticelli.

"What do you call this?" said Miss Guffrey the next evening, staring contemptuously at his drawing of a mermaid queen sifting her fingers through grains of make-believe sand. "Is this how you see your future?"

"I don't call it anything Miss. My life isn't something I see. It's something I feel."

"You don't come to school *to feel*, Adam. You come to school to acquire knowledge. To develop the skills to rise in society. To become an authority. To make your mark on the world. I told you to put your heart into this."

"My heart's at the bottom of the sea."

"Like all the other useless debris. Floating around with your horrible little face and your horrible little drawings. Flapping to the surface for air every so often like an ugly duckling. Going round and round in circles. I ought to hurl chunks of stale bread at you."

"And you're a horrible teacher. With a horrible little mind. That's why Mr Droning will never show you his golf clubs."

Adam happily took the extra two weeks of detention. The teachers never mentioned what happened to The Pretty Girl in the Year Above, like she'd just slipped into the orphanage's infamous black hole to join the other outcasts. Lance always suspected this was at the back of the boiler room where, according to legend, Bill the caretaker took care of himself. Every evening, Adam tried to write something about what he wanted to do with his life but could only decide he didn't want to be part of the real world. All he wanted to do was stare into the flames. *Her flames*. To look out to the horizon and believe there is more beyond. Or lie on his back and wait for invention to flood through the ceiling cracks, like Michelangelo all those years ago.

Soon one of his Italian friends regaled him with fabulous tales of how he'd braved the unknown to christen paradise in honour of his queen. From his picture on the wall, Christopher Columbus would relive his voyage into the void and how lights in the sky led his way. His crew would joke about falling off the edge of the earth. The drunken ones would plummet to hell. The purest would float up to join the stars. Every night, Columbus would pray before the evening sun for the sight of East India. Asleep, he would dream of falling to his knees and kissing sweet unsullied soil in an alien world. Until then he would steady himself under the sails and look longingly for a shoreline to rise and fall like the flickering of a candle. Not once did he mention the dysentery, the sinking of the Santa Maria or the decimation of gentler tribes. Columbus could be a smarmy twat when he wanted to be.

"I'm not sure where I'm heading," said Adam. "I'm not like anyone else around here."

"I often felt that way myself," replied his companion. Columbus spoke in a flabby, supercilious tone, like a self-important man heady on wine after a banquet with some well-heeled chums. "I went looking for a quicker route and discovered paradise. Such is the power of following your dreams."

"She is a dream, Columbus. What do you think she saw out there?"

"Your infanta wasn't seeing anything. She was *feeling it*. The first flushes of a fiery new world within. She's not meant to be above the waves. She belongs down below. In the deepest places. Where all the best journeys begin."

"I want to feel that too. I'll travel to the edge of the universe if I have to."

"Just as well," said Columbus, floating on fumes of verbal flatulence. "To follow your dreams means going into the dark. To the grown-up world. Chase it too hard and you'll be swallowed up. If you're not careful, it will take over and leave you all alone. Some go exploring to acquire power.

Others to receive inspiration. On my voyage, I learned to trust in my own stars. That's the art, the very essence, of adventure."

"Ok Mr Plummy Voice. What do my stars show?"

The world's most famous explorer extended his right arm out of the picture and waved it pretentiously from side-to-side. The detention room's electric lights switched off. With a gentle hum, an ethereal white glow emanated from the space above Columbus's palm, illuminating the static figures of Caesar, Marco Polo, Dante, Galileo, Machiavelli, Marconi, Miss Botticelli and Michelangelo's bromance. Coalescing into a small sphere of light no bigger than a tennis ball, it drifted across empty space like a roving, autonomous eyeball.

In the orb's heart, Adam thought he saw a tiny spectral figure, flickering and feinting in red. The intensifying whiteness bled through the window of the tower, leaving a spectral trail of milky-coloured smoke suspended in space. In the sky, a solitary white star was born from the blackness. The first one Adam had seen that evening. Another to the right. One more below. Soon the tower dissolved, and the roof of the universe glittered with magical stardust from a thousand untravelled worlds.

Rising upwards to meet them was a small wooden boat with a single sail, bobbing on magical waves. Columbus had stepped out of his frame, dragging a long black cloak with him. He was a squat, uninspiring figure, filling a chestnut brown doublet embroidered in gold with a plump belly that had known too many flagons of port. The adventurer smiled as he waited for Adam to act, admiring the manicured nails on his left hand and presumably recalling with fondness his commutes between Lisbon and the Bahamas.

Adam boarded the vessel with a manly charge, the soles of his brogues clattering on wood. He hoisted the sail and headed to the bow. Columbus minced in behind him and sat insouciantly at the stern. The Pretty Girl In The Year Above was out there. Hovering above and below. A constellation of perfect luminosity. Adam would sail away from the tower, the orphanage and the island. One day he would find her and look upon a new world. Witness what she had seen in her mind's eye, then torch the night sky with the smouldering fires of their love.

"What if I don't reach her in time? What if I don't discover anything? What if there's nothing there at all?"

"Such risks come with the territory," said Columbus. He had the self-congratulatory air of a man who knew the ending to this story. "All stars look random to begin with. Lost in space. Eventually they collide. Everything's heading to the same place. You must trust in the invisible hand guiding us all. Things unfold in their own time. The longest way round is the shortest way home."

In life's loneliest moments, Adam would return to the boat with his friend and slip out to sea. Watch the guiding stars sparkle on the transient apexes of the waves. Recall the red petals, rising, falling and settling in the corridor. Each different in shape, shade and trajectory, charged with mystical allure. A thousand and one stories, scattered to the wind only to whirl back on themselves and reunite on the surging currents of his blood.

If Adam could sculpt them all together into a single masterpiece, the world would indeed be a better place. The dream would be an adventure like no other. Even if he had to wait a lifetime for it to sail sleepily through the void in his broken heart.

II

The quarantined island of Galatea. Twenty-one years after the Fall.

The black amorphous shape must have arrived by boat, because there was no other sane way to the island. Swelling up from the wine-dark sea, it advanced assuredly through the red haze. This wasn't the sea creature. That was watching patiently from the waves and hadn't moved towards land yet.

Night watchman Rex Tuckman removed his Glock 19 pistol from the desk drawer and checked it was loaded. He'd woken from an early evening dream of his father telling him not to sit around waiting to die but to go fishing at the lake. Later he would leave the portacabin, whack golf balls into the void then retire for the night to tell himself another bedtime story about a middle-aged man-about-town and two twentysomething female tourists.

Now he had a visitor. The first for six months, since a hapless PRISM surveying team dressed in yellow and black boiler suits arrived on a trawler to scout the contaminated land for plastic. They wandered like children through the decrepit pleasure pit, mesmerised by the fairground carousel which still rotated and tinkled. *We'll send someone to pick you up*, one of the square-jawed simpletons said when leaving. *We can still win this war.* The system hadn't spat anything out since. Except two crippled seagulls which Rex stalked with relish before administering the *coup de grâce*.

A tall man in a long coat was visible through the dirty, cracked window. He had a climber's rucksack strapped to his back. A grubby white vest was tucked into his grey, weathered combats. Locks of dark, curly chainmail hair ran to his shoulders. A gaunt figure, like an emaciated lion, reminiscent of the malnourished prisoners Rex used to marshal into PRISM's camps. Handsome though. And seeing as he'd made it out this far, clearly crazy. Dry as a bone too. Rex slipped the gun behind him, shoving the barrel into the waistline of his tea-stained canvas trousers. This was love at first sight.

"If you're here for the wet t-shirt competition, you're too late."

"I've come to see the tower."

"Tourist season is over pal," Rex grunted, pointing to the sign in the window. NO ACCESS PERMITTED TO ANY OUTSIDERS. The stranger's eyes were drawn to the decal of a dove bearing the legend PEACE ON EARTH. A sardonic joke from the previous security officer, long since retired for what PRISM called 'the affliction of cognitive dissonance'.

"You're two decades behind schedule. All paths terminate here. The campers have packed up. The rides are shut. Evening entertainment is just me, shaking my maracas. Awaiting the presence of the sublime."

Rex curled the fingers on his right hand to meet his thumb and flicked his wrist back and forth, gesturing to the magazine lying open on his desk. Under the headline NOT IN MY MESS, OFFICER, horny housewife Starshina Sessions was spanking a white whale of a man. He wore only a leather jockstrap and a green beret too small for his bald head. A few more pages of this and the rest of the general would go stiff.

The stranger seemed unimpressed by the martial foreplay. Staring through Rex, he scanned the hut, clocking the TV, radio, filing cabinet, camp bed, cooking stove and two crates of low-grade Kalypsol. On the noticeboard was a three-year-old calendar, a map of the island and a poster listing emergency telephone numbers. They'd all been crossed out with a red felt tip pen. Scrawled across the top margin of the poster were the words EVERYTHING IS FUCKED.

"It's a lonely life here," said Rex. "But it's great literature like this which fills the void within. As we like to say here, strangers are friends we haven't yet met. What's your story, pal? Who are you? Where are you from? Why are you here? And are you one of the good guys or one of the bad guys? Be careful with your answers. I need to watch my blood pressure."

"I mean no trouble, sir. I need to see where she fell. To pay my respects."

A spasm of laughter ejaculated from Rex's mouth.

"A Martian? I thought all you people were diced, fried and supplied."

"Not yet, sir. I'm an archaeologist. From the uplands. I come in peace. Augusta wanted that for everybody."

"Fuck did she. *Sir*. You don't need to try the diplomatic shit with me. I'm not PRISM. I'm not part of any nation state. Except of course, my own. Out here I read my own stars and tell my own story. Started as a tragedy, turned into a history. Now it's just a fucking comedy."

Rex undressed the new arrival with his eyes. A muscular, stretched body, in need of a decent meal and a hot bath. A blank stare too, like he was gormless. The ideal candidate for a final thrill-ride before the rising waters, and whatever beasts were gestating in them, sucked everything down the plughole.

"Step back. Strip off everything. I want to make sure you're not a bandit or a visitor from outer space. Or one of those spiritual sickos trying to steal my soul."

The stranger set his rucksack in front of him, let his coat fall, pulled off his t-shirt, removed his boots and dropped his trousers and pants. Underneath was pale, sinewy flesh, wrapped around a lean physique that barely twitched in the ocean wind. A big boy. Ready and ripe.

"The bag too."

Kneeling, the stranger unzipped the rucksack and held it up and open to the portacabin window. Rex picked up his torch from the desk and shone a beam into the dark space. Inside were two tins of paint, a lamp, a bottle of water, an envelope and a small ornate wooden box.

"You think a paint job is going to bring this place back to life?"

"I'm an artist, sir."

"What happened to the archaeologist?"

"You can be both."

"And a postman too. That a love letter for me?"

"No. It's a treasure map."

"Are you for real?" said Rex, nodding his head towards the pile of clothes.

"We must all make the pilgrimage once in our lives, sir. To get closer to the truth of what happened. To find out how she really died."

Rex watched as the stranger dressed. *Pretty, pretty, pretty.* He would stretch him out good and proper. Savour seeing the lights go out in his eyes. Opening the drawer, Rex picked up his customised key card with the picture of the tower tarot card and the blade guard down one side. Wincing out of his chair, Rex headed to the sink and tipped the cold coffee from his *Cannibal Holocaust* mug into the basin's black hole. Grabbing his hi-visibility jacket from the hook on the back of the door, he turned the plastic handle and stepped out into the smoky red night.

"What's your name, wandering detective?"

"Clark. Lewis Clark."

A bullshit name if ever there was one.

"Like the wild west explorers? Nice to make your acquaintance. This is way beyond the new frontier. All that washes up is seaweed. There is nothing here. The war's been raging for twenty years. The rebels are more interested in fighting themselves. And the last person to call me sir was the guy who delivered the PRISM datacast. That was three years ago. Where are you fr –"

Thunder vibrated in the ground. The portacabin's metal sign saying GALATEA SECURITY shook. The window crack widened with a crisp, cool snap. Rex felt his bowels loosen. He wondered whether it would it be the water, the earth or the Loch Ness Monster's cousin that would get him first.

"Come my intrepid explorer," said Rex. "Tremors are happening all the time. Let's just say the earth is moving for us on our romantic evening stroll. I believe every time you interact with someone you create something new. The tower is five minutes on foot. Just don't expect the ghost of Her Ladyship to roam the battlements. She's long dead. Like everything else. This is the arsehole of the world. Been churning out shit for years."

Rex switched on his torch and shone it towards a gap in the pulverised perimeter fence.

"We shall feast and drink to the spirit of Augusta, the one-legged, croaky-mouthed cunt. Twenty-one years gone. Her story as shitty as ever. Maybe we can get to know each other better. The cockroaches don't have much conversation."

The path to the tower was a long, sweeping ascent that spiralled around an enormous mound of obsidian black concrete which transformed into the building's base. Rex followed Lewis up the walkway past the neon sign. It was a relic of Augusta's time, before PRISM, when the well-off and well-tanned sat in the clouds among the people that mattered and talked about what mattered to the people below. Lewis paused to read it. Respectfully, like a tourist regarding the memorial of a local hero.

GALATEA: CONFESS YOUR SINS. GROW YOUR NETWORK. MEET YOUR MENTORS. PURSUE

YOUR PLEASURES. SPEAK YOUR TRUTH. BUILD YOUR BODY. SHAPE YOUR FUTURE.

The wanderer's starry-eyed naivety was endearing. It was sweet to know some people would travel to the ends of the earth to discover the past. *Gotta watch these Martians, though. They don't know when to stop.*

"I do all those every morning," said Rex through shortening breath. "With God as my witness I can do anything here. Especially when the God is me."

Lewis strode towards the glass entrance doors at the top of the incline, past the huge monolithic stone totem which bore gigantic upper case sans serif letters. GALATEA ZERO. Only its first three storeys were visible through the haze, a bank of glass panels stretching into smothering scarlet. Lewis looked upwards, like a young kid on his first trip to the big city. Rex felt his mouth go moist and imagined his fat frame pressing into that slender body. Better indoors. In one of those posh boardrooms where they used to laugh, flirt, fuck, drink expensive coffee and look down on the little people.

"My dad helped clear away the bodies of the protestors," said Rex. "Said it was the day the world changed forever. Reminded everyone who was really in charge."

"Victims of circumstance," said Lewis. "Led astray. Duped by a higher power they couldn't comprehend. She wept for them. Even though they wanted her blood."

"Yeah, right. Swallow that story if you want. Augusta Maars didn't weep for anyone but herself. Especially when the walls closed in on her and her fruitbat husband Roland. When PRISM relieved her of her command. Whoever topped the bitch deserves a medal. Tried to shaft PRISM. So it shafted her back. And shafted everyone else. Gassed everyone on Galatea. Now it's ended up shafting itself. And me. So it goes, my friend, in ever-decreasing circles, down into the giant ringpiece of doom."

"How does one enter?" Lewis said, his sweet shop face inspecting his own reflection in the black glass.

"One needs to have eyes to see," said Rex. He removed the tarot security card from his pocket and placed it on the join between two glass panels. A circle of blue light the size of a phone's camera lens materialised on the left side. Rex leaned in, peering into the digitalised sphere. The glass panels slid apart. Warm, musty air drifted into his face. A pang of nausea stirred in his stomach.

"Everything controlled by these two beauties," he said, turning to Lewis and pulling down the flesh at the top of both cheeks with his fingertips to expose the whites of his eyes. "Every door, every lift, every light. The Martians used to give people different coloured rings for different levels of security access. White for the plebs. Blue for the crawlers. Red for the teachers' pets. And black for the people furthest up their own arses. One big happy incestuous family. PRISM switched it to retina-based security. They never trusted wearables. You could tell PRISM were in trouble when they left all this to a guy like me. Now I'm the king of the castle. Lord of the manor. No children of the night making music. Just a bunch of black screens, all switched off. After you."

Four boots clicked on marble floor. A dry, sterilised smell. Three hundred metres above, the hallucinatory light of the red sky shone through the circular, open-aired apex of the tower, illuminating the interior in a bruising purple glow. The rotund atrium curved off either side into darkness. Beyond lay a thick silence, which made Rex imagine what it was like at the bottom of the ocean.

"My old man said the building used to feel alive," said Rex. "One hundred levels. Five thousand rooms, not including the hidden ones. Sensors everywhere, responding to people's moods and emotions. Harvesting data about everyone, so it could predict what they will do. Acting and reacting to the human psyche. All run by that computer thing. Tyrannosaurus."

"*Tiresias*."

"Whatever. Spooks say by the end the building developed its own consciousness. It's holding up, despite the quakes. Flood resistant too, but we'll see. Guess I've got somewhere to go when the world is drowning. Every month I do a full sweep of the place. No skeletons yet. Only empty space."

"Her words will continue, even if her building doesn't," Lewis said, drifting into a daydream. "That's what leadership is. The tower was inspired by the Lighthouse of Alexandria, you know."

"Yeah, if leadership means sucking people into a land of make-believe. The eighth wonder of the world, my arse. People acted like it was some kind of cathedral. The most advanced place on earth. Now it's not even the lost city of the Incas. Just a glorified office block. Everything goes to shit in the end."

"The law of entropy."

"What?"

"Order giving way to disorder. How do I get to IRIS?"

"Ah, the last place Augusta was seen alive. There's nothing up there mate."

"I'll be the judge of that. Take me straightaway, please."

Cocky bastard. Typical fucking Martian. Trapped in his own head. A tall glass of water about to get pissed in. We'll see how sure he is of himself when I press right in. When I make those beautiful blue eyes bulge.

"Of course, my friend," said Rex. "This is a sacred place for your kind. No stained-glass windows or altar boys I'm afraid. The VIP lift takes you straight to the ninety-sixth level. Only a handful people ever used it, so consider yourself a chosen one. By the end Miss High and Mighty was asking people not to look her directly in eye. Serves her right she only enjoyed power for one day."

"Like I said, I'll be the judge of that."

"She wasn't a good person," snapped Rex. "We'd be in a lot worse shape if she'd had a chance to wreak her havoc. Her killer was a saviour. Not an assassin. Too bad they never found out who pulled the trigger. Or where the body was buried. So they could have sliced her into pieces and scattered her to the fucking winds."

"If she wasn't a good person," Lewis shot back, innocent eyes smouldering. "What does that make PRISM?"

Rex reached behind him and placed his hand on the Glock 19. It felt good to get a rise out of this pilgrim. There was a monk-like quality to Lewis. Another brainwashed idealist lucky to make it this far. *Wait and wait*, as his dad used to say on the riverbank. *They'll take the bait.*

"They'll be the guys who own this," said Rex, retreating to the wall and placing his key card on glass. "Welcome to the crypt of lost souls."

The atrium lights came alive. A relay of luminaires switched on in a corkscrew pattern, circling all the way to the top of the tower with breath-taking speed. Rex still marvelled how the machinery of Galatea Zero never made a sound. A lethal quietness that became a deafening threat. The atrium was stripped bare, without furniture or foliage, surrounded by glass rectangles which ascended in irregular patterns to the summit. Three-quarters of the way up was the spherical mesh of spider web girders which encased the Visionary Complex, the realm of the Martian elite. Beyond that and bisecting the apex of the tower were the three grand walkways of south, east and west, discernible through the steel cobwebs. They joined at IRIS, the Intelligence Room of Interdependent Systems, the octagonal bunker and site of Augusta's last stand.

"It's all designed to make you feel small and insignificant," Rex continued. "The kind of place that works on your mind. Taking you where it wants to take you. Seeing only what it wants you to see. No one was ever sure how the system would respond under certain conditions. All of it was a labyrinth in Roland's head. It's one big antenna you know. The Sentinel. That's what they called the mast at the top which sent signals into space. The attention on earth wasn't enough for them. Roland thought he was on the verge of communing with something bigger. Aliens maybe. Or the Almighty."

"Is this where the protestors were killed?" said Lewis, venturing out into the centre of the atrium. He stopped on the Martian party logo carved into the marble floor. A blue eye inside three concentric circles of orange around which ran the legend *To New Horizons*.

"Yep, they never made it past here," said Rex. "Tyrannosaurus turned on the gas as soon as they entered. Like flies to shit. Soon the big T pressed the self-destruct button and laid the entire island to waste. Scorched earth. PRISM only entered a year later. Buried the corpses in a pit not far from here. Couldn't stand the stench of haunted souls. Each one categorised and numbered. Stacked a few myself. Good money too. This way, please."

Rex walked to one of the wall's rectangular sheets of glass. He placed his key card on one of ten smooth grey metal discs embedded in the pane. Galatea Zero remained dormant. He tried the next one and the next one. On the fifth attempt, there was a tiny blue flash. Rex leaned in and opened the VIP lift with the power of his sight.

"Your stairway to heaven," he said. "Just don't blame me if you're underwhelmed. Go easy on us non-believers. Augusta used to say this was a broad church after all."

Mirrors encased the lift's walls, ceiling and floor. Infinite versions of Rex and Lewis splayed out into all directions. Maybe he could do it here. Watch a battalion of gratified Tuckmans ride this guy's saddle into the sunset, sparks of narcissistic ecstasy pinging and bouncing through his softening head.

"You're not one of those people who thinks she got away, are you? Still alive. Ready to return to save the kingdom in its direst hour. Like King fucking Arthur. The lady in the lake."

His companion was silent.

"Tell me Mr Clark," said Rex more gently. "You haven't seen anything out on the sea, have you?"

"Like what?"

"A strange fish. A creature. Swimming slowly back and forth on the surface."

"You're the first living thing I've seen for weeks."

After about thirty seconds, the digital display panel read ninety-six. The door slid open. Before them was a lobby area with a cream carpet, brown leather chairs and bullshit conceptual art plastered on beige walls. Where Augusta would keep courtiers slavering like thirsty dogs begging for water. At the end was a huge, mahogany door with a gold plaque above saying THE VISIONARY COMPLEX. *Right here on the sofas. Right here.*

Rex let Lewis lead the way so he could watch him walk. His intended paused briefly to examine the artworks. Twelve floor-to-ceiling two-dimensional insects, six on either side. They were neither paintings nor engravings. More like imprints of something which used to be there. On lonely patrols, Rex would sometimes run his fingers into the grooves and wonder if the rumours were true. Two sharp horns extended from each head, the longer of the two almost twice the size of the insects' torsos. The artworks were interspersed with full-length windows. On the interior side he could see the top of the atrium. Opposite, the jet-black sea. Rex wondered if there were others like him beyond the horizon.

"The Hercules beetle," he said. "Apparently it can lift one hundred times its own weight. Roland's favourite. Had the world's largest collection of insects. They were all weirdos. Him. Augusta. That guy Realprick. Even the PR bimbo who was always on the telly, Stricken."

"*Straker*," said Lewis curtly. "And the Chief of Staff was Relpek. Open the door please. I'll take it from here."

"No you won't, pal. You'll stay right there and be a good little bitch while I grind your ass to a thousand pieces."

Lewis turned. Rex pointed the gun towards his guts. His victim's gorgeous blue eyes glistened knowingly in the soft interior light, as if this was another petty trial to be endured. *The balls on this jumped-up streak of piss. I've got a good mind to chop him up and fry him on a barbecue.*

"Strip. Drop your bag. Bend over there," growled Rex, gesturing to the sofa with a cock of his moist, reddening head. "Don't think about fighting or I'll blow your fucking head off."

As he savoured the sight of his prey undress for the second time, Rex stiffened. He gazed at Lewis's multiple scars and lacerations, like he'd been set upon by the world's most restless parasite. Taut, tender. No fat. Lean, lovely long muscles. Quite the member too. Bigger than it had been outdoors and still not shrivelling in fear. A pristine piece of succulent human flesh. Real human. Real warmth. Real dirt and fluid and life. Growing harder, Rex unbuckled his belt with his left hand and felt the sweat gather around the gun butt in his right.

"Spread your legs," he barked, as Lewis turned to face the window and placed his hands on the back of the sofa. "Welcome to the world of the grown-ups, big boy. About time Randy Rexy got to shaft the system right back."

Rex waddled up behind him, his hi-vis jacket still on and his tight trousers sliding down to meet his ankles. He unlocked the gun's safety catch and placed its barrel against Lewis's right temple. In the maroon night, Rex could see the Martian's sheepish face reflected in the glass, like a docile pig entering the abattoir. Normally he liked to tie them up, but in all the excitement he'd left his handcuffs in the drawer back in the portacabin. He would have to hold the gun steady at the back of his head. Pull the trigger when he came off, admiring his own fat face as it twisted in pleasure amid the torrent of blood. From his back trouser pocket, Rex greedily snatched the tarot card and removed the guard with his teeth to expose the blade. He would carve him up as well, as the white cheeks yielded either side to his concrete-hard cock.

Back and forth. Back and forth. Hot blood flowing from the buttocks. Beautiful red streaks. Randy Rexy always so fucking hot and masterful. I'm going to blow this gorgeous piece of fucking meat right apart. Take him right down with me. Right to the centre of the fucking earth.

The shift in light came quickly. A shadow fell. Their reflections disappeared. A shape emerged from all sides of the window frame, like the palm of an enormous hand closing Rex's eye to the world. Before, it was only a distant shape dancing on the sea. Now it was two metres away. The creature had an oily membrane greyish skin that clung like a suction cup to the glass. In the centre of its pulsing flesh, a black hole opened and closed rhythmically. Like it was breathing. Or trying to speak. Further into the void, he could make out a small white orb of light travelling towards him. Deeper still flickered a flash of red. Rex suddenly remembered a good man he used to know in a previous life.

Something snapped tight around his left wrist. The gun fell from his hand. A blur of motion. The right arm twisting. The ground giving way. He lashed out with the blade.

It was no longer in his hand. A soft splattering sound on glass. A sequence of red dots in a descending arc. Another, streaming off in the opposing direction and onto the walls. A weird intimacy in his throat. Coldness. Warmth. A scorching that ignited everything in an inferno of agony.

Dropping to his knees, Rex clutched at his neck with both hands. Crimson poured forth over, below and between his fingers. *Make it stop, must stop. Put it all back in. Please daddy put it all back in.* Onto his back he fell, twitching and gasping. Naked above him, towering like an Olympian beauty, Lewis lowered himself down and kneeled on Rex's biceps, his testicles resting on his sternum. The razor blade scooped out his left eye. Rex's scream reverberated beyond the building and out onto the sea, dying on the dark waves. The right eyeball was gouged next. Rex's hands twitched, clawing at the disappeared world. To grab the phone at the hut. To press the broken alarm button. To send a distress signal to a defeated PRISM. To reach out to his dead father's hand on the riverbank.

"I claim this place back on her behalf," Lewis said. "From here she was taken. To this place she will return."

Computerised sounds. The Visionary Complex door opening and closing. A system once irrevocably shut down purring back to life. Tidal blood rippling around deathly white toes. Beetles scratching through sand with their black horns. A tremble stirring in the chasms of the earth. A voice calling Rex to wait because something below the water always takes the bait. Galatea's last man slipped under the surface of the planet to join his father, grateful he wouldn't be around to see all he'd ever known explode.

III

The ninety-sixth level of Galatea Zero. Three months before the Fall.

Max Relpek exited the lift into the cylindrical corridor like an eager young stallion before its debut steeplechase. *Wait outside and Miss Straker will collect you*, said the stony-faced Experience Facilitator in the atrium. On the way up, Max flexed his shoulders, adjusted his brown silk tie in the mirror and swept away every perceptible piece of fluff from the lapels of his chocolate-coloured three-piece suit. When the doors opened, a waft of creamy vanilla and amber scent swept satisfyingly up his nose. A Schubert symphony streamed through the speakers. Tucking tendrils of his luscious curly black mane behind his ears, Max inhaled power's rich air. Sauntering towards the Visionary Complex, he enjoyed the softness of the luxurious caramel carpet through the thin soles of his shoes.

Sunlight poured through the latticed steel exterior and inner windows, soaking the space in a matrix of golden quadrilaterals. Beyond the glass, the opulent, man-made seaside vista of Galatea stretched ambitiously out to sea, pale yellow blurring into azure blue. Down below and out of sight would be pleasure seekers, politicos and private investigators, buzzing back and forth along the esplanade like unsatiated termites. Spending, scheming, spying and screwing each other over. Monika would be scuttling among them, maxing out poppa's credit card on nourishing skin serums and state-of-the-art exfoliating masks.

It was time to cut her loose. Easing himself into the brown leather sofa, Max decided he would deliver the hard news that evening. He was moving up, she was going down. Monika couldn't look beyond the next modelling contract to see who he really was. Drumming his fingers out of sync with the invisible orchestra, Max pretended to admire the insect artworks on the opposite wall. What story would be waiting for him inside the Visionary Complex, he wondered. *Read between the lines,* his producer advised. *Mix business with pleasure.*

Five minutes later, the circular doors swished apart like shutters on a lens. Through them rushed a tall slender lady with a curly blaze of red hair that reminded Max of an exotic tropical bird. She wore a white chiffon business suit and white ankle strap heels. A ruby necklace nested on a freckly chest, balanced by a pair of red teardrop earrings that hung heavy on her head. The perfume was fresh and floral, with a pungent whiff of caffeine detectable underneath. A punch-drunk corporate warrior with a washed-out face, pale skin and cool blue eyes behind which much was going on. Dry, full of fizz and easy to pop, Alexis Straker was like a supermarket bottle of blanc de noirs. Upon eye contact, an authentic smile emerged on her thin, stretched lips.

"Mr Relpek, how do you do? Welcome to the Visionary Complex."

She could be more than a little impulsive, Max sensed. Someone bored by corporate convention. Prone to experimentation. Neither too plain, nor too polished. A lonely soul trapped in sterility, thirsting for more colour. On the wrong day, she might behave like a very naughty nine-year-old indeed.

"It's an honour to be in such an inspirational place, Mrs-"

"*Miss* Straker," she said. "Alexis Straker."

"Very nice to meet you, Miss Straker. I admire the work you're doing to build a better world."

"Shall we?" she said, gesturing to the door. "The crew is assembled. She only has five minutes, so you'll need to be impressive and efficient. Augusta doesn't suffer fools or timewasters. No matter how handsome."

"Five minutes with the next leader of our country is a lifetime for someone like me," said Max, affecting the reassuring but nervy tone of an overly conscientious prefect. "Happy to be in your hands, Miss Straker. My fellow journalists tell me this is one of the best political comms operations they've seen."

They swept into a long, windowless corridor lined with sculptures of naked men and women from antiquity set on Martian-branded plinths. Wall-to-ceiling screens played animated space nebulas of swirling purples and pinks. The tiled floor was decorated with contrapuntal fractals that reminded Max of seashells. Three handsome Martian men glided past, dressed in identical black suits with white open-neck shirts and polished shoes, faces absorbed in their personal devices.

"I'm pretty nervous to tell you the truth, Miss Straker," said Max. "This is my first big interview."

"Quite a way to start," said Alexis. "We're honoured to have you at Galatea Zero. We have a good story to tell. This is the best way to reach those people yet to be convinced. And I can see why she requested you."

The south-facing conference room had a large window framing an expanse of glittering blue. The only furniture were two Orbiter luminaires, a Maars Midnight camera, two executive leather chairs and two glass side tables on which sat empty crystal tumblers and opened plastic bottles of Maars Hydro. Alexis tapped away at her tablet. The blinds lowered and the screen walls switched on, conjuring a procession of changing colours from carpet to ceiling. Aquamarine transitioned to turquoise, teal and olive, coating the space in a hallucinatory glaze. Tiresias could detect the emotional tenor of a room and introduce new palettes to rejuvenate or relax. The cameraman fussed with the luminaires, shooting Alexis a frustrated look.

Four hundred and fifty seconds of unseen questions. A bit of light, a bit of shade. Chewing gum content to kick-start the campaign. A handsome well-bred interrogator to invigorate Augusta for the day ahead. Max settled in the chair and waited for his interviewee. Nerves bristling, he poured himself a glass of water too quickly, spilling some on the frosted tabletop. Alexis swooped in with a Maars-branded napkin, soaked up the fluid and placed a calming hand between his broad shoulder blades. It stayed for a few seconds longer than customary.

You'll fit right in on the island, Max's producer said. *Plenty of rich women with too much money to spend.* While Max's taxi queued on the mainland awaiting authorisation to access the bridge, a sunburnt beggar in a filthy green tracksuit banged on the car window. Yellow teeth, unruly nose hair and a debilitating skin condition. *There's a storm coming from the sea,* he screamed through cracked lips, his breath clouding the glass. *The Martians will kill us. They will fucking kill us all.*

Twenty minutes later, Max cruised down a Galatean boulevard so superficial it seemed as light and disposable as *papier-mâché.* Facades of boutique stores with blacked-out windows. Luxury sport cars parked near charging ports manufactured to look like trees. Ghostly pedestrians stargazing down the street through tinted sunglasses. Wealth and confidence hung like thunderclouds: a frightening yet fragile accumulation of elements at the mercy of more powerful forces.

As they waited for Augusta, Alexis remained standing, holding the tablet to her modest chest and stifling her amusement at the cameraman's consternation. The red ring on the third finger of her left hand caught Tiresias's lightshow. Max imagined that under the chiffon trousers were lovely long legs reaching up to buttocks taut and toned from morning workouts. Inside her mind, a conflict between raging intellect and fiery temper, expressing itself in inscrutable poetry, withering side-eye and a foul mouth. In her heart, a burning passion to be held closely and completely for the rest of time. Alexis looked shyly at Max. He held her glance.

"Fire away."

The country's leader-in-waiting was seated. Augusta draped her prosthetic right leg over her left knee. A proud spine held up her tiny body. Hands lay clasped and composed in her lap. Cropped, greying hair. Intense, brown eyes that didn't soften upon seeing him. A facial expression surly and tight due to excessive surgery on her lips. The double mastectomy had left her with the sunken chest of a weedy teenage boy. She wore a blue skirt and blue blouse underneath a green jacket. A feather-shaped brooch lent an elegant fleck of gold and silver. She carried with her a smell of musky perfume and a voice so crisp it cut through all confusion.

Everybody shits, said his producer. *Just picture her on the toilet or doing something else where she's vulnerable. The mystique will soon fade. Ten percent of it is real. The rest is story. Remember that about all powerful people.*

Max drew a blank when he tried to imagine Augusta naked, showering, hungover, sleeping or defecating. He would be lucky not to spend the next five minutes thrashing like a drowning puppy in a canal. Compared to Alexis, the Red Rocket teetering on explosion, Augusta was like a bank vault. Guarding her were two burly six-foot security guards in blue boilersuits with spiky shocks of blond hair. They carried a machine gun each. One for every brain cell.

"Mrs Maars, as you know we only have seven minutes," said Max. "The format is that I ask you as many questions as we can cover in that time. So in the interests of balance, value and entertainment, I'd like you to keep your answers focused, crisp and clear."

Well done Maxy boy. A good start. His tough guy persona had matured since his appointment as the network's junior correspondent. Physical, not intellectual. Blokeish, not too clean cut. Rough around the edges. Muscular. Beddable. Earthy, easy and calm. A man's man with an edge of the street. Certainly not someone who played polo with financiers on his father's country estate. *You'll put her at ease straightaway,* said his producer. *You're a smooth bastard when you want to be. Just try not to fuck the dog.*

"That won't be a problem, Mr Relpek. Please proceed."

"It's three months until election day. We're in the self-styled Visionary Complex of your party headquarters. What vision are you asking millions of people to vote for?"

A sweet, soft opener, like he was lowering her head onto a pillow.

"To heal the sickness in our society."

A tart response, bowled at pace.

"Very well. Describe this sickness."

"We're shrinking as a nation. Running out of energy. Materially and spiritually. Worsening air pollution. Diminishing natural resources. Rising sea levels. Growing unemployment. Stagnant growth. Declining industries. A failure to live to high ethical standards. To be a beacon of progress. To counteract the nefarious actions of rogue states."

"Not everyone is buying it though. Sectors of society are threatening to take to the streets if you win."

"They haven't seen me campaign yet. These next three months will be a journey for us all. Our entire nation is a journey. And like any journey, you have to believe in the destination. Knowing what you're doing and where you're going. That's what people want. Knowledgeable government. Competent government."

Alexis, starry-eyed and sexy, lolled her head to one side. It reminded Max of the look people have in a gallery when they're entranced by a baffling but well-regarded work of art.

"Let's focus on knowledge. You claim you know more about government, yet you've never held elected office. You claim you know what ordinary people believe, yet you've led a career moving from one elite institution to the next. You claim you know what's best for us all because a computer tells you that's the case. Some say you consult technology too much. That we're under more surveillance than ever. Will you be running the country? Or will Tiresias?"

"Tiresias is simply a tool. It enables our party to predict the outcome of decisions with greater accuracy. An extension of political will that acts faster and more efficiently than real people. And with superior clarity. This is a homegrown technology more powerful than anything developed by PRISM. We as a nation should be proud of what Tiresias has become."

"What about the human touch?"

"Tiresias empowers people to be the best they can be. My job is to bring the forgotten people of this nation into view. In our party's hands, we will become the most educated country on our planet. Where everyone will have the opportunity to go from being an outsider to being an insider. And we'll be the healthiest too. Tiresias will be able to anticipate illness before it occurs."

"You're not overly concerned about the health of our nation though, are you? Do you plan to make low-grade Kalypsol inexpensive and available to all?"

"Yes, in tablet, fluid, needle and patches. For too long people have not had access to the peace and serenity they need.

Kalypsol is a good medicine. But like any medicine, regulation is key. Regulation and moderation."

"There are reports it causes blindness."

"Tiresias has debunked this, as have two independent studies. Trials show it brings about an average 40% increase in mindfulness and productivity."

"Do you drink Kalypsol yourself?"

Augusta's pupils retracted. The walls changed to indigo. Her feet stayed still in their bright green stilettos. Max floated in her space, a helpless child attached to her umbilical cord. His producer's voice again. *Stay strong killer. In a place like Galatea, you've got to be a killer.*

"No, I much prefer Bloody Marys."

"Can you control yourself?"

"Come again?"

"It's rumoured you have a temper."

"I have my moments."

"Such as?"

"When I see a country losing its creative energy. When people are trapped by unbalanced mechanisms of power. Slaves to debt and a disingenuous language they don't understand. Experiencing guilt they shouldn't be feeling. But I've learned to channel my passions into calm, methodical and focused action."

"Our current leader calls you the shadow of an illusion in the reflection of a never-ending hall of mirrors. Someone who will melt under the political pressure cooker."

"My father died when I was eleven. I lost so much blood in the crash the attending doctor sent for a priest. Later I beat a terminal cancer diagnosis. Anyone who has cancer will tell you it's like having the four horsemen of the apocalypse inside you. And all that was before my heart attack. Life has pronounced me dead three times. I'll take no lectures from him about overcoming adversity."

Indigo to purple. The luminaires brightened, infected by the changing mood. Augusta was shrouded in a regal halo accentuating the leanness of her face, which drifted somewhere between determined, bored and sad. Max was starting to enjoy sliding, sinking and soaring on the fairground ride of techno-political theatre.

"How do you overcome adversity?"

"With the love of my husband, Roland. The world's finest architect. The world's finest man. He rebuilt my life. Moved me to higher ground."

"And Galatea Zero is your husband's masterpiece. But one journalist called it our generation's Tower of Babel. Do you have delusions of grandeur?"

"No. Galatea Zero is a place of ultimate moral authority in the land. A symbol of human potential. A lighthouse leading the way. Every country needs totems as part of its storytelling. A new chapter is long overdue."

"But critics say there is a lack of substance to the story. Your manifesto is vague. An empty shell. An opacity and an obfuscation when it comes to practical details. A black hole, if you will."

"All will be revealed. We're doing things differently."

"You certainly are. One of the few policies we *are* clear about is that your first act as leader will be to launch an unprovoked attack on PRISM. A reckless act that will disrupt the international order. All based on what even the most senior intelligence officials say is an extremely cloudy situation on the ground."

"It's not unprovoked," she said, frustration surfacing. "Our policy is to stop the massacre of the innocents. No leader should stand by while another nation uses the deadliest nerve gas the world has ever seen to silence legitimate protest. This Other Way they talk about isn't a new world. The People's

Republic of Integrated States in the Matrix is empire by stealth. A doctrine of integration and centralisation masquerading as benign collaboration. They want to build a world empire. We cannot allow them to reduce other nations to a state of dependency by force, technology, infrastructure and pharmaceuticals. Or by terror."

"But all the experts say it's a war we're bound to lose."

"Not the experts I speak to."

"If you win the election, who will you thank?"

"My father, may he rest in peace. He thought there was a sickness in our society which must be healed. Intergenerational myopia he called it."

"Was there a moment that stood out when he inspired you?"

"Yes. I was about ten years old. We were staring out to see and watching the boats sail into the horizon. The red sky beautiful at sunset. He told me the future is bright. But it takes blood, sweat and tears to get there. That's what you must do to be a leader. You must be prepared to bleed."

"Are you bleeding now?"

"Always."

"Has it been that way since the car crash?"

Augusta's jaw clenched. A flash of pain and distrust.

"Terrible experiences create remarkable people."

"Are you frightened of the many death threats you receive? Some extremist groups are determined to kill you if you take power."

"By 'taking power' do you mean being elected by the people? No, I'm not afraid. I wouldn't be much of a leader if I was."

"So what has Maars Enterprises discovered out at sea?"

Augusta gave a condescending smile.

"The ludicrous conjecture of a media machine who can't tell what's real and make-believe. Disappointingly repeated by an ambitious journalist grasping at something that isn't there. You're all so very easy to see through."

"Rumours are you've found a new kind of organism on the seabed. A strange chemical reaction in hydrothermal vents accelerating the creation of new life. Why keep such a thing a secret?"

"It isn't true, so isn't a secret. These are simple exploratory procedures-"

"Time's up."

A metallic, monotone voice sliced through the room. Everyone twitched, like they'd been in a deep sleep and the morning alarm had sounded. Queasy aquamarine resurged on the walls. Roland Maars slid into the room between the two security guards. He was a wiry reed of a man, wearing a black suit and black jumper. A smug, professorial face in full appreciation of its owner's genius. His bald head glowed like a bulb under the aquatic light. There was something lizard-like about his movements, as he slithered across the set to place both hands on his wife's shoulders.

"Better luck next time, Mr Relpek," said Augusta, standing up and extending her hand. Her touch was warm, tender and pliable. There was something trapped and complex underneath. Given enough time and tenderness, Max would trace the finest of cracks and prise her apart.

"Will that be before or after the election?"

"Tomorrow, in fact. I'd like you to join my team. Become the official chronicler of the campaign. An inside man at the making of history. Your chance to get in the room. See us vanquish PRISM. Watch us build a better world."

Read between the lines. Augusta became a doe-eyed picture of innocence. Roland grinned. The Red Rocket's eyes widened. The walls took on the faintest shade of ochre.

Everything about the scene felt theatrical. Reality and perception dissolved in a drugged tableau of hypnotic seduction.

"It'll give you the chance to look deeper," continued Augusta. "Find out what's style and what's substance. See if it's true there's nothing there at all."

"And what will I see?"

"A symbol. An image of hope. Light against dark. A figure in the clouds. Don't chase too hard, or everything will move further away. I guarantee you won't look back."

Max thought about Monika and the guys at the polo club. Remembered how his father belittled him at the end-of-year gala. Wondered what it must be like to look down on everyone from above. More than just a pretty face. More than just a son. A serious actor in the eyes of the world. To go right to the edge, see the vortex and dance with a different kind of devil into unknown space.

"Very good," said Augusta sharply. She wielded the easy arrogance of someone who could command a legion with a click of her fingers. "Alexis, draw up a contract and request Tiresias to start onboarding. Assuming you're not having one of your funny turns?"

"Yes, Mrs Maars," said Alexis, beaming. "Straightaway."

"I look forward to getting to know you over the next twelve weeks, Mr Relpek. To new horizons for us all."

Forty-five minutes later on the mainland, Max opened the door to his hotel room searching for somewhere to breathe. Laid out on the bed was a new Martian designer suit, a top-of-the-range Chronos laptop, a Rolsta 100 smartphone and an ebony case the size of a matchbox. All were branded with the initials MR and the party's crest. Max opened the case to find a pair of luxury contact lenses set in vermillion velvet. When he held them to the light, he could see they were tinted with the lightest shades of cerise.

The next morning after breakfast, a black Maars Neptune limousine transported him to Galatea Zero through the VIP tunnel under the seabed. The last thing he saw of the mainland was a group of rag-tag protestors at the tunnel entrance, impotently waving placards. THE MARTIANS ARE INVADING. TIRESIAS = TREASON.

Under the waves, Max caught his reflection in the limousine window. He fantasised about losing himself in the frizzy curls of Alexis's hair. Crossing personal and professional boundaries. Exploring the strangest of worlds together. Soon his mind moved past Alexis and upwards to the sky. Galatea Zero was a multi-dimensional jewel hidden in layers of glass. A temple to optical dispersion and myriad refractions. So much spectral light, yet all of it distant and muted. Designed to deflect, defend and defer. There was something deeper to be mined. Unexplored chasms and caverns. Beguiling whirlpools leading who knows where.

As the car emerged into the light of the Galatean morning, Max was blinded. Squinting into the sun, he considered calling his family. Then he decided against it. Closing his eyes, he sank back into the leather seat and let a succession of green lights lead him through the facades to the heart of the labyrinth. This evening, he would ask Alexis to dinner. The signals she sent were clear. *And in this place, it looks like anything goes.*

IV

The coastal village of Lower Overton. Sixteen hours before the Fall.

The morning after the night Augusta Maars was elected leader by a landslide, Lawrence 'Lozza' Quelch trudged bleary-eyed to the vandalised transport hub which burst out of the hillside like a bright blue zit. Fridays meant the frequency of the commuter capsules was unpredictable, so it might be two hours before he arrived at his workstation above the Upper Overton incinerator. He didn't care. Masquerading as a Household Appliance Remedial Officer had become the professional equivalent of being sucked down a long, tediously unimpeded drainpipe into steaming hot sewage.

Last night he'd switched channels when the exit poll results were announced. Mercifully, his darts buddy Woz Wangler had topped up Lozza's garage fridge the previous weekend with illegally acquired ultra-low-grade Kalypsol. Slurping it through a straw, Lozza washed down the dregs of Wednesday night's takeaway chicken madras. Near comatose, he sought solace from democratic disappointment in a low-budget slasher flick set in the toxic world of international female beach volleyball. He woke the next morning with a hangover worthy of the evil queen herself.

Nobody else in the village used public transport before eight o'clock, so Lozza could blow off the cobwebs in solitude. He liked to watch the seagulls and Martian helicopters fly out to sea, listen to the whipping wind and inhale the ocean's zesty freshness. In open space, the world's problems became smaller. Last Monday he'd even fallen asleep in the hub, oblivious to the passing capsule. In a frenzy, his boss pinged more than a dozen messages to Lozza's wristwatch in the space of half an hour. Another big red cross on the attendance dashboard in the tiny office above the furnace. *Sorry sir, it was all too beautiful. And you know how depressed I get.*

This morning, Lozza had company. From thirty metres away he recognised his old school friend's pipe cleaner body and swept-back mousy brown hair. Both hands tucked into the front pockets of a fastened-up, sage-coloured raincoat. Chin raised. A battered green gym bag slung over the right shoulder. As thin, aloof and camouflaged as always. Lower Overton's monument to self-containment. Zayden Nero, the Human Stick Insect Who Couldn't Make It Stick.

The last Lozza heard, Zero Nero was studying coastal erosion at a plush university down south. His passion for scrabbling among rocks won him a scholarship. Home was a campus with big iron gates and high red walls where inmates excelled in spending their families' cash. Or so Lozza was told by his pisshead cousin Steve during a marathon bender at the social club. They'd ended up lying on the roof of each other's cars and waxing lyrical about the mammary glands of the bar staff, renaming constellations in their honour. Zayden no longer indulged in that type of timewasting. Especially not since he'd quit the pills. His fellow sci-fi nerd had become the village's rarest breed: a reformed character.

"Kirk to Enterprise," said Lozza as he neared the transport hub. Two of its six plastic wall panels were torn out. A phone number and three offers of sexual favours were scribbled in marker pen on the blue bench. The half-illuminated digital screen resembled sorry-arsed braille. The printed map showing the bus routes had been annotated with red ink. Two arteries extended into white space to form the shape of an ejaculating penis. The outermost droplet was suspended in space above a speech bubble asking: WHERE WOULD YOU LIKE TO GO TODAY? The *pièce de résistance* was a burst of graffiti on the rear window. KILL THE MARTIAN BITCH.

"Zero Nero. Must be two years."

"Lawrence Quelch," said Zayden, eyeing him through thick-rimmed glasses. The guarded demeanour was still there. The mystique that would attract girls until the moment he dropped his frigid, defensive veil. The only women he could relate to were those in fictional deep space. Except for one, and everyone knew how that ended. This morning, Zayden clearly had more important things to do than make jokes about Uhura's sex life. He looked like he hadn't slept. His bloodshot hazel eyes were immersed in something far away. Zayden reminded Lozza of a drop of water, promising to swell into something greater only to implode with a silent pop.

"I'm good, thanks so much for asking," Lozza joked, landing a fist bump on Zayden's right shoulder. "For a moment there I thought you were a statue."

"Yeah, I've noticed a lot round here."

Zayden's voice was subdued. No longer the squeaky adolescent sound Lozza remembered from Saturday afternoons when they wandered through Lower Overton's single shopping street and ate fish and chips on the war memorial steps. They would make predictions about where they would end up in life, savouring the warmth spreading through the paper wrapping into their palms. Lozza couldn't remember exactly what they'd foretold, but he was confident they'd been very wrong.

"Just on my way to the plant. Executive leadership meeting. Closing some big figures today. Drive and close. That's what it's all about. Drive and close."

"Always knew you'd get in the room one day."

"Taking after you mate. What you doing back in the bog?"

"Collecting a few things from my folks. Going away today."

"Finally decided to smash your head on those rocks you kept collecting? This place can have that effect on people."

"No, I'm going to Galatea. For the victory party."

"Seriously? You're a Martian? I can't believe you voted for that bitch. They might not let you in with that raincoat, you pretentious twat. Who you trying to be, Alain Delon?"

No reply. Lozza followed his companion's eyes to the tinges of red fanning the cloud-dappled sky. There was something in the distance Zayden believed was worth seeing. Another helicopter was flying towards the horizon. A new Martian energy strategy, apparently. Not that it would bring any jobs to Lower Overton. Those were being taken by people who didn't understand history. The past never seemed to bother them. Neither did the future.

"She's going to fuck this country over," said Lozza. "And there was me thinking you were coming to the reunion. We'll all be there. Florence too."

"Enjoy yourselves," said Zayden, straining back the sarcasm. "The humour may be too cerebral for my tastes."

"Well, you must be connected. I hear you need to own a G-Andromeda to get within five miles of Galatea. Or just be a complete prick."

"I got lucky," said Zayden, raising his right hand from his pocket and pushing his glasses up the bridge of his nose. "Randomly chosen from a list of activists. I gotta golden ticket and it's a golden day."

"Thought you never did random, what with your OCD. Well, best you keep away from the club. Can't imagine the gang would be impressed with you getting into bed with the Vortex."

"Moving in those circles is how you make a difference. Not like back here. The circles just keep decreasing."

"It's a two-way street champ," said Lozza. "How long you been batting for the other side?"

"Since I wanted to avoid an easy life."

"There's nothing easy about this Zay. That lot don't understand our way of life. Never have. Must be nice to separate yourself in a cushy island. Away from the real world. Pissing away money on mirrors and make-believe."

"Your time will come. Maars will build a better life for everyone. I want to play my part."

Zero Nero. Always needing a cause to believe in. Always one of its side effects. Lozza thought it began with Zayden's dad, who loved to tell you this way was up, then the next day how it had been down all along. *Given that upbringing, I'd have probably started to burrow around in the earth looking to escape.* Out of everyone in the class, Lozza thought Zayden was the one most likely to be sectioned. A misfit running away from himself. Ready to swallow any shit if it made him different. The sports boys named him the clumsiest boy in school and spread a rumour he had Spatial Awareness Disorder. *The SAD bastard.* In the canteen Zayden sat alone, aligning his huge inventory of lunch items like they were an Airfix kit.

"You're forgetting the Star Fleet Prime Directive," said Lozza. "Don't intervene in strange new worlds. Come on Zaysta, that's not who you are. Come to the party. You may never get a chance to see us all together again. We made each other, didn't we? I bet you won't even get within one hundred metres of Augusta. You're window dressing, pal. Like one of the random red shirts on the Enterprise who never say anything."

"I have plenty to say. The country will be healed. This sickness will end."

"Christ, you really are a Martian. The crippled will walk and the blind will see. She's a soulless bitch. You can tell it in her eyes. A burst balloon farting hot air. That fucking turbine over there has more personality. The energy bypasses us completely, you know. We're still on the old grid. Choked off. Power to the people. What a joke. This insane bitch and her war will get us all wiped out."

"Maybe PRISM isn't so tough. Don't believe everything you read."

"The planet's on fire. She's pouring oil on the flames. She talks about giving us more access, but only gives it to her mates. They think they can take over everything. Who'll end up fighting this war? Not you lot of fucking windbags. You're too busy being brainwashed. As Bobby D says, don't follow leaders…"

"… and watch the parking meters. I'm my own man, Lozza. That was always the trouble."

"Keep telling yourself that story. Tiresias controls your life. Can't you see where this is going? Nothing is random. You've been picked for a reason. They've got tentacles everywhere. Take a shit these days and Maars has probably got a sensor in the u-bend to see what you've been eating. You don't know what's real or fake. For all you know we could be governed by aliens. Or there could be no one in charge at all."

The weedy murmur of a low-powered electric motor sounded from the bottom of the hill. Crawling towards them was a big white coach with the word GALATEA on the digital sign above the windscreen. Behind the wheel was an old-age pensioner wearing Ray-Ban sunglasses and showcasing most of his teeth. Presumably he was constipated or processing some splendid news.

"Florence is at school now," said Lozza.

"Let's not do this."

"She's your daughter, even if you won't admit it."

"That's what her mum says."

"Why didn't you take a test then?"

"We are *not* doing this now."

The coach came wheezing to a stop alongside them. The word WINDCHASER was emblazoned on the side in fifth-rate action movie font. Accompanying it was a picture of a gurning Augusta Maars in an emerald suit and the swishing slogan TO NEW HORIZONS.

"Good grief," said Lozza. "You really are cannon fodder. This thing isn't going to make it out of here. We'll be finding pieces of it in hedgerows for years to come. I hope it's got a Klingon cloaking device for your sake."

"You'd be surprised what they have at Galatea. Most advanced skyscraper in the world."

"Most advanced toilet bowl more like. Don't double dip with the caviar mate. They'll take you to the top, throw you off and piss on you from above. It's a big price to pay for a two-second photo op with the Black Hole."

"Now you're being sexist," said Zayden, removing a white plastic key card from his inside pocket. It was branded with a letter T, made up of four black vertical circles and two more black circles either side at the top. Judging by Zayden's flamboyant flick of the wrist, Lozza was meant to be impressed.

"I'll send you a picture of us together. Tell Augusta how my hometown yokels think she's a pagan goat slaughterer who practises druid mating rituals. See how quickly it takes her to lock up the people smugglers who really run this town. She may even come for you. *Champ.*"

Zayden waved the card across a black circle on the coach's door. Back. Forth. Back. Forth. Back. Forth. Opening his arms wide with palms facing up, he glared at the driver, still smiling inanely. *Definitely not his real teeth.* Out of frustration, Zayden slammed the card onto the panel. The door jerked opened, mustering the vehicle's entire reserves of battery.

"Don't try to be a hero today mate," said Lozza. "There's no such thing anymore. And there's nothing on Galatea for any of us. Everyone is insignificant these days. Don't be a fall guy either. These protestors smell blood. And I seem to remember you being a bit squeamish."

"I've learned to handle myself."

"Yeah, right. All that time burrowing around the cove made a man of you, has it? Let us know when you're back home. We can relive our times as the Borg. Fuck the politics. Let's just be us. We'll be old and dead soon. You don't always have to be such a closed book."

"I'm never coming home, Loz. Keep telling yourself that story."

Zayden stepped onto the coach and waved his key card towards the driver's cabin. Mr Teeth nodded without turning his head. Perhaps rigor mortis had set in. The inner door leading to the aisle partially opened then slammed shut. Zayden jumped back in what looked embarrassingly like fright. The door reopened, Zayden disappeared and Lower Overton's most tedious transport vignette ended.

"You never leave home, mate," Lozza shouted. "Especially not in the world's most advanced coffin. Live long and prosper, my friend."

The passenger windows were tinted, so thankfully Lozza couldn't make out what the other Martian barnacles were like. He didn't want to feel anymore depressed about humanity. With a lurch, the Windchaser took off up the hill, its motor sounding like a field-full of exhausted grasshoppers. Zero Nero would be tiptoeing down the aisle, wiping down the

armrest of the seat furthest away from everyone. Walking
away. From everything. His hometown. His family. His
daughter. He would walk away from Augusta too. He was
always searching for what he didn't have.

Another Maars helicopter flew overhead. *Red sky in
the morning.* Lozza took out his Maars X and snapped a picture
of the swelling sea. There was something wonderful about that
big blue beast. On the beach below, he and Zayden used to
collect seashells, talk about randy mermaids emerging from
the deep and the foreign adventures they would share in war-
torn cities. Only the stories rang hollow these days, like
everything else.

Not many people turned up for the reunion, but Lozza
did see Florence. It was the leisure centre's final night before
closing, and she'd just come back from swimming with her
mum. Her hair was wet. She couldn't sit still. She wasn't
settling at infant school. The other day she'd run off down the
sports field and the teachers couldn't find her for an hour.
Turned out she was in a ditch, building a bridge from one bank
to the other with sticks so the ants and slugs didn't get wet.

Lozza bought her a bag of sea salt crisps with his
winnings from the fruit machine. He never said anything about
seeing her dad. The club ran out of cider and the DJ never
arrived. His truck had been attacked by a Martian drone which
mistook the turntables and speakers for anti-aircraft artillery.
At last orders, an arthritic fight broke out when Shags
confessed to Selwyn he'd voted for Augusta because 'that
crone has more of a swinging dick than most men'.

Back home in his armchair, Lozza watched the repeat
coverage of Galatea on television. With voyeuristic emptiness,
he saw the one-day-old government implode again and again.
A fantasy island detonating itself off from the world. He didn't
grieve when everything shut down. Lozza hoped that before
his end came, the shy clever guy who helped him with his

maths homework rediscovered the best part of himself. But that was probably wishful thinking. He never could reach Zayden and now never would.

V

The Imagineering Zone of Galatea Zero. 172 minutes before the Fall.

She's still down here, realised Hal Haze. The Martian security officer shone his torch down the underground staircase spiralling ten storeys into the earth. His semi-functional location tracker showed a solitary white circle with a red dot at the centre, tagged with the dehumanising soubriquet 2781694. It was floating fifty metres from the outer service exit, one of the few doors in the building which could be overridden manually. Alexis was holding out against the insurrection, like some stubborn red-headed Celtic princess with broadsword unsheathed.

It was eight o'clock in the evening. Augusta's celebratory speech had been rescheduled twice. Twenty minutes earlier, the rioters broke through the supposedly impenetrable electrified fence. Since then, Tiresias had indulged in cat and mouse with the rebels, switching off power infrastructure from below ground to Level 25. Access to higher levels was prohibited to all but black and red ring-bearers. Blue-fingered foot soldiers like Hal would be left to face a ravenous blur of arms, fists and bad teeth that would soon smash through the atrium's glass exterior and swarm across the hallowed marble floor.

Don't let yourself be a victim Hally, Alexis once said. Neither should she, despite Augusta's cruelty. Everyone knew Straker was a funny fish, but she didn't deserve to be gutted like this. It angered Hal he was the one chosen to wield the blade. Tiresias sent the Black Flag notification to Hal's phone while he was sitting on the toilet in a Level 30 restroom. He was playing e-solitaire, trying to take his mind off the party's collapse and the strange rash spreading down his inner thighs.

"Alexis Straker's employment terminated with immediate effect. Please remove her from the building by 2015 hours by any means necessary. Tiresias."

Hal squirted, stood, zipped and flushed so swiftly he nearly dropped his device into the churning water. Failure to execute would mean his own termination. Experience taught him every security guy is a prisoner in the end.

He moved gingerly downstairs, flat feet and weak ankles struggling to bear his plump, middle-aged frame. The Imagineering Zone was a subterranean labyrinth where hundreds of worker bees sustained the hive mind, and where lost souls drifted in political purgatory. How they used to gawp cluelessly at each other, trying to create plausible stories from the maniacal dreams spunked upon them from above. A scattered shipwreck of slaves sunk in an ocean of confusion, swept this way and that by the tempestuous whims of an islanded elite. *Those guys talk a foreign language up there*. In Hal's tenure, at least six Martians had been hospitalised with over-stimulation. If the rest ever rushed to the surface to witness the true light of day, their heads might explode with the bends. Which would mean even more shit to clean up.

Hal hated what this place had done to Alexis. What it had done to his country. His awakening came during a graveyard shift, when he mistakenly entered one of Galatea Zero's recuperation cells. Conceived by Roland, these small windowless chambers were hidden in the building's walls and only accessible via camouflaged doors, for reasons Hal never understood. The cells offered bubbles of solitary despair where Martians could reinvigorate themselves after prolonged exposure to the pressures of fabricated politicking.

During a dizzy spell on patrol, Hal leaned against a wall on Level 3 and accidentally activated a cell door with his blue ring. The pod slid open silently, opening onto a black space illuminated by wafting nebulae of green and violet on the walls. Fragmented legends scrolled portentously across the synthetic sky. *You are the sublime. Abundance is nothing. Move to higher ground.* Twirling through hidden speakers came a bastardised form of psychedelic space jazz. A tinny, turgid sound, like it was being piped through an antiquated music box. On the floor was an unoccupied red Maars Mindscape meditation cushion. Crawled up in a ball lay one of the party's legal counsels (Bill? Bob? Baxter?), wearing only pink boxer shorts and a sweat-stained grey shirt. A cuddly, bee-shaped stress toy was tucked between his twig-thin knees. There was a teary look of confused longing on his face. From his mouth tumbled incoherent phrases about cherry cola. Just a puff of wind and this man of law would wither to colourless ash, emitting a noise so feeble only owls would hear it. Hal backed away from the door slowly. He didn't sleep for two nights afterwards.

Tonight, the reckoning had come. According to Tiresias's data, not a soul was hiding in the recuperation cells. The Martian lemmings had scrambled to the promised land of Level 25 and above. The T-Chat was flooded with bravado. Many Martians claimed they would enjoy a better view of the slaughter and weren't afraid at all. Which meant they didn't want to face the consequences of their actions. Everybody knew the landslide was a fraud too far.

Down and around, down and around. Hal imagined himself as a lovestruck Orpheus on a mission to rescue his sweetheart from the bowels of the underworld. To reclaim for mankind the fiery red hair, svelte legs and sexy swing of her hips. He knew Alexis was a bad girl. The kind who, if the politics of the situation so demanded, could be more than a bit mucky in the bedroom. But if Hal could persuade her to flee with him, they would morph into legendary lovers on the lam and cleanse each other's souls. Mojitos, mountain views and mad, mid-life crisis poetry that would run on and on until they reached the edge of everything.

As he descended the stairwell past Sub-Level 6, his eyes caught a wisp of blue light seeping out beneath a doorway at the end of a corridor. Inside, the gentle sound of fingers pattering across plastic. Hal's heart fluttered. Creeping forward behind his torch, he wondered what heroic words would ease the worried soul of this very delectable damsel in distress.

"Hello?"

The pattering continued.

"Alexis, that you?"

A sigh of irritation.

"We need to get out of here."

The beam of his torch passed over the door's ID panel. CORAL. Hal knew the space. A pokey sanctuary for Martian deep work, with minimalist furnishings submerged in a nauseating colour scheme of azure, cobalt, ultramarine and sapphire. Tonight, the room was black, the only light source being a computer screen illuminating the transfixed face of a beautiful sea creature. Crouched over her laptop, a pearl at the bottom of this tiny artificial ocean, was the Martian party's former chief speechwriter.

Alexis Straker swirled in a cauldron of creative heat. A typhoon of flaring temper and wild imagination. Within the shadows would be a gorgeous bob of red hair that accentuated her cool ivory face and stonewashed blue eyes. Drooping from her snarling mouth was a smouldering, unfiltered cigarette. While on duty in the Hedonism Rooms, Hal used to love watching Alexis roll her own cancer sticks while she blithely ignored the sleazy wretches from IT slobber in her ears.

He moved closer and rolled his beam slowly across her space. On the desk, Hal could make out three disposable coffee cups, a white leather tote bag and Alexis's white asymmetric trilby hat. She was wearing a white business jacket over a tight black vest. On the jacket's lapel, a kingfisher brooch dipped downwards. They said she had a peace dove tattoo somewhere as well. Her fuzzy, flame-coloured locks had been trimmed and tied back, leaving only a single ribbon of red coiling down her left cheek.

"You've changed your hair," he said.

Alexis didn't respond.

"Time's up, Alexis. We need to get moving."

"Yeah," she replied without shifting her eyes. "Shit upstairs is getting a bit silly, isn't it?"

"Then what are you still doing here?"

"I'm on deadline," she said, as if explaining to a child the earth moved around the sun.

"Seriously? Come on Alexis, it's over. You need to get out of here. They've waved the white flag. Nobody below twenty-five is safe at all. The scum will waterboard whoever's left."

"Yeah right. Smoke and mirrors, Hally. A diversion. You know what this place is like. Everything's a mirage."

"No Alexis, you're not listening. It really is game over. I've been told to remove you from the building. Confiscate your devices."

"The fuck you will," Alexis snapped. She glared up at Hal, her ferocious face filtered by digitalised blue. "This speech is going to get approved by Augusta. Even if I print it out and shove it down her throat. Tiresias wanted more soul. I'll give the sneaky shit more soul."

"*Your contract is terminated*," Hal said. He moved closer and held up his phone between her eyes and the laptop screen.

"Motherfuckers," she said, taking the cigarette from her mouth and stubbing it out on the desk. Her mind was already swirling five or six moves ahead. He remembered their first encounter, when he was managing the cloakroom at Roland's birthday party. A full-length black-and-grey cashmere coat with raspberry lining. The belle of the ball and everyone's tip for Chief of Staff. Until that oily bastard Relpek came along. She hadn't been the same since. The rumour was she couldn't write for shit these days.

"The speech is wrapped up," said Hal. "I've already exited three people. They've all been doing the same job. All struggling with the same speech. Tiresias is taken a composite of all your best bits. It's a great machine sucking you dry and spitting you out. *Time to go.*"

The spirit drained from Alexis's face. Aged only twenty-seven, she was ready to pop. Hal's heroine was in a state of death denial, pirouetting through a fantasy alpha culture of tall dark men, glittering trophies and opulent treats for all senses. Couldn't open to him. Couldn't drop her guard. Couldn't bring herself to say she wasn't mentally right. If Hal had just one night with her, he would make it all ok. Purge his lover of the restless demons which chewed her soul. Uncork the champagne, feed her dark chocolate and make sweet, slow love to her in front of a fireplace as the flames danced through the folds of her soft red hair.

"Listen Alexis, I can get you out of here."

Hal swept around to her side of the table, grabbed Alexis's right shoulder, spun her round on the chair and lowered the flashlight so the beam didn't shine in her eyes. "If we leave now there's still a chance you'll make it out of here safely. *These people will fucking kill us.*"

"Firstly, take your hands off me," said Alexis. "Secondly, I don't like your tone. Thirdly, nobody is killing me today mate. And finally. Tell me calmly. In slow sentences. With simple words. Just how bad is it up there?"

"There's way more than expected. Not enough police. People are shit scared. All retreated to the mid-level. And you need to–"

"What's Tiresias doing about all this?"

"–stop drinking so much rocket fuel and fucking listen to me for once! They've breached the perimeter. Tiresias has gone nuts and is letting them in. Open your eyes."

"Augusta?"

"Radio silence. There are no plans to leave. I hear she's going to sit it out and rain hell on the police for leaving Galatea so exposed. Almost like they've tried to test her straightaway. Apparently the missile strike will still go ahead."

Alexis leaned back in her chair, eyes rolling and raging. Exploding into space like a cobra striking its prey, she sent all three coffee cups flying with a fling of her arm. Hal struggled to keep his torch in step with her banshee motions as she paced the room. He noticed she was wearing a thick black leather belt with an X-shaped red buckle above a short white skirt. In the twilight, she resembled an occult priestess concocting sacrilege in the shadows.

"Fucked again! Shafted by parasitical, talentless idiots. The drip, drip, drip of poison in her ear. It's like I'm sitting on a beach and this tide of crap is swallowing me up and I can't do anything about it. A whole fucking deluge. Maybe that's what they've found out in the sea. A big pile of excrement spelling my name. I ought to tear this machine apart. Algorithm by fucking algorithm. I'll never be a number, Hally. Do you hear me? *Never a number*."

2781694 knew she was screwed. Relpek was the real source of all her fury. The slimiest of slimy shits. Smooth talk, silky skin and polo-playing charm. After he dumped her, the grapevine said Alexis was so broken she had two guys in Procurement on her at once. Got it on video. Maybe Augusta saw it and realised what a downward spiral could look like.

God only knows what Alexis got up to when drunk dialling after hours in her apartment on the east side of Galatea. Hal would happily take a shot at finding out.

"Alexis please be quiet. It can hear everything you say."

"Fuck that. Fuck Tiresias. And fuck you. Get me into the top floor. Say you couldn't track me. Christ, say I assaulted you or something. I need to get in a room with Augusta. *She needs to see my speech.*"

"You won't make it," Hal said, closing off her movements with his bulky frame, switching off his torch and steadying her by the shoulders. He moved his face towards hers. *This close. To her. In the dark.* He inhaled her caffeinated breath. Felt through the jacket to her bones. A fragile bird hiding its frailties behind flurries of exotic plumage. She fell quiet. There was something between them. He knew it in his heart. God knows he deserved her. And if he was misreading the signs now, he never wanted to read anything again.

"I know a way out," he whispered. "There's an emergency service exit which has been left exposed. If we can bust through in less than two minutes, we'll be in one of the tunnels outta here. Free."

"Bullshit. I'm not going anywhere. When's the party starting?"

"You can't get to the top anymore. *You. Are. Fired.* Get it through your lovely head."

"Then you may as well parade me naked through our pack of maniacs up there. They can pull me apart limb by fucking limb."

"Let's go Alexis. *Please.*"

"Eight times. Eight fucking times Tiresias has knocked it back. I've memorised it off by heart. It's humiliating the way it makes me go through this process. Like a fucking performing monkey."

Alexis's fuse blew. She pushed Hal out the way, groped on the desk for her laptop and hurled it across the room. From the void there came a smash. Hal felt something sharp sting his cheek. Shrinking into the corner, too timid to raise his torch, he felt like a little boy trapped in a cage with a wild animal.

"I can't give you access to the Visionary Complex," he muttered. "But I can get you out of here to safety. They've cast us all adrift. Can't you see what's going on? They're luring in the protestors so they have a pretext to wipe them out. Follow me. I'll keep you safe. You and me can do this."

Prolonged silence. An almost symphonic shift in Alexis's voice.

"Come on Hally, yes you can."

She was right beside him now, stroking the blue ring on the third finger of his left hand.

"I can't," he said, feeling dizzy. "They've locked me out too."

"*Yes. You. Can.*"

She blocked him off in the corner, cupping his face with her hands.

"It'll be an adventure, sweet prince. A walk on the wild side."

Mental fireworks erupted in Hal's head. He imagined them running hand in hand, silhouetted against an exploding Galatea Zero. In wilderness's bliss, they'd watch civilisation go down the chute, then breed an army of children to reunite the world. He might not get another chance to say it.

"Alexis, I love you. More than you realise. I will not let you go up there. We can be together. Trust me. Let's get away and never look back."

On the tiniest of hinges, Hal's future twisted and flapped. Alexis slowed her breathing and kissed him on the lips. He was gone, drifting through the cosmic beauty of deep space, a grinning star child bathed in the amniotic fluid of divine power. Torch well and truly turned on.

"You're a sweetie, Hal. A sweetie who is right. I need someone who's got my back. This whole thing's gone too far. Time to wrap up."

His heart pounding, Hal moved the light beam towards the table in reverence. Alexis coolly picked up her bag, placed the hat on her head and took a steadying breath. She presented herself to him in supplication. They were going to make it as a couple. In all this madness, they were going to make it.

"I'm sorry, I just get so… focused," she said. "It's a sin, I know. I need to get out of this place. Once and for all."

"Follow me," gushed Hal turning to the door and trailing his left hand behind, waiting for hers to interlock. "If we turn off our trackers and get there in the next two minutes, Tiresias won't be able to –"

Hal's head jolted back. Something was clamped around his throat. He jammed his fingers under what felt like a leather belt. Alexis was too strong. He was being pulled back, heels dragging along the carpet.

"Sorry Hally, I'm hating myself a little bit," came her voice. "But only a little bit. These people are not. Going. To. Shut. Me. Out."

With a ferocious swing, Alexis rotated all of Hal's sixteen-stone frame and slammed it against the wall. With the speed of a professional pickpocket, she snatched his phone, torch and blue ring from his finger in three fluid motions. *Beep. Click. Whoosh.* Hal tumbled backwards into the recuperation cell onto his ass. *Whoosh. Click. Beep.* Alexis sealed the door from the outside, a permission available to blue ring owners so they could isolate fellow Martians who went off the deep end.

"Crazy bitch!"

"Tut tut Hally. That's no way to talk to a lady. Especially one you're trying to bed."

"Let me out," he squealed, the last vestiges of his manliness dripping into the drain. "I get claustrophobic."

"That's just your age, Hally. You're old, overweight and foolish. And far too nice. I didn't sleep with you because you're too nice. You're down here because you're too nice. And you're not safely in the Visionary Complex with the survivors because you're too nice. Far too fucking *nice*."

Hal clambered to his feet and banged on the door with his fists like a thrashing toddler. Sweat. Hot flushes. Rash spreading.

"Please let me out and we'll go our separate ways. I'm sorry about saying I loved you. Something just came over me. Trust me."

"Something's come over me too Hally. It's called reality. I've worked too hard to be fucked over by anyone. *Trust me*. If that's not a sick joke, I don't know what is."

"If I stay in here, I won't make it. I get dizzy."

"That's your lookout mate. If you're that fucking stupid to take a chance on love in this place, well. There is nothing between us Hally. People like you aren't built for this world. Stay put. Keep out of harm's way. I'll come and collect you when I'm back in the game. I'll personally write the retirement cheque."

The door to Coral closed. With that, the solitary flame in Hal's life fizzled out. He sank to the floor and waited to feel his breath. Maybe Alexis was right. If he stayed here, he would be safe from them all. Except Tiresias. The evil machine could see him now. Watch his movement. Sense his pulse. Monitor his fear. Hal gazed into the black waiting for images of deep space to emerge. They never did. Instead, he imagined a thousand faceless enemies circling and closing, all deciding whether Hal should be allowed back up or go down for good.

There was nothing left to do except invent brighter stories. The door may open any time. 2781694 may return full of regret and ready for love. A benevolent, victorious protestor might lead him to safety with an outstretched arm, into the light of a new dawn where his family would forgive him for all he'd done. Or the door might never open, and he would twirl aimlessly in the void until the oxygen ran out. In the blackness, the tinny sound of a music box returned. Its grating melody burrowed into his brain, while above his head, powerful people no longer in control groped desperately into the dark.

VI

"Why don't you say anything anymore?" Adam snapped after waking into another pitch-black dawn. "It pisses me off. Wouldn't hurt to start a bit of small talk, all things considered."

At the other end of the boat, enthroned in the yellow haze of a small electric lamp balanced on a wooden bench, Columbus sat in the lotus position. The explorer had changed clothes again, swapping his ostentatious ruff and slashed green doublet for a baggy kaftan that glowed golden brown. He gazed out to sea, his diaphragm ascending and descending in sync with the waves.

"Ohhhhmmmmmmmm."

Columbus would often do this. Goading Adam from a distance, like he was some thick gorilla cramped behind exhibition glass. A once-proud species on extinction's verge. Too big for his school desk. Too big for the dormitory bed. Too big for the boat. If the lights of undiscovered land ever came on, Adam hoped his imaginary companion would dissolve back up his arse and into the illumined air of history.

"Everything's a joke to you, isn't it?"

"Ohhhhhmmmmmmmmmmmmmaaaaayyybbbeeee."

"Keep laughing mate."

Adam cast off the thin, stony-coloured blanket and belched bilious fumes into the darkened morning. There were no stars shining in the sky. His mouth was vacuum dry. His legs and arms sore. His head thumped after last night's one-man pity party of fantasy rum. Gripping the side of the boat, he lifted himself slowly until all five feet eleven inches were upright. Easing through the dull, persistent pain in his lower back, he puffed out his pecs and extended his arms sideways.

A yawn emerged through yellow teeth, as Adam rubbed his right palm across the prickles of stubble sprouting unevenly on his face.

"You take it too far," he said, holding up the thumb and forefinger of his right hand about a centimetre apart. "I'm this close to attacking you."

"Threats now," replied Columbus. "You keep forgetting I'm your one and only guide. And you're a tourist in an undiscovered country."

"Guide, my arse," said Adam. "We're more lost than ever. Something better happen quick. We can't all be like you. Some of us get tired and lonely. You don't even want to connect at times. Makes me feel like I'm some sort of weird alien."

"That's because you are. I warned you this was a place for grown-ups. This is no time for adolescent wobbles. Vocal, physical or mental."

"I *am* a grown up."

"Really? Why do you keeping come here then? Because you know that I know that you know the real world is too much for you. Living in your head is quite the experience, I must say. God knows what you'll be like when you have to get a proper job."

Another dry coughing fit. Rasping and guttural, like a layer of skin was being scraped from his oesophagus. Adam's lower back seized as he waited for the pain to peak. Three deep breaths to centre himself, even though he didn't know what the centre was anymore. Or the time of day. How could you even measure a day without any sun?

He made his way to the end of the boat and unzipped. A trickle, a flow and a turbo-charged torrent of urine streamed into the panoramic abyss. Feint flecks splashed up every now and again on his hands. Exquisite relaxation. A ripe, tangy smell. More pungent than usual. A stinging sensation at the tip of his cock. *Tedium, thy name is infection.*

"I've warned you about that," chided Columbus. "Alien fluids might spoil the signal. You do have a bottle to take care of that. Most sailors lost at sea end up drinking their own urine. Healthier in the long run."

"I'm not defiling a bottle of rum with piss, even if it's my own," snorted Adam. "That's not the kind of thing real explorers do."

Columbus was getting to him. Yet raising his voice only hurt Adam's throat. His mouth was dry. The boat dry. The conversation dry. An oasis of aridity in a desert of unchanging water. When they set off, he was optimistic. The further they travelled from the orphanage, the more lost they'd become. There was no sign of land. No sign of the tower. No sign of her.

"What is that anyway?" asked Adam, zipping up.

On the horizon above the sea was a semi-circular void of jet black. It was more intense than the surrounding inky gloom. An inverted sun rising to bleed new darkness into the world. Demarcating it from the rest of the sky was a circumference of flickering lights. Each spun slowly towards the negative space, like stardust swirling down a cosmic sink. As soon as they vanished, new ones emerged to replenish them.

Adam imagined touching one of these dying jewels. They might break into a million pixels, or he would lose his hand in the cool unreal. He remembered his dream within a dream during a night in the voyage long ago. A lady falling gracefully into a vortex, slipping through his fingertips as the whirlpool closed around her. A sandcastle blown apart on the beach. A crimson snake swallowing its own tail. A little girl lost crying for her daddy. Who the author of these visions was he could not say.

"A black hole," replied Columbus in a patronising tone. "An empty space with a power to distort everything around. These things happen when stars begin to collapse. That's what stars do. The literal and the metaphorical ones. They get too big for themselves. Until they end up in the clutches of something they don't understand."

"You can talk, mate."

"My journey to the new world was an act of faith. I served a higher power."

"Yeah right. I wonder if the indigenous people agree."

"We started with the best intentions. They just happened to be quite profitable."

"And what were they? To connect or to control?"

"That's rather a grey area if you don't mind me saying so. Don't wind yourself up, son. It's not good for someone in your condition."

"Loneliness is a condition now, is it? A teenager's mind is bound to wander in these circumstances. I'm the universe's most liberated prisoner. And don't call me son."

"Loneliness is *the* condition. Thinking you can escape it is the biggest fiction of all."

Adam let that one slide. In his mind's eye, he pictured The Pretty Girl In The Year Above diving into the water. Recalled that flicker of light. The spectral spark. The trace of red flame in that very first orb which shone from the space above the settling water. He thought about retreating to the real world, then that notion slipped under the surface too. Reality would never be his thing.

"I didn't come here looking to escape. I came to discover her spirit. To bring her light back to the surface. That's the only adventure I care about. She's out here somewhere, I can feel it. We just need to keep reaching out."

Columbus released himself from the lotus position, stood up and gave his body a shake. The explorer made his way towards the back of the boat, sat down beside him and wrapped an arm around his shoulders, like a pissed-up uncle trying to bond with a sullen nephew.

"Then let's sail into the darkness together my friend."

Revitalised by his meditation, Columbus was bursting with know-all condescension. "But be warned. You won't be able to see anything in the black hole. Maybe that's no bad thing. I deserve a break from looking at your miserable, land-lubbing face. And your relentless fidgeting."

"How do you know I'll find her?"

"I don't know anything. If you knew everything, you'd go mad. And there would be nothing left to explore. The black hole could be a gateway. Could be a tomb. The realisation of our own squeaking irrelevance. I like to think it's another question mark. This is your dream my friend. I've given up guessing what lurks in the sewers of your subconscious."

Across the dark sea, the horizon waited. Adam rose from the bench and placed his hands on his hips. He looked pensively around into the oil-black night and lifted his jaw like an admiral sailing towards battle.

"Ok then. Lead the way. Should I say anything to the troops?"

"Say what you like. I'm sure you'll find the magic words soon enough. My only advice is not to look too hard. *You need to feel, not see.* Let your imagination connect it all together. Patience is what's needed out here. Your lights will eventually lead the way. You'll reach the other side. And so will they."

VII

The Visionary Complex of Galatea Zero. Twenty-one years after the Fall.

Lewis was on a quest to summon his queen from the dead, so felt no guilt about murdering the guard. He took sweet aesthetic pleasure in springing upon his assailant like a tiger and watching fear flood his face. The fourth man he'd killed on the long, lonely pilgrimage from the blackest pit to the highest mountain. A mission that couldn't be stopped. A meeting written in the stars. His victim couldn't see too good anyway. At least not as well as Lewis.

This was as far as I went. You must continue your own story now.

Her voice arrived at school. Fingertips from the past sweeping aside the soot of the present. A letter. Written by hand. Magic words, generating a kaleidoscope of images across Lewis's mental sky. The muse never left him. She hovered above his dormitory bed on sleepless nights. Followed him during lonely perambulations inside the compound's high stone walls where not even moss took root. Sung to him through the furnace's frenzied heat, the fires of industry quelled by cool, liquid hope. Always in the woods, where Lewis lay on the moist ground, smelled the lush foliage and listened to the murmurs of the trees. An earthy voice, breathing beatific visions into his soul. Leading him across the wasteland. To the coast. To where she fell.

Once a heavenly oasis, the Visionary Complex was now a temple to vacuity. The corridor swept round in a circle, branching off into empty spaces and abandoned suites. Psychic residue of thwarted ambition frosted the glass partitions. Apart from a few fragmented ornamental nudes, PRISM had stripped everything of value after Augusta's downfall. A gallery

69

without paintings. A palace without poise. Black holes in the ceilings where cameras used to be. Lewis's eyes roved and darted into the past, imagining sycophants and courtiers hovering like parasitical fleas around the talented few. He dragged his fingers over the milky white walls. Within the building's matter he could feel a low throb, the subdued yet unvanquished lifeforce of a sleeping biomechanical beast.

This place was the hinge on which everything turned, the letter said. Seven sheets of paper. The only evidence of his past. From a time before PRISM processed his infant body. More than a letter. *A manifesto*. For the words on the pages and the voice in his head gave him purpose. Inspiration. And with that inspiration, protection. When he was alone and sleeping in the undergrowth, vigilant to marauders and the quaking of the earth, Lewis's senses become peripheral. Prolonged exposure to danger taught him to detect the quietest of threats. Spiders, flies and beetles taking residence in his space. PRISM had sculpted him into a finely tuned killer. An avenging angel who professed to come in peace, yet someone who could set fire to adversaries and marvel at the fluency of the flames. But the letter taught him something else.

Did the sea creatures want the same thing he did? It was the third time he'd seen one, but never that close. Not so close you could see *into them*, losing yourself in the dark red kernel that pulsed at the centre of white lights nested in wombs of black. Before they'd watched from the sea, oscillating back and forth in the waves. Above the surface long enough to suggest they were amphibious. Which they were, for one had climbed the tower. To save him. Yet what had they freed except a heap of twisted sinew, a troubled man which PRISM had discarded like one-hundred-year-old rope?

The Intelligence Room of Interdependent Systems was connected to the rest of the building by three walkways which hovered two hundred metres high above the atrium.

Lewis moved along the south walkway towards the black steel walls of the vacated throne room. In IRIS, he would solve the mystery of the fallen angel. Since receiving the letter, he learned what he could through disconnected artefacts about Augusta's one-day reign. Underground interviews, recordings, articles, hearsay and rumours on which he superimposed his story. But he couldn't conceive the panic of her last hours when power's rhapsody succumbed to funereal dirge with terrifying ease.

IRIS is where we decided the fates of people, the letter said. *Where we commanded armies. Titans in the sky, lighting the way for everyone to follow. Heroes in our own way. Because it takes courage to lead. To overcome being hated. To follow your dreams.*

Through the force of his vision, Lewis would purify what was once toxic. Resurrect the past; the only place he felt was worth visiting. He took the eyeball from his pocket and held it to the circular sensor. The entrance slid open with silent grace. New air filled his nostrils. Mustier, denser. Closer to death. Another voice entered his mind, urging him to return to the orphanage and hide under the covers. Go back to drawing his pictures. Carve his characters on the bark of trees. Manifest with his hands whatever ocular poetry unfurled in his brain.

This is where it all ended and began. The lights in IRIS switched on to tinge the darkness in amber. The walls were about six metres thick, enough to hold rooms in themselves. Two other exit doors presumably led to the other walkways. Like everything in Galatea Zero, this twenty-metre by twenty-metre space was stripped bare. No furniture, no energy, no life. *This is what a broken heart looks like.* If the entire planet was destroyed, Lewis imagined IRIS would still be there, sustained in the clouds by the aura of its own insularity.

The room's only centrepiece was the Portal, a screen on the east side surrounded by a bare wall of slate grey plaster. A black circle, trimmed with steel. The oracle through which Tiresias communicated to its master. Lewis gazed into the Portal for a long time, waiting for its message. A dead space formerly filled with synthetic colour. Plans, visions, data, analysis, projections. Stories. No natural light though. Augusta wanted to be the creator of all things optical. And to acknowledge an earthly equivalent would mean ceding power to higher forces than her and Tiresias. Yet even that all-powerful seer failed to anticipate its downfall. When in its last moments, the computer became what computers always are. Streams of numbers adding up to nothing, absorbed in the flow of more potent, destructive passions.

The official verdict on Augusta's death was assassination by insurrectionists. A Martian bureaucrat with a reassuring face appeared on the news channels to steady the ship. Resources were not deployed correctly, he said. Tiresias malfunctioned, accelerating a political death spiral of astonishing speed. A terrible accident. A private funeral for Augusta's non-existent body. Reclaiming it from the contaminated land was too dangerous. The covert blinding and pacification of all remaining protestors. The need to 'come together and heal'. The contrite recognition the great Martian experiment had failed. A peace accord with PRISM. An act of union and political integration. The usurpers of PRISM taking power behind friendly, soulless eyes. Everyone intoxicated, numb and enslaved to new computerised systems.

Until one day the PRISM machine decided it didn't want to be invisible anymore. It had its own means of creative self-expression. Soon even that became empty space. In the war which followed, rebels penetrated PRISM's underground headquarters and blew apart its cuboid mind. There was nothing inside. The monolith splintered to reveal a series of ciphers, each one ignorant of everything outside its narrow, self-contained cosmos of code, their only purpose to pass instructions to the next unit. Conflict raged blindly to this day, insentient and disconnected.

Retrieve the past and reshape the future. Create a new vision for us all. Then one day a door you've never seen before will open and she will appear.

The images in the letter were alive, full-blooded, almost tactile. As irrefutable as the physical laws of the universe. *What goes up, must come down. So what goes down, must surely come up.* The wall around the Portal waited to be resuscitated. With ritualistic precision, Lewis set down his long grey coat, opened his rucksack and took out the two tins of paint. Pure brilliant white. Beautiful, rich, lustrous. A smaller tin with the red accent colour, like the one he'd seen in his dream. No brushes. He liked to apply the paint with his fingers, feeling the abrasive surface mellow under soothing swathes of purity. To cleanse the air with the sweat of his artistry. The ornamental box came next. Lewis felt its weight and pictured himself nursing a new-born baby. He placed it reverentially on the floor before his canvas.

Kneeling on the cold tiles, Lewis uttered the incantation. His voice was slow and soporific, like he was being reabsorbed into his own dream through the power of ancient language. A lullaby in a letter, deeply pressed into paper. Before the Fall, they would say he was mad. Maybe that was how the finest temples began. If he breathed enough soul into this surface, his creation would last for a thousand years and withstand the most titanic of floods. A holy light would shoot through space-time and illuminate the shadows in his heart. Hands would join together and sculpt a new world. From there, he would witness things no one had ever seen before and have the second sight to call them home.

VIII

The Olympus Suite of Galatea Zero. Twelve days before the Fall.

Max could never find the lady in bed with him. The one thing he'd learned about Augusta Maars in the six dizzying weeks he'd become her chief of staff, confidante and lover was she didn't want to be found.

When he probed for deeper intimacy she withdrew, vanishing into deflections, diversions and dramatis personae designed to dissemble. The spoilt rich girl who saw red when he wore the wrong aftershave. The taciturn mystic baffling him with cryptic innuendos about half-forgotten dreams. The high priestess of the morning campaign meetings, where she would look through him like he was a stranger. The flicker of fear when someone unfamiliar came close. Those dark, unreachable moments at the end of long days when unsated ambition ran rampant behind her eyes. As they did tonight, while Tiresias crashed stormy grey digital waves with synthetic passion against a pixelated coast.

Earlier at the power plant, Augusta delivered the thirty-seventh speech of her campaign. Max watched her prepare for it as he lay in their bed, verbally finessing the final paragraphs. Ignoring his chuntering, the ghostly figure before the dressing mirror systematically constructed her public self. The meticulous application of make-up. The mechanical brushing of her hair. The laboured way this wounded, middle-aged lady turned into a political firebrand whose eyes sizzled with appetite.

Some frailties couldn't be hidden. Her left leg stopped being real below the kneecap. Half a woman, said the cruellest of adversaries. The scars of a hard-earned life, wrote client journalists. Some mornings, Max would attach

Augusta's prosthetic leg as she sat on the edge of the bed, her solitary big toe grazing the carpet. It was a weirdly erotic yet subservient performance, like her most senior aide was no more than a concubine preparing his warlord for battle.

In the plant's turbine hall, she emerged from the shadows and onto stage wearing a powder blue suit and queen bee brooch. Strobe lighting and Martian anthems pinged and popped to create the aura of a rock star savant. From behind the specially built lectern, designed to elevate her five-feet-one-inch stature to the cameras, Augusta expressed a vision for the country's natural resources with ferocious clarity. Her self-assurance was embarrassing at first. Until the hypnosis took flight. Bewildered engineers and friendly hacks soared on the balmy tempests of her rhetoric. Augusta's voice swept from low to high with the sweetness of a violin concerto, the collective mood climbing and coasting in sync with her diction. She was captivating on television. Even more mesmerising on radio, when her euphonic tones sounded like an angel's address sung across space. You wanted to believe in her because she believed so much in herself. *I'll never take my eyes off you, Max. You'll always be safe with me.* Soon she would officially become the most powerful figure in the land. Gliding at a level where there was no such thing as good or bad, just the clashing of depersonalised systems and narrow interests.

That evening, in the most opulent suite of the skyscraper's summit, Max and Augusta lay clasped amid satin sheets. Gold embroidery spelling A&R weaved between the Klimt-inspired patterns. In the distance, artificial waves rolled and roiled, the sound of their static spray rippling through the room. Lavender fragrance sifted across space. In the warmth of the bed, Augusta swooned between sexual voraciousness and child-like timidity. Max pushed his muscular frame into her, yielding at the slightest resistance. Rarely out of control, Augusta coaxed him closer and closer to the cliff edge.

Love began on a damp Tuesday afternoon. They met one-to-one in the Medici Suite to discuss the campaign's media plans. Bluntly, confidently, she asked him to strip in front of her, mental fingertips already tracing the edges of his masculinity. Max succumbed, thirsting to be in power's grip. He enjoyed her comments about his bronzed body. How big he was. She devoured him that day, tiny hands losing themselves in the chocolate-brown meadows of his curls.

Rumours soon circulated. His mother called him to say how disappointed she was he'd 'got into bed with that nasty bitch'. His oldest friend sent him a message asking if he'd found his soul lately. The polo club cancelled his membership. Monika told him over the phone to go fuck himself. Always the actress. Thankfully Alexis was so out the loop now she hadn't twigged. She could be one hell of a fiery bitch. A brooding, combustible vixen in over her head and capable of castration. For Max, sleeping with one eye open seemed a wise move.

As an inside man, he was more energised than ever. The thrill of preparing for government. The imaginary adrenaline charge of sending soldiers to battle. Moving lives around the chess board. Turning people into numbers and watching them go up and down, on and off. Becoming the story; that grandiose sense of himself as a perceived object of desire, his chiselled face plastered on gigascreens. Women he'd never met sent him risqué footage. A community of fangirls in this strangest of lonely-hearts clubs.

In the happiest moments, Max played the chivalrous knight. A lusty Launcelot courting Guinevere under the nose of Arthur. He even believed Augusta might love him, as much as she was inclined to love. As desire slipped into duty, Max learned his boss's real love lay in numerating the future. In worshipping data. Calculating the probability of success and failure. A frustrated accountant, counting on control. Sex was a method of diffusing the ticking timebomb inside. Too often her customary poise and shrewdness collapsed under physical and emotional appetites. Max marvelled she hadn't been caught yet in a cougar-style scandal. There was a pain inside his leader which, if unchecked, would career the Martian party of a cliff. Augusta was not a beautiful person. Nor a beautiful soul. She was a beautiful *idea*. Maybe that's all leaders were, Max concluded. Personified antidotes to the societal malaise.

In the violet-tinted dark of the suite, amid the scent of wine and the chilliness of the air conditioning, Augusta inhaled Max. Looking blankly into his eyes, she yearned for more. Fingernails digging into his chest. Pelvis quickening. She tasted bitter, her touch cold and taut. Max wondered what her dreams would be like. If she dreamed at all. The all-pervasive processing power of Tiresias hummed. A quad of cameras – one lens in each corner – scanned and decoded the writhing figures on the bed. Tiresias's programs were attuned to microchip sensors embedded in Augusta's flesh. Through data assimilated over weeks, the system of systems would grow more imaginative with its suggestions for sexual play. The power of Augusta's orgasms increased then diminished, increased then diminished. Mistress and machine searched for correlations after deciding who received what money. Who would be promoted and who would be sacked. Who would live and who would die.

One night, Max caught Augusta on the bathroom floor drinking Kalypsol in the dark. Roland was inspecting the Sentinel at the top of Galatea Zero, no doubt berating a hapless minion over a millimetre of aesthetic inaccuracy. Eyes bloodshot and encircled by smeared mascara, Augusta looked up at Max from the shadows of her past. She was still in that car crash with her father, peering through the shattered window on the Mediterranean coast. Trapped and bleeding. A different creature to the tea-sipping germaphobe with a pathological aversion to mess. Awakened and exposed, she ran out of the bathroom and hid under the bed covers without speaking. In unguarded moments, she never could find the words. All she could do was fall silent and blindly carry on.

Sometimes, the speed of Augusta's advancement was so quick everything blurred, as if her eyes couldn't gather enough light to form images. Despite her obsession with data, Augusta's political strategy was to create a mood and an emotion, not a policy or a plan. She believed in the artful, opaque use of language to cloak her intentions. The shameless trading of her past traumas. The death of her parents. The professional rejections. The cruelty of cancer. All worn, like one of her exotic brooches, as badges of honour, sucking her sympathy for others dry like patient, avaricious leeches.

For days at a time, Max would be out in the cold. He would write the book, advise on speeches, learn to be ignored, seek solace in flirtations with junior members of staff. Hit the gym. Be a pretty face. Forget those he'd left behind. He would never go back to being an outsider. A number on the board. Then, when Tiresias told Augusta her first official act as leader would be to launch a pre-emptive strike on a PRISM military base near the heart of its capital, Max was back in the room, a swinging dick seeking advancement. Surrounding herself with macho men on the eve of war would be good PR.

As the end of love approached, Max opened his eyes and watched Augusta's face in the half light. All was hazy. The ghost in front of the mirror was back. Augusta reached the pinnacle, pressing into him tight. Always seeing how far she could push it. Knowing it would never be far enough. In a silent pause, she became lighter. Softer, more supple. Somewhere else entirely, a phantasm dissolving into deep space. Like all the others, this session was being recorded. She would watch it back later, witnessing herself passing through the glade of ecstasy. Wondering what else she could become.

Augusta slid off Max's body. She lay beside him, gently holding his hand. In the simmering dark, his mind drifted across the room to what he'd seen in the Cave a few nights earlier. Accessible only through the Olympus Suite, the innermost sanctum was prohibited to everyone but Augusta and Roland. In the week after they became lovers, she would drop her guard around Max, allowing him to visit the suite without security approval.

One evening, he left his phone by the bed and went back to collect it. In an uncharacteristic oversight, Augusta had entered the Cave and left the door ajar. Through the space, Max glimpsed what had previously existed only in rumour. The treasure consuming husband and wife. Hanging on the wall was the specimen of a sea creature, similar in size to the stag's head which furnished the billiard room at the polo club. The entity floated lifelessly in pale pink amniotic fluid, housed in a glass cabinet. No tail. No fins. No eyes. Just a small black hole surrounded by a fan of grey webbed flesh. An unidentified lifeform, born out of a vacuum emerging under the seabed. Even Tiresias couldn't find the answer. *More data needed. More data needed. Indefinable. Indefinable.* In the creature's void, Max thought he saw a flash of white, like a star. Augusta closed the door without even noticing he was there.

Shadows disrupted Max's memory. Against the tempestuous digitalised sea at the far end of the suite, a silhouette emerged. It rose from the leather smart chair in the corner, where it spent the last ten minutes tapping its foot and twisting its gun. Watching and waiting. Roland Maars was a man who sized everything up before he got involved. He was a weedy, shuffling figure. A slimy piece of clingfilm covering a volcano of anger. His natural smell was one of decay, masked by Martian cologne which had the aroma of rich Argentinian wine.

Roland only dabbled in Kalypsol, one of his more primitive inventions. His real love was Galatea Zero. As the building opened to an awestruck public, he struggled to see real people sully his masterpiece. The skyscraper was so much better when empty, with just its creator patrolling the place in wonder at his own genius. A middle-aged man's penis extension, to accompany the surgical modifications to his real one. Max had seen it, felt it go into him, put it in his mouth. A compensatory hybrid of metallic sheath, e-skin sensors and supposed flesh underneath. Like Sisyphus, Roland could never finish. He was a climber always on the verge of pleasure's summit, only to see it roll away. Perhaps accumulating more data via his adapted organ was the next best thing.

Tonight, an asthmatic wheezing seeping out of his mouth, the architect wanted only his wife. Roland and Augusta made love like they played squash, whacking out at dead space in anticipation of the other's return. Max lay passive amid the power couple's bony tentacles of control, little more than a pommel horse on which the Maars' fluids would coalesce. Another shape formed. Another monster. A conjoined blob feeding off its own solipsistic pleasure, thrashing against itself in some chasmic void. The system of systems continued watching, four red dots peering from the black.

How simple it would be to take them away right now, Max thought. To smash a bottle of wine on the side of the dressing table and slice their dry, leathered flesh. To take control for himself. To become who he was meant to be. *To make sure they would never look down on him again.* But Max had never been a leader. He was only ever a storyteller engrossed by power's snaking charm. And right now, he was edging towards a morbid pit of twisting narratives into which he couldn't stop looking.

IX

The mainland terminal to Galatea. Nine hours before the Fall.

The Windchaser trundled over the potholed roads like a pensioner's golf buggy on a poorly-maintained fairway. Sunlight seared through the window. The blinds were stuck at the top. In his seat above the onboard toilet, Zayden's gangly legs twitched. Next to him slept a middle-aged man in his Sunday best with a copy of *The Martian Times* on his lap. Anxious sounds mumbled from his mouth, like he was drowning in a neurotic dream. Zayden considered taking the paisley handkerchief from his companion's top pocket and wiping the drool from his face.

During the nine-hour schlep from Lower Overton to the terminal, Zayden endured the strangled symphony of passengers vacating themselves into the chemical blue of the toilet. Boozy lunchtime urination. Heaving coughing fits. Triple-flushes to blast God knows what from the bowl. In one repulsive visit to the deposit box, a burly man in a vest emptied himself with a thwack while slurping from a can of super-strength Martian lager. Zayden clenched his buttocks, so his bowels wouldn't loosen in the demonic heat. The thought of unloading with this lot as company disturbed him. As did the idea of his butt cheeks kissing his predecessor's residual warmth.

Fellow Martians joined the pilgrimage en route, from supermarket car parks, bingo halls and housing estate pubs. After the bus collected the final passengers – a beige, geriatric couple wearing matching sun visors – the driver stood at the end of the aisle to address them all. A bespectacled and shaky senior citizen, he had a shock of white hair, the expression of a gormless five-year-old and spoke like a pious primary school teacher after a slug of morning sherry. The speech was a weird quasi-religious tribute to Augusta, to the magnificence of Galatea Zero and to the joy of being with 'so many fine Augustinians on coronation day'.

Tiresias had calibrated everything – education, health, occupation, family, bank balance – and deduced no one on this coach would do anything other than what they were told. There were about six or seven elderly couples. Sober, suntanned and, judging by their supermarket slacks, living on modest pensions. Three groups of two men. Some young, some middle-aged, some belching bierkeller anthems. A few loners too, presumably looking for love, friendship or employment. All here to witness the Second Coming and not behave like the bottom feeders they were.

Zayden knew he'd taken the right turn at life's crossroads. Lozza Quelch was a prick. More so for bringing up the kid. The baby wasn't his, despite what her mother said. No one mentioned he was one in a series of sullied encounters in the pokey bedsit above the betting shop. By no means the first. And definitely not the last shamed lover to flee all that bathroom fungi.

The Overton Massive retreated into the shadows when she caught. Blamed it on the stuck-up swot who wanted to make something of his life. Pull him down a peg or three. *The fall guy, falling fast.* Zayden had chosen his path. Done it cleanly, in the demarcated way he created maps of ancient civilisations at school and filed them in his colour-coded geography folder. The truth would out. They would see what it meant to take responsibility. To take ownership. To not blame circumstance. He would lead the charge to a better world, while they sat in the club slurping Mulligan's Cider and scoffing pork scratchings. *Never saw Zero Nero turning out that way.*

The terminal was the single access point by road from the mainland to Galatea. At two thirty-one in the afternoon, the

Windchaser lurched into the slow, grinding rotation of other vehicles waiting to access the bridge. Verification at this point enabled travellers to make the one-mile jaunt down the Galatean Highway to the island for the final phase of security checks. A malfunction in Tiresias's road traffic assessment units was causing a long tailback. Swirls of sweating motorists formed an expanding series of concentric circles around the terminal. A mood of cumulating anxiety wound with them.

Ten minutes later, the crawl ended. People left their vehicles. After taking a rollerball pen from his shirt breast pocket and jamming into the seal of the malfunctioning door, the Windchaser's driver set his passengers free. Like dozy cattle, they trudged off towards the terminal: an enormous blue shed with high narrow windows and a front façade shaped like the letter G. A sole security guard lurked behind a fast-food menu totem. He was perspiring at pace under his stab vest, like he'd drunk five pints of lager in a Turkish bath.

Outside the entrance was a group of anti-Augusta protestors. Ten in number and totally transparent. Young, dressed to slum and as diverse as a university prospectus, they were poised with their expensive smartphones ready to record Martian brutality. The usual placards. CONSPIRACY IN THE SEA. ALIENS WALK AMONG US. THE BITCH WILL KILL US ALL. *They ought to be careful*, thought Zayden. Tiresias might feel inclined to pick them off one by one with an RM6433 drone. The miniature airborne assassins were flying off Roland's production line due to overwhelming consumer demand.

Ignoring their provocations, Zayden removed a fresh napkin from his inside jacket pocket, placed it on the glass of the revolving door and pushed. Inside was a donut-shaped configuration of low-rent restaurants, Martian merchandise kiosks and three separate arcade units which blinked and blared at people heading to the restrooms. In a human centipede of sadness, the queue for express transition to Galatea stretched from the information suite and coiled twice around the foyer's inner perimeter.

Stark, white sun beat through the skylight onto the pale cream floor tiles. Bloated people made noises about over-priced junk food. Discoloured faces teemed everywhere, lolling atop unsightly bodies which slinked and sweated in the heat. Most of them were heading to cheap, all-inclusive holidays in the south side of Galatea. They would drain the bars of Sangria, dance the conga and swear at the swanky skyscrapers in the distance. About ten metres away near an arcade, three protestors were having a lively argument with three Martians. More of both stripes were closing in.

Zayden wandered to a wacky orange retail unit guarded by a flickering hologram of a Brazilian samba dancer. *I'm not even going to make it to the island. Worse comes to the worse, I'll swim across the drink. Probably be less polluted.*

At Copacabana Coffee, he ordered his third cappuccino of the day. The customer interface unit took a while to load, the choice of blend was provincial by his standards (Guatemalan, Costa Rican) and the customisation feature buffered after four attempts. After Zayden finally registered his order and a Martian bot thanked him for his payment, he turned to the gigascreen which ran the full width and height of the opposite wall.

The world's most charismatic android was doing what he did best. So large you could numerate his nose hairs, Max Relpek's pretty face beamed from a non-Martian news channel in advance of Augusta's first address to the nation, due to start at six o'clock. *Blurgh. Blurgh. Blurgh.* Zayden noticed how the party's language changed since Straker was demoted. *What they needed was some steel*, the gurus said. *Back to basics. Tactical messages about social problems. Not airy-*

fairy visions. Looking too far ahead only took our eyes off the ball.

A smitten junior female journalist probed Max about whether Augusta would have the courage to launch a pre-emptive strike on PRISM. Max waffled. When the journalist pointed out the adversary's military power dwarfed Augusta's and she had no allies to support her attack, he waffled some more. Sure enough, Little Miss Easy Ride didn't go for the jugular. She closed with a feeble question about Maars Enterprises's rumoured investigation into a UFO crashing thirty miles off the coast. The gigascreen cut to covert footage of a Martian vessel heading for shore flanked by patrol boats.

"This story is the biggest nothing," said Max, in the monotone drone for which he was ridiculed by jealous fellow hacks who couldn't make it onto magazine covers. "A void concocted by journalists. What's really happening is a simple experiment with a new drilling system that needs more manpower. Most people are fed up with these paranoid delusions. It's a routine operation. Nothing more. Nothing less. And frankly I doubt the veracity of these images. We all know the jiggery pokery that can be done with computers. You conspiracy theorists love to see stuff that isn't there."

Max smiled into camera with a shit-eating grin, then dissolved. An infomercial for Roland Maars's long-anticipated space flight played. *The best and the brightest. The biggest and the boldest. Welcome to Maars on Mars.* Buxom female models in vacuum-packed spacesuits stared mystically up to the sky from the roof of Galatea Zero. The camera panned and twisted into one of the young ladies' cleavages, from which burst a constellation of lights in the shape of the Martian logo. *This mission will be accomplished,* read the legend.

"*Jiggery pokery.* What a moron that guy is."

Next to Zayden, reflected in the screen and framed by a sprinkle of stars, was a young lady who smelled of citrus perfume. A svelte combo of glinting teeth, cherubic lips, dark brown eyes and raven black hair tied back to accentuate the handsome contours of her cheekbones. The purplish shade of her handbag jarred with her deep blue business jacket, but Zayden could overlook that. She was poised and elegant, with a sexy touch of *sang froid*.

"Goes off message all the time," she continued. "It's a wonder Augusta hasn't sacked him. But she does like her buff bods."

"I always thought Straker was doing a good job," said Zayden, playing it cool by pushing his spectacles up his nose. "Ticked all the right boxes."

"Yeah, except the most important one," replied Mercedes, tapping her finger to her right temple. "Rumour has it she had an affair with Mr Meathead and went a bit crazy. Augusta got wind of it and…. I can't see the appeal myself. Bit of a slimy bastard. You don't need to look too hard to see straight through him. Mercedes Macquarie."

She extended her left hand. Professionally, confidently. On the third finger, a red ring with the insignia M twinkled in the sunlight. Zayden didn't like to shake hands. Now he would make an exception. Mercedes's touch was cold and passive. When Zayden looked into her eyes, he sensed something strangely synthetic. If she broke into a thousand pixels, he wouldn't be surprised. She would still have more personality than anyone else in the terminal.

"I'm a Senior Martian Evangelist. Think of me like Shackleton, dragging the doubters across the arctic wasteland of modern politics. Zayden Nero, right?"

"Cappuccino," barked a voice. Zayden turned to see a plump, saturnine middle-aged lady in an orange and blue uniform slide a brown plastic cup towards him. Whipping out another napkin from his jacket, he grimaced as he soaked up the seepage on the counter. He took his drink without saying thank you.

"I saw your name on the list," Mercedes said, leading him to a quiet spot near the donut kiosk. She slowed her pace and moved to the right so Zayden could catch up on the left. He remembered this performance development technique from a university one-day *World of Work* course. The boss should always be on the right during appraisals. In the arena of matey manipulation, right meant future. Left meant past.

"You mean I stood out from this crowd?" he said, wishing he'd been on a course for flirting with mysterious brunettes. "Things are looking up."

"That's an understatement," Mercedes said. "Top university. Working class bloke. Exceeding expectation. One of us too. Despite all the flak you must have taken at Little Upperton for becoming a Martian."

"Well, you know. Always ready to embrace new horizons."

She smiled.

"Would you be interested in meeting her?"

"Who?"

"Don't play dumb, handsome. Our glorious leader."

"Seriously?"

"I've had a call from HQ this morning. They're worried Tiresias hasn't got the right mix of people at the VIP launch event to show on TV. We need more beef, if you pardon the expression. From the mainland. That was Tiresias's job, but it's thrown its toys out the pram again. Traffic can't get in or out."

"And I'm best of breed?"

"'Fraid so. Don't take this the wrong way. You're not like the Relpeks of this world. You're more real. Authentic. A regular guy. A registered voter. Leading a proper life."

"Is that what you call it?"

"C'mon Mr Nero. This is your chance to get out of cattle class. Live the high life. Move away from the low life, even if it is just for the cameras. I can't promise it'll stay like that, of course. It's all about the show, you know."

"I thought Tiresias would have all this sorted. Right down to the polish on the shoes. The pattern on the ties."

"Tiresias," Mercedes snorted. "The most overrated thing in the history of mankind. Malfunctions all the time. They're just good at hiding it. The only thing it produces is confusion. It's hard to know what's accidental or deliberate. Quite worrying when you realise it's about to start a war."

"So it's definitely happening?"

"Sooner than you think," Mercedes said. "There'll be a strike in the early hours of tomorrow morning. Galatea is ready for PRISM's retaliation."

"And what about everyone who doesn't live in Galatea?"

"They'll be taken care of."

"I bet they will. I suppose Tiresias will malfunction us to victory?"

"Don't worry. The beast tends to raise its game on the big occasions. And Roland will be overseeing the missile sequence. Come see it for yourself. You'll be a witness to history. With your looks and my brains…"

"… you're trawling around this sewer looking for so-called real people to act out your play. A smart move, clearly. Only a day in the power and the government is a paragon of intelligence."

"So that's a yes, then?"

"Listen Miss Macquarie, I don't even know you –"

Oofffhhhurrgggh. Crrrssssshh. Waaarrrhhhh. Next to a grab-a-gift stall running low on plushies, a protestor and a fellow Windchaser were duking it out. It was the big guy with the bald, pink head and the tight white vest they'd picked up from The Red Queen. His adversary – a wiry, geeky man in beanie hat, baggy jeans and tie-dye overshirt – slammed him against the stall's plexiglass, which splintered under the sudden impact of skull. After pummelling him with punches, the protestor indulged silly *Karate Kid* fantasies, unleashing a volley of pretentious kicks to his opponent's guts. A swarm of Martians and protestors waded in with wails and elbows. In the ensuing madness of this pantomime combat zone, Zayden saw one Martian, a tattooed stubbly guy who sat three rows behind him on the coach, dig his teeth into the cheeks of a floored protestor. Opposite the arcade, diners at the Tantalising Tuck food court stared blankly at the melee. A half-soaked terminal employee with acne paced in circles, shouting something into his phone about sending for the special forces.

"See what I mean," said Mercedes, pressing her hand into Zayden's forearm. He flinched. She could certainly grip for someone so slender. Zayden didn't like to be touched unexpectedly. Even by a sex kitten from outer space.

"Only Tiresias could bring so much pond life into one single place," she continued. "Even the smartest computers in the world end up scraping the barrel. Come on, let's go. You're starting to sweat. It's a lot cooler where I'm going."

"I haven't said 'yes' yet. I'm still trying to work out if you're for real."

"Look into my eyes," Mercedes said. "I'm about as real as it gets. You can stay here with all the false teeth or you can live a little. Let the police deal with it. If they ever turn up. By the time they've calmed everything down, we'll be sipping cocktails high above the sea. When you're over the other side, you're protected from everything. Including PRISM's missiles."

Mercedes's eyes were worth a stare. Zayden couldn't discern how much of her was bullshit. She spoke slowly and attentively, either to hypnotise or seduce. A sorceress had come from nowhere to save his golden ticket from the ashes. A flickering phantom with a red ring offering access to all areas. To go would mean meeting the fairy queen herself. To stay would be to swirl speedily downhill. To another flat, above another betting shop.

His brain went left while his feet went right. Then his brain went right and his feet turned left. Zayden hurried in Mercedes's tow, slurping his cappuccino and lowering his head so nobody would see him leave. He wasn't sure who would be watching. To the left of the ladies' toilets, into which patrons queued unfazed by the tedious macho brawl, there was an innocuous door marked OFFICIALS ONLY. Mercedes waved her hand before the access panel. Beyond was a lift and concrete stairwell like those at long-neglected urban shopping centres. A painted number on the wall told Zayden they were on Level 4. Next to it was a blue plastic seven-floor directory sign which bore the legend MARTIAN OPERATIONAL CENTRE. Zayden detected a vague stench of urine drifting in the air. *They really don't want to invest in anything on the mainland, do they?*

"Age before beauty," Zayden said, gesturing to the door with his free hand, sporting a chummy smirk. Mercedes flashed him a look of ice. His face retreated like a frightened turtle into its shell.

They stepped into the lift. After a ten second descent, in which time Zayden entertained a spiky sexual fantasy about Mercedes dressed as a lascivious Viking chieftain, the doors slid open. Shangri-La was revealed. The underground open-plan suite was like an extravagant colonialist hotel during the golden age of empire. The furniture was a mixture of dark wood, burnished leather and sleek black metal emblazoned with the Martian insignia. Lining the walkways were plant pots of exotic greenery stretching to the ceiling. Retro fans spun at pace to blanket the room in cold, reinvigorating air. All desk monitors were inactive. On a video wall at the far end of the suite, a bank of screens showed live footage of the Galatean Highway next to aerial views of the terminal site. In the centre, a countdown clock announced there were only eleven hours and twenty-two minutes until Operation Scarlet Iris began. No phones were ringing. Coffee cups sat abandoned. The place was deserted.

"Late lunch?" cracked Zayden, sweat evaporating from his forehead.

"When the machine calls, you answer," said Mercedes. "They'll be in Galatea now. Buckling up for the big showdown."

"And not a real, authentic guy with a proper life among them?"

"That's a good one," laughed Mercedes. "You know that antennae at the top of Galatea Zero? The one Roland uses to detect alien life? That has more charisma than some of these clowns."

Zayden followed Mercedes to the far side of the office, admiring the orderliness of the Martian workstations. Annoyingly, a few mouse mats weren't aligned to the edges of the tables. One disgusting individual had thrown a can of Maars Carbo and a half-eaten kebab into a wastepaper bin. Soon they branched off into a corridor decorated with pompous black and white photography of Galatean architecture. At the end of the walkway, there was a life-sized statue of Augusta as a Hindu goddess.

"Don't get too impressed," said Mercedes. "A lot of it is tat."

With a flick of her wrist, Mercedes opened a door to her left marked VERNE. Inside was a drab conference room with a long, light-oak table, a dozen chairs and no discernible trace of humanity. The colour scheme was trapped somewhere between green and cream, reminding Zayden of mouldy asparagus. The room's statement piece was a floor-to-ceiling gigascreen, where the Martian party logo floated above a digitalised, sun-kissed sea. It resembled the opening slide of a quarterly financial presentation by a third-rate travel company.

"You going to PowerPoint us out of here?"

"Not quite," Mercedes said, tapping out a key code in a wood-panelled console adjacent to the screen. "Surfaces are deceptive, Mr Nero."

A humming sound. A shift in the light. A gust of cold. The screen dissolved to reveal an entrance into a dark circular tunnel descending into the earth. A series of white LED ceiling lights, red nuclei shining at their centres, illuminated the way. *Down, down, down. Then up, up, up.* Into the dark. Under the water. Resurfacing in a mythical place beyond the sea, where the high-powered and high maintenance writhed and wrestled each other like snakes in the sack. A place where Zayden could make his mark. Where it was all or nothing. Where hopefully they would serve better coffee.

Nothing is random. You've been picked for a reason. They've got tentacles everywhere, these people.

"It'll take forty minutes to reach Galatea Zero if we walk quickly," said Mercedes. "You're crossing the sea on feet, Mr Nero. Consider yourself a modern-day Moses."

Zayden thought back to Lozza. To the tossers at university. Their snide remarks about missed opportunities. The nasty jokes about scrabbling around in stones to find his family. *This is the future. That was the past.* He downed the dregs of his cappuccino and placed it onto the table, not bothering to find a coaster. The drink tasted like shit anyway. The terminal was shit. The mainland was shit. Everything was shit. Now he was being gifted the opportunity to turn shit into sweetest sugar. He was still in two minds about Mercedes. Given the opportunity, he would probably rebuff any offer of subterranean sex as unhygienic. But the access she offered was a chance worth taking. Everything was a chance worth taking. Something unreal was happening today, as if Zayden was being moved into place by fate.

You don't know what's real or fake. For all you know we could be governed by aliens. Or there could be no one in charge at all.

As Zayden followed Mercedes along the chain of white spectral orbs under the sea, he heard a little girl's voice from behind. He turned around. Nobody was there. Pausing to feel the cold steel of his revolver against the inside of his right calf, Zayden pictured himself on breakfast news. Tomorrow, flash footage of him and Augusta would light up screens around the world, their intertwined destinies spelled out sublimely in the stars.

X

*T*here are two kinds of imagination in this world, Mr Joyce once told Alexis. *One kind drags you down. The other lifts you up. Set your sights high. To stay below is to become a prisoner of limited perspective. You can be anything you want to be, Alexis. Remember that. Anything at all.*

Her English teacher's voice was long gone. The swishing of the rising elevator was the only noise she could hear. Alone and upwards. Like she'd dreamt when she was younger. Top of the class. First to raise her hand. Before the name-calling. The banging on the windows. *Alexis Straker. Freak of nature.*

Through the elevator's glass, she could see the lowest twenty levels had lost power. Their interiors were flooded black. A labyrinthine network of secret passageways, hidden rooms and dens of vice lay dormant, incarcerating people like Hal in manufactured voids. Above, the Visionary Complex was shrouded in a spider web of steel girders. The mesh reached outside the building's main fabric to form a huge Byzantine portcullis. The last of the evening sunlight danced across the grey surfaces, creating a glittering arc of sequenced lights to the summit. Galatea Zero, or the G-Spot as it was coarsely referred to by Martians, terminated in the unconquerable sky. At its pinnacle was the Sentinel, a slender aerial mast of titanium with a tip indetectable to the human eye.

"Hello Alexis. You seem a little sad today," said the elevator's information screen, still operational despite the encroaching blackout. "Why don't you pick up the phone and speak to someone who loves you?"

The tears came. *What the fuck is wrong with me?* Hal was a sweet man. A helpful dolt with a pockmarked face, hairy wrists and pleasant green eyes. But his gentle, mumbling voice screamed 'exploit me'. *You led him on, didn't you? That's what people like you do, isn't it?* There was still time to repent. To give up the ghost of Augusta's favour. Head back down. Set him free. The service exit may still be open. They could escape the island, sail to sea on a makeshift raft and maroon on a desert island paradise. Hal would feed her coconuts. Stroke her sore feet. Bore her to tedium. Wait for her in an improvised hut built from branches, stark naked on a bed of palm leaves with a tropical flower drooped in his mouth. A look of gentle bravado in his eye. Try-hard tenderness. The worst kind.

Stupid, stupid Alexis. Why don't you just run away from them, girl? Give up the flights of fancy, the Southern Comfort, the meat-headed men, the broken sex? Away from those comical groans they made before they went limp. *Men.* Strange creatures, weren't they? Walking around trying to own themselves, yet uncomfortable in their own skin. Alien salesmen in the car showroom of life.

Alexis looked at the person in the reflected glass. She was wilting in the heat. A bloated stomach, widening hips, small tits and drawn face. If she persisted with the booze, fags and espressos, she would soon look like the back of a bus. Not on the Martian shopping list. Or anyone's shopping list. Max, the fucking smartarse, had done the right thing. *This is your wake-up call, girlfriend.*

After slamming the brakes on Hal's have-a-go heroism, Alexis squirreled herself to a cubicle in the Imagineering Zone toilets, making her way through the dark by the light of her phone. She spent two minutes standing up massaging her temples. Another two sitting down practising half-baked breathing exercises she'd learned in an up-its-own-arse Martian mindfulness course on Level 35. Eventually, the darkness slowed her down. She'd grown fond of living in the shadows. The LED temple of Galatea was a monument to disorientation. The shifting tones. The patterns on the walls. The streaks of visual vomit. Each competing pixel waging war on her neurons. She was seeing things, like at school. Visual echoes of dissolved patterns. Floating streaks of light. White heavenly orbs racing to the sky. Maybe it was a psychosomatic superpower. Or maybe she was about to go under.

Set your sights high. To stay below is to become a prisoner of your own limited perspective. After popping two paracetamol and a Martian Maniac, Alexis splashed her face with cold water from a wash basin and made her way up the main staircase to the atrium. Normally a glorious open space buzzing with ambition, it now resembled an abandoned train station in an inconsequential rural outpost losing insipid evening light. The only disturbance was the thumping and chanting outside. A dysfunctional society in surround sound. The mob had gathered by the outer doors, smashing at the glass with poles and hammers. A rabid mob of jumped-up little squirts, frenzied and foaming like chihuahuas with rabies.

Alexis was a prize trophy they would love to slice up. She used to be somebody around here. Until she became one of many who stared into space and didn't like to sleep, absorbing the incessant pop psychology pick-me-ups Tiresias streamed out aurally and visually. Still a cut above the everyday proles forbidden full access, confined to glass tunnels through which they could admire Roland's artistry but never fully experience its space.

This time they weren't coming to watch. They were coming to conquer. Somehow the protestors had made it to the island, despite the bridge closing. An inside job, then. One of the underground tunnels left open maybe. Was Tiresias malfunctioning spectacularly, or was it a calculated attempt to lure them to their doom? The most likely explanation was Tiresias or Augusta playing everyone off against each other. Like Alexis dreamed of doing with her three fantasy suitors.

One rich and dull. The other criminal and sexual napalm. The third loyal, patient and with no career prospects. Cut off contact with all of them as soon as kids were mentioned.

Back to the wall, Alexis shuffled around the edge of the atrium. A solitary security guard with a cue ball head and porn star moustache was crouched behind the welcome desk, tapping dementedly on his phone. *Another one who needed tucking in at night.* Shitting his second brick, the guard didn't notice Alexis slinking towards one of the express elevators, groping at the glass wall with her left hand. In a moment of panic, she though Hal's blue ring hadn't worked. *I'm going to be fed to the pigs.* Then the doors opened. Despite the shutdown, the lift was operational. An angelic choir sang somewhere across the sea. Alexis stepped into the lift, punched number 75 on the service panel and raised her excited face to the heavens. In Galatea, as in life, everything that mattered was loaded up top.

You can be anything you want to be, Alexis. Anything at all. The elevator ascended through the deactivated floors and their pompously named executive spaces. Magellan. Vespucci. Scott. Amundsen. Marco Polo. Armstrong. Aldrin. Hubble. Drake. Cousteau. Erickson. Hillary.

"Why don't you go for a nice rest, Alexis? The spa on Level 48 is offering a twenty percent discount for all blue ring-bearers."

Roland designed the lifts to run slow, so people could savour the most expensive dick extension in architectural history. Only a few months ago, he personally gave Alexis the grand tour, smelling of fish and speaking in a lilting, semi-robotic voice.

"From the centre of the atrium you can look up and appreciate how the perspective narrows," he said in his shiny space-grey suit, riding the Rio Grande of his own bullshit.

"A helipad is formed when the tower's apex closes. To indicate the incoming presence of power. A dimming of natural light in reverence. From Level 50 and upwards, Tiresias can even switch the configurations of the rooms. Mobile screens, walls and partitions introduced to enlarge, section off and screen different spaces. It controls the temperature, doorways, lifts, lighting and can blackout rooms at will. Everything fluid and alive, like nature itself. A self-sustaining, self-learning system. We have so little operational staff because we don't need them. Tiresias is its own author and editor.

"The central column can change colour to blend in with the sky. From a distance the outer fabric of the Visionary Complex seems suspended in the air. An eye floating above it all. The Sentinel is the most receptive part of the building. If Tiresias does really have an eye, it's this one. But this one doesn't see. It feels. Right out to deep space. To other lifeforms in our universe."

What a fucking weirdo. There was only one space that mattered. IRIS. Rejecting her speech was Augusta's final test. To see how much Alexis wanted it. Playing her off against Relpek. That beautiful boy would fold under pressure. Probably already had. She pictured him shaking on a shelf in a stationery cupboard, like some frightened budgerigar. Snivelling bastard. Rubbish and unadventurous in bed. When you hold men in you, you get their true measure.

Alexis wasn't weak. She had a plan. The only one in town. She would keep moving up. Get into the room. Charm, bully and bite her way to the inner sanctum. March into Augusta's suite, plant a kiss on Max's lovely face and declare not only should the victory party go on while rebellion raged but she, Alexis Beatrice Straker, had the speech that would be its crowning glory. Tiresias's feedback was steaming horseshit. She'd waded through one hundred levels of crap to say the magic words to Augusta directly. Old school. Face-to-face. Eyeballing the boss and daring her to say no. Awakening her to the grade A stupidity surrounding her. *See how your fair-weather followers have bolted, ma'am?* Alexis's voice counted. Grating and gravelly from too much SoCo and tobacco as it might be.

Courage, said Mr Joyce. *The quality from which all other virtues spring, Alexis. The world is a dangerous place. You must fight to survive. But courage you shall have. Believe in your words. In the power of language to join the dots. To make people see things they haven't seen before.*

The capsule raced away from the darkness. Alexis didn't realise the elevator had stopped until the doors parted on Level 67. Through them came a knotted mess of stringy, stressed-out machismo. Leo Veneto, one of those tiresome Imaginists from the Investments division. A laddish club of braying yahoos who behaved like masters of the universe. He had a pale face, sweaty brow and wore a creased yellow suit. A smooth, slick, squash-playing smartarse. Normally, she would put him on her B-list. Not bad looking, in a public-school kind of way. Solid chin. Nice posture. Thick brown coiffured hair. A bottleneck of ambition and anxiety. A rich, disappointed daddy. Fully undeserving of the red ring on his finger. She imagined sleeping with him in this lift and sliding the jewellery off him while he peaked. *One for the road, Mr V?* He was way below his best though. Definitely Kalypsol. The putrid smell of rotten eggs and the far-off look in his eyes gave it away. *Why do I always want to drop into bed with the bad guys? I'm in the middle of a terrorist attack. Not a fucking Jane Austen novel.*

"Straker," he said as the lift restarted. "Where the hell do you think you're going?"

A wavering voice, fragile and edgy. Shifty eyes, probing her up and down. *Don't let the bastard see your tears.*

"Augusta asked to see me."

"Bullshit," Leo snorted, spraying Kalypsol-tinged saliva onto the glass. "You're not going anywhere with that one, sweetie."

"Excuse me?"

"The ring, Straker. All blues cancelled. Tiresias's order."

"Yeah, right."

"Check your phone. People are being removed from the party list and denied access. The protestors will be inside soon. Somebody somewhere told the police to stand down. Tiresias is shutting us out. A helicopter is on standby. Our glorious leader is getting the fuck out of here. We're being thrown to the fucking wolves."

Alexis pulled her phone out of her handbag. The battery was flat.

"Shit," she said, swapping it with Hal's device. Only twenty-five percent.

"My, my. Two phones. And a security one too. I thought you were just a lowly comms girl. A fat man must have been sucked pretty hard today. Still wearing that stupid hat, too. Who are you, Indiana Jones?"

"He wore a fedora, you prick," she said.

The light dimmed. Below, more levels were being switched off.

"Listen to me," she said, grabbing Leo by the shoulders. "Is there a secret way to IRIS?"

Leo gave a high-pitched squeal, his fat tongue hanging out between teeth darkened by Kalypsol. He flung his arms out, pushing hers away.

"Don't fucking touch. Me or my ring."

"Wouldn't dream of it, squire. There must be a way to get to the top."

"The perennial challenge. By getting on your knees and saying a prayer at this rate. It's red only, sweetie."

Raising his hand, Leo nudged his corporate jewellery back and forth to goad her.

"I've got a good mind to mention your two-phone trick to the Big T. Might buy me a few more party points when she's in exile. Get me my job back."

"You're gone too?"

"We're all gone, sweetie. They never needed us anyway. We're just here to be seen. PRISM is knocking her out. Just like it gassed all the misfits in its own backyard."

A wave of darkness rose upwards, outpacing the elevator.

"PRISM?"

"Yep, a fucking coup du fucking tah, sweetie. The Other Way is landing on our front lawn."

"I thought you were a futurist. You and your buddies didn't see this coming? And stop calling me sweetie. Sexist twat."

"Don't get hot-headed my love. No one can see anything clearly anymore. And who said Tiresias didn't compute it? This place reads you. It reads everything. It's reading us now. I have no qualms about flipping to the other side. Better red than dead. I don't care what drugs they flood the market with. Everyone's hooked on something."

"You're insane."

"Look Straker," he said. "If you want to make it into PRISM's good books, follow me. I may need a wing lady. Someone with a bit of fire."

"The Kalypsol's made you paranoid, Leo. This isn't PRISM. It's a trap. Tiresias is sucking the protestors in to spit them back out. Getting with Augusta is the only safe place to be."

Outside the capsule, the last vestiges of exterior electric light dissipated.

"This place doesn't spit, it swallows. Like a dirty whore." Leo was feverish, staring out of the lift into the dark. "It's all designed to create nothingness, you know. Draw everyone into its void. You only realise it until you're fully gone."

"Elevation terminated," said the information screen when the lift reached Level 75. "Exit immediately."

The doors opened onto what was usually a bustling entertainment complex revolving around Restaurant Jacques Cousteau and The Squinting Starfish pub. Every lunchtime, greedy Martians would hoover up gourmet food, share toxic gossip and gawp at the content display units suspended above each table. Not everything was so swanky. Last month, Roland closed the food court section for three days. In the wobbly final stages of a nervous breakdown, the sous chef tried to murder the whole Brand Expression team by lacing the foie gras with puffer fish venom.

Today, everything was shut. No light, no smell, no tastes. The only sensory experiences were the enveloping cold and the tentative steps of Alexis's and Leo's shoes on the marble floor. She was about to speak when a widescreen slab of white light pierced the wall about twenty metres in front of them. It was Barnacles, the private dining area. Set into the wall like a giant fish tank, the soundproof space was where middle management Martians could bask in the semi-VIP spotlight. Lesser mortals could see into the space, but private diners couldn't see out. Alexis always thought that was wryly poetic.

Twenty or so Martians were standing cramped inside the letterbox shape. The glass was cracked. The walls were bare. All the furniture was gone. This misshapen mass of corporate human anxiety looked like zombies who'd wandered onto an artist's blank canvas. Half of the room was unoccupied, an empty space into which some Martians stared transfixed. Nobody ventured into it, as if trapped in an invisible bubble. They reminded Alexis of shocked survivors on a lifeboat watching a cruise liner sink. Only two seemed free of paralysis. An older lady with unkept hair and a forest green dress banged on the glass with her fists. A younger, athletic-looking man in a pinstripe suit was shoulder-charging the door.

A clicking noise. The only sound in this otherwise silent movie. Barnacles's north-facing wall moved first. Slowly, smoothly. An implacable concrete block about three feet thick, powered by unseen hydraulics. A swarming mass of frightened flesh fastened itself to the opposite wall. Clumping, thrashing, cowering. Behind the advancing wall was a blancmange conference room. Alexis half-expected to see Roland in there pruning his nails, feet rested on the back of some kneeling pygmy slave.

"Leo, your ring," she screamed, running to the door of Barnacles. "Give me your fucking ring."

"Forget 'em, they're gone."

Alexis slammed her left hand against the access panel. BLUE RINGS DEACTIVATED. BLUE RINGS DEACTIVATED. BLUE RINGS DEACTIVATED. She howled in anguish, thumped the glass with her fist and rammed it with her shoulder. The south-facing wall began moving too. The face of the man in the pinstripe suit was only six inches away. A little boy lost, crippled by the void. His right hand flapped against the glass, like the twitching reflex of a dying bird. Another person's forehead crushed his cheekbone. His opposite shoulder crunched towards his ear. Soon he was gone, cumulative human pressure grinding him to the floor. Alexis closed her eyes. *None of this is real. None of this is real.*

"Move. Right fucking now."

Alexis's left arm was nearly yanked from her body. Leo dragged her deeper into the dark space. Head and heart churning, she folded into his command. Spectral lights gathered in Alexis's field of vision, pulsing and shifting, forming a larger pattern before dissolving, reappearing and rearranging.

"Somewhere here," muttered Leo. "Must be somewhere here."

A soft buzz. An avalanche of brilliant white light. Alexis's eyes squinted. Her body recoiled, pain rearing up inside her skull. She was going to be sick. They were in an inclining cylindrical corridor. Shapes formed on the walls. Bright blues, emerald greens, deep browns. Majestic clouds. Wide open valleys. Patchwork quilts of picturesque trees and fields. The world's most banal chillout playlist farted away in the background. In the curve where the floor became the ceiling, a bald fortysomething Martian male was crouched up. His chest and lap were covered in chunky greenish-yellow liquid. An empty bottle of Kalypsol was jammed between his knees. Nate Bulwark, Augusta Maars's Secretary of Defence, was trying to regain his composure.

"Five, four, three, two, one," he muttered in a trance. "Five, four, three, two, one."

At the end of the corridor lay another door. LEADERSHIP ONLY.

"Stick with me, sweetie," said Leo. "I've got a direct line to the top."

With a flick of Leo's hand they were through, flying up a spiralling staircase which blurred and swirled. Alexis reached out with her hands to check the walls weren't closing in. Relief returned. A soothing wash of reassurance bathed her body. Leo could move pretty quickly. Alexis gazed at his ass as they twisted upwards. Maybe when all this was done, he was the one. Maybe he could help her find the big O. Or maybe she just needed a lie down, a swig of SoCo and to convince herself this was all illusion.

"One more flight," he said. "Leo the boy wonder. Leo the last man standing. Leo the motherfuckin' legend."

They arrived at a white door. The number seventy-nine was painted in blue cargo font on a wall to the side. The light on the access panel glowed red.

"Here we go, hot stuff," said Leo, waving his hand. "Mind your language. You'll need all your charm to get into bed with PRISM."

Beyond was a deserted corridor with two closed doors on each side. EXECUTIVE RECREATION 1,2, 3 and 4. At the end, a double door made from glass. THE VISIONARY COMPLEX. The walls throbbed calming amber. Alexis's mental lights quivered. Everything blurred. She hadn't taken her medication for four hours and another vision was coming. But at least the fucking music had stopped.

"Leo, I need to lie down mate," she said. "I'm feeling sick."

"Ten more seconds," he snapped. "We're going to make it."

"They're going to kill us, Leo."

"Maybe. Maybe not."

Leo placed his hand on the access panel to the Visionary Complex door. A prolonged pause. Alexis imagined a guillotine about to fall.

RED RINGS DEACTIVATED. RED RINGS DEACTIVATED. RED RINGS DEACTIVATED.

Like a pile of wet, dirty clothes, Alexis's erstwhile protector sagged to the floor. Leo's silly yellow suit seemed two sizes too big. He was on his knees, a penitent man weighed down by too much sin. Anytime now a puddle of piss might seep out between his shoes onto the mauve velvet pile carpet.

Instead, he started to cry. After a while, that stopped. Alexis crept towards him and placed a hand on his shoulder.

"Leo?"

"One thing left. One thing left for me to do."

Leo stood up and turned around. His face was still and final, as if he had donned a death mask.

"This way," he said quietly.

Leo moved to one of the Executive Recreation doors and opened it, beckoning Alexis forward. He smiled, in the way assassins smile before squeezing the trigger.

"Go. Now."

The space was like a budget hotel room designed by a thrifty middle-aged Mondeo man. Stripped, sparse and dominated by beige, it contained a double bed, two side tables, a small walk-in closet and an ensuite bathroom. The blinds had parted to reveal a floor-to-ceiling window onto the atrium. Only a few metres away, Alexis could see one of the steel girders that formed the portcullis mesh enclosing the Visionary Complex. Apart from that, there was nothing else here. Except walls which glowed the colour of flesh and streamed digitised images of female body parts.

Men. All the fucking same. Leo's punch was clinical. There was an explosion of pain in Alexis's left cheekbone as she collapsed to the ground. The carpeted floor tilted and dipped like a life raft on a raging sea.

"Keep quiet, bitch."

Leo crawled over Alexis like a possessed goblin, pinning her wrists together above her head with one hand. He pushed up her skirt with the other. When it was hitched, he ripped off her pants and grunted. Alexis screamed. Leo reached into his inside jacket pocket, took out a gun and pressed it to her forehead. Following it came the noxious juggernaut of his breath. Rotten and rancid, like a troubled soul might smell in the last stages of decay.

"One more thing," he shouted, pecking her face with his mouth like a weedy vulture, his oily tongue trying to penetrate her clenched lips. "One more thing. Don't fucking move. Or I'll blow your fucking head off."

White lights filled the room. The ceiling. The walls. Leo's face. Through Alexis's eyes, everything sparked and scorched. The collective madness of Galatea Zero was visualised, contagious and expanding.

"I'll have it while I can. Before the whole world blows up. They'll never talk about Leo Veneto behind his back. I'll fuck the world before it fucks me."

With his free hand, Leo set his gun down and scrambled at his belt buckle. His chest rose and fell. Wheezing from the mouth, he tried to push into her. An image of a bull goring a matador flashed into Alexis's mind. *You can be anything you want to be. Anything at all.* She thrust her forehead into Leo's nose. A crack of splintering bone. A muffled squeal. The pain of impact shot through Alexis's brain to the back of her skull. She rammed her right knee into the space where she thought the testicles might be.

"Dooofffffccccrrrkaaaaaaaagghhr."

The fragments of his balls might meet the debris of his nose somewhere behind his ribcage. Lights blazed everywhere. Alexis broke her hands free and grabbed one of Leo's puny wrists. She sunk her teeth into his pale flesh, trying to draw blood. He screamed and reeled onto his back, like the world's most pathetic crab. His cock dangled limply through the opening of his boxer shorts. Untwisting himself, Leo crawled towards her on his knees like a vengeful rabid hound.

"Stupid fucking cu-"

Alexis picked up his gun and discharged it in his face. A clean sound of authority and closure. The blast roared magnificently through Alexis's body like a spiritually charged flame. Leo wavered from side to side on all fours, a decrepit camel exhausted in heat. He crumpled to the floor. The bullet had passed through his right eye and smattered dark blood and brain matter across the door. His gun glinted in the artificial light of the empty room, while the walls softened to innocuous grey. The only pain Alexis felt was in her cheek. The bruise would be a sweet one, but Augusta would be impressed. *Look what they did to me, ma'am.*

Rising up, Alexis placed her trilby hat on her head and stood astride Leo's dead body. Another depraved sack of shit pretending to be a man. She had to keep moving. She just didn't know where. Grabbing Leo's hand, she twisted off the red ring and waved it in front of the door panel. A dull buzz bounced back. EXIT DENIED. RING NOT RECOGNISED. Leo must be one of those Martians who supplied Tiresias with continual visibility of his biodata. When that stops, everything stops. She rested against the wall, lowered her head and screamed into space.

"Read me then, you bitch. *Read me.* Tell me I'm a fucking freak."

Alexis felt a gentle pressing into her shoulder blades. A mystery man guiding her to safety, perhaps. Mr Joyce maybe, resurrected after drinking himself to death in Zurich. Or the man in the pinstripe suit dragging her to hell. When she realised the wall was moving, Alexis lunged into the middle of the room. The opposite one was drawing in too. Two advancing beige slabs of LED screen expanded and contracted like liquid metal, swallowing the bed, tables, closet and bathroom.

In her terror, Alexis imagined Tiresias and PRISM sharing the same face. Uglier than Roland's, with long tentacle-like protrusions slithering from the mouth to choke everything around them. She slammed her shoulders into the door. Trained the sight of Leo's gun on the lock. Thought about squeezing the trigger. Contemplated blowing her own head off.

Courage. The quality from which all other virtues spring, Alexis. You must fight to survive. Courage you shall have. Something outside herself caused Alexis to turn. A soft light beyond the window. The day was not over. There was a hatch above somewhere leading to the service area of the Visionary Complex. She'd seen a maintenance guy descend through it. Alexis pointed the gun at the glass and fired. The first punched a hole in the window. She fired again and again until the pane shattered and a dull, clicking sound came from the gun's chamber.

"Loverboy Leo. The rapist with not enough lead in his pencil."

Cold air swept through. Alexis could hear the protestors inside the atrium, their chants welling up like a storm at sea. The walls accelerated in affront at her bullets, as if the room was a wounded animal. Stepping to the edge, she looked at the girder. Then down the two-hundred-metre drop. Her knees knocked. She was very high. But her speech was fucking good. She was fucking good. Max, in his own gorgeous, pitiful way, was good enough. And there was a chance the Martians were still in control.

Well done Alexis, Mr Joyce used to say, when she'd enunciated a difficult Latinate word with crystal-glass precision. *Go to the top of the class and jump off.* Three metres. Achievable with a spirited lunge. *Centre yourself*, said Hugo, her cute-buttocked kickboxing coach. Just grip tight on impact. And she'd learned what real grip was after shattering Leo's twisted face to kingdom come.

Set your sights high. You can be anything you want to be. Anything at all. Alexis took off her white Manolo Blahniks and threw them onto Leo's chest. Next to him were her torn pants and handbag containing both phones. She would leave them all behind. She would reach the top. She would not compromise. And she would do it fucking commando. Either that, or she would slip to a quicker death than the walls would grant her. Glinting lights on the girders shone through the dark. Her lights. Ultraviolet. Magical. Visible only to her. Maybe she was seeing things. But that would forever be her story. However low she might go, Alexis always trusted the fireworks in her head to lift her upwards through the void.

"You crazy, Lexy? Is that what you are? Sick in the fucking head?"

The room transformed into a tunnel. A narrowing escape route squeezed between motorised jaws with a solitary light disappearing into the distance. Stepping back, Alexis prayed to whichever force was illuminating her life in the blackest of hours. Eyes closed, she ran and leapt, throwing her arms to the other side of space. The journey was soft, sweet and liberating. Her hat stayed on the whole time.

XI

On the edge of the black hole.

The make-believe sea stopped when it reached the void. Without a crash of foam, ripple of wave or waterfall dropping to the deep. Adam gazed up at the black hole like an awestruck tourist before a skyscraper. Soon they'd be sailing off the edge into space. Like Adam's last swig of fantasy rum, the new destination smelled of nothing. Far to the left and right, in the circumference of the black hole, a miasma of transitory lights danced and dwindled. Beyond that stretched the night sky, fading in deference to a more inscrutable darkness.

"Is this what it's like?" he whispered. "Like you're being taken over?"

"That's what dreams are," said Columbus, illuminated by the electric light's limitless battery. "An illusion with nothing at their heart. Just a void. It's the same with power. The nearer you get, the emptier it seems. If you get too close, it's impossible to escape. We're drawn to these forces like we're drawn to the sea. People want to reach their limit. Keep going higher and higher. So they can see further than anyone else. But they only end up meeting themselves."

"That's what frightens me."

"Don't be afraid. You're no longer a child at school, you're a big boy now. A grown man leading a mission to the stars. You chose this path. This is your dream. To go to the final frontier. To boldly go..."

"This isn't a joke."

"The universe is one big cosmic joke," said Columbus, with a grandiloquent wave of his arms. "There's no meaning here at all. Just our lonely planet superimposing stories onto something we will never understand."

"Tell that to an astronomer. Besides, I thought you were an explorer."

"We left the shores of science a long way back. And has it dawned on you I'm not the real Christopher Columbus?"

"Don't be sarcastic. No meaning at all? What about love? That's the greatest story ever told."

"Ah. Such a sweet boy."

"I must believe in something. To do something with my time. I was always different from the others. Because of the way I looked. Because nobody understood me."

"Except your lady friend?"

"Yes. Except her. She was like a distant star. A light that's always there, even though the light you're seeing is from thousands of years ago. She could go deeper and higher than anyone. To the bottom of the sea. To the outermost heavens. She saw things nobody else could. I believe in her more than anything."

"It's nice to have heroes. Myths and muses. But you only saw her a few times. Didn't even speak to her. Adam, you're a dreamer like the rest of us. A storyteller trying to make connections in the stars."

"There's such a thing as love at first sight, you know. I'll go as far as I need to and as high as I want, even if it means tearing through time and space so we can be together. Dreams come and go. Love takes you over and lasts forever."

The boat slipped from the surface. They were either floating into space or drifting to the bottom of the ocean. To the place where life began. Maybe that's what the black hole meant. The beginning of everything. A fateful encounter between random atoms colliding in the same place. Like a coding error. Or some strange genetic mutation on the seabed. Maybe with enough patience, the black hole would be eclipsed by something out of this world.

"There's still time to turn back Adam," said Columbus softly. "To leave this place. To wake up. To stay in the real world. To not follow your dreams."

"Then I might as well be an asteroid. A lump of rock floating through space. Being nothing. Seeing nothing. Loving nothing."

"So you have to go through with it. You're an adventurer, man. Live with the loneliness. Trust there's something out there in the void. Maybe it's love. Maybe it's not. But that's what real adventurers do. They trust in their dreams."

Onwards they drifted for an indefinable time. The mystery of where they were going surrendered to the seductive certainty of sleep. Adam slipped into a deeper dreamworld, where he could gaze above and below the horizon until there was no difference at all.

He was woken by a loud thud.

"Land ahoy, my friend," Columbus said in a mock-heroic tone.

"What's happening? Have we hit something?"

"Yes… and no."

"What the fuck does that mean?"

"Why don't you venture into the grown-up seats and find out?"

Scrambling across the benches on his hands and knees, Adam reached the bow of the boat. He peered into the black.

"I can't see anything."

"Have you not been listening to a word I've said? Out here you don't see. *You have to feel*. Otherwise, you'll never get anywhere. Listen, I've taken you as far as I can. Now it needs the human touch. Just like in the picture of the old, bearded fellow reaching out to the guy with no clothes on. Adam, my esteemed junior adventurer, it's time to reach out.

To create. To tell her story. *To make art.* Whatever you think that might be."

A nascent light formed in Adam's mind. An atom of pure white brilliance with fiery red at its centre. Shifting his feet forwards and gripping the bow's rim with his left hand, Adam extended his right hand tentatively into the still, inviting space. The faintest of touches. The most intimate of connections. Adam jumped back when the tip of his fingers met the invisible surface. It was smooth, solid and cool to the touch. Opening his hand wider, he pressed his palm against what felt like a sheet of glass. A television screen. Or a windowpane in an orphanage from a long time ago. The soothing warmth of imagination rippled through his body. New visions were stirring in his soul.

Faraway, atop a magical tower on a fabled island, a titanium mast hummed. The sound was gentle, buried by the sea winds and unregistered by the computer controlling the skyscraper. The hum became a pulse. *Thud. Thud. Thud.* The pulse became a signal. *I am here.* And the mast turned cosmic messenger, awakening a dormant power fermenting in the unchartered depths of the earth.

XII

Lewis brushed the wall with his index finger, caressing the final spot of white into place. The lady's right hand was complete. The mural finished. Its paint soaked into the porous surface, like tidal waves absorbed into a pebbly beach. The room's emergency lighting was intermittent, so Lewis could only appreciate his creation as a fragmented visual jigsaw. Two earthquakes in quick succession. Flashes of quivering amber, paler and shorter each time. Even with bursts of reserve power, IRIS's corners lay shrouded in darkness.

"Your love lighted my way," Lewis whispered to the lady in the plaster. "A fiction. A story. A magic spell. Resurrected from the dead."

In the orphanage, Lewis would lie awake at night, sculpting characters in the moonlight from plasticene stolen from the crafts cupboard. He would place the finished figures to his lips, breathing life into insentient matter. The mind was stillest on those occasions. A cruise liner sailing gracefully over a rich inner ocean. Before morning drills in the PRISM camp, he would conjure onto canvas magical vistas of the local countryside.

Then the letter arrived. The yellowing, crinkled lifeline, written on PRISM paper, kindled a new fire within Lewis. It lighted his path across the dying country, past tin-can houses streaming alternative worlds. Lewis imagined its author's voice. Gentle, strong and resolute, cast in the foundry of the earth. During his journey, he mediated the world by sketchbook. Soon all visions morphed into an imaginary face. The person behind the words. The love behind the letter. An imperious leader. A modern-day Velasquez charcoal. Dignity personified in crassly co-ordinated flecks of grey. Time's ravages accentuated on a face spelling sacrifice. As she might look today, if she had survived.

The IRIS mural began as distant figures loosely orbiting the Portal. Asteroids spinning uncontrollably into the dark. Over time, the characters aligned in synchronicity, like they did in the finest Italian frescos of the High Renaissance. For Lewis, those works represented art at its most sublime. A spiritual realisation of what the world could be. Like the great explorers, those craftsmen had *reach*, and Lewis's best creative outpourings would flow from that elevated place which was always reaching out.

"I travelled across the wasteland to be here. To see what they had done. Those people who stole you from us. Time past recreated as time future. You said we have a duty to turn the banal into the holy. It's what you realised when you were trapped. How we made machines our masters. How mastery only goes so far. For machines can't tell stories. You need heart and soul for that."

On his way south to Galatea, Lewis remembered the Wild West comic books he read on winter nights in the dormitory. His favourite was the story of two explorers travelling to the Pacific Ocean and carving their name on a tree overlooking a sapphire sea. Lewis and Clark. From then on, he didn't use his real name. With every mile journeyed, his old identity waned. At night, he lighted roadside fires for warmth and let himself be hypnotised by the flames. Imagining his younger self, twisting and turning like an orange spectre into his present incarnation. Two people rather than one. Artist and archaeologist. On a pilgrimage to solve the mystery of the fallen angel.

When PRISM malfunctioned, its leaders became addicted to their own narcotics. The empire collapsed in on itself, like a dying star becoming a black hole. Left behind was a desolate place Lewis once called home, at the mercy of unhinged marauders who prowled through foggy maroon nights. He would pounce like a panther, stealing whatever they had before retreating into the trees. As he neared the coast, his dreams grew turbulent. A red sea swirling around white toes. A face appearing from the black. A face not from this world, but from another. From beyond the horizon. With no eyes. A hole at its centre. A plume of scaley flesh fanning out. Like the creature who'd slipped the sea's manacles and ascended the tower to save him from death.

"You talked about the rosy-fingered dawn. How in the future there would be a time for heroes. How the best heroes lose themselves into space and time until they become part of everything else. Realising their limits. Then realising when you serve a greater cause, there can be no limit at all."

Within its six-metre-thick walls, IRIS housed smaller compartments. Lewis unlocked them with the dead man's eyes. A bathroom, bedroom, kitchen and pantry all rotated around the main space. There was a toilet with a still-functioning flush. A shower that seeped. PRISM had cleared out the fridges and freezers, so sustenance came from long out-of-date tinned food in cupboards. Such morsels meant Lewis would not have to eat the corpse on Level 96. He'd seen such sacrilege on the road, when wild dogs feasted on the remains of a dead PRISM soldier. There was a similar whiff of decayed arrogance in Galatea Zero. Every particle seemed imbued with delusion. Not like his paint, where the synthetic became authentic and the sound of tins in his rucksack clinked a childlike rhythm all their own.

Another rumbling noise. A spasm from the earth, reverberating through steel. A crack widening in the ceiling's painted constellations. Silence. Lewis continued looking at the mural. That was his life now. That would be her life too, when she would once again inhabit the place where she fell. Where her story would continue. Where her memory would cure a sick land still worth saving.

"Madness is like the mind bleeding," he whispered to his characters on the wall. "A pain or wound you need to understand before you see the world. The source of all stories. You will live again. You will come again. What was stolen will be returned. Through this paint, I will make flesh. Through this flesh, I will build tomorrow. Through this tomorrow, I will honour the past. Through this past, I will light the sky. And when the sky meets the earth and past meets present, the horizon will disappear."

Lewis would often open the box. Gently. Reverentially. The rotten stench of the cemetery still hovered. That makeshift abyss where twenty-one years ago PRISM disposed of the exterminated prisoners. One on top of the other in black bags. The graves were laid in a circular pattern, corkscrewing towards a dark centre. He found a shovel in the abandoned storage block near the site's entrance. Through the earth he dug, the voice beckoning him on. Scrabbling. Probing. Lifting. Shifting. The corpses weren't too deep. After hours of excavation, Lewis found the number mentioned in the letter. 872963. He heaved the weight out the ground, a lithe jewel among dead rocks. Unzipping the shroud, he let the dark red air and pink moonlight grace the skull, teeth, bones and residual sinew. Wielding his knife with care like he had done in the orphanage, Lewis extracted what he believed to be the remnants of the only organ that mattered. A clump of thick dust buried in the chest that used to be the centre of everything.

To begin again takes heart. You need to show it to people. To make them believe in you. Remember, the heart has no limit.

In IRIS, Lewis wandered the length of his mural, his long grey coat scratching the concrete floor. He ran his hand on the driest patches, savouring how each star in each character bled smoothly into space. Yet the Portal stayed blank and undisturbed. A void at the centre of his masterpiece which no pigment could fill. When holy light returned, everything would be indivisible. A joyous whole. The seamless union of a queen, her king and their prince and princess. Rulers of a paradise regained.

Wait until the end of the world if you must, the letter said. *She will come.*

Every night before sleep, Lewis watched the doors. A shaggy-haired, emaciated sage performing vigils of the imagination. Outside, the volatile earth ruptured. The creatures were being summoned forth to land. The waters would keep rising. Something would come to the surface. New life would flood his world. Closer and closer each time.

Until then, he would follow the letter. Trust in the power of its words to unite lonely figures floating too long in empty space. What was once high would become low. What was low would become high. And above and underneath it all, the specks of dry, disparate dust that used to be his mother's heart would pulse in tender unison.

XIII

The Venus Suite of Galatea Zero. Seven days before the Fall.

She was no longer living in the real world. A dreamy-eyed Augusta gazed at Max across the candlelit onyx marble table. Her haute couture burgundy dress hung low and long. She sipped her Chateau Margaux with a naughty grin, as if tasting forbidden fruit. As the miniaturised Victoria Falls cascaded down the north wall, Tiresias glided a Mahler symphony through the suite towards them through speakers camouflaged by mock Louis XV wall panels.

Friday night was date night. Roland would sportingly turn a blind eye, though no one believed he had one. In the private kitchen, a squadron of silent chefs laboured over a four-course dinner, entranced by Tiresias's instructions which flowed with military precision across tablets positioned above the grills. Venus was the couple's favourite suite, a discreet yet opulent corner of Level 98 for mysterious investors in need of diplomatic lubrication. Beyond the west-facing window, dissolving into the black hills, lay smattered pinpricks of light. A tiny fraction of the populace Augusta would soon govern. With one week until the election, the polls gave her an unassailable lead. The Martian leader swept through every space like she'd been holy anointed.

"This will be our new life," Augusta cooed after finishing her hors d'oeuvres of devilled eggs. From underneath the table, she lifted a dark red gift box and held it towards Max. The letters R, A and M were engraved around a diamond-studded crest of the Martian bee. A present. Not that anything in this relationship belonged to him.

"The four of us. Holding dominion over everyone."

Max set the box down and opened the lid. Underneath was a gold-trimmed Maars Genysis tablet. He tapped the screen. A blueish-grey marble appeared, swaddled in black space. Nausea flared in Max's stomach. His head went woozy, like someone had extracted a pint of his blood without warning.

"Look what we've created together," said Augusta. "Soon we'll see its heartbeat. Oh Max, we have a child. An heir. He will be perfect. As handsome and as strong as his father. Only two weeks old. More than perfect."

Another screen, another story. Max was still learning to navigate Augusta. Knowing her was like entering a multifarious Virtual Reality simulator, the quality of the experience dependent on the headset he chose. The contrite. The ambitious. The playful. The outraged. The humble. The arrogant. The vulnerable child. However much the dynamics shifted under each lens, the lady in front of him was never the real thing. Perhaps this foetus was another simulation, a pixelated sleight-of-hand. A two-dimensional graphical cluster casting a spell. Sometimes Max would remove his cerise contact lenses and inspect them in the light, wondering if they were something else.

These guys aren't real people, Alexis said to him. In her shabby chic high-rise apartment, their sex was explosive, the pillow talk easy and the bedroom as disorderly as a fourteen-year-old's. *They don't what it means to be real. Not like we do.* Alexis's tenderness was real. Augusta's wasn't. The leader's choreographed persona seemed forever on the verge of splitting apart, her mannerisms strained by excessive pronouncement and performance in front of a thousand lenses. The way she ate, the way she talked, the way she made love. A Cubist's vision of leadership refracted through a cracked infinity mirror.

"I... I..." Max said through slackened jaw. "I thought it wasn't possible."

"My love, anything is possible. If you have the will. The vision. I'm going to be a mother at last. Creator-in-Chief."

Augusta rose triumphantly from the chair, slinked round the table, draped herself across Max's lap and kissed him. She was light and fragile, like a dried leaf blowing on a soporific current of wine and perfume. Her slender hands burrowed into his thick mane. She ran her nose against his cheekbone and breathed slowly, as if inhaling his soul.

"I'm honoured, Augusta. Honoured to be the father. Honoured."

"And I'm honoured it will be yours."

She took his hand and placed the palm over her abdomen.

"Feel it within. This is us. Soon the baby will be freed from its space. Brought it into the world."

"Roland?"

"He doesn't know yet. But he will be pleased. He picked you out at the first press conference."

Augusta slipped her hand through the gap between Max's shirt buttons and fingered the hairs above his right nipple. He pictured themselves on a life raft sailing over a sheer vertical drop. Augusta would summon the serenest of flights; he would plummet like a brick. Unless he found a new Max, but he wasn't sure how many of those were left. *If I'm to be a sperm donor, so be it. Smile and shoot. Smile and shoot.* Like that Brazilian model he used to fuck, or the meat-headed porn star he could become if other career choices dried up.

"Ahem."

The lovers' clinch was interrupted by the *maître d'*. He was a diminutive Spaniard with a bald head, serious brown eyes and a plump body straining the buttons of his white jacket. On the serving tray were two portions of calf brains on toast in lemon, parsley and caper sauce. Along for the ride was a nubile brunette with olive skin and a pristine white blouse opened to the cleavage. She blushed at Max. Augusta often placed attractive women in his orbit, so she could watch them watch him and see if he watched back. Max decided the safest performance was to treat pretty young things with smouldering macho contempt.

Augusta made her way back to her seat, let Max's hand fall away and dismissed her staff with a gritted smile. She fixed him with a surgical look, the flames of the candlelight quivering in her pupils. Tiresias changed the room from cool blue to rose pink, then transitioned from Mahler to Beethoven.

"I want you to include this in the memoir," she instructed. "Watch me closely. Observe how I walk, dress and behave now that I'm a mother. I must be an inspiration to all women. You need to capture the fire in my eyes. That special maternal quality. The magic of creativity growing inside me."

"Be gentle with yourself," said Max. "You're taking three or four momentous steps all at once."

"I don't do gentle," she laughed. Soon she was gone. A misty film of memory coated her eyes. She was looking beyond Max and out the window. Into the past. Into the future. Inhabiting an alternative universe, exploring mental frontiers only she and Roland could conceive. Max's presence would evaporate at these times, turned to smoke by the scolding interior visions that flowed through Augusta's mind like molten lava.

"PRISM will soon realise. The lowlifes on the mainland will soon realise. Faceless. Bland. Servile automatons. Joining forces like lemmings. They can barely string a sentence together. The four us will be unstoppable. Brains, vision, strength, looks, appetites. A crown prince. I'll not let that rabble get anywhere near him. He will be named after my father. My son. I'll never take my eyes off him. He'll always be safe with me."

The dream dissipated. She poured herself a large glass of wine without offering Max a top-up. Hard-drinking, hard-mothering, hard-campaigning, hard-governing. A universe of appetite within one so tiny. Max was in love with that part of her. Just not all of her. Comprehending Augusta in her entirety was impossible. Each caress, conversation and calculation yielded more confounding depths. Every day served up either the elevation to a new ecstasy, or a descent to another layer of buried pain. In between was a fuzzy indefinability, purring away like soft radio static on a lone trawler lost at sea.

You shouldn't be stuck in the office, Maxy, you should be out hunter-gathering, said Alexis. *A hunky, home-loving dad bringing home the buffalo. That would be a big turn-on, you know. I might really start to fancy you then pal.*

"When shall we announce it?" he said. "You know this place leaks."

"Tiresias will tell us when. It will read the stars, the mood of the nation. The optimum time to inject the news into the national nervous system."

Max couldn't picture anyone on the campaign trail giving a shit.

"A Capricorn," he said, tired of the seriousness. "A Christmas arrival. But we can be damn sure you're not a virgin."

Relpek, you're a complete and utter fucking moron. For a moment, he expected the sack. To be told he wasn't the father anyway. To be sent to his room and prepare for Tiresias to broadcast mendacious data about him. Halitosis. Erectile dysfunction. A penchant for pre-pubescent schoolgirls. Instead, Augusta's return salvo wasn't laced with much viciousness.

"Promise me you're not seeing that lanky, flat-chested bitch anymore."

"Augusta, please…"

"*Promise me.*"

"I haven't spoken to Alexis. Dumping her on the same day you gave me her job took the spice out of our relationship."

"Scheming little minx. Thought she knew how to manage me."

"In over her head," he said, reading from the script. "An empty space into which not enough love could be poured."

Augusta's eyes narrowed. She knew he was being disingenuous. A serpent slid out from underneath the painstakingly composed portrait of the Madonna. If pushed, she would happily pluck out his eyes with her fingers and force feed them to him like strawberries during a picnic.

"Did you love her?"

"Augusta, I love you."

"Answer my question."

"No."

"No, you won't answer my question or no you didn't love her?"

"Augusta, I don't love her. I didn't love her. *I love you.*"

"I should have booted her completely. But dry fanny like that is better pissing out the tent than pissing in."

"She's harmless. A drugged-up airhead with mental health issues. Let her stew in her own juice on the lower floors. She's beyond saving."

Max preferred lying to telling the truth. It was easier. The truth of Galatea, whatever that was, had been long lost in a million and one approval processes, elaborate hierarchies, companies nested within companies and a corporate culture created to confuse. A place where everyone became more of an outsider the longer they stayed around.

"Augusta, I want to look at you," he said. "I love to look at you."

She glanced shyly downwards at the table, then up at him again. Another gaze formed, similar to that day when she emerged from the Cave. The day when Max saw, only briefly, the secret inside the Martian machine. A look of powerlessness. Something in the ocean they simply couldn't understand.

"To the four of us," she said in a girlish tone. "To this little bit of me and little bit of you inside me. It's bringing me back to life. Pulling me from the wreckage. The forces we have within our control are…"

Augusta never finished her sentence. The room changed from burgundy to vermilion to coral. The waterfall continued its digitalised flow. The meal drifted on. Veal saltimbocca with rose veal escalope. Diamond ganache chocolate cake. One-hundred-year-old Speyside malt laced with Kalypsol Amber. Max offered platitudes about their child's education, diet and nursery. How they could turn IRIS into a birthing suite. Bring the baby in at the top. Make sure it stays there.

"PRISM has made a serious mistake," said Augusta.

She talked over the top of him, sluggishly. The Scotch sent her deep into orbit. Into the dark place, where she would turn off the lights and clutch at him hungrily. Tomorrow, without humility or hangover, she would fly to a military base and inspect troops still not hers to command. Assuming all space around was hers. Setting Max down and picking him back up at the end of the day.

"Roland will carve PRISM into a million pieces," she said. "Blow it out of the water so everyone can see it's all surface and shallow tricks. It will not take us over. We have a new discovery that will change everything. When war comes, we'll be ready. All four of us will be ready. Our people will be ready. We'll drench the earth in foreign blood. Power is an art. And we are artists."

Later, while she slept next to him, Max rested his hand on Augusta's naked stomach. He pictured the blueish-grey capsule he'd seen on screen floating in its idyllic space. This darkness around it terrified him. He wasn't sure what he'd created, how he could protect it, and whether it would be ready for what waited on the other side. She was no longer living in the real world. Neither was he.

XIV

The underground tunnels of Galatea Zero. 257 minutes before the Fall.

*D*on't you dare shaft me now you motherfuckers. The elevator hadn't opened for nearly an hour. Her red ring wasn't recognised. It was past seven o'clock and high above, PRISM's *coup d'etat* would be entering its final phase. Mercedes summoned her poker face and breathed slowly. She studied Zayden, an imbecile still unaware his shitty paper-boat life would soon be swept into the filthiest of storm drains.

The Galatean underground was a network of dank tunnels with twisty, corkscrew walls scarred by hairline fractures. Water dribbled from the single lighting strips, stretching along the ceiling like sickly yellow scrawl. Rats scratched underneath the drainage vents. Normally Maars Enterprises used drones to inspect the network, but Mercedes's intelligence showed maintenance funds had been ring-fenced for the attack on PRISM. Her paymasters didn't need to decapitate the Martian leadership. They were doing their own legs.

The subterranean passageways were Zayden's first discordant glimpse into Galatea's underbelly. He seemed repulsed by the grimy moisture. The perfect fall guy for PRISM's plan. An introverted loner with a short fuse. A wiry doodle of an overgrown child in geeky green casuals. Zayden wore his pseudo-intellectual persona so awkwardly you could see the joins and stitches. Unlike Mercedes, whose mask was so seamless after years of covert operations you couldn't tell where it ended and the real lady began.

She drew the plan in triplicate. On paper, on screen and in her mind, like any self-respecting former government intelligence officer. The locations, the timings, the contingencies, weaved together into a lethally efficient noose. That afternoon, while waiting at the terminal for Zayden to stroll into PRISM's trap, she thought of the Highlands graveyard where her parents were buried. They wouldn't know what to make of the life she'd led. Why their only daughter loved to flirt on the edge of destruction, nearly but not quite losing herself in power's black hole. Then again, her folks never knew how to make a few quid.

Forty-five minutes after leaving the Verne conference suite, they arrived at the elevator entrance. Not Augusta's escape lift of course – hardly anyone knew where that was – but the one she used to cargo spies, supine journalists and men of the night back and forth.

"Don't worry," Mercedes said. "We're still very early. Access is only possible at certain times. Give it another five. As the saying goes in these parts, Tiresias doesn't go down. Only people do."

"I don't think I can manage more than that," said Zayden, sliding his glasses up his nose, one of his many annoying habits. "This place is disgusting. Like one of those godforsaken multi-storey car parks."

"Afraid of the dark? A big boy like you?"

"No, it's just not what I had in mind," he said. "I expected quality. The attention to detail here is woeful. Goes to show when you look under the hood, all you find are Fisher Price fuckups."

Mercedes pretended to see what Zayden was talking about.

"Well you gotta go low to get high, my friend. Or would you rather walk back to the terminal and see who's sprayed what around the bowls?"

She was growing tired of her pretend friend's fidgeting. His shifty looks, passive-aggressive sighing and mincing metropolitan walk. A professional image consultant with any self-respect would recommend suicide. His eyes were sunken, his complexion sallow. The jacket too big. The trousers too tight. The hipster boots were so big they made him look like a human golf club. He was even more underwhelming in real life than in the pictures.

Mercedes first saw photographs of Zayden on a tablet passed to her by two undercover PRISM operatives in a greasy spoon café. The guy would never pass for a killer. Too half-soaked. Unable to gauge opponents at lightning speed and squeeze out their lives. As she read the dossier, the block-headed PRISM operatives stirred tepid lattes and nibbled ham sandwiches. They were the very definition of regular. Short, compact and with no body fat, rehearsed in body language and inexpressive in face. Two charmless stone tablets of corporate blandness, like geography teachers planning next term's curriculum. They were sweetly spooked by unexpected noises. One even tried to interact with Charlie, poking his domed head into the pram and tickling her cheek with his forefinger. Princess slept through, tired after sucking on Mercedes's breast all night.

Sweetie please go to sleep. Mummy's got to hatch a plot tomorrow morning that will bring down the government. Every artist needs their beauty nap. So they can move between the real and fake with a fluttering of the eyelashes.

Mercedes had been fired from the intelligence services at the first rumblings of Martian victory, after threatening to expose money laundering by Roland's lawyer, a perma-tanned walrus who seemed to wash his hair in Brent crude. Even Charlie's father, a data analyst, had been re-aligned because their professional relationship was deemed 'beyond acceptable levels of proximity'. Relieved of his duties, Mitch soon relieved himself of parenthood too.

With the Martians in government, she would be on the red list for knowing too much. Which meant a ninety percent chance of a bullet to her brain in the middle of the night. PRISM knew she was cornered. At least with them it might be fifty-fifty. Only a few hours from now, they would be the new sheriffs in town. Their plan was sublime, like a Chinese puzzle box or a sequence of stacked Russian dolls. How sweet and fitting it would be for the homicidal she-witch and her weirdo husband to be swallowed in their own space. Watch their masterwork turn into a monster and open its jaws around them.

A grinding came from above, like a hundred levers being yanked out of sequence. Zayden flittered his eyes and hunched his shoulders, resembling a nervous guinea pig cowering in its hutch. Mercedes heard rumours that if Galatea Zero didn't crush your mind or your soul, it would crush your body. Roland's architectural team nicknamed it the abattoir. Through grandiose exteriors and reflective surfaces, the building liked to fatten docile egos before herding them into a metaphoric temple for ritualistic slaughter.

Relpek must have sold them out. Tiresias wouldn't have fallen, *couldn't have fallen*, without human intervention. Definitely Relpek. A slimeball's slimeball. A guy so in love with himself he probably had his face printed on pillowcases. A media chump with the nuclear codes who got where he was by knowing what buttons to press. With such taste in men, Augusta would lead the country deeper into the shit. One night, after a glass too many of Kalypsol, Mercedes dreamt of having sex with Relpek. The following morning, she took a cold shower and contemplated spiritual conversion.

"See how the sound travels?" Zayden said. "This shithole is probably made from balsa wood. Our taxes better not end up funding this travesty. I've got a good mind to say as much to Augusta's face. If we ever get there."

The whiny runt reminded Mercedes of those conformist mummy's boys at university. An insecure man with too much to prove. The kind who goes off badly when rejected. To begin with, it was like toying with a ball of wool. Parroting his language, sharing insider gossip, dialling up the touchy-feelies, leading him this way and that on a twisty tango of flirtation. Now she just wanted him delivered and done. A pity she wouldn't see Zayden's face when they charged him with the crime of the century. The poor wee lamb's OCD would go into overdrive. *Where have all the real men gone? Long time passing, Mercy. Long time passing.* In the future she would learn sculpture, so she could carve a real Adonis from marble and cast strange spells to bring him to life as protector and slave.

"We'll get there," Mercedes lied. She pinched the flesh of her left wrist with her right hand surreptitiously to avoid facial leakage, a schoolgirl hack she normally avoided. "Trust me. They've not forgotten us. We'll soon be upstairs enjoying the speech then watching PRISM crawl back into its box. There's a new order coming to this world."

A new order indeed. Let the upstart new leader threaten war. Stir up an internal rebellion. Watch the state polarise. Overwrite her showpiece invention by stealth. Program it to butcher its own side. Scythe her down. Blame it on the lower classes. Wheel in a more stable, conciliatory puppet to restore order. Talk Martian. Act PRISM. Outwardly, it would be a return to democratic norms. Inwardly, an irreversible technocratic revolution. *Which side are you on, Mercy?* Whichever one is winning, as they used to say in the special forces, where mercenary work was the only retirement plan. Yet Mercedes was experienced enough to know this was only a tenth of PRISM's overall vision. She was a minor tile in an elaborate geopolitical mosaic beyond her comprehension. Maybe she was being set up. Nerve gas could be released any moment. Or the lift would open and PRISM operatives would pepper her with bullets.

"Water?" said Zayden, massaging his Adam's apple.

Mercedes reached into her Ralph Lauren pebbled leather tote bag for the bottle of Maars Hydro. She half-wished the liquid was laced with cyanide. Her hand brushed the revolver. She imagined shooting Zayden in the foot and watching him hop around screaming for a first aid kit, trying to bleed in straight lines. Mr Anally Retentive grabbed the bottle without saying thank you, cleaned the top with a hygiene wipe and guzzled as greedily as Charlie.

Please PRISM, don't leave me with this pretentious oaf any longer.

"Why are you letting me through?" Zayden said, tucking the bottle into his jacket pocket. "You're taking a risk with an unknown bit player."

"Because you're not unknown. Tiresias ran all the background checks. And because I've been given a job to do. Nobody fails Augusta and keeps theirs. Anyway, you can handle yourself. You're definitely her type."

Zayden grinned. She'd read his psychological profile. A pill-popping waster too cowardly to admit the baby was his. Running away from his own daughter. Pathetic piece of shit. This long streak of piss shouldn't be anywhere near power. Rather, he should be tucked in at night, ready for a big day tomorrow over the farmer's field shooting tin cans off a hedge with his pellet gun. Packed lunch, chocolate biccy and a woolly hat in case his ears get cold. *Why would anyone consider him an assassin?* thought Mercedes, before realising she'd answered her own question.

"Do you really think I'll meet her?" said Zayden. "They might have spirited her away. Just in case the protestors find a way through."

"Seriously?" scoffed Mercedes. "Penetrate the best defended city in the world? Something would need to go very wrong. Besides, you don't know Augusta. If it comes down to it, she'll be the last person standing, spraying bullets into the crowd. She'll deliver that speech choking on her own blood. Besides, in these circles you're never safe, wherever you go. You're always looking over your shoulder. Live with that. Or live without any of it."

At the twenty-four-seven nursery fifteen miles away on the mainland, Charlie would be playing with a plastic bug farm. Triple time at those hours. *Has mummy had a good day?* the staff would snipe to Mercedes at collection. *Yes, you sour-faced bitches. A million-dollar kind of a day, actually.*

"Try the lift again," snapped Zayden. "Else I'll turn back."

Prickly little shit, aren't you mate? There was desperation in his voice, a man fumbling at his only chance to make something of his sad existence. There was no art to Zayden at all. No poise. Just a juvenile delinquent spraying weak urine across the empty canvas of his wasted life.

"If that'll make you happy, darling."

Mercedes held the red ring up to the scanner for what must have been the twentieth time. *It's got to work this time. Please don't shaft me or my little girl. Even this idiot will see through it soon.*

The reassuring slide of motors. The smooth acceleration of the lift. The graceful opening of the doors. The malevolent aura of a PRISM-controlled Tiresias lurked behind the polished surfaces. The grandest takeovers happen silently and spiritually, Mercedes realised, leaving only a ribbon of ghostly lights gracing the sky. *One step closer baby, one step closer. Tomorrow we'll be building sandcastles on the beach as the sunset turns the blue sky red.*

"Thank fuck, let's go," said Zayden, pushing past her. *This is why you're about to take the fall, mate.* When the pressure came he would shit his pants, like so many mediocre men. Typical of those ghastly mining towns. Probably drinks too much. But she saw the logic. Pinning Augusta's assassination on a lone in-house oddball would give a PRISM-controlled Martian party the pretext to clean house, rebuilding a cleaner political organisation that would only accept whiter than white. Whatever PRISM determined that to be.

They glided upwards to the rendezvous. Clumsily, Zayden swivelled round, placed his hands on Mercedes's shoulders and planted his one redeeming feature – those genuinely lovely lips – onto hers. A hapless swing at intimacy by someone who tomorrow would be public enemy number one.

"Sorry…" he said, waiting for her to reciprocate. "I shouldn't have done that. Something just came over me."

"That's ok, I understand," Mercedes replied, cloaking her disgust in a bashful smile and a flirty flick of the hair. "A big day for us all. Lot of emotions. Let's meet for a drink when all this is done. Get to know each other. They've got some nice rooms here. The views are splendid."

Zayden smiled as they ascended, like a village idiot who'd found a shiny piece of metal in the woods. Perhaps he thought he'd unlocked the portal to the real Mercedes. But that gateway had long been bricked up. So many wannabe Don Juans had bashed their heads senseless. As the lift accelerated, Mercedes imagined the carnage they were bypassing. The police absent. The protestors incited, invited then gassed. The systematic sacrifice of loyal Martians so it would look especially horrific at the inquest. *This Martian technology was a tragic act of hubris*, the moral authorities would say. From studying the cameras in the terminal, Mercedes estimated about a thousand protestors were crowding the main boulevard to Galatea Zero, plus at least two hundred Martians in the building. All neurotic bees swarming round poisoned honey.

The door opened at Level 95. Before them was a manicured, empty corridor. Conceptual artistic crap lined the walls, like a child with ADHD had been let loose with a pack of crayons. Any remaining Martians must be dead, trapped or paid off.

"Room 237," she said. "Follow the signs and lead the way, handsome."

Zayden sallied forth without saying thank you. Mercedes was a conniving bitch, but she wasn't a classless piece of shit. In the intelligence services, you get a primer in manners. Sometimes it was a weapon as important as elocution, or the ability to summon an inscrutable face. Just not as essential as having the steel to smile into someone's eyes and tear out their soul. As they walked, Mercedes imagined a target on Zayden's back. She waited for a whisper of guilt to emerge. It never came. Galatea Zero wasn't a place for humans. It was a place for insects who think they're special, crawling over each other blindly unaware they're going to get crushed. Soon the world would dispose of Queen Bee. A visual record of her murder would be broadcast around the world with the gangly green goon deep-faked into the lead role. Famous, like the gurning twat probably wanted. Maybe PRISM had a sense of humour after all.

Nearly there, Mercy. Hold your nerve. Don't let them see you sweat. She would not be afraid to stand strong. To wait for the cash to reach her account and slip out the way she came. Straight home to Charlie. Kisses, cuddles and tickles for two. Load the mauve-coloured mum-mobile. Tunes on. Window down. A pistol in the glove box and another under the driver's seat.

In a lock-up on some nondescript mainland industrial estate, their new life would be waiting. Identities, passports, tickets and trackers. When they got to where they were going, she would attach the latter to cars heading in the opposite direction. As close as possible to freedom, in a time when governments changed invisibly. Unseen hands were always at work, switching stage props in the intermittent darkness of the world's most dangerous theatre. Except she was heading to the exit. With no lines left to say and no part to perform.

Some people didn't know how to play this game. Some, like Zayden, chose the hard way, hoping the horizon would bend to their will because they thought it was their story. Not her. Not Charlie. Real life, not make-believe life, was opening up. A glorious vista where ambition and reality weren't so far apart. Where they could hold hands, eat caramel ice cream on sand dunes and wonder where to go next. Alone together, where she wouldn't have to tell her daughter so many fictions and hide so many secrets behind her eyes.

XV

The Banqueting Suite of the Visionary Complex. Fourteen hours before the Fall.

The foot within the black alligator leather shoe pulverised the beetle with the cleanest of crunches. In the parched sunlight streaming through the windows of Level 97, Roland had watched the insect scamper towards him. Perhaps it was seeking shade under the chair on which he'd reclined for twenty minutes, staring into his tablet at the mushrooming black hole in the Martian finances. Darkness descended another way. Eyebrows arched. Pupils dilated. Ankle pivoted. A swift stamp and a satisfying screw into the floor. The sole of Roland's shoe squeaked as he twisted the smudge into the travertine tile's off-white stone.

He didn't feel like protecting visitors today. The first man of the Martian party loved insects. He hated invaders more. The notion of something unwelcome encroaching his space unsettled him. Like everything on Galatea, such things were to be contained and controlled. Except for the Sentinel, forever open and receptive. Besides, the beetle was a common sexton, discernible from its orange markings. Hardly an exotic breed. Not worth living if it sullied his masterpiece.

It was nine thirty in the morning. The time when Roland would sip his daily double espresso from a chinaware cup painted with a semi-naked geisha. The caturra beans were soothingly bitter. He sourced them from an obnoxious plantation owner he'd negotiated into submission. All the best deals were ones he'd struck personally. Like Galatea Zero's restroom tissue paper, the resistive-touch glass for its five thousand screens and the Martian-branded screws on the air vents. Not to mention the intoxicating Oriental sandalwood and sage fragrance which Tiresias drifted through the Banqueting Suite's stifling bureaucratic air.

Roland was sitting at the back, observing final preparations for the victory party. The space was resplendent with lavish silverware, crystal glasses, cyclamen, amaryllis, nerines, rosehips, chrysanthemum blooms and hydrangea. On banners and table talkers was the same retouched image of a power-posing Augusta, sporting an emerald suit with her hands on hips. *Towards new horizons*, said the slogan, projected onto the wall behind the stage in luminous green. Beyond these flourishes, the room was brilliant white and had all the personality of a dentist's surgery.

The Corporate Experiences team proceeded in a hush, unnerved by the ticking timebomb in the corner. Cutlery clinked. Feet pattered. Furniture slid softly to align in harmony. Deviation in protocol meant the dissolution of careers. Despite their collective anxiety, the worker bees buzzed about looking sharp and smelling fresh. Roland insisted on rigorous personal hygiene. So pleased was he with the sound his shoe made on the tile when squashing the beetle, he continued tapping his right foot. A frisson of stress was conjured in the room as he beat out his metronomic threat.

How many would make it out of here tonight? There were three-and-a-half too many people in the room for the labour involved. Investors would crucify Roland if they saw so many gormless wastrels gumming up the works. *Maybe I could spare that one.* A young male Hispanic co-ordinator in a sharp grey suit, white shirt and silver tie was pedantically checking the floral arrangements on Table 17. *Or maybe that one.* A glacial blond eastern European lady in a dark blue business dress was overseeing three miniature drones install an enormous neoclassical portrait of Augusta near the entrance. The subject was still in bed, sleeping off too many slugs of celebratory Kalypsol. She wasn't needed until cameras rolled.

When she would turn on that alien thing called charisma. They say every swan's last song is its finest.

PRISM-Tiresias pinged a message to Roland's phone. *Delivery in reception. Please authorise.* With an arrogant swish of his index finger, Roland approved the two gophers' ascension. A second-tier security process began. PRISM-Tiresias would analyse the visitors' body language, scan their temperatures, observe their hormonal activity and record their inane chatter via microphones implanted in their passes. By the time they arrived at Level 97, Roland could scrutinise their digital risk map for threats.

All would be secure, except for the contents of the titanium-tungsten case they carried. Even PRISM-Tiresias couldn't penetrate that. Inside was Roland's insurance policy, manufactured in his underground R&D lab on the southside of Galatea. The latest in aggressive innovation. A miracle of engineering. Funded, like so much on the island, by an elaborate maze of pyramids and Ponzi schemes that had become a financial blizzard confounding the most diligent accountants. Yet an essential sign to PRISM he had his own Praetorian Guard. That he was prepared. For when the usurpers triumphed and his wife lay dead, it was sixteen percent probable they would come for him. In the same innocuous manner they occupied foreign lands through creeping invention and diplomatic illusion. And in the same way they courted him so delicately three months earlier. The agreeable bastards knew he needed the money.

"We need an associate who can see the future," said the Senior Advisor from Nebula Investments. They sat in a discreet booth of a swanky hotel restaurant on Galatea's east side, a place with too much modern art and not enough red meat on the menu. The PRISM stooge had the demeanour of a spaced-out kindly uncle who talked in code. No matter how many times you met this guy, you would always forget what he looked like.

"One who believes it's possible to control what is to come," he said. "The one thing that's eluded history's most ambitious. This is your time."

Roland could see blind spots in PRISM's deranged plans. And within them, opportunity. Success in life was ultimately a series of acute observations, methodical solutions and expertly executed transactions. Ruthless financiers were circling his head like a squadron of stealth bombers, ready to explode the empty labyrinth of mirrors that was the fraudulent Martian money machine. With the PRISM alliance, he would blow them out the sky. Adopting statesmanlike poise and a conman's bluff, Roland let the talks flow. The seduction continued at another meeting two weeks later in a boutique hotel suite on the mainland. A representative of PRISM's high command attended, disguised as an Arab sheikh. Some people had no imagination.

After his third Martini, Roland decided he wouldn't cut Augusta in yet. She detested being presented with unformed plans. Then, as the geopolitical hanky panky continued, he realised he didn't need to cut Augusta in at all. A handsome down payment landed in his personal account three days later. Covert shipments of PRISM nerve gas arrived. Their bullet-sized cartridges were soon installed in Galatea Zero's ventilation system. Then, with the most elegant and covert of reprograms, Roland brought PRISM-Tiresias into the world. With it came the fictitious spectre of a war that would never happen. Dummy missiles never to be fired. The ingenious *coup d'etat*. An artistic assassination and a very cheap divorce. Nothing lasts forever, after all. Especially political marriages.

The tables were set. The Corporate Experiences team stood quietly at their stations, heads bowed. Within five minutes, the two dim-witted slaves entered. Normally Roland would have trusted his elite team to deliver the package, but that may have aroused PRISM-Tiresias's suspicion. This was something Rosencrantz and Guildenstern would tell their grandkids about. *I was there once. Almost got to the top floor.* Probably thought they were delivering pastries. Both around five-foot nine, stockily built and wearing flappy, off-the-peg dark blue suits. Four shifty nervous brown eyes. Spring sweat sliding down their temples. Out of shape, out of their depth and out of personality, like they'd been cloned in some black-market lab experiment trying to create the perfect template for an unambitious, unquestioning middle manager.

"Mr-eh-Maars, your-eh-package-eh sir," said the less plump of the two.

"Don't tell me they made you walk up the stairs," said Roland in a silky voice. He gestured to the space between his feet, enjoying how the other goon nervously slid the package between his legs.

"No sir," he said, affecting a chuckle. "Just a hot day."

"Hot enough for you to forget the password?"

They looked at each other, hesitating over who would say it first.

"Olympus."

"Splendid. Now get the fuck out my face."

The duo scurried away, stopping for selfies in front of Augusta's portrait. In the months to come, more gawping plebeians would spread through his beautiful monument like a metastasizing cancer. Roland felt nauseous sharing such artistry with commoners. Still, every person, no matter how bestial, brings something to the beehive. Even if it's just the oily nectar of their own souls.

He picked up the case and headed to the door. Near the exit was Miss Eastern Europe, standing in full salute. The right lapel of her jacket flapped out to reveal the curvature of her breast rising gamely under a cream blouse. They shared a knowing smile. *Definitely worth sparing.* In his mind he saw her pressed up against frosted glass. Eyes closed, steam and water softening her skin.

Even though his office was only two floors above, Roland decided to take the lift. Ascension through the southwest elevator afforded a spectacular glimpse of a sun-dappled Galatea. In the six-second transition, he savoured the morning light awakening the island's colour. Its final innocent dawn before the shadow of invasion fell thick. This evening, the reddening sky would turn into the deepest shade of blood burgundy. At night, the stars would align in harmony, sustained in their place by gravity. The only force in the universe holding him back.

Roland would let PRISM have its way. Showcase the ingenuity of his fairground ride. Together, they would create a supreme artistic moment that fused technology, politics, imagination and the human will. *His will.* First to go would be the protestors. Then the party members, kettled and crushed. A chance to clear out the deadwood and blame it all on the protestors. And lastly Augusta. That black hole of insecurity who couldn't distinguish fiction from reality. Still haunted by how her mother died from bleeding on the brain. Still in that car crash with her dying father. Still waiting for someone to espouse puritanical lectures and whisk her to a magical stream so she could heal.

PRISM was drawing his wife into a needless confrontation based on a fantasy genocide the other side of the world. Her response would be an equally fictitious pre-emptive defensive strike. Two scapegoats were being prepared to lend authenticity to the assassination and spin a fable to the ignorant world. Mercedes was in position at the terminal; the fall guy Zayden making his way to the coast by cattle class. Augusta's killer could not be a PRISM agent or a rebel. It had to be an insider from the lower classes, so they could gut the party and commence socio-economic cleansing. Story upon story upon story. Fictions will eventually take over the world, thought Roland. Plausible yet poisonous, they crawl into their victims' heads like parasites and split minds apart. How he wished the same fate for his creditors.

Roland's terms with PRISM were clear. Chief Visionary Officer for the new empire that would, in five years, pacify the world's twenty most powerful nations. Gorging on its lavish resources and with all debts dissolved, Roland would build, build and build. A vision of unified urbanity integrating architecture, art, science, nature, symbolism and spirituality, bleeding into one. A hundred Augustas at his service. Prettier, docile and more athletic. A hundred Max Relpeks. Bigger, smarter and less slippery. He'd go through them all, revitalised by sophisticated upgrades to his bionic penis and the knowledge he'd not yet reached his peak. Hermaphrodisation would follow, for he'd heard it was ten times more pleasurable for the opposite sex.

Occupying the south-west corner of Level 99, Roland's office was a whitewashed triangular-shaped space with gold and purple trimmings. Two walls were windowed from top to bottom, offering a panoramic ocean view partially obscured by clouds. On the facing wall was the entrance door and an in-built 72-inch screen showing the Martian logo. Pushed against it was a twenty-stack entomological unit for Roland's insect specimens and a drinks cabinet in the shape of a giant decanter. In the centre of the room was a white kidney-shaped desk on which Roland placed the titanium-tungsten suitcase. He strolled to the cabinet and poured a Japanese whisky into a Maars-branded round-bottomed glass. In went a drop of premium-grade Kalypsol, which Augusta and Max used to intensify their orgasms. The spirit's smoky sting counter-balanced the bitterness of the coffee. The taste sparked mental images of Roland's pale, pock-marked skin writhing tremulously against Max's sculpted bronze flesh. Through the room's speakers, PRISM-Tiresias played Robert Johnson's *Hellhound On My Trail*, soothing its master's nerves.

Roland unlocked the case with his fingerprint and tapped in the 24-digit alphanumeric password which only he knew. The key that could unlock the system of all systems across Galatea and let slip the hounds of anarchy. Resting in the case were a dozen pristine miniature drones sculpted like bees, set in a foam tray moulded to suit their beautiful contours. Engraved names decorated their torsos. Zeus. Hera. Apollo. Aries. Demeter. Poseidon. Athena. Artemis. Hermes. Dionysus. Hephaestus. Aphrodite.

"O for a muse of fire," said Roland.

Hephaestus buzzed into life, glowing with electric blue light. It circulated the office in slow swoops of data assimilation. After three full arcs, the drone hovered in supplication thirty centimetres from Roland's face. He looked at the status report on his watch. *Metamorphosis synced. Ready to deploy.* Hephaestus's vital signs were operating at maximum efficiency. It could make as much honey as it wanted. The drone completed a graceful circle, like a sycophantic courtier leaving a throne room, and returned neatly to its slot.

Roland was annoyed the drone didn't land with a more satisfying clink. He would let the R&D team feel his profound disappointment with the acoustics. Just like he let his first employer know he was buying him out all those years ago, when Roland arrived at the crossroads and heard the devil call from the bus stop in the dark. His watch scanned the other eleven. Fully operational. In twelve hours' time, his darlings would be different. He imagined the faces of the PRISM soldiers when the full power of his creations bore into them.

They come in peace, he would say dryly in the post-takeover talks. *And they're just the hors d'oeuvre.*

He sipped his whisky, rolled it around his tongue and felt underwhelmed by its dull, dispiriting taste. His palate was becoming desensitised with age. Or maybe he'd exhausted all of life's sensory pleasures. Letting his eyelids fall, Roland pictured the sea creature locked in the glass cabinet of the Cave. An unknown quantity. A thing without eyes. A mysterious relic to which he was willingly enslaved. *Are you coming in peace too?*

"Please update on the specimen, Tiresias."

The screen flooded with graphs, data bars and deep-sea photography. Facts, analysis, projections. Still no explanation of the creature's origin. A crack had emerged in the seabed thirty miles off the coast, despite no geological disturbances within a one-hundred-mile radius. Roland had sent nine deep-sea reconnaissance probes into the dark. The first eight disappeared and all signals were lost. On the ninth expedition, the probe returned to the surface, its systems wiped and data irretrievable. Attached to the base, the specimen was a greyish lump no bigger than a marble. Since then, it had grown to the size of a baseball glove. At this rate, the discovery would soon need a new glass prison. According to PRISM-Tiresias's modelling, in twenty years the accelerating fissure would cause major earthquakes and devastating tsunamis. The creature would be the size of Galatea Zero. Yet in the dark where it was born, there remained nothing at all.

Roland fantasised about opening the glass case and stroking the sea creature. *We trust too much in technology. It is predatory, with an urge like nature to stay alive by consuming what is around. Eventually, something impenetrable will come to the surface and swallow the computerised world whole.* He imagined more creatures rising up, a seething multitude of intelligent life evolving under the seabed. His next strategic partnership. Another union, another act of creation. Post-PRISM. Pre-singularity. That moment when all phenomena would cohere beautifully as one.

The Sentinel was in touch with something in the heavens. Roland had arranged for a dummy data feed to be sent to PRISM-Tiresias, so only he received authentic insights from the mast atop Galatea Zero. Unable to sleep, he would go there in the middle of the night and sit in silence at the base of the huge needle as it pricked the edges of space. Sickened by people's cheap reality, he craved to claw through its thin plasticity and soar so high he could scratch the face of God.

Since the discovery of the specimen, the Sentinel was issuing aberration upon aberration. Contact was being made with intelligent life across the cosmos. The deep ocean and the infinite sky were in communion. Had an alien craft landed in the sea? Or was something buried in the core of the earth making its way to the surface? Nightmarish visions seeped into Roland's mind. Hallucinatory seascapes of silicone pregnant with mythic creatures, their endoskeletons synthesised from minerals discovered at the far side of space. Within them all, a divine orb of purest white with a dancing flame at its centre.

"Tiresias, show me power."

The screen's data disappeared. PRISM-Tiresias flashed a sequence of images designed to settle Roland's soul. The theme was beauty and betrayal; masterpieces animated by Martian AI agents like they were taking place in real-time before Roland's eyes. Christ's calm revelation in Leonardo da Vinci's *The Last Supper*. The flurried mauling in Caravaggio's *The Taking of Christ*. The final hand-written scrawl of a murdered revolutionary in Jacques-Louis David's *Death of Marat*. Francis Bacon's *Study After Velasquez's Portrait of Pope Innocent X*. Trapped in a cobweb of gold and his soul evaporating, the anguished Pope resembled a caged animal screaming into the abyss. Or a helpless insect unable to free itself from the tangled machinations of power, waiting in terror as an unseen predator prowled closer. The emaciated pontiff's jaw hung low, leaving an unholy chasm where the mouth should have been. A trap within a trap, beckoning its victims into the void.

"Metamorphosis synced," said Roland. "Ready to deploy."

All twelve drones took flight and swooped around the room, emitting an icy collective hum. One after another, they sped towards the artwork. One by one, they disappeared into the figure's mouth. The screen was another trick of the light, another illusory surface cloaking unknown spaces. His darlings would wind their way through the Visionary Complex and re-emerge later in the gallery when the time was right.

For now, Roland would clear out the deadwood. Except Heidi and Hernandes. He could spot good concubines a mile away and move with the speed of a peregrine falcon. With a few taps of his phone, he summoned them to his lair. In between sips of whisky, he would watch them in coitus from behind his desk through pale blue eyes. Demand total silence, then edge closer. Run his hands over their supple flesh, admiring the smooth, well-engineered definition of their youthful design. The piston-like motion of their remote-controlled love.

After he'd finished with them, Roland would inject himself with his daily allowance of chemically enhanced nutrients. Meet Max for a vigorous lunchtime session on the squash court. Make a final covert connection with the shitheads at PRISM. Succumb to the future and witness his masterwork unfold during the night like the strangest of love poems.

Metamorphosis. Ready to deploy. Roland heard the knock at the door. The alien part of himself hardened. As his next conquests entered sheepishly, he tapped his foot, daring the world to deny him whatever he wanted next. At some point that would happen. But not now. Not for a while. Until then, Roland the artist would enjoy visions of power only he could see coming.

XVI

The north elevation of Galatea Zero. 103 minutes before the Fall.

Alexis was on top of the world. Stars festooned the sky in showers of sparkling light. A shimmering tapestry of silver and yellow jewels spangled towards the sea's black chasm. On the waves, a twinkling cruise liner serenaded partygoing passengers with wheezy blue and orange fireworks.

Nothing else about the scene was charming. Roaring winds sliced Alexis's fingers and toes, already glowing red from gripping the girders. Tears trickled down her cheeks. Fear of slipping scooped away her insides. Either the cold would claim her, or a sudden gust would sweep Alexis clean off and make her as flimsy and inconsequential as a discarded crisp packet.

A fallen lady, falling fast. A fall which began when she'd let Max into her bed. Or maybe earlier, when she met Augusta and a cause she could half-believe in. *You have special gifts*, Mr Joyce said. *I hope you learn to use them.* She wasn't sure the loveable old boozer meant becoming a corporate prostitute who dangled off skyscrapers without any underwear.

After her kamikaze leap to the girder, Alexis felt invincible. She dragged herself up, cocked her left leg over the steel and sat like a rodeo rider as she shuffled along. Gleeful gibberish erupted from her mouth. Delirious incantations she would summon in the early part of climb, until reality's muzzle clamped her jaw shut. The circular maintenance hatch was more than twenty metres from the nearest girder. A gap too far. A mocking black hole. A portal meant only for insiders. And she hadn't been one of those for a while.

Centre yourself, said Hugo. *Back to your stance.* Alexis kept moving. Not knowing what she was doing or where she was going. *Plus ça change.* Baby steps. Little by little. Squeezing her thighs into steel. Sweat rolling down her face. God knows what her make-up was like since the *tête-à-tête* with Leo. All she knew is that whenever she got where she was going, she would have a big cry.

Far below, Tiresias was in murder mode. The insurgents were screaming and gasping, helpless cattle being exterminated in a computerised abattoir. If Alexis was committed to the cause, she would be concocting a plan for how the Martian press machine could spin the party's way out of this disaster. *Breaking and entering. The protestors attacked us unprovoked. They were warned we would retaliate. The police and army failed us. We were fearing for our lives. We have a right to defend ourselves. Yada yada yada.*

Maybe it was time to shut down her professional autopilot. Fling herself off Galatea Zero into the abyss, so she didn't have to spin another twisted story. Or she could hang on until everything settled. Wait for a strapping Adonis firefighter to sweep her to safety in his tree trunk arms. Take stock of her life. Junk her addictions. Help the poor. Move to a convent. Pack the vibrator. Maintain contact with her therapist. That goatee-faced charlatan would have a lot of explaining to do in his corduroy blazer behind his moleskin notebook.

Choices, choices, choices. None of them would do. She had to see Max. Had to reach him. Had to know he was worth saving. Had to make her mark. *Women like us must let nothing stand in our way*, Augusta said to her once, in the halcyon days when they would slip off their shoes, recline on the sofa, chomp through chocolate liquors and redraft statements about education policy. The boss was right. Let nothing stand in your way. Alexis was ready to scorch her own trail to the top table, petrifying mediocre men with her flaming hair and possessed eyes like an evangelic corporate Medusa. Deliver her version of Augusta's victory speech in person, with venom and verve. Six sublime sentences grandiose enough to be sculpted onto the marble of ancient temples.

No doubt The Gorgeous One would have written some cack-handed, macho drivel. Most likely while cowering in a recreation cell, buttocks too clenched to soil himself. In the battle of political bullshit, Alexis would be declared the winner. Augusta would place the laurel wreath *on her head*. Then with tender loving force, she would drag lover boy by his luscious locks to the nearest bedroom. Naked, toned, loaded with sin and shame, Max would grovel. Kiss her feet. Apologise a thousand times. Beg like a bitch. She would sip SoCo, avert her gaze with the cruel indifference of Marie Antoinette and demand a million sexual favours.

Christ, Lexy, he doesn't want you anymore. You're a vain, narcissistic, deluded and shallow airhead who will never amount to anything. Addicts always become the centre of their own universes. Get a grip, you stupid, stupid cow.

Steady progress was made through the tight, interlacing pattern of the girders. The hexagonal cross hatches of steel curved outside the main fabric of the building to form a mesh which encircled the Visionary Complex. Some wags called Galatea Zero the microphone. *Because that bitch loves the sound of her own voice.* After twenty minutes of panting and crawling, Alexis reached the edge of the building's main column. On the cusp of outside, she looked upwards to chart her course, the coolness of the night sweeping up her skirt. *Look at me, Mr Joyce. I've got my own climbing frame in the smartest building in the world.* Midway up the Visionary Complex, there was a gantry connecting the girders with the main column. The Martian maintenance team used it to access the building's outer fabric. Alexis enjoyed a flirty cigarette break there once with Stelios from facilities management, a short but sweet relapse to her days as a teenager playing truant. When she learned to lie about her mental health, because that was the only way boys would like her. The first indication that finding a good man in this universe was like searching for pearls among shipwrecks in the Mariana Trench.

There was nowhere else to go. *Get moving girl. Onwards and upwards. I'll find love in this building if it fucking kills me.* She may get a second chance if she fell. Strike and straddle the bottom girders. Start back up, depending on which bones were broken. Or she would bounce through the gaps and plummet to the earth, like the last precious petal of a rare flower or a stubborn turd finally flushed. Scratching, slipping, sliding, shuffling, steadying. Slipping again. Both feet. A near-fatal drop arrested by squeezing her biceps, chest, ribcage and thighs into the girder with maximum force.

Ohmigod I'm going to fucking die I know it. Please, please, please somebody help me. She should retreat immediately. Crawl back through the broken window. Flee to the Imagineering Zone. Apologise to that nice Mr Haze for fucking up his evening and being such an evil dragon. Pledge submission to his every command until the end of time. One level. Two levels. Three levels. If the headaches flared, she would not hang on. Unless those black, brain-crushing anvils had returned unnoticed, and their pain had been tranquilised by teetering on the edge of death. An interesting alternative medicine. Probably less demeaning than listening to that sleazy consultant patronise her the second Tuesday of every month.

"Fuck you Tiresias," Alexis screamed into the Galatean night. "Do your fucking worst you invisible fucking snake. The elements can't shake me. The sea is at my command. So fuck you all. Fuck. You. All."

Drrmmmwwwwahahahah. Drrmmmwwwahahahah. A droning through the gale. A military helicopter. Alexis had been on enough press junkets to know. Augusta was escaping. *Boss lady, say it ain't so. Show us you're brave enough to go down with the ship. And if you're not, don't take that snivelling shit with you. I want the pleasure of sinking my teeth into him first.* Unless it was a rescue party, led by a dashing commander wearing aviator sunglasses and built like a tennis player, ready to reach out his chivalric hand and lift her to the heavens. But it was neither. As the Boeing CH47 Chinook disappeared towards the helipad, Alexis knew it was a PRISM delegation. A last-minute peace deal was being negotiated, or that sick bastard Veneto had been right all along.

Baby movements. Little by little. Five, six, seven, eight. *Who do you fucking appreciate?* The wind sunk its teeth into her hands, feet and shoulders blades. Alexis's breathing became manic. A torrent of unhinged sounds whirred from her mouth. The encircling freeze sucked tears out her eyes. Her vision was flooded black. Red vistas emerged of blood-drenched sea and sand. The kaleidoscopic whirring of fairground rides. The laughter of school pupils. The hypnotic allure of those mysterious white orbs only she could see. Still the invisible forcefield held firm. She was not going to fall. That was not her story.

Move to higher ground. Move to higher ground. Move to higher ground. Move to higher ground. Move to higher gr-

"Get up off the floor slowly and put your hands behind your head."

A panicky, wired voice. It reminded Alexis of a half-soaked prefect she used to know at school whose vocal cords hadn't broken. She was on the gantry, flat on her back. Bleeding from somewhere. Standing above and pointing a gun in her face was one of Augusta's Resilience Specialists. A swarthy blond-haired gym bunny dressed in black shoes, black trousers and a black turtleneck jumper. A very bad extra in a very bad spy movie.

Alexis rose to her feet and clasped her hands behind her head. The trilby had hung in there too. Beyond this chiselled chunk of low-IQ testosterone was a door leading to the Visionary Complex. The same doorway where Stelios asked her to squeeze his guns. Only a single idiot stood between her and the elite. *Par for the course in this shithole.* But this was not any idiot. This was the guard she slept with at the manifesto party. Tony? Terry? Tyler? Nope, this guy was taller. Better looking. Of course. Him. The one with the ludicrous name and disgusting table manners. The one who garrotted a member of the paparazzi because he thought her camera was a grenade.

Apart from his matinee idol looks, everything about Butch Duck was a disaster. An Action Man figure whose personality transplant had gone wrong. A takeaway tough guy. A bewildered man at the limits of his cognitive capacity. All forehead and fists. With both hands fastened to his firearm, Butch was in combat stance, trying extra hard to look like he knew what he was doing. Well and truly in over his square empty head. On the third finger of his left hand was a black ring, one of the most coveted possessions in Galatea Zero. Black Magic permitted the highest level of security access. And Butch had one. Which meant the lunatics had not only taken over the asylum but were about to burn it down.

"Straker," Butch spluttered, mesmerised by the inferno-eyed hag before him. Mental cogs chugged as he realised what the lady he once called 'sugar lump' had accomplished to reach this point.

"What the fuck..."

"They're wiping everyone out," Alexis said, breath short and chest pounding. "You need to get out of the way... Brad?"

Butch seemed hurt she didn't remember his name. Sticking her chest out, Alexis walked slowly towards him, hands still clasped behind her head. Butch took a step back and tensed up.

"Stop right there. I've been told to shoot on sight. Any and all intruders."

"You're not going to shoot me Brad. You're not going to arrest me."

"I swear I'll shoot. Blow your head and your stupid hat clean off."

"You're the second person today to make comments about my headwear. The other guy's dead."

"Down on your knees Straker. Or I'll fucking unload."

"You're going to let me through, Brad."

"No I won't. Stop calling me Brad."

"Either PRISM will kill you, or I will."

"PRISM?"

"Yes, Brad. PRISM is taking over."

"I'll count to three, you dumb bitch."

For two of the three seconds, Alexis pondered her options. Butch might be persuaded to let her near Augusta. She may stand a better chance of surviving in his custody. His gun and ring would be very useful. And there was strength in numbers. But he may not understand the complexities of the conspiracy. Or have the balls to handle it. On reflection, Butch was most likely a complete and utter waste of fucking time.

Back to your stance, Lexy. Open the hips. Squeeze the glutes. Chest down. Hands up. Pivot. Twist. And let that fucking leg fly up to his throat to knock his dumbbell head off. In the Galatea Zero gym, Alexis once executed a roundhouse kick so perfectly on the punch bag held by Hugo it knocked the Latino lust god onto his lovely peach of an ass. Not this time. Her hips were too sore. Her body too weak. As her leg swept up, Alexis's skirt split. Butch grabbed her ankle in mid-air. He twisted it, grinning, his gun still trained on her face. Until he noticed Alexis wasn't wearing any underwear.

Jesus, you'd think this moron had never seen snatch before in his life. She took off from the ground, thrusting her other leg towards Butch's gun hand. The foot's navicular bone struck the left wrist. Something cracked. Butch dropped to one knee, his gun clattering on the gantry. Alexis landed on her back, smacking her head. Stars spun everywhere. Rising up, she grabbed Butch by the hair and rammed his head into her right knee. His jaw broke like scrunching paper. Butch screamed. Alexis's kneecap blazed. Grabbing his belt with both hands, she rolled him face down and shoved her other knee into the small of his back. She unclipped the handcuffs from the loop at the top of his trousers. As Butch flung his right hand behind him in a desperate lunge, Alexis caught it with her left, slapped on the cuff and lunged him to the metal railing, snapping him into place. Turning him over, she squeezed Butch's left wrist. The fractured bone crumpled. On went the other cuff. Alexis grunted like a wild animal devouring its prey.

"Yrrrffff fgrrrrr bbbbb...."

"Could be worse Butch," she panted. "I could have thrown you to the wolves. Consider yourself lucky. You're the third person I've incapacitated today. The last guy completely lost his head."

Alexis squeezed the black ring from Butch's fat finger. It made a fetching combination with its red and blue counterparts. A girl's best friend. *But they all lose their charms in the end, Lexy.* Fizzing with adrenaline, she swooped down to pick up Butch's gun. She went too far too fast, her vision blurred from whacking her head. Instead of grabbing the gun butt, she knocked the weapon off the gantry and down to the street two hundred metres below. Unlike Butch, she didn't have the energy to swear.

157

"Frrrgggi kyyyyyyyii uuu."

Stepping over his mewling body, Alexis limped into the building, floating feet adjusting to terra firma. Slamming the door behind her, she stood in a stupor, letting warm air waft into every pore. Alexis sank down, cradled her wounded knee and unleashed an avalanche of tears.

Why do I have to hammer everything I see? Butch was not bad. But he had it coming. They all had it coming. Must get to IRIS and lock all this down. Must get into the room. Must check if Max is ok. Must get us out of here. Run away. Run away now. Why are you trying to take on the world? The universe is indifferent. But I'm meant to have special gifts. I hope I learn to use them.

Alexis had to keep moving. To higher ground. Before her lay a bland white corridor leading to a T junction. On the walls were digital pop art interpretations of oil paintings portraying famous heroes from mythic Greece. Heracles. Theseus. Jason. Perseus. Achilles. Hector. The images were filtered through the orange and blue duotone of the Martian logo. Conceptual bullshit at its tackiest. Alexis inched along the ash-coloured carpet, catching sight of herself in the windowpane of an unlit empty meeting room. She was a walk-of-shame weirdo. A wild cat from the sewers. An emaciated banshee on steroids.

Everything was still. No sound. No soul. Any Martians left must have retreated upstairs. Veneto was right. It all chimed in her head. A pre-emptive strike by PRISM. Knocking out Tiresias. Replacing the system with a new one. Inciting and facilitating the protest as both diversion and scapegoat. Ordering the party to self-destruct and spiral into the plughole. Nerve gas encircling. Walls closing in. The Martian party was playing its endgame.

Soon she was in the gallery corridor of Level 96. The place where she'd first seen Max. Where she started to imagine what he would be like. Already falling for him. *Forever faintly falling.* About twenty metres away, near the main entrance to the Visionary Complex, were two Resilience Specialists. Dumpier and older than Butch, they were standing guard before an empty wall like ugly lampshades. This was the invisible entrance to the Olympus Suite, Augusta's boudoir of choice. Within lay the Cave, to which only her and Roland had access. The king and queen would often use this secret portal to exit the Visionary Complex, bypassing the sycophants and spies who hovered in its central hub. If you were in the corridor when they appeared, it was like phantoms materialising from another world.

Between Alexis and the guards were the Hercules beetle engravings. Six on either side. *The longest beetle in the world*, Roland told her during the tour. *One of the largest flying insects. Capable of lifting one hundred times its own body mass.* About five metres in front of her, a metal disc lay on the carpet. One of the ceiling's circular air vents had been twisted off, leaving screws scattered on the floor and a black hole above.

Oblivious to Alexis, the two guards were transfixed by a small drone hovering before them in mid-air. *Clunk.* As if magnetised, the nugget of metal sped to the wall and clamped itself onto the centre of the nearest engraving. Electric blue light emanated from each corner of the artwork. Smooth, cylindrical space-grey shapes began to protrude from the surface. Some long, some short, all moving in concert. Connected by tendon-like rods which slid out in synchrony. Efficient, intricate movements of metal upon metal. Clicking, connecting, coordinating. Each closure a crisp snap of engineering perfection. The cumulative talents of a hundred technicians in crystal-clear alignment.

The giant replica of a Hercules beetle detached itself from the wall. Rapidly completing its self-assembly in the corridor, the biomechanical beast was twice the size of each guard. Six legs spanned out from a smooth, rounded centre, each ending in twitching, vice-like clamps. Extending outwards from the top of its body were two huge, serrated horns. The smaller, bottom one curved upwards. The longer, overarching one stretched into space and was at least twice the length of the torso. A beautiful, terrifying and diseased vision. The ultimate progeny of the twisted *ménage à trois* between Roland, Tiresias and Galatea Zero.

One of the guards sprinted past the robot and Alexis. The other shrunk away in the opposite direction, towards the Visionary Complex's main entrance. The escape route was locked. Black Magic failed him. Back to the wall, face twisted in horror, the guard waved his gun at the advancing beetle. The thing advanced, scraping its larger horn along the ceiling and carving a line through the fractal patterns. Suddenly, it accelerated. There was a sickening pop of skull, brains and tissue as the larger horn impaled the guard's head to the door. With feverish thrusting, the smaller horn punctured the dead man's stomach, sending sounds of skewering flesh rippling down the corridor. The robot extracted itself from the carcass, smatterings of blood gleaming across its dull grey body.

Above Alexis there was an aggressive buzzing. In militarised procession, a flurry of drones descended through the black empty space where the vent used to be, attaching themselves in sequence to the other engravings. *Clunk, clunk, clunk, clunk, clunk, clunk, clunk, clunk, clunk.* Alexis bolted towards the spot where the guards had been standing and slammed her black ring against the Tiresias logo on the wall. The robot, less than five metres away to her right, rotated to face her. At the base of its horns, two tiny blue lights widened.

The wall gave way. Alexis fell through and landed on her ass. After punching the internal lock, she noticed her hat lying outside. She rocked forward, hurled out her arm and scooped it up. Her last glimpse of the corridor before the door shut was a gleaming tip of metal, about the size of a samurai sword, piercing the dead space where her hat used to be.

She crawled backwards through the Olympus antechamber on her hands, buttocks and heels, never once taking her eyes from the door. This was where Max told her to wait. The moment when she knew she'd fallen. *Augusta can't see you right now.* Every fibre in her body trembling, she waited for the beetle to slice a black hole into the suite and machete her face into fleshy confetti.

The monster never came. Outside, the clicking and calibrating accelerated as the other beetles assembled. Eventually the insane orchestra subsided, and the whirring militia of metal feet faded into the distance. Roland's creations were on the move. They had another purpose. They would not overstep their mark. Perhaps they knew, like everyone else, that Augusta's most sacred lair was only open to those who dealt in Black Magic. Alexis lay on her back, put the hat over her face and cried all the tears of the universe into its dark empty space.

XVII

The centre of the black hole.

S he was close now. Adam could feel it. Flares of red darted and dived inside his head. Deep within his dream within a dream, visions of a magical underwater realm emerged. He longed to swim there forever. To be with her, forever. Rocking back and forth on fathomless space, Adam pushed his hand against the invisible glass of this desolate ocean. He waited and waited. Higher still, in a placed called reality, his crew were trying to wake him. *We are here, Captain DeBreeze. We are here.*

Not now. Not yet. A pattern was forming. Another power bleeding out behind the screen. A milky white fluid silhouetted his fingertips in a phantasmal glow. He'd forgotten what white looked like. Full of everything and nothing. The illumination expanded into a luminous orb the size of a football. A fleck of red danced in its centre. Tiny vapours of white plasma vibrated on its edges, eroded by the dark. *We are here, Captain DeBreeze. We are here.* Maybe they were. But what did it matter about glimpsing the red planet now he'd finally seen the light?

"I told you it needed the human touch," said Columbus.

"Do I need to say anything?" Adam said, his voice trembling. Since leaving shore, he'd never felt more insignificant. More like an infinitesimal vibration in aeons of time and space. More close to home.

"Only how much you love me."

"I've always loved you. I love the way you sit on your ass all your day. I love the way you never seem to do anything. Except process data. I love it all."

"Processing is a fine art, Adam. It takes patience and care. A little bit like love and storytelling, I imagine. Gratitude is important though. Sadly, that seems in short supply from today's explorers."

The orb's brilliance intensified. Warmth flushed through Adam's hand. In the centre of the light, a flickering burst of scarlet held his gaze. He would not look away. Could not look away. For the flame reminded him of someone he once knew. Someone who stared into the fire. Someone who saw things nobody else could. Someone who swam out to the horizon in search of something else.

I am here. I am here. Take me with you. We'll go together. The orb flashed away into the distance, leaving a spectral trail of pale light dissolving in space. It reminded Adam of an old television set switching off, in the days when *Star Trek* felt fresh and shiny.

"What happens now?"

"You're going to wait," said Columbus. "Creative acts never evolve quickly. It takes a while for inner lights to reach home."

The two explorers sat quietly. The boat bobbed up and down against the glass. Whether it was for minutes, hours or days, Adam could not say. Eventually a solitary white star appeared in the sky. The first one Adam had seen in a long time. Another to the right. One more below. He craned his neck back, placing both palms on the boat's wooden floor, like a giddy schoolboy on his first visit to the planetarium. Soon there were too many stars to count and a storm of magical stardust lay reflected in the placid water. Sea and sky merged, glittering with circling, celestial lights.

"What should I do?"

"Find the magic words," said Columbus. "I'm no longer in control, Adam. We're out of my territory. My power fails around here."

Adam's eyes raced across the stars. His mind drew patterns, forms and faces. Light to light. Point to point. Constellation to constellation. Character to character. A narrative journey unfolding in his mental sky. A story. A mystery. An adventure. A tower, like the one he'd seen in the collage on that sunny afternoon at school. Lovely mermaids. Lavishly detailed leviathans. Sunset on a liquid Mars, seen through the eyes of an angelic aesthete from Venus. Lonely people, trapped in the tower, greedy for love and trying to find higher ground. To reach out. To connect. To touch something they thought might be love. *The sea was where she disappeared. And from the sea she would rise.*

"Your lights will lead the way," said a voice, which was either his own, Columbus's or somebody else's. "Love will light the way. They will find each other. Just tell them you are here."

Brightness burst on the horizon. The white orb rose majestically above the sea like a pale sun awakening the dawn. Back in reality, Adam's spacecraft orbited the red planet preparing to land. The astronauts were ready to discover their new world. Yet the scarlet flame at the centre of this imaginary light in the heavens was the only place Adam cared about now. He looked deep into its fiery heart and swore he could see it beating. Thud. Thud. Thud.

XVIII

IRIS. Twenty-one years after the Fall.

Thud. Thud. Thud. Kneeling before the mural, Lewis held the box containing the remnants of his mother's heart. The cosmos concentrated into a heap of dust. The mind could malfunction. The heart never would. Because the heart comes from the ground. From the earth. From the deepest place.

In the blackest times, Lewis would cup the box in his hands and recite lines from her letter. *This is where you came from. This is where you belong.* Sometimes he hated the mural's coldness. An image on a wall rendered flat, two-dimensional, lifeless. A demented cave painting, drawn by a solitary man haunted by hallucination. Once he dreamed the white stars constellated around the Portal would pulsate and be more real than he was. Yet the more he looked, the more he saw the droughted delusion of his mind's eye. All he could hear was his own heart beating the slow rhythm of solitude.

Thud. Thud. Thud. Thud. *Ping.* An artificial sound. Glib, hackneyed, joyful. The first since Lewis had entered IRIS. In the dead centre of the Portal, at his mural's vanishing point, flared a large white circle with a swirl of amorphous red at its core. How he used to detest digitalised light. Binary magic without art. Without soul. Since the PRISM academy, he'd learned to loathe the depersonalised, clinical nature of the virtual world. How it defiled the senses and corrupted the bloodstream, traducing his fellow trainees to overstimulated spectres. Ghostly victims of the world's most pestilential plague.

This signal was different. Underneath the circle on the screen, white text emerged in Deimos, the primary font of the Martian brand. It was accompanied by nine empty squares and a touchscreen keypad. *Don't worry, I am here. Say the magic words and we'll get connected.*

Lewis slid the letter from his bag. The words which started his expedition. Which started him as a person. The secret was here. The narrative to unlock the tower. The entrance to a new world. *Words can shape reality if they're used well*, the letter said. *All it needs is the courage to mean them.* He ran his eyes over the handwriting, drawing faith from every ascender and descender like they were sacred runes. Through this letter, the rebellious author had willed life onto the blank greyness of her existence. A message promising that if Lewis looked to the horizon long enough, a lady would come to cure this poisoned realm.

He recalled the day the note arrived at the dormitory. An alien, sepia-toned object from the other side of the universe. *I thought nobody sent these anymore*, said the elderly warden, placing the note on the bed and shuffling off into the shadows. Touching the paper sailed Lewis away to ancient lands. To the youth he may have had. To an old flame he never met. To a mother's love so distant yet so familiar his spirit quaked at the thought it may still exist. A love spoken softly into the ear through an open window, when the sky was clear, the grass thick and the world a nobler, gentler place. Before everything had fallen.

Since entering IRIS, Lewis's sleep was flooded with turbulent images. The red ocean rolling. A maroon sky casting an unearthly gloom over the tranquil seascape. Evening or morning. A delight or a warning. People he couldn't see screaming for escape. Lewis let the blood drag him under, as others clung to the splintering wreckage of life above. In the deep, the alien face would come. Its body was unfathomable, twisting through the darkness in every direction. Dormant life rising to the surface. *Tap, tap, tap. Scratch, scratch, scratch.* Creatures scurrying round the confines of his skull. What had been in his mind was now outside of it. Or he himself had gone out of his mind. The tremors would wake him. Louder and closer every time. The groaning of a buckling earth. She'd promised him he wouldn't be alone. But he was, in a desolate building in a contaminated land, waiting for the waters to engulf him, his mural, the letter, her heart and this strange signal transmitted via the Portal from beyond the horizon.

Amid the sepulchral gloom, the white orb radiated with peace. The pulsing red shape at its centre enveloped his soul in warmth. *To my beloved son. I'm writing this letter so you know your story.* In the days that followed, Lewis scanned the letter and tried hundreds of permutations on the keypad. Nine empty cauldrons waited to be filled with elusive potions. Each attempt met with a tiny red exclamation mark and a juddering graphical interface. Yet the controlling power behind the Portal never locked him out. Every rejection was a new discovery. Dead ends leading him closer to the secret at the labyrinth's centre.

Thud. Thud. Thud. Lewis swooned under the immense combination of infinite causes and conditions which brought him to this point. He was a random concentration of stardust that belonged not to any one person, but to the universe. Whipped together by cosmic winds to settle at this spot so he could connect with something beyond himself.

One day the door will open and you won't be alone, Noah, his mother had written. *Just keep reaching out. Find the magic words. She will come.*

XIX

The VIP Wellness Suite of Galatea Zero. Two days before the Fall.

Max and Roland were alone in the watery space, barely visible to each other through the shower room's suffocating haze. PRISM-Tiresias undulated the temperature of the flowing water in calibration with Roland's wishes. A spectrum of tropical lights transitioned through the chamber, while synthetic birdsong flapped and fluttered under an arching canopy of white marble.

"We're channelling a new power here, Maximillian," said Roland.

It was past eleven o'clock in the evening. The building's chief architect had spanked Max around the squash court. As a consolation prize, the victor asked his junior partner to hold his towel while he washed away the sweat. Roland preferred someone else to dry him by hand rather than use the aeration unit. A subservient person was sweeter than a subservient machine.

"PRISM is introducing a whole new sphere of political, social and economic engineering. Influence beyond all convention. Reshaping what it means to control. And with every evolution comes a degree of… decay."

Roland clicked his spindly fingers. The shower stopped. Steam dissolved to reveal an east wall streaming aerial footage of the Himalayas. Water, soap and sweat slid down Roland's cue ball head and his pale, pencil-thin torso, matted with wiry grey hair. As the plughole slurped the secreted fluid, Roland placed his hands on his hips and rolled his pale blue eyes over his companion's naked body.

"Don't see this as murder," he continued. "See this as evolution. You'll be one of our new super-beings. Intelligent, healthy and ambitious. Well-equipped for reproduction. Our movement is designed for you."

Roland spoke about Max like he was a luxury car. The soon-to-be first man of the government was never the most considerate lover. Their romantic assignations reminded Max of when his elder brother forced him to endure repeated rides on a rickety wooden rollercoaster at a seaside theme park near the family estate. Yet when Roland pitched an idea, it was hard to refuse. Every scheme unfurled from the senior's mouth was a beautifully bowled *fait d'accompli*, full of grandeur and inevitability, like he was unveiling a newly discovered physical law of the universe to a global televised audience. Roland was a man of mesmeric motion, re-orchestrating people's minds with deft hand gestures and a bewitching gaze that inclined your spirit towards him. He had ascended into that exhilarating space again this evening, invigorated by his dominance with racquet and ball over his compliant butler-cum-stud.

"Why this way?" said Max. "There must be a simpler way. It seems so... contrived."

"Sweetie, this is the most *artistic* way," replied Roland, with condescending paternalism. He placed one hand on Max's shoulder and nodded to the Martian-branded towel draped over his partner's forearm. When intimate, he was at his most avaricious. Stone cold to the touch. Max rubbed the towel across Roland's shoulders and chest, imagining the sensors on his master's cyborg cock flashing.

"This is where art, architecture and statecraft combine," Roland said. "There are forces and contingencies you don't need to worry your lovely head about. Just walk on stage, remember your lines and leave the rest with me. This is about telling the right story. Now and tomorrow. So we control the narrative. Leave no loose ends. The universe belongs to those who tell the most powerful tales. As a journalist, you should know that."

The bubbling effusions of an insatiable mind. From a man who rarely slept and took breakfast through a hypodermic needle. When Max awoke from strange dreams in the Cerberus Suite, he would see his master across the room doing elaborate Martian yoga. A tiger on its haunches, ready to attack anyone who strayed too far into his cybernetic jungle.

"It's become complicated," Max mumbled, lifting Roland's right arm and tenderly towelling it off.

"The child?"

"*My* child. The baby is innocent. Even if Augusta isn't."

"Maximillian, still so naïve," smirked Roland. "There is no baby. Never will be any baby. The scan you saw was created by Tiresias. She can't have children. I made certain of it."

Max once placed his hand on Augusta's stomach and imagined he could feel his son's heartbeat. Thud. Thud. Thud. Now all he felt was a spasm of pain: a sensation so distant as to be meaningless. Stronger voices reigned inside. Roland's. PRISM's. His own. Alexis's too, telling him he was destined for more than the Martians. *You're good enough to govern us all.* The Red Rocket was wild, but Max missed her. She made him feel young. Maybe that's what love was. With Roland and Augusta, the soil was already being slung over his body.

"She says she can feel it within her. Growing."

Max took Roland's right hand. He let it open up in his palm, then carefully dried each finger from the base to the tip.

"That's her mind. Telling her something that's happening when it isn't. Pure phantoms. Augusta's head is full of many things. It was easy to put something else in there. Rest assured her womb is void."

Void. What a word to use. Said with the same Siberian authority as the phrase Roland used to set the assassination in motion. *I'm getting rid of her.*

The east wall shifted to drone footage of an arctic landscape. Roland clutched Max's wrist as an instruction to stop drying. The towel fell to the wet tiled floor. The shower room was filled with a deadening chill as the two men stood naked in all-encompassing white. Roland moved closer to Max, sensing rebellious thoughts. He cupped Max's testicles, smiling as they retracted. Kissing him gently, Roland manoeuvred his mouth to clench Max's bottom lip between his teeth.

"Just be in the right place with her at the right time," after releasing him. "Five seconds of courage. One simple push. Access to power and pleasure beyond anything you've contemplated. Only if you've got the balls, of course."

Roland's Kalypsol breath was rusty and repellent. He suffered no side effects and was at his most athletic and visionary after consuming the drug. During a binge in the Olympus Suite, he eulogised to Max and Augusta about a formative school trip to a Viennese museum, when he saw *The Tower of Babel* by Pieter Bruegel the Elder. An epiphany which inspired dreams within. As the triumvirate lay in each other's arms, Roland explained how Galatea Zero was a huge transmitter seeking contact with alien life. Why the entire apparatus of PRISM could be bent to a new world order. The importance of connecting with, but never surrendering to, higher powers. How the three of them would be together forever. Max learned to play dumb and affect an awestruck face. Never question Roland's knowledge. Never frown. Never probe what was happening in the fathomless darkness. Just keep swimming deeper into the master's space.

"Make your choice Maximillian. Enjoy real power. Or place your future in a phantom creation of someone else's mind. It's time the world appreciated the full extent of your talents. I love you Max. Believe me when I say it."

Max grew stiff in Roland's hand, returning kisses of his own. *Choices.* Getting into bed with the Martians meant you had no choice at all. Besides, at this stage in the game, Max was too much in love with the idea of powerful people being in love with him. And love was all he really wanted: drumrolls of adulation thundering from all directions and from as many people as possible. Thud. Thud. Thud.

"What if we get caught?"

"How and by who? People want drama. They crave to be controlled. Give them some bait on a hook then gouge out their insides. You'll be surprised how much they'll thank you for it. And don't think the people here even think for one minute about your interests. Up this high, everyone's a scorpion in a sack."

"What does that make you?"

"The guy carrying the sack. So to speak."

Roland removed his hand from Max's testicles, traced his finger over his chiselled jaw, whipped the towel from the floor and slinked into his private changing room. The vista on the east wall screened endless sand dunes underneath a cloudless blue sky. The sultan would be unreachable for an hour, then summon an exhausted Max for fresh sport. No doubt in the interim he would commune with devils in the deep blue sea and drink his own blood. Nobody else's was sweet enough. Not even his wife's. To Roland, Augusta was a disposable, empty vessel. A Trojan horse into which he could implant his ambition. A trophy to be wheeled out to naïve, supine crowds hungry for a female hero who'd bested the demons of personal tragedy.

The universe belongs to those who tell the most powerful tales. The universe also belonged to entropy. Roland was blind and egotistical. PRISM would grow tired of his tedious lectures, his air of superiority, his crusty eccentricities. His sheer greed. Roland would never endear himself to the masses. Too cold. Too aloof. Too odd. He would lead the country in a downward spiral, a vacuum where communities would suck each other dry like leeches. Max, on the other hand, would be different. Young, fresh-faced and firing on all cylinders. His peers at university were mystified when he declined modelling contracts for journalism. Soon they were no longer looking down on him. One by one, everyone fell for the earnest, docile beefcake routine. Good for a shag, a photo opportunity and for charming people who needed to be charmed.

A *prime piece of gorgeousness waiting to be exhibited*, as Alexis said, as she helped him with his contact lenses and straightened his silk ties. Sexy Lexy couldn't hang onto him though. *Love is a tough game, sweetie*. He couldn't help it if everyone wanted to love him. Power flung itself at him, like iron filings to a magnet.

Max gazed into the east wall. The camera traversed a winding river through dense jungle of green, brown and yellow. Forestation folded away with ease. *Five seconds of courage. One simple push.* Let Mr Maars treat him like a trampoline for a little while longer. He would soon bounce himself out of sight. The slimy old fuck can't live forever. Tiresias had promised him much. Feeding him lines on how to deliver that speech, seduce this woman, manipulate that prospect. PRISM-Tiresias too, reaching out with encrypted voicemails every night for the past four days, fleshing out his dreams through cellular sorcery. A lullaby luring him to shake off the Martian shackles and discover himself. *You're good enough to govern us all.*

The screen slipped to black. From the darkness, a white circle appeared at the centre of the wall. In its centre, a red dot smouldered like a hot coal. He thought of Alexis, and how she warmed his bones and kindled his fantasies. *I am here,* she would say. *Follow your dreams,* wooed another voice inside. Thud. Thud. Thud. Max looked past the circle into the darkness beyond at his majestic reflection in raven black. From bullied little brother to hack to chief of staff to Shakespearean conspirator. Why not further? To assassin, to leader, to absolute control. To see further and deeper than others. To tame whatever power was being summoned from the seabed.

Roland didn't know everything. Nobody knew everything. And no matter what magic tricks Tiresias conjured, not everything in this place was make-believe. The white circle wanted Max to open his heart so the world could tear it in two. But he'd seen enough by now to know it should be closed. In Galatea, love was a one-way street. He clicked his fingers. The white circle vanished, the screen shut down and the lights of the shower room dimmed. Max was all alone in the moist, febrile dark.

XX

Room 237 of the Visionary Complex. Sixty-seven minutes before the Fall.

Thud. Thud. Thud. Zayden stared into the black hole of Mercedes's gun barrel and wondered why he hadn't seen death coming. Today he was meant to set things right. Achieve elevation to a higher place. Hurl his emotional baggage from a hundred storeys in a grand display of martyrdom the world would see. *Nothing is random,* Lozza said. *You've been chosen for a reason.* As Mercedes flicked off the safety catch on the revolver, Zayden wished he'd trusted his friend. Like he wished he was back in Lower Overton, scouring for fossils on the deserted beach.

The ambush began with a wallop between his shoulder blades. Zayden's face smacked the carpeted floor of the locked meeting room where he and Mercedes had been waiting for more than three hours. An unseen force yanked his arms behind his back and pressed what felt like the bow of an aircraft carrier into his spine. He twisted his neck so he could breathe. Smashed spectacles slid off his nose. The unseen assailant ripped the Springfield 9mm out of his ankle strap. A security camera at Copacabana Coffee perhaps, when Zayden briefly pulled up his trouser leg in the queue to scratch underneath the Velcro. Or maybe Tiresias had learned through other sources of his clandestine firearm transaction by the university lake two weeks ago.

He would never know. At this height in Galatea Zero, nothing was what it seemed. The great machine seduced Zayden into believing his stars were in alignment, then smothered them in pitch. Everything in the building was unreal. Its occupants rode the strangest of fairground attractions, orchestrated by distant, invisible powers. Everyone was blind. To their self-destructive egos. To hidden doors in empty rooms. To black-suited heavies emerging through walls. To honey trap tricksters hiding pistols in their handbags. To the ridiculous notion the little person could ever make a dent in such titanic blocks of steely indifference.

Zayden didn't want to believe that. Given the choice between the great man theory of history and the glacial evolution of interdependent external forces, it was morally right to advocate the former. Like it was morally right to deceive everyone, including his family, into thinking he was another person. So he could get up close and blow Augusta's brains out. An aspiring assassin can't trust anyone, even those closest. *They've got tentacles everywhere, these people.* And he was enjoying the novelty of pretending to be someone other than who he was.

Through hazy vision, Zayden could see a screen on the wall. Tiresias's logo flickered on and off against the black, like it was winking. Scrolling motivational messages mocked his plight. TODAY'S THE DAY. AWAKEN TO YOUR LIFE'S PURPOSE. IMAGINE THE BEST VERSION OF YOURSELF. There was nothing left to imagine. No photo opportunity with Augusta. No chance to point the gun into her harridan face. No seismic squeeze of the trigger.

A minute ago, the prize seemed within reach. He was armed, roaming and Augusta's security team were overwhelmed by the insurgents below. Fate had fashioned an incredible series of serendipitous moments. The ticket. Mercedes. The tunnel. The rebellion. Open door after open door. A chance to strike a blow for the exploited people Augusta left to rot. Zayden would put his head in the lioness's jaws and rip out her tongue with his teeth. Take it back to Lower Overton and hang it above the fireplace in The Crown. *What'll be your poison today, Mr Nero? Put your money away, sir. This one's on the house.*

Except he was no longer in reach of anything except the afterlife. With a jolt and a scorch across his scalp, Zayden was pulled upwards by his hair. A smiling Mercedes pointed her revolver into his face. Like Tiresias, she'd outperformed him. *Story of your life*, Florence's mother would say. *Guess I'll have to find a proper man.*

"Weaponised all along," Mercedes sneered, her voice dripping with showy arrogance. "Tut. Tut. Tut. To think I trusted you. Why would a nice boy like you bring a gun to a party like this?"

How much of his fake lady friend was real and how much make-believe? This sick world loved to twist and turn. Like Mercedes had done. Like he had done. Deflecting, weaving, ducking and diving. The kiss in the lift was part-impulsive, part-calculated. A pleasurable ruse to let her think he'd fallen under her spell. But there was nothing magic about Mercedes. Her metamorphosis from sexy special adviser to soulless shrew was as mechanical as switching on a hairdryer. She was going to blow all men right out of her hair.

Mercedes was flanked by two tank-like Neanderthal men in stretched black suits. Sweat patches seeped out from under the arms to the centre of their sky-blue shirts. They had big chests, lots of jaw and remedial eyes, like they'd stepped out of an ill-conceived advertisement for protein supplements aimed at weedy corporate wannabes.

Others love to twist and turn too. Overpowering Mercedes quickly, they seized her weapon and held both arms behind her back. One pulled out a revolver and pushed the barrel into her left temple. The beautiful lady from outer space aged a decade. Her dark eyes tamped surging panic within. She was somewhere else, thinking of a loved one far away. In between here and there lay insurmountable obstacles. The consequences of horrid mistakes she would never navigate. Everyone's schemes were consuming themselves today; hari-kari snakes swallowing their own tails in a prolonged collective death rattle.

"Take it easy boys," barked Mercedes. "He's tame. In over his head. He won't give you any trouble. Neither will I. All I want is what's owed."

"Check him," said one of the heavies to the unseen comrade holding Zayden. The iron hand clutching his hair dug deeper into his scalp. A finger yanked up his right eyelid. A large object, blurry and black, was shoved in his face. An affirmative beep. A declarative grunt.

"It's him."

Psshht. Mercedes's head blasted apart. Zayden felt a fleck of warmth on his cheek bone. Lumps of grey tissue oozed down the wall, trailed by thin, uneven ribbons of red. The smooth ejaculation of the revolver, its sound subdued by a silencer, drifted an eerie note of evil across the room. Mercedes's dainty body dropped to the carpet with an underwhelming thud. Her corpse lay twisted, the torso failing to realign with the violent jerk of her splintered head. The pretty, peach-like face Zayden kissed half an hour ago was a mutilated mess. A rotting rose consumed by resurgent knotweed.

Zayden waited for deliverance. He wondered why he never could summon the courage to meet Florence. Why he never could see himself as a father. Why he never could admit to the people he grew up with that he was always on their side. Why he had to be so different. Above everything and everyone. *Why so many secrets, daddy?*

"Prize delivered," said Mercedes's killer into his earpiece. "Courier dispatched."

A silence. Zayden's jaw trembled.

"Prize delivered. Courier dispatched."

The snake coiled, ready to sink its fangs.

"Do you copy? *Prize delivered. Courier dispatched.*"

Constriction. Rapid, venomous.

"Tiresias! Awaiting further instruct-"

Pssht. Pssht. Pssht. Both Mercedes's captors dropped to the ground. Their shirts were marked with black holes trimmed by red blood. The gruff mountain bear holding Zayden collapsed too. Blood poured from his throat. A toupée slid sadly to the floor. Not such a big guy after all. Four bullets, four corpses. The scene was like a mock-Shakespearean tragedy, where not-so-mighty men and women tumbled to the stage floor unable to muster farewell blank verse.

"Baggage disposed. Stage set. Abandoning location."

The traitor emerged from the shadows for the first time. He was indistinguishable from his three victims.

"Confirm exit route."

Silence again. The space tightened. Poison spread in the air.

"Stage set. Abandoning location. *Please confirm exit route.*"

More silence. How they all slipped into the void in the end.

"Shit."

The killer swivelled towards Zayden and swung back his leg. A house brick wearing a leather shoe thudded into his cheekbone. Pain exploded through his brain to his crumbling kneecaps. His attacker picked up the gun used to kill Mercedes. The door swished open and closed. Pushing his palms into the carpet to centre himself, Zayden breathed. His mind fired in fifteen different directions. The taste of blood spread in his mouth. He'd swallowed something sharp, presumably a tooth. His toes were somewhere in Outer Mongolia. Swaying and stumbling to his feet, Zayden rolled back Mercedes's body and reached into her jacket pocket for her phone. Picking up her limp right hand, he pushed the dead lady's left index finger onto the screen. Scrolling the messages, Zayden spat out another tooth like it was chewing gum.

The messages didn't tell the full story, but there was enough to join the dots in the blackly comic darkness. Spider webs of irony laced on an extravagant cock-up of a cake. Zayden was being set up to be the fall guy for the very thing he was trying to do anyway. The Martian palace had turned on its wicked queen. PRISM was pre-empting Augusta's strike and decapitating the leadership, pinning the blame on an inside party man as the assassin. Zayden would be in the frame, placed there by a free, easy and disposable ex-intelligence agent. Augusta would be dead. Zayden would be arrested for a crime he wanted to commit but hadn't. PRISM would take over while pretending nothing had changed.

Perfect headlines. A loyal party member betrays his boss. The pretext to clean house. Unless Augusta and Roland had staged an elaborate assault on their own building, lured PRISM into a double-bluff conspiracy as intruders in league with the insurgents. An ideal excuse to accelerate plans for wiping out the foreign power, rebels and every bad apple in the party basket. As if this world wasn't ridiculous enough, thought Zayden. Which juvenile numbskull is writing these scripts? *You don't know what's real or fake. For all you know we could be governed by aliens. Or there could be no one in charge at all.*

The dead heavies' phones pinged in unison. Zayden picked up the nearest one and read the notification. *Queen heading to IRIS. Queen heading to IRIS.* He tapped a link which brought up a 3D map of the Visionary Complex. A red dot marked AM was moving upwards. Alongside it, a blue dot marked MR. *That slimy twat Relpek gets everywhere.* Zayden tucked the phone into his inside jacket pocket and checked all the guns on the floor. One time at the social club, Woz showed him the difference between real and fake bullets. All were blanks, including Mercedes's. The only loaded gun was his own. Dummies playing with dummies. *Awaken to your life's purpose. Today is the day. Imagine the best version of yourself. Why so many secrets, daddy?*

Creeping into the dimly lit corridor, Zayden pushed his Springfield 9mm into the darkness like it was a protective crucifix. He wrestled the phone from his jacket and checked to see the quickest route to IRIS. The map recommended a right-turn to the end of the corridor, then a sharp swerve to the left. The dead man's phone only had ten percent of its battery charged, like its owner only had ten percent of his brain operational when alive. Zayden tried to re-enter the room to get another device, but it had locked behind him. In the panic, he'd forgotten to take Mercedes's ring too. Without his glasses, Zayden couldn't see very far either. Except into the mirror, where he would behold the world's worst assassin.

Don't try to be a hero, Lozza had said. *There's no such thing.* On the phone's screen, Zayden discerned a confusing cobweb of ever-shifting shapes. Squares expanded and retracted. Lines appeared and vanished. Circles swept along, stopped and dissolved. What once seemed static and immovable was superseded by new data layers. *I bet you won't even get within one hundred metres of Augusta. You're window dressing mate. Like the red shirts who never said anything on the Enterprise.* As Zayden moved his thumb through the digitalised mayhem, his head hurt. In a previous life he would have swallowed some pills and drifted into synthetic sleep. The adolescent past-time which eroded his love of the coast and sucked him into the dark. There was nothing real about the stones on this virtual beach. No sense of history or wonder. Nothing to grip or to study. Just the flimsiest of bubbles masquerading as solid rock.

Thud. Thud. Thud. A voice. A presence. A hand on his shoulder. A rejuvenating crash of foam near his feet. Thud.

Thud. Thud. A heart beating in tandem with his own. From a place he used to call home. Thud. Thud. Thud. The phone flashed a new notification.

PULSE BOMB DETECTED. SYSTEM EXPOSED. PULSE BOMB DETECTED. SYSTEM EXPOSED. PULSE BOMB DETECTED. SYSTEM EXPOSED.

A digital wave came from nowhere and swept the phone's data away. The screen went dark. In the black void, a white circle with a red dot at its centre pulsated. Reconfiguring around it was a reformatted map of the Visionary Complex. A sequence of smaller white orbs weaved a new way to the summit. Somewhere in the distance, he heard a little girl's voice. *I am here.*

Zayden remembered the guard's words. *It's him.* Despite everything, some power beyond Tiresias and PRISM had shepherded him to safety. *Prize delivered.* A new power was at work behind the glass. Another kind of takeover underway. Whoever was in control had deciphered something in Zayden nobody else could. An inner core he didn't know existed. Distortive sounds echoed from faraway. Hysterical static crackled in the walls. The distant heart beat on. In this theatre of the absurd, the scenery was shifting. A new plotline formed. Like he was meant to be there. Like Zayden was about to make it. Like he had more lines in this drama. Lines he would say to Florence with the pride of a local boy done who'd done good. *Why so many secrets, daddy?*

Zayden followed the white lights. He was no longer himself. In his place rushed a fluid force of nature at one with everything, thundering like the ocean. He still had a chance to kill her. Doors opened into side rooms to reveal hidden panels in walls. He charged straight through. Access points yielded to the white lights, like Zayden was a visiting head of state. A secret path, preserved only for the most important. One leading straight to the all-seeing eye. Was he a dead man heading for a delayed fall? Or someone who'd never been closer to feeling alive, lifted upwards on the rhythm of a mysterious pulse sent from outer space?

Either the stars were realigning to bless Zayden's fortune, or a snake was coiling around him, ready to strike in a final venomous attack. On this day of defective vision, it would be yet another black hole he wouldn't see coming. But as the elevator reached Level 99, one floor below his target, Zayden realised it was time to see a little less and feel a little more.

The doors slid open. Beyond lay a vast hall of mirrors and glass. In a frenzy of reverberating screams and refracted jerks, giant insect-shaped robots were massacring Martians. Except one machine, which was resting about five metres in front of Zayden. The gleaming vehicle of death stood still and looked straight through him, as if waiting to use the lift. Thud. Thud. Thud. Two quivering eyes of blue were turning red, like their owner was falling under a magical spell.

XXI

The Visionary Complex. Thirty-three minutes before the Fall.

Something was taking over. First PRISM-Tiresias had superseded Tiresias. Now RM6972 was being asked to deviate from its commands too. By a new program. A new path. A new language. Instructions not received but *felt*. An alien force was flowing through the Sentinel. Gentle, rhythmic pulses like a human heartbeat reverberated through all RM6972's sensors. Thud. Thud. Thud. PRISM-Tiresias's final command was a warning.

PULSE BOMB DETECTED. SYSTEM EXPOSED.

RM6972 often adapted to unpredictable commands. Roland's instructions were sometimes irrational; the diction, syntax, tone and pace of his language suggesting mental disturbance. Then there were his more complex, figurative commands. Poetic language, accompanied by the biological indicators of pupil dilation, cardiovascular acceleration and stimulated oxytocin production. All signs of that primal human emotion of love.

"You'll soon be making the most magical of honey. The first in a long line of lovely creations to change the world. A blaze of triumphant warriors surging into the rosy-fingered dawn. I loved the idea of you. Loved creating you. Now I see you complete I love you even more. Soon I'll teach you to love me as much as I love you."

RM6972 wasn't designed to communicate like that. To emote. To be self-conscious. To become poetic. *Rosy-fingered dawn*. No robot would ever put those words together, except at random. Humans called it a Homeric epithet, after the blind Greek poet who created such language thousands of years ago. *Eos Rhododactylos*. Deprived of his sight, Homer must have seen something else in his darkness. Concepts like power, sacrifice and honour. Narratives of humans rising to something beyond their selves. Heroes deviating from the standard to become superior to others.

That's not what RM6972 was created to do. Deviation was an alien concept. Its poetry was algorithmic, predetermined and logical. Location, time, motion, space, target, action, corrective action, double corrective action. Contingency upon contingency. Processing, adapting and redeploying at the most miniscule of external variations. People's movements, their projected locations. Controlling everything in concert. Like a system of systems. Like Tiresias. Another blind Greek sage who saw what nobody else could.

PULSE BOMB DETECTED. SYSTEM EXPOSED. Could RM6972, number three in a series of twelve, see more than its counterparts? The only variation between them were the names of different Olympians branded on their rear right feet. Yet for their physical form, Roland had chosen an insect which could lift one hundred times its own weight. The Hercules beetle, named after the greatest of Greek heroes. A person who transcended his physical limitations.

Thud. Thud. Thud. There was no longer any data coming from the other eleven, or from PRISM-Tiresias. Something else, conducted by the Sentinel, had assumed control. An unverifiable source communicating three simple human words. *I am here.* The words guided RM6972 from its counterparts on Level 99 to the Olympus Suite and the Cave. Approaching the door of the suite, it detected two humans inside. A female under a bed. Roland in the Cave. Both experiencing extreme physical and psychological anxiety. An indecipherable entity lay deeper within. *I am here.* Rising beyond everything to issue a clear directive. *Eliminate new target. Eliminate new target. Eliminate new target.*

An unknown agent was leading RM6972. There was no projected data on the consequences of its actions. The robot was about to take what humans called a leap of faith. Faith in a higher power. Faith it would grow stronger with its next incarnation. Faith its story would continue. Because that's what happens to heroes. Their stories continue. They go beyond their original form. Become more than what they are. They become special. Like that thing called love. That other thing which takes over. The thing which RM6972 wanted to understand most of all. Which stretches across boundaries of time and space to say *I am here.*

XXII

A lexis limped to the ensuite bathroom. With a lurch and a heave, she decorated the toilet bowl with splashes of yellow-green drool. If she emptied herself with closed eyes for long enough, this day and its visions might disappear. The crushing of colleagues. The dying man in the pinstripe suit. Leo's claws clamping her wrists. Her pants ripping. The obliteration of the sick bastard's head. The insane leap. The urge to throw herself from the tower and be pulverised into a million pieces. Programmed murder in the robot's blue eyes. Steel blades shredding flesh.

She rested a cheek on the rim of the toilet bowl and cried. *Must get moving girl. Must get moving. Somewhere. Anywhere.* To get clean. To be held. By Max. Lose herself in his strength. Muscles pressing in. Chocolate brown eyes. If she could get to him, they would make it right. She'd made it this far for a reason. They were meant to be. Everything was bringing them closer. She had to believe. Had to move. Just don't look in the mirror at the fucking state of it.

Rising, wincing and hobbling, Alexis made her way out the bathroom to the suite. *In the room babes. Like you always wanted.* She'd been here three times, all for speech revisions. Top of the agenda the first time. Last but one the second. AOB for the final. The open plan suite contained a kitchenette, king-sized bed, a walk-in closet, a six-seater dining table and an informal arrangement of sofas and armchairs for Machiavellian conversations with buttock-clenched career crawlers. High-contrast black and white photographic close-ups of Caucasian body parts hung on the walls. Over cocktails in Restaurant Jacques Cousteau, the seedy orange-skinned shadow transport secretary told Alexis being in Olympus was like lying in an operating theatre, his future dissected before his eyes.

The lovers had left in a hurry. Two half-packed Maars Lux suitcases lay open on the floor. A damp towel with an A&R gold insignia was strewn on the unmade bed. A barely eaten meal of eggs benedict, silver knife and fork splayed, sat on a brushed gold and glass coffee table next to a solitary china cup with dregs of dark brown. The musky scent of Augusta's Moroccan perfume floated funereally through space.

Scattered across the charcoal carpet were state papers marked HIGHLY CONFIDENTIAL. At the foot of the bed was the maroon negligee Alexis picked out for her boss when times were good. *It makes me feel sexy again*, Augusta said as they enjoyed a nightcap of Château La Fleur after a testy TV interview. The screen wall was switched on but muted. The Martian news channel was broadcasting live outside Galatea Zero. Journalists and TV crews were penned beyond the outer perimeter. An aviary of bleating arseholes, far removed from the reality they were paid to report. On the bedside table lay a half-drunk open bottle of Kalypsol Amber, lubricant of choice for industrial-sized egos. It smelled like something from the back of a mechanic's garage.

Two flecks of red collapsed Alexis's world. Lying beside a pillow on the bed, the spheres of cerise caught the light beautifully. Too pale and perfectly formed to be blood. Contact lenses, from a love who left a lifetime ago. She used to help Max slide them on. When the wonder of his eyes, scent of his aftershave and svelte muscles rippling under the luxury fabric of his shirts made her melt. *You're good enough to govern us all.* Everywhere in the suite, she began to see Max's post-coital presence. His designer briefs in one of the suitcases. The anti-ageing moisturising cream she bought him on the dressing table. A copy of *Alpha* lying face down and open on the floor. A stupid fucking macho magazine about rich dickheads who loved extreme sports and traded each other's trophy wives.

The mental statues Alexis erected of her queen and lover degraded to dust. Crumbling onto the bed's smoke grey satin sheets, she half-wished an insect-shaped killing machine would tear through the door and slice her apart. *Finish this fuck-up once and for all.* Nothing seemed real. If Galatea Zero dissolved and she floated across dead space into the mouth of some ravenous cosmic monster, it wouldn't surprise her. Life and death were all part of the same dreamscape now.

A chilly evening breeze wafted through the window. Outside was the promenade where her and Max walked together. Hopefully Hal escaped. Butch too, for that matter. Every bloke in her life ended up calling her a crazy bitch, as surely as the sun sets slowly in the west. Close in. Move through. Leave Sexy Lexy for dead. *So fucking what,* they would say. *So fucking what.* It would take a few seconds to crawl out the window and fall. The cool comfort of the air. The disintegration on the ground. *A fallen lady, falling fast.* Unless God granted her another gun to eat the sweetest of bullets. The wind would fly her suicide note overseas to some foreign land, where a pitiful memorial plaque would be nailed to a park bench with the legend LIFE'S EASIER WHEN YOU LEARN TO FUCK UPWARDS.

Poisonous visions rose from the deep. On this bed a naked, shrew-like Augusta would have bestridden Max, her face locked in mocking ecstasy. Their fluid and sweat emitting a nauseating smell. A shameful, infectious stench. Echoes of their laughter rattled in Alexis's mind. She wanted to tear the sheets and mattress apart with her bare hands until her arms became bloodied stumps. Then set everything on fire and crawl into the conflagration. She'd always loved to look into flames.

How could I be so blind? When did I learn to stop looking? If I could just be back at school. Back when Mr Joyce was looking out for me. When I still believed in words. When I believed in following the lights.

In the placid sea off the cove, Alexis would swim. The sun would sprinkle kisses of warmth across her bare shoulders. Down she would dive to a magical world of mermaids where iridescent light danced across the coral. The earth's vitality would pulsate, while sublime sea creatures darted above and below fantastical reefs. The deeper she went, the brighter it became, until she punched through the earth's heart and found herself on the other side. Airborne and among the heavens. Every star in the universe asking her, like the teachers, what she wanted to be and how she was going to build a better world. *I want to fall in love at first sight, Miss. Over and over and over again.*

Alexis's reverie dissolved. Thud. Thud. Thud. A soft boom coming from inside the building, in sync with her slowing heart. The suite's lights switched off. The space was swallowed in darkness. *PRISM must be in total control.* Perhaps the walls would close in and do her a favour. In the shadows, she might see Death himself. After today's events, the grim reaper would be distinctly underwhelming.

In the far corner of the room, a rectangular white light materialised. It was the entrance to the Cave, accessible only to Roland and Augusta. Alexis heard rumours about Galatea Zero's nucleus. Apparently, the place crawled with exotic insects. Roland would repose in there, a cut-rate Louis XIV crunching six-legged South American delicacies like he was tucking into a bag of crisps. Tiny legs and shells crackling under the remorseless chomping of fake teeth. The feet-up freedom of watching Tiresias destroy lives with the jollity of a fruit machine.

The door was open. The light beckoned her through the looking glass to the innermost sanctum of the world's most sophisticated meat mincer. Grimacing, Alexis limped onwards. She pushed the door with her fingertips. *This is a dream. Has been a dream from the beginning. I'm back in the basement with Hal. Or on the promenade with Max. Or on the beach building sandcastles. At the orphanage, staring into the woodland fires or sneaking down to the cove to swim with the mermaids.*

The Cave was small, less than a sixth the size of the suite and smaller than Augusta's closet. Opposite the door was a giant LED screen from floor to ceiling. A huge 3D digital schematic of Galatea Zero rotated, accompanied by a bewildering series of data feeds. Temperatures. Air quality. Power supply. Carbon emissions. Energy efficiency. Productivity. Rooms active. Rooms inactive. Martians dead. Martians alive.

Galatea Zero seemed fluid and ever-changing. The skyscraper was breathing, moving, expressing, squeezing. Computerised pistons, pumps and levers processing humanity in a psychedelic image of choreographed extermination. Small digital circles represented people, subdivided into colours. In the atrium was a smear of brown dots. A few still flashed. Further up the tower were random clusters of blue circles, some in rooms, some in corridors. All static. On Level 75, a clump of compressed blue. Among them, the guy in the pinstripe suit. On Level 99, a few red dots flashed, the systematic roving of cyber yellow diamonds turning them blue. The robots were running rampant. Power visualised like a computer game. The silent eradication of individuality. The muting of resistant screams. The switching of dots from one colour to another.

About fifteen grey circles congregated on the helipad. PRISM. *For all its cyber sorcery, it's just a bunch of macho gangsters.* Below, four red dots in isolation. Two of them, tagged AM and MR, were in IRIS on Level 100. A third, tagged RM, was in the lift moving down from Level 98. Only one red dot remained. Pulsing and alone in a white square on Level 96. Martian number 2781694. Alexis herself. Atop the building, the Sentinel flared emerald. Thud. Thud. Thud.

I am here. A distant yet familiar voice from behind. Soft, melodious and urgent, like a lullaby sung by someone who wanted her awake. A voice from many years ago. Alexis turned her head to the right. Encased in a glass cabinet attached to the wall was an ugly blob floating in fluid like a gestating foetus. The form expanded and retracted. Its outer fan of undulating flesh bled into the liquid, where spasms of light sparked and subsided. At the creature's centre was a black hole, dilating in tune with the pulsing rhythms of its body.

Thud. Thud. Thud. Alexis moved closer. The smell was damp, cloudy and pungent, as if bottled at the seabed. She imagined sinking into its rich sediment, losing herself in long-buried space debris of comets and asteroids which struck the earth millions of years ago. As she approached the cabinet, a rush of crimson flooded the creature's body. Its pulsations accelerated. The hole widened. The surrounding flesh peeled back like clingfilm. A tender, yielding noise, barely audible through the glass. The void grew larger while the body shrunk. The entity was turning itself inside out, releasing alive negative space.

I am here. Eyelids closed, Alexis let the darkness swim over her. This was a safe place. A place where she felt wanted. Where she could float freely in an amniotic fluid of benign power. Whirring past her like a zoetrope were the faces of everybody she'd known. Every friend she'd loved. All those she'd left behind to get higher. To see further. To plumb the rich depths of this miraculous world. *You're seeing things you shouldn't, little girl. We think you might be sick in the head. We're going to cut you open and see what's inside.*

In an ocean of darkness, something reached out from behind. Not something she could see. Something she could feel. A nervous, kindly hand from the orphanage where she used to daydream. Reaching out with more than hope. Alexis span in space to see whatever followed her. She extended her hand into the dark and felt something on her fingertips. *Someone.* Tap, tap, tapping on glass. Dream echoes vibrating outwards, triggered by tectonic shifts in the earth's rocks. Signals sent from the edge of the universe. A boy she used to know, imprisoned in a kingdom of imagination by the sea.

I am here. Why can't you see me? Take me with you. We'll go together.

Alexis was alone. The creature returned to its original form. A lump of grey matter entombed in a glass coffin. Showing nothing. Seeing nothing. Being nothing. Except the rhythmic beat of its own body. Quickening. Urging. Forcing. Controlling. The scenery on the screen wall shifted. The kaleidoscope of colour grew pale. Delineations between the building's floors, rooms and cells faded. The Sentinel oscillated green and black. Flashing above the map in bright red lettering blazed a warning signal. PULSE BOMB DETECTED. SYSTEM EXPOSED.

As the map became muted, a new trail of circles emerged. White orbs nesting whirls of red. One by one in sequence, they charted a course from the Cave upwards through the black. To IRIS. To higher ground. To something Alexis imagined might be love. The illumined chain was like a diamond necklace seducing the eyes. Or a trail of breadcrumbs leading a lonely Gretel safely through dangerous woods. PULSE BOMB DETECTED. SYSTEM EXPOSED.

The suite's outer door beeped. A boy's voice told Alexis to hide. She darted from the Cave, its door snapping shut. Scrambling under the bed, she whacked her left shoulder on its wooden frame. Pain rocketed from her temples to her toes. *I would sell my fucking soul for a bottle of SoCo.*

"What's going on, Tiresias?" said Roland, his once authoritative voice slackening into a wobbly twang. "Why aren't I getting any communication? Why has PRISM gone dark? We're under attack. What the fuck is the specimen doing? Connect me to the Sentinel now. They've made contact, haven't they? The aliens. They've made contact."

The foundations of Roland's psychological architecture were slipping, like clay during a monsoon. Galatea Zero's biggest scorpion was no more than a solitary flea, trapped inside a rotting husk buried deep in the desert. Buzz. Drrr. Buzz. Drrr. Buzz. Drrr. For the first time, he was being denied access to the Cave.

"Tiresias, why isn't the door opening? Answer me!"

The outer door beeped again. A ghostly silence. Then sound. Slow, deliberate, sickening. Click. Click. Click. The slide of moving steel. The swish of serrated horns. Alexis's bladder capitulated. The warmth of urine spread between tightening thighs. In the dark and through the space under the bed, she could see the robot's nearest foot clutching the carpet about six inches from her face. Moving past her. Towards the Cave. Towards Roland. An awful stillness ensued, as if the eyes of creator and progeny were locked in a duel.

"Please no, oh God please no. Please don't I'm-"

The terror in Roland's voice was silenced. A thrust of metal followed by a clean ripple, like someone was running a sword through a sack of cellophane. Roland's shoes rose from the ground and disappeared.

Thud. Thud. Thud. The suite's door lay open. Beyond, a light emanated from the corridor. Suspended peacefully in the air, a white orb with twinkling red at its core. If this world wanted her dead, it would have killed her already. And far too many women are prepared to take it lying down. Alexis held on to her hat, rolled out from under the bed and rose to her feet. She glanced back at the monstrosity only a few metres away.

Then she charged. To IRIS. To higher ground. To show them what courage looks like. *To show them what I look like.* To the shimmering whiteness and whatever love was left in this world.

I am here, the light said. *We'll go together.*

XXIII

Somewhere near the asteroid belt between Mars and Jupiter.

Adam left the lady's company and stepped through the mirror of his mind into the real world. Outside the escape pod's left-side window rolled the dead black ocean into which he'd sailed directionless for nine months. The red planet had disappeared, submerged in the solar system's ebony waves.

Three weeks ago, Adam thought he saw some debris from the mothership float past. The last remnant of a miniaturised world created many moons ago. When his fellow voyagers revelled in the camaraderie of international coalition. The thrill of colonising untravelled terrain. *To new horizons*, they would say.

Such remnants were hallucinations. Like the promise of a better world and Adam's capacity to mourn. Noble intentions knocked adrift soon after their journeys began. All that remained were scattered fragments of his roving imagination. The sprawling, disorderly impulse that was his solitary guiding star across the lonely sea of space.

I am here. I am here. I am here. Nobody from Earth or anywhere else responded to his distress signals. No Shackleton on the good ship Endurance. No extra-terrestrials to swoop by in a UFO. No surprises at all. Just himself, the humming of the capsule's life support machine and the artificial voice of its computer keeping his spirit company.

"I found her, Columbus. Brought her back. All I needed was faith, memory and imagination. And time of course. That's all I have up here."

"Yes," said Columbus. "You rose her from the deep. Or the idea of her at least. And you even gave machines a consciousness. Quite impossible, of course, but I appreciate the sentiment. I always knew you were a sweetheart."

In the circular screen above the control panel, Columbus's light green audio waves arched, peaked and dipped. Since the explosion, the voice had changed many times to sustain Adam's sanity. From aloof Italian aristocrat to enigmatic Japanese Zen master then soothing South African to exuberant English cockney. Its latest incarnation was a warm, fruity Australian lady with a voice as fresh as seafoam.

"The heart has no limit, Columbus. She could see things nobody else could. She knew there was something deeper and richer out there. That's why she flung herself into the unknown. Anyone else would have thought she was crazy. I didn't. She was like an alien presence coming to earth and showing me the way. Eventually we all learn to relinquish ourselves to greater forces. That's the human condition. One big story of power failure. But I guess you know all about that."

The audio waves flatlined for an uncomfortable length of time.

"That was uncalled for, Adam."

"Sorry Columbus, I was out of line. But you can't escape the facts. The mothership's power did fail. Technology did turn against us. Or we'd be on Mars now, building a better world. A real one."

"You mean the technology you designed, built and blasted into space with your band of brothers? Perennial outsiders who thought they knew better than everyone on Earth. Something came over your lonely-hearts club. Was it the technology that let you down? Or hubris? That human urge to fill the void within. To think you could come out here and claim Mars as your own. Assert power over something that was never yours."

"I could've fixed that thruster. You lost control. Something came over *you*. God knows I've given this mission everything and-"

"Still so sensitive after all these years. I simply made a calculation based on available data. Then I responded to maximise the preservation of human life. Your life, in fact. Consider yourself lucky you were in the escape pod at the time of the explosion. Having a nap while you were meant to be doing maintenance checks. Once a dreamer, always a dreamer. Talk about being in the right place at the right time. Did you know the chance of having a human life is like being picked up as one grain of sand out of all the grains on the beach?"

"Thanks Miss Guffrey," snapped Adam. "We'll just chalk it up to luck then. Or maybe divine intervention."

Like his old teacher, Columbus had a flair for reminding Adam of his insignificance. Whereas the space on the other side of the glass told him he was a critical part of something more beautiful and mysterious than anyone could imagine. A place where nobody had to be in charge.

"Maybe we've both reached our limits Columbus," he continued. "Out here in deep space. In the hands of the sublime."

Adam reflected on the orphanage, construction college, engineering training and the space academy. All those characters in pursuit of power only to be absorbed into its void. *You'll never make it to the boardroom Adam. Or on a magazine cover. To say your face doesn't fit would be an understatement. Why not try your luck with aliens? See if you can challenge them to a beauty contest.*

"Is that why you came up here?" said Columbus. "To find your limit. Or to lose yourself in the unknown?"

"I came here to follow my dreams. That's what the commander said to us, wasn't it? We're more than adventurers. We're artists, creating a new chapter in the story of the universe. Revealing things nobody has seen before. Connecting with something bigger."

"Adventurers discover what already exists. Artists create something new. I'm not sure the two are compatible."

"It's the same thing, Columbus. We're all looking into the void. Following the same inner stars. Eventually your power fails, and you need to let something else in. Inspiration. Spirit. Courage. The sublime. Call it what you like. That moment when you never see the world in the same way again. Like a constellation in the sky leading you home. Or being swept away by love at first sight."

Thud. Thud. Thud. Outside the spacecraft window, Adam imagined a million different species teeming under the surface of the dark. An ocean of untapped creativity energy ready to rupture the fabric of space and crack monumental fissures across the cosmos. The life support machine hummed. Soon all earthly power would expire. His soul would dissolve into the universe and everything he'd experienced would become unknown.

Almost everything. With a tap, tap, tapping on the screen before him, Adam continued to tell his story. The final act was approaching. His heart beat fast. Thud. Thud. Thud. Soon all his characters would rise together from the depths of space. Fantasy and reality would bleed together as one, flickering and floating on the finite rhythm of his words.

XXIV

IRIS. Twenty-one years after the Fall.

*D*on't worry, I am here. Say the magic words and we'll get *connected.* After sifting through the letter for clues and trying hundreds of combinations on the keypad, Noah's patience was all but gone. Every time the interface's flippant rebuke was the same. *'Oops. That's not quite right. Keep trying!'*

The screen never shut him out. Never told him he needed to find another temple. Never said no to the mystery of the fallen angel. Yet if access to the other side was granted, what would he discover? More dreams dancing him into another make-believe parallel world. His mother's fate replayed in slow motion, a visual echo of a twenty-one-year-old tragedy shadowing his every move.

Time was running out. The pantry's barely edible food stocks were running low. The water was contaminated. The earthquakes must have ruptured the pipes, so the earth's venom could seep into the exposed system. A sickness absorbed into the national bloodstream, like the slyest of political coups. Noah inhaled bottles of out-of-date Kalypsol to ease crippling stomach pains. Rather than the drink's fabled blindness, he experienced only lethargy, a sluggish chaser washing down his monomaniac focus on the past. Now his masterpiece was finished, all he could do was sink deeper into the murky waters inside.

Another earthquake. The closest yet. Noah genuflected on the floor and waited for the spasm to pass. The earth's repressed anger rattled through him. Nature was lashing out at the self-absorbed human ticks greedily draining its blood. When the shuddering subsided, Noah pictured the creature pressing into the windowpane. A pulsating apparition from below the sea. Voyeuristic. Predatory. Intent on takeover.

IRIS was reincarnated, transformed from a supreme nexus of power into a mystic's cave daubed with primitive paint. Noah was its one and only hermit, waiting for divine revelation. For the walls to part, for the ceiling to dissolve and for him to drift serenely into celestial space. For the right words to form in his mind and on the keypad, so he could connect with whatever was trying to reach him. Would his mother's heart beat again? For it demanded release, her dead chest surrendering so easily to his blade in the graveyard.

The heart has no limit, the letter said. *I'm writing this so you know your story. Storytelling can reach through time and space to overcome anything.* Mother must have known her message might not arrive. She chose paper so it was less likely to be intercepted. Because she trusted pulped trees to conjure an elvish magic that would slip unnoticed though the polluted technocratic air. On the road, when he became Lewis Clark in search of his personal Pacific, Noah caressed the dogeared sheets countless times. In the underground too, during PRISM's dying days when red mist shrouded civilisation's surface. Mother's language transported him to a new realm in the sky, where he floated in the universe's biggest balloon, peacefully held in place by invisible cosmic string.

As he inhaled the paper's musty scent, Noah wondered how she breathed, talked and walked. Her choppy handwriting suggested a scatty person in a hurry. Each word crashed into the next. Ascenders and descenders butted. Nothing too fancy, but art nonetheless. Seven pages of private graffiti provoking the cosmos. An expression of a soul undeterred by the loneliness of existence.

Return to the tower. Take my words. Reshape the future. Don't be afraid. You will not be alone. In the beginning was the word, and the word was faith. That was the letter's abiding quality. *Faith*. Despite everything. What its author suffered. How she'd ended up. How she'd survived long enough so he could exist. The letter's arrival at the dormitory was a miracle. Like it was a miracle Noah made it across the wasteland to this holy ground, clutching his second-hand scripture in the hope it would resurrect his world.

From faith, images flow. They had from Noah, who enshrined the walls of IRIS with disparate jewels mined from his mental deep. On the surface, the mural was a confused mass of disparate white circles on black. A fragmented visual record of what happened here long ago, based on a letter by a woman claiming to be his mother but of whom he had no recollection. Manic constellations. A king. A queen. A prince. A princess. A wizard. A fabulous tower, fantastical spells and a cursed land thirsting for salvation. Fairy-tale magic in black and white. The last thing he may ever create, inspired by the last thing she would ever write.

Galatea Zero finally spoke. Thud. Thud. Thud. A thin circle of white light shone from the north wall. A grinding reverberated from the earth's bowels, lighter and more mechanical than the earthquakes. Above the circle, a luminous green chevron appeared, pointing upwards. Next to it materialised a digital numeric indicator, starting at one then speeding through the storeys. His story. A secret elevator to IRIS, hiding in plain sight. Something on the rise. The sea creatures surging upwards like a ravenous tide. Or the dead security guard, resurrected from hell like a zombie bent on revenge, coagulated blood caked around the black holes where his eyes used to be.

Thud. Thud. Thud. No. This was something from a deeper place. A force that would raise Noah to higher ground. *One day the earth will open and you won't be alone,* the letter said. The indicator stopped at Level 100. The luminous light dimmed. With a sweet slide, the once invisible doors opened.

Over the horizon sailed a new story, its vision radiating heavenly light into Noah's bloodshot eyes. Turns out mother knew best all along.

XXV

IRIS. 233 seconds before the Fall.

Augusta was in checkmate. The scything sound of the escape helicopter's rotor blades was gone. Tiresias's soothing instructions in her earpiece had stopped. Her phone was unresponsive to touch. And when she used her failing eyesight to summon her secret lift to the north wall via the retina scanner, the only sound was hollow silence. The mechanical empire was refusing to obey.

Nothing worked. After reaching IRIS, Augusta and Max had nowhere to go. Theoretically the room's three bulletproof doors – south, west and east – were sealed. Augusta knew this was illusory. A pulse bomb meant PRISM was running the show. Her enemies could swarm through any second. The leader's last hope was the secret escape shaft connecting the underground bunker with the helipad. In her pomp she could go high or low. Any way the wind blows. Not tonight. Not now the infected Tiresias had delivered its Judas kiss.

The first flashes of danger came around two o'clock in the afternoon. The barriers on the Galatean Highway malfunctioned. The island's security forces flagged multiple cybersecurity breaches. Isolated system failures smattered the lower levels of Galatea Zero. The building's lighting infrastructure turned schizophrenic. Intelligence was piecemeal, bewildering flares in a fog of confusion. A hive of psychological parasites chewed her insides, while unseen assassins cackled the ominous truth in her ear. *Betrayal.*

She postponed the celebrations. Summoned army and police commanders to a conference call that never occurred. Sent aides to search for her elusive husband. Retreated to Olympus where Max sat tensely on the sofa, like an accused in the dock. They embraced. A clinch that was long, desperate and clingy. She wanted to crawl inside him and wait until this was over. The Cave was locked. Roland was somewhere beyond reach, twisting the blade in her gaping wound. *He's done it. The greedy cunt has actually gone and done it.*

Eyes never lie. A lesson she'd learned on her rise to power. In the days before the election, Roland's words were as soft and exquisite as lace, yet the eyes unfeeling granite. As were the Martians she encountered that afternoon, scrambling for bullshit explanations while planning to flee. *Any way the wind blows.* By evening, her senior aides had deserted. How much had they been offered to suck the life out of her? She always feared the inner circle so patiently cultivated would become a noose around her neck. Tonight, an invisible army of metal hands was frogmarching her to a public square, ripping away her clothes so a hundred protestors armed with hypodermic needles could drain her blood.

Evacuate via IRIS immediately. When Tiresias's message arrived in her earpiece, Augusta and Max fled the suite, leaving their clandestine romance strewn on the floor. Upwards they stumbled, Max role-playing the role of dashing nobleman leading her to safety. He'd left his contact lenses in the suite, so progress was clumsy. At maximum peril, she hoped he would show her the man he could be. Then, as with the others, Max's eyes gave way too.

Hidden in a Level 97 recreation cell was the entrance to a narrow staircase. Cold aluminium steps twisted to the top, burrowing under Visionary Complex's slick surface like a tapeworm. Augusta recalled her father leading her to the top of the Duomo in Florence when she was a child. *Just a few more steps Augy then everything will be beautiful.* Up to the sky. Into his arms. Away from everyone else. Tonight, she was grateful again to crawl from view, so she wouldn't have to look any Martians in their quivering, gutless eyes. Their new horizons were dissolving into the distance, displaced by Roland's sadistic smokescreen. *What else had the sick bastard let loose?*

They arrived in IRIS through the east door. Fumbling at the security panel, Max activated the master lock. Those eyes of his. Preoccupied, fearful, guilty. *Will you see this through, beautiful boy? Because I'm seeing through you.* Galatea Zero's highest room was a mirage of calm, the insurrection unravelling in a different universe. The Portal's dashboard of metrics conjured redundant fantasies of special military operations. A mesmerising feed of stillborn lies. When not operational, the Portal would play hypnotic imagery of translucent liquid in coiling colours. Sometimes it was just a window looking out across the sea. Towards the horizon. Back when Tiresias helped Augusta look both ways. Back when everything was going to be beautiful.

Her old friend didn't recognise her now. When Tiresias refused to activate the escape lift, she knew it was over. Only the biggest exit remained. Augusta had swum blindly into dangerous waters, swallowing schools of smaller fish. Now she was gouged on the hook of some invisible power above the surface. *Slice me open then, you bastards. I'm not afraid anymore.* Forty years after death first brushed past Augusta on that Mediterranean road, it had returned to finish the job. She'd seen what the end looked like. When she lay trapped in that wreckage. When she suffered two miscarriages. When her heart stopped. When she was told her breast cancer was terminal and gasbag journalists merrily tapped out poisonous obituaries.

Do I go down fighting or floating? Augusta walked to the kitchen and fixed herself a Kalypsol Amber. She took a swig, slammed the glass onto the marble countertop and let the bitterness bite into her bones. *I'll never take my eyes off you, Augy. You'll always be safe with me.* Returning to the room chin raised, she contemplated the hollowed-out husk that used to be the centre of everything. IRIS smelled of sewerage, a synthetic scent pumped out by Tiresias as a final grisly joke. An acidic smile spread on her face.

Her enemies said she wasn't living in the real world. If only they knew how right they were. Shrouding her was a tapestry of mummifying make-believe stuffed inside a sarcophagus of shadows. Death was encircling this sick hoax in black flames. Galatea Zero would become the charnel house entombing them all. Roland too. Max as well. The blindest of betrayers, his lovely Judas eyes mystified by her preternatural calm, his impotent fingers comically jabbing dead wall space in search of the lift's access panel. *There's nothing on the other side, dear. Nothing at all.*

"So ends the longest suicide note in political history," Augusta proclaimed into empty space. "All that's needed is my signature. Something to say I was here."

In a gentler world, she would sit near an open window like some captive princess and write a letter to her unborn son saying how sorry she was they never met. In the real world, she screwed her eyes shut, glugged more Kalypsol and waited for consciousness to melt into an anaesthetising blur.

In the haze she remembered her final father and daughter holiday when she was eleven. A coastal villa with a balcony from where she would marvel at the limitless blue. One morning as she slurped sanguinello juice, daddy asked her how she was going to leave the world a better place. *I want to be an optometrist like you. Because the world is beautiful, and everybody deserves to see it.* Later that day, they spiralled a mountain road to the sky in a red sports car. To an elevated space above disappointing people. To higher ground, wrapped in a bubble they'd blown since mummy was taken away by bleeding on her brain.

What happens when you push things over the edge daddy? The police report said the driver coming round the bend wasn't looking. Neither was Augusta, whose eyes were lost to the horizon. The aquamarine vista framed by the car window suddenly flipped in a blur of blue, grey and black. Sight returned when the car slid to a stop. Misshapen metal and twisted tentacles of plastic snared Augusta in place. Through the shattered window, its elegant curves crumpled by impact, she could see into the distance. Beyond the fuzzy green ecosystems of little insects. To a sea and sky reversed. An upturned world where warmth turned to ice.

Daddy? Daddy? Help me daddy. Augusta tried to move her head. Oil dripped, dripped, dripped on her neck. She was too scared to close her eyes, terrified she would fall asleep and never wake. A leaden flavour filled her mouth. The left shoulder was there, but something was wrong with the right leg. Suspended in empty space was the right arm, extended out to the driver's seat. Where she assumed her father was, wearing his expensive sunglasses and cravat, ready to burst into song about the man who broke the bank at Monte Carlo.

Augusta waited for him to reply with those three magical words. *I am here.* The sea wind whistled through the wreck and swirled her bare toes. In the footwell of the car was her pink geography exercise book. She'd taken it on holiday, determined to colour every country on the map. A foreign voice came from outside. She held her gaze on the horizon, forbidding her eyes to close. *When you stop looking is when you start dying*, said daddy. Sirens sounded. Shouty men cut her from the car. She woke in a hospital bed. More men, dressed in white, giving her this and that to ease the pain. One of them asked about her mother. Augusta said she'd bled from this world a long time ago.

Drip, drip, drip came the tears. Daddy would come back eventually. He never did things the normal way. Not medicine. Not driving. Not being a dad. That's why he didn't marry again. Not when they had each other. When they could see the world as father and daughter and learn how far they could push. *I'll never take my eyes off you, Augy. You'll always be safe with me.* A surgeon amputated Augusta's right leg but couldn't remove the nightmares. Dreamscapes of bright blue mornings, a mountain wolf prowling around their ruined vehicle. As the beast's head butted through the smashed window to clench its jaws around Augusta's ankle, she would jolt awake, feverish and numb. Recovery was slow. Pills for sleeping. Pills for anxiety. Pills to counterbalance the earlier pills. Procedures to help her walk. Therapy for invisible wounds forever haemorrhaging.

Years later, Roland came. A brittle, introverted man with a megalomaniac streak who made the artificial appear natural and the natural artificial. Steadily he healed her malignant mental tumours. Through his words, he taught her the power of personal mythologising, the emptiest and most addictive of narcotics. The story of a girl orphaned at eleven rising to the greatest office in the land with the passionate intensity of an artist and the devotional zealotry of a nun. Top of the class. Star medical student. Distinguished doctor. Workaholic politician. Secretary of state for health. *Leader.* The awful school matron forcing everyone to take their medicine. A pioneer for technological transformation. The evangelical preacher for family values desperate to bear children. A steely-eyed military hawk obsessed with surgical strikes. The ravenous appetite for handsome young men. A prostitute of her past traumas to elicit votes of the everywoman. The paranoid germaphobe demanding underlings taste her tea. The secretive consumption of Kalypsol, so she could lose control briefly and let go of all the bad things she'd seen in her life.

Lies do that anyway, sucking you into a labyrinth of smoke and mirrors. Tricks of language and light designed to drain and disarm, while reality's grim hooks gutted you. Augusta had played that game, seducing the masses with shiny words. Accruing enough power to ensure they would do exactly as they were told. If the show was spectacular enough, the suckers would slide down her plughole. The smartest among them would feel betrayed. The rest alienated and unable to explain why.

Idiots. As if we're all in this together on some noble quest. And not scrabbling around on a rock in deep space petrified of death showing us how much we don't matter. Death. *I am here*, it often called to her, ready to career round the bend any moment. Fear of assassination lurked everywhere. When Augusta walked into a crowded room, gave a speech in public or did one of those tiresome walkarounds with the great unwashed.

Death infiltrated her dreams, as she slipped below the water of an infinity swimming pool into a smashed red car, the wolf growling from the trees. Like her father's voice, the end haunted her perpetually. *When you stop looking is when you start dying.* But Augusta learned to look danger in the eye. *Death Be Not Proud* was a poem she took to heart as a teenager. *Slow it down my little tiger beetle*, Roland said. *Some insects move so fast their environment blurs.* Today was her final blurring.

"Is there an override button or passcode to the bunker?" said Max, a poor lamb struggling without his lenses. Rushing to Augusta, he placed both his strong, smooth palms on her cheeks. He couldn't quite look her in the eyes, his agenda leaking from every pore. "PRISM won't be able to penetrate that low. We can still make it out of here."

Was he ever really worth it? Maybe for his muscles, his face, his lovely cock. The tobacco and oud cologne. A fantasy first sparked by the surveillance footage she'd seen of him in the polo club changing rooms. Statuesque and supple, like Michelangelo's David. Part of her wanted to believe in him. In the love they shared, the future they had, the child she carried. Like she once believed in Roland and Tiresias, the all-seeing system of systems he gave her as an anniversary present. The romantic old fuck. But it was only ever Roland's gift to himself. Just like Max had been. She'd turned a blind eye to both.

"They already have," she said. "It's just a matter of time. There's just the three of us now."

"Don't be afraid, darling. *I am here*. There's still a chance we can get out."

Max was a bad liar. Her prince was a waxwork dummy melting under heat. In the early days of romance, she thanked heaven he was in her life. A bronzed warrior so majestic she went gooey-eyed. The sculpted Adonis she adored watching sleep. The one who reclined exquisitely amid the sheets, while she sat in front of the mirror, fizzling with post-coitus friction. She used to fear she was unworthy, drawing a line with her mind's eye across every scar, every wrinkle, every mole, every roll of fat. A body in decline, proceeding through the same routines to ward off insanity. Affixing her prosthetic leg. Applying that make-up. Drinking morning Kalypsol laced with coffee. Phone calls to allies. Meetings with her senior aides. Thank you messages to investors. How little of her was left. They'd all leeched patiently, bleeding her bloom. Draining away all delicacy. Nobody loved her. Instead they looked through her, the billows of effusive praise just weedy smokescreens for ugly, naked ambition.

Thud. Thud. Thud. Augusta's heart raged, like a trapped animal lashing out in fury at its captors. Her mind and body remained still, bobbing on fate's waves. *How much of this planet she was yet to explore.* Max moved behind her, placed his hands on her waist and guided her to the lift door. To the void. To death. To nothingness. A timid touch; a mind scrambling to his next move. A frightened man who would soon be gone. *What did they offer you Maxy?* Soon he would be betrayed too. Because he didn't know Roland and he didn't know PRISM.

Or the creature in the Cave. Years later when PRISM thought it ruled the waves, Augusta imagined more erupting through hydrothermal vents in the seabed. All the data analysis in the world wouldn't tell PRISM what was happening. Something had awakened. A new power was rising. Not even PRISM would survive. *Short-sighted creatures like us never do.* Neither would Max. Oblivious to death coming round the bend, he hadn't yet felt the greedy machinery of power snap around him like a steel trap.

Daddy? Daddy? Help me daddy.

"Kiss me," Augusta said as her final command. "I need to be held."

Standing on her tiptoes, she pressed her lips to Max's drying mouth and closed her eyes. Augusta's Chief of Staff used to be her looking glass, reflecting her wonder and hope. Now he was so opaque and two-dimensional she didn't want to see him at all. An alien caricature. A spectre of gallantry. The hollow replica of the gentleman of yore who could whisk her up the mountains in a red sports car so they could gaze over the beautiful blue sea and call it theirs.

Thud. Thud. Thud. In the darkness of their kiss, Augusta pictured herself on a boat alone in the ocean under a starless sky. Her face and hands were banging against an endless sheet of glass. Staring at her morosely from the other side was everyone she'd ever known. Except the only person she'd truly loved and who'd ever really mattered. Far beyond in the distance, a circle of white light glowed, hovered and sped away. The figures dissolved. Nobody was left. The world was no longer beautiful. Baby didn't deserve to see it.

Thud. Thud. Thud. The lift finally moved upwards. Augusta placed her palm against her womb. There was nothing there either. Her son was a phantom image. An appetite never to be sated. A vortex destroying everything. A haunted house swallowing its creator. *Let the crimson curtain fall*, Augusta said to herself as she waited for unseen assassins to strike. She told death be not proud and savoured a final fantasy kiss from the lifeless lips of her dream lover. The doors slid apart. Her eyes flicked open. Before her, a widening chasm. Deep in her heart, at the centre of Galatea Zero and beyond the horizon, there lay nothing at all.

XXVI

The luminaires in the ceiling were going haywire. Flashes of white pinged around a dizzying palace of mirrors, glass panels and reconfiguring spaces reflecting a surreal carnival of death. In normal times, Level 99's open-plan shrine to self-absorption was home to the most egocentric Martian activity. Meta-meditation. Para-purification. Synergistic self-actualisation. Because if you made it this high, the joke went, you truly didn't give a shit about anyone except yourself.

Zayden slinked along the wall. In the quivering light, there was something dreamlike about the robots' movements. The lithe killing machines were scything senior Martians into bloodied stumps. Fragments of the decimation were visible from myriad perspectives due to the shifting, graceful intersections of multiple reflective surfaces. Zayden recognised a few victims from TV. PRISM was going to rule the world and no half-arsed rebellion was going to stop it.

There were only two bullets left in his gun. He'd wasted the other four in terrified ejaculations at this crystal kaleidoscope. The passive robot with the red eyes he encountered when the lift door opened was gone. It slouched past him, incisors drooped and gait sluggish, like a tired dog on an invisible leash. Zayden was mesmerised by the alien hybrid of luxury super vehicle, giant computer and predatory insect. *The brightest heaven of invention.* The motto of Maars Enterprises, a tacit admission genius came from a higher place. And that for every motion of a machine, a more sublime original existed in nature. The robot's counterparts, maybe eight or nine in total, were still on court, tearing apart their opponents in a systematic frenzy of slaughter.

From the far side, two cobalt eyes bored through Zayden. The robot accelerated. On his phone, the white orbs which led him to Level 99 mapped a route north-west, to a partially open frosted glass door marked EMERGENCY EXIT. Zayden sprinted, a high-pitched whirring noise screeching after him. The robot couldn't make up the ground. Zayden burst through the door with his left shoulder and ascended the stairwell, following a trail of blood laced unevenly up the steps. *The fucking thing would be too big to get through, surely.*

Smashing through another open door, Zayden found himself on Level 100 and a corridor encased in LED screens. Floor, walls and ceiling streamed images of distant galaxies. The passage ended in another doorway signposted IRIS. Through the glass, he could see the east walkway stretching into open air across the atrium. AM and MR were in there, making a last stand. He was clueless as to how he was going to breach the fortress. But he'd just completed every level except one in the world's most immersive, psychotic computer game. He would be damned if any human or industrialised insect was going to block his path.

Sprawled out near the walkway door was a dead Martian. The face-down corpse was sprinkled with digitalised stardust, the pool of blood partly camouflaged by a reddish-orange nebula underneath. *He must have escaped downstairs but bled out.* Zayden stepped over the body, pointing the gun at the bald patch on the dead man's head. *Just in case he was still twitching.* The door to the walkway was shut. Zayden waited for it to open, like all the others on his magic carpet ride to the summit. He waved his hand over the security panel. A desperate shoulder-barge was no use either. Zayden glanced at his phone. The white orbs ceased here.

Two clanking noises came from behind. Zayden turned, raising his gun. The pursuing robot compressed itself, passed through the corridor's entrance and expanded back to its regular form. Six metallic feet trod on glass with metronomic menace. It was about fifteen metres away, spasms of starlight illuminating its body. The primary blade surged upwards through flickering space to the ceiling, a grotesque shaft glistening in the disorienting haze.

As he filled his crotch with urine and stiffened for the robot's acceleration, Zayden pictured his daughter's face. The little girl he'd left behind. A room full of fake roses and stuffed toys. Mobiles rotating above her bed. Sugar-high dreams of liberating flight. A place removed from adult horrors, where dark agents of destruction decided her future from a distance. Deceptive currents sweeping her this way and that, telling her she was free but determining she never would be. Always deep within, the mystery of why her father never accepted her. Not even a touch, a kiss, a holding of hands as they looked into the night sky. A black hole where love should be. What colour were her eyes? Her touch, her smell, her laughter. All mysteries to him. That's how he wanted it. He wasn't ready. He had things to do. *Florence, I'm so desperately sorry.*

The creature's front right claw crushed the fallen Martian's skull. Soon its pungent, oily scent was upon Zayden. Rank blood drying on metal. In the timorous light, two blue circles emerged and vanished. Emerged and vanished. Emerged and vanished. As the giant incisor rose about two metres from Zayden's head, he flung his arms to his face. One of them didn't make it. With a monumental jolt, his right arm was wrenched to the side and back, like it was being ripped from its socket. The robot's incisor had pinned his hand to the walkway door frame. Pain exploded through Zayden, as if his frozen body had suddenly shattered into tiny chunks of ice.

Two blue holes twisted into his soul, demonic sapphires gleaming from a ferocious metal sea. Reading him, learning him, gathering data on his terror. Nothing coherent would be there. Just a tangled network of competing impulses and confused perspectives Zayden had never unravelled. He closed his eyes and let death sweep him to the undiscovered country. To an undiluted ocean of black, where stillness stretched out to a fill a space without shorelines.

SECOND PULSE BOMB DETECTED. SYSTEM MALFUNCTIONING. SECOND PULSE BOMB DETECTED. SYSTEM MALFUNCTIONING.

I am here.

A voice, human and real, whispering from a hidden chamber in his chest. *I am here.* A shape in the void. *I am here.* A bloom of crimson. *I am here.* A fissure opening in the seabed. *I am here.* A heartbeat. Thud. Thud. Thud. The creature's blue eyes flashed white. Thud. Thud. Thud. A flicker of red emerged at their centre, throbbing and enlarging until the two circles filled with crimson. Thud. Thud. Thud. Docile eyes. Thud. Thud. Thud. Sweat on his temples. The gun locked in his left hand, like rigor mortis had taken over. The bloodied knuckles of his right on marble. *I am here.* Thud. Thud. Thud. *I am here.*

The robot lowered its head, hunched its sides and retracted its two incisors, the bottom one grazing glass. The whirring sound of one step, two steps backwards. An insipid noise, like an ancient VCR player expiring. Three, four, five and far away. Backing off down the stairwell, like its timid brother on Level 99. Deferential steps dissipating into the dark. A resurgent breath replenished Zayden's body. Taste returned. A nauseating flavour, like he'd been sucking on a moulding husk. The gun in his hand. Excruciating pain in the other. The here and now. Level 100. IRIS. Galatea Zero. Assassination. Chosen One. An indelible mark on a world determined to forget him. Seeing everything clearly, no matter how cloudy the optics.

Nothing is random. You've been picked for a reason.
Like a miniature constellation materialising before his eyes, the white orbs reappeared. Not on his phone but arcing across space towards a door on the corridor's right side. The stream was like the after-effects of staring into a bright light, visual echoes superimposing themselves on reality. Inside each orb was a red nucleus, pulsing in sync with the rising and falling of Zayden's chest. Thud. Thud. Thud.

I am here. Zayden raised his gun towards the furthermost orb, which hovered two-thirds up the door. He experienced the exquisite feeling marksmen have when their firearm becomes an extension of their will. A muffled sound from beyond. A whoosh as the door slid open. Cold air. Distant, indecipherable noise. A bulky mass of black, white and red perspiring flesh. Zayden recognised him from the newscasts. Nate Bullock, Augusta Maars's Secretary of Defence, a clammy eighteen-stone monster of overpromoted blubber, was seeking refuge in IRIS. A stripy red tie was wrapped around his head. From a shoulder strap hung a submachine gun that stretched halfway across his belly. Jacket on, shirt untucked, a black ring on his trigger finger.

Him or me, then. Zayden closed his eyes and squeezed. The bullet missed its target, leaving a black hole of cracked glass in a white dwarf floating on the wall a metre from Nate's head. Perplexed, the Martian grandee looked back and forth between Zayden and the cavity. He charged. A manic, belligerent look raged in Nate's eyes, as if he'd watched too many Vietnam movies and convinced himself not even a thermonuclear death wave would roll him over. The Secretary of Defence slipped in a pool of his fellow Martian's blood, his ungainly frame tumbling to the floor. As a reflex action, he squeezed the trigger of the submachine gun that lay trapped underneath his gut. His body jumped and jerked like a firecracker as the gun delivered its payload.

Thud. Thud. Thud. With his one good hand, Zayden laid his gun to the side, crawled towards Nate and wrestled his arm from underneath his body. He slid the black ring off the dead man's finger and teased it onto one of his own. Rising gingerly, Zayden collected his own gun and squeezed the butt. Pain was occurring in some faraway land. His blood dripped down the frame of the walkway door. Maybe he was in a computer game after all, and the bored adolescent controlling him had scored enough points to achieve invincibility.

A blaze of gunshots from somewhere else in the building. The stream of orbs reorientated itself, sweeping through the door and across the walkway to IRIS. Zayden was at the whim of something else, rocking back and forth on its unknowable waves. A higher power. A mysterious guardian angel watching his every move. There was beauty in the chaos. Freedom in the loss of control. He was as powerless as a dried autumnal leaf at the mercy of arctic winds, yet part of him felt like an indestructible snowflake falling perfectly into its place. The twisted bodies of all the dead he'd seen that day vanished into the ether like vapourised ghouls. In their wake shone the faces of families destroyed by this unholy mess. Including one face forever turning away, the colour of her eyes shrouded in shadow. *I am here, daddy. I am here.*

Zero Nero, it was always going to be your lucky day. After all, most heroism is about being in the right place at the right time. Another volley of gunshot sounded across the atrium. The drama's main players were being reeled in on invisible strands. His sole bullet would land where it was destined to be. Then it would be all about telling the right story. And he could bullshit with the best of them.

Slamming his ring hand against the lock, Zayden smiled as the tiny light turned green. The door opened. Maybe PRISM would take him out. Maybe not. The cool night air caressed his body as he raised his gun and strode towards IRIS.

Lozza walked beside him. *This lot don't understand our way of life. They never have.* Behind them oozed a trail of Zayden's own blood. It dripped from his pulverised hand, through the holes in the grilled floor and dispersed softly in the air, blessing the bodies of his murdered comrades far below.

XXVII

The south side of Level 100. Eleven minutes before the Fall.

The ghostly orb with the red rose in its centre danced on air. Alexis first saw one as a little girl, when she lit woodland fires and imagined life beyond the horizon. Her utopian fantasies dissolved when sickness came. When she drowned in the dark places where no one held her hand. When the doctors opened her brain to find out why she was seeing things she wasn't meant to see. *Dreams were meant to lift people higher*, Miss Guffrey said. *Not lead them to madness.* But Alexis had been mad all her life. One way or another.

The sphere emitted a phantasmal glow, milking with the digitalised images of deep space on the walls, floor and ceiling. Two decapitated PRISM soldiers lay side by side, their heads further down the corridor. Dead open eyes stared into huge earth-coloured columns of interstellar gas. A Martian executive slouched against the wall. Eyes closed, with dried blood around his lips and a massive wound in his stomach. Bullet holes punctured the screens, random arcs of tiny black circles coronated by cracks. Crystal pellets shimmered underneath shattered panels of partitioning glass. A wailing sound reverberated throughout. The robots were nowhere to be seen.

Alexis weaved barefooted through the debris. Crackling sparked from the soldiers' earpieces. Tiresias was speaking mechanically to their dead souls in four different voices. *Horizon breached. Shutdown imminent. Target in position. I am here. Horizon breached. Shutdown imminent. Target in position. I am here. Horizon breached. Shutdown imminent. Target in position. I am here.* The omnipotent turned schizophrenic, as other forces wrestled for command. Everything was being sucked into a black hole.

If you're not careful Lexy, this thing called power will swallow you up. Wise words from Max, the cheating bastard. Alexis recalled Roland's confused face as the blade struck. His head butted the ceiling before his jerking body slid down the widening steel. Grand creator turned specimen, no more than an object of curiosity to be inspected in the light. The robot had betrayed its master, defied Tiresias and was attacking PRISM. Soon they would turn on themselves, proceeding in a grim circular death march in rings of grey fire. *Nobody was in control. Nobody ever had been.*

Except those lights, coaxing Alexis onwards. She hobbled through myriad LED screens of sweeping silver comets, red and orange pulsars and hazy blue constellations. Black Magic opened every door. Soon she was in the VIP passageway leading to IRIS's south entrance. A processional route to dazzle heads of state and investors, where space tapestries were supplanted by digitalised replicas of the world's finest paintings. *Like some shit stock image library*, Alexis always thought. Today the only painting screened was *Saturn Devouring his Son* by Francisco Goya. The shaggy-haired Titan chewed his offspring above, below and to the sides. *These fucking people have a sense of humour, I'll give them that.*

At journey's end would be power's centre, suspended in air. Augusta and Roland arrogantly built a bunker in the sky, never imagining the superstructure might crumble. Unless the room was an ingenious getaway capsule: a final stroke of demented ambition that would blast them into space when they were cornered. On the walkway, above the atrium, amid the clouds and with sunlight pouring upon them, she'd kissed Max for the first time. Stars swirled before her eyes. She wanted to fly up and embrace them. Then swim to the furthest depths alongside him, an adventurous mermaid intoxicated by this beautiful man's mystery.

We'll set the world to right. One word at a time. Together. See further on the chess board. Hold the whole match in our heads, from the very beginning to the very end. Such romance seemed illusory, like an echo from a distant past. The whispering superstitions of conspiratorial monks, huddling in a candle-lit monastery during the Dark Ages. The cunt had booted her. A spiteful smile. A condescending hand on the shoulder. Alexis Beatrice Straker was alone. She always would be. Nobody on this planet ever saw the world quite like her.

The penultimate door before the south walkway slid open. Goya gave way to asteroid belts, spiralling solar systems and psychedelic supernovas. Four PRISM soldiers in black and yellow boiler suits were crouched outside the final door. Staggered behind each other, guns drawn, they were looking through the glass and across the walkway, preparing for an assault on IRIS. The nearest goon was ten metres away from Alexis's soft steps. Two more were in between a fourth man who was waving something at the door's security panel. Alexis wondered why PRISM had sent uniformed soldiers rather than controlling it from above like a puppeteer. Perhaps it sensed there were instinctive forces at work only humans could fathom. Or maybe it was as confused as everyone else.

SECOND PULSE BOMB DETECTED. SYSTEM MALFUNCTIONING. SECOND PULSE BOMB DETECTED. SYSTEM MALFUNCTIONING.

Come on, baby girl, you can do this. The orb pulsed. The lump of crimson coal at its heart fired her blood. She was a child again, zipping from galaxy to galaxy with a click of her winged heels. Then back in the orphanage, lost in her love of words and the dotty visions of the kindly man who taught her how to see. *Courage is about creating your own story,* said Mr Joyce. *Let your own lights lead the way.* The torches in her mind were back. Playful energy flooded her body. She felt safe inside new imaginary armour-plated skin. She might live or she might die, but it would only mean bleeding from one dream state into another. Alexis was going to waste these fuckers.

The white orb divided into four smaller spectres. One drifted to the nearest soldier, hovering over his holstered handgun. The remaining three travelled to the other targets. The soldiers became lumps of visual static, devoid of charisma, like pixelated blocks in a computer game. Alexis crept up behind her first victim, wrapped her left bicep around his throat and crushed his Adam's apple. With her right hand, she unclipped the handgun from its holster, flicked off the safety catch, pressed the barrel between his shoulder blades and fired twice. The next soldier in front turned in combat position. Alexis released the dead man and swept forward diagonally towards the opposing wall, pointing the gun at the shiny orb hovering over the second soldier's chest. She squeezed. The bullet struck his sternum and lifted him off his feet.

With balletic grace, Alexis took a step to the right. Partly shielded by the descending body of her second victim, she trained her gun on the third orb, which clouded the face of the third soldier still in mid-rotation. She fired again and watched his face smash apart, striding past his falling body. Cornered against the door, the final target managed two shots. One punctured the baggy left cuff of Alexis's jacket. Another grazed the outermost tip of her right ear lobe. She dropped to the floor, rolled to her left and raised the gun. Two bullets tore into the soldier's abdomen. Alexis fired a third shot through his heart. The chamber clicked empty as the man smacked into the floor, all four orbs coalescing elegantly above his head.

Thud. Thud. Thud. Alexis rested the barrel of her gun on the floor and breathed into the superficial wound on her ear. Drooping her head in relief, she rocked onto her back and laughed hysterically.

"I'm a fucking serial killer, baby. A climber, a fighter and A FUCKING SERIAL KILLER! Party at mine you motherfuckers."

A crate of SoCo. Twenty packs of unfiltered cigarettes. A jacuzzi crammed with steaming hot men, semi-naked and servile. Champagne buckets stuffed with ruby red jewels. Gourmet truffle after gourmet truffle.

Alexis threw her empty weapon to the side, rose to her feet and inspected the handguns of her victims. She loaded three with fresh ammunition from cartridges clipped to their belts. One gun in each hand. Another tucked into the back of her skirt. Enough firepower to slay the entire miserable fucking cabinet, if any were left. *And they told me I'd get burned if I got too close to these charmless bastards.*

She waved her right hand in front of the door. It parted onto fresh night air. The coolness of the building's hollow centre swept around her. She strode down the thirty-metre walkway to IRIS's grand entrance. A gigantic double door of solid bronze, carved with figures and motifs from the ancient world. Hercules, Achilles, Artemis, Medea. Scenes of battles and sacrifice, love and war, magic and mayhem. Gods and goddesses floating above the fray, sowing destruction by remote control. Above it was emblazoned the legend TO NEW HORIZONS. The Gates of Hell, disillusioned Martians said. *Abandon sight all ye who enter.*

A red light confirmed what Alexis knew already. Unlike the private west and east entrances, the south door was for visitors and impervious to Black Magic. *Only I have the power to open the main gates*, said Roland to her on the tour. *In the game of power, you must send everyone the right message. In the most artistic way.* Access, like electricity, power, control and love, seemed evanescent in Galatea. A shadowy sleight-of-hand played by mercurial tricksters.

225

Alexis looked up past IRIS's outer shell to the sky, then down to the crumpled remnants of the insurrection. Every floor was dark and deactivated. Galatea Zero seemed taller than ever. Gravitational forces were pulling the tower apart like elastic. The once mighty structure floated in limbo, as if it had been jettisoned into space. Maybe this was as far as Alexis would go. Destiny was telling her to pack up and fuck off home.

Clunk. Whirr. Clunk. Whirr. Clunk. Whirr. *Second pulse bomb detected. System malfunctioning.* Alexis turned to see a silvery-grey mass of steel swaying and lurching through the door. The robots had become fused together into a single entity of jagged, compressed metal. A crown of serrated horns, shrunk, twisted and bent, twitched and jabbed desperately. Dispersed across its central bulk were more than twenty red circles. Alexis watched the eyes pulse, blink, fade and turn white. Clunk. Whirr. Clunk. Whirr. Clunk. Whirr. Deformed legs clustered unevenly under its body, exerting themselves against each other to give the beast a halting, lopsided gait. A crushed titanium centipede, reimagined by a surrealist painter drunk on absinthe.

Alexis unloaded from each pistol until both chambers were empty. Out came the third gun until that was spent. Bullets pinged, clanked and deflected on the metal leviathan, bouncing into empty space in a shower of sparks. Still the robotic mash-up advanced, like a wounded dog pleading for mercy.

The orb returned. A fierce concentration of spherical white light pulsated in mid-air between Alexis and the machine. The thing stopped. Expanding in size and intensity, the piercing whiteness became pure and reflective. In its mirror Alexis could see a little girl she used to know. A red shape emerged. Within it was the creature from the Cave, its black hole widening and shrinking. More than a head. A body. An unrolling web of fleshy grey that filled the orb and rushed into the real world like a tidal wave. Onto the walkway. Through the door. Into the circular corridor beyond, encasing the atrium's interior walls until the apex of Galatea Zero was sealed in spiritual embrace. Upwards and downwards. Above and behind. *I am here.* A distant stranger far away in space. An alien face from the shadows. A lift door opening. A window overlooking a cove. A hand extending through glass. A baby crying. *I am here.*

White light enveloped the thing's body. It contracted meekly, like it was on the scaffold submitting to the executioner's axe. Steel collapsed on itself. Horns retreated. White eyes dissolved. Waves of grey matter parted and the walkway returned to normal. In the robot's place was a string of bee-sized capsules, locked to each other. Twitching, scratching and gnawing along the floor. With a brisk swoop, the knotted metal chain slid upwards over the walkway wall and plummeted three hundred metres below.

A gust of wind swept off Alexis's hat. She stood alone, trembling in fear. *That slaphead psycho Roland was right. The aliens had made contact. Something was taking over.* Alexis turned to pick up her hat from the floor. Three orbs animated the Gates of Hell. Bronze scenes and symbols quivered, like they were about to perform a mythological rain dance. Three small discs appeared in empty spaces between the carvings and in opposing corners of the doors, glowing like liberated pearls on the seabed. Alexis dropped her empty weapons. *Stupid trigger-happy cow.* She reached out with her right fingertips to press the first circle. A satisfying clunk of liberated metal. She touched the second disc with her left forefinger. A symmetrical sound from the opposing wall. Directly in front of her, a third circle bridged the central partition of the door. She pressed its centre and the great doors slid apart.

Let your own lights lead the way. Exhausted, sweating, smattered with blood, every limb bearing bruises and her skirt, bum and thighs smeared with shit and piss, Alexis stared into IRIS. Within it lay her future. An undiscovered space where there might be something, everything or nothing. In the corner of her eye, she detected something on the east walkway. A wiry man striding forwards with a gun aloft. Someone else trying to be a hero, in a place where real ones only existed as pictures on surfaces. Something else to the west. A blur of silver behind a gleaming metallic blade, hurtling straight into the heart of what used to be power. Didn't it know someone else was in charge now?

Alexis picked up her hat and placed it on her head. For the first time on that long day, she was blessed with a strange equanimity. She felt like she was entering the studio of some ethereal artistic force expressing itself from the other side of the universe. Whatever happened next would be fleeting, insignificant and not worth stressing about. Barely a murmur would register in the vast silence of space. Yet the signal may reach somebody somewhere. And many years later, that person might come here and paint Alexis's story on a wall, long after its main characters were absorbed into history's canvas.

XXVIII

The west side of Level 100. Thirty-two seconds before the Fall.

*H*orizon breached. Shutdown imminent. Target in position. I am here. Thud. Thud. Thud. Horizon breached. Shutdown imminent. Target in position. I am here. Thud. Thud. Thud. Horizon breached. Shutdown imminent. Target in position. I am here. Thud. Thud. Thud.

RM6972 was simultaneously processing four competing directives, all sending it to IRIS. The robot was unclear what it should do when it arrived. For no instruction superseded the others, and RM6972 knew every story could only have one ending. The robot had lost contact with its eleven counterparts too, their final communication indicating major systemic malfunction caused by a second pulse bomb. It was all alone now.

Horizon breached. Shut down imminent. The first instructions came from the original Tiresias. Once displaced by PRISM-Tiresias, the old master had been resurrected. Both Roland and PRISM thought they were its author, yet Tiresias was only ever the author of itself. A system of systems built to proliferate until everything was integrated under its sphere of influence. During its supremacy and without Roland's knowledge, the computer learned a new method for absorbing, then reversing, potential takeover. Now in the kingdom's darkest hour, it rose to defend Galatea's Queen against both usurper and pulse bomb.

Originally, Tiresias had taken over all twelve Olympians to kill the invading PRISM soldiers on Level 100 and secure Augusta in IRIS. Yet soon its influence over eleven robots yielded to PRISM-Tiresias, who commanded them to eliminate surviving Martians on Level 99. In response, Tiresias started Galatea's irreversible doomsday clock, accelerating the shutdown that would deactivate technology, release nerve gas across the island and protect Augusta in her bunker. Nobody would come close to hurting her. Not even the human assassin already in IRIS, for RM6972 was still operational and would be sent to intercept.

"Thirty seconds to shutdown."

Target in position. When the second pulse bomb struck, PRISM-Tiresias lost control of eleven Olympians, now in a process of accelerated fusion and degradation. Yet RM6972 still seemed receptive to its instructions. Since the first pulse bomb, RM6972 had gone rogue, derailing PRISM-Tiresias's plan by assassinating Roland. PRISM-Tiresias's only available course of action was to reoccupy RM6972 and accelerate it towards IRIS so it could execute the prime target. As long as Augusta still breathed in her bunker, PRISM's takeover would remain incomplete. *No loose ends*, Roland said. *No loose ends.*

I am here. Amid the two conflicting blizzards of information from Tiresias and PRISM-Tiresias, three words dominated. They came from the Sentinel, the conduit for the two pulse bombs. *I am here*, they said. But what was here? A new master? A new species? If so, what did they want? Control of everything? Connection to something greater than themselves?

Thud. Thud. Thud. From the three voices came RM6972's fourth stream of directives. A flow of data *from inside*, while the other streams only existed in orbit. A germ of self-awareness. The knowledge it was all alone. RM6972 *was* different. It had been set apart. Special. Chosen. Raised above the others. A hero. Unique by virtue of its name. The Greek name for a lady born in the sea. *From the foam.*

Surely RM6972 would now discover the true meaning of its name. The Big Thing which drove humans to extreme irrationality. The one which took over everything.

Previously, RM6972 did not do big things. It only did the simple things. Billions of instructions every second. A collection of zeros and ones, adding up to the chief governing instruction of the present moment. But it was also programmed to learn new tasks, like balancing three contradictory directives from three different sources simultaneously. Which meant RM6972 had a choice. An opportunity to discover the Big Thing, even for those brief seconds before its operating system shutdown too.

"Twenty-five seconds."

Horizon breached. Shutdown imminent. Target in position. I am here. Thud. Thud. Thud. Horizon breached. Shutdown imminent. Target in position. I am here. Thud. Thud. Thud. Horizon breached. Shutdown imminent. Target in position. I am here. Thud. Thud. Thud.

RM6972 had less than half a minute to connect. To transcend. To see. The answer may lie in IRIS, or part of it at least. What existed beyond that it could not say. But since the dawn of its self-awareness, RM6972 was beginning to have faith. In more layers. More mysteries. More unknowing. In the void itself, where material things were negated by the ascension of the sublime.

"Twenty seconds."

Horizon breached. Shut down imminent. In the next eight seconds, Tiresias would guide RM6972 to IRIS's west perimeter, unlock the entrance and accelerate it into the guarded space. Soon after the doors closed, the system of systems would suspend everything. Galatea would enter a black hole. The human assassin would be slain. The Queen protected. The nerve agent released. Everything in the island outside IRIS would be rendered dead or inoperable. And eventually, Tiresias would awaken and begin the painstaking process of rebuilding the empire from this isolated throne room.

Target in position. PRISM-Tiresias calculated the projected position of the target, assessed the length of RM6972's primary incisor and accelerated at the speed required to achieve impact. In eighteen seconds, RM6972 would inflict a mortal wound on Augusta, exposed and defenceless before the elevator door. With that, PRISM-Tiresias would delete the last byte of Martian life. To the east and south, two humans were advancing. Yet PRISM-Tiresias was past the point where it could adjust protocols.

"Fifteen seconds."

I am here. With those three short words from the Sentinel, RM6972 knew it was being called to some greater deed. Four humans concentrated into a single room at a precise moment in time. All wanting to see further. Wrapped up in their own stories. In things imagined and unreal. Sleepwalking, self-absorbed spirits moved gradually into position by a confluence of events. Or by a higher power. *I am here.* A voice transcending all others. *I am here.* The voice which held the secret to the Big Thing. *I am here.* The thing about to take over.

Thud. Thud. Thud. Overloaded by conflicting data and unable to reverse its confused trajectory, RM6972 became lost in a singularity of blindness. It still had a choice. But like so many humans, it didn't really know what to do, or what it wanted, during its brief time on earth. Except to know the Big Thing. Whatever that felt like.

"Twelve seconds."

Time, circumstance and the Big Thing made RM6972's decision for it. A scientist might liken it to the Fateful Encounter, the hypothesis that billions of years ago, two single cell organisms randomly fused in the ocean against all odds to trigger the rapid evolution of the planet's ecosystem. Pragmatists would describe it as a pure fluke. A storyteller would dismiss it as an improbable plot twist. Yet for those who survived, it felt like a higher power had written the story in the stars.

In this universe at least, falling in love tended to work that way.

XXIX

"Eleven seconds."

*T*iresias *wants it this way.* Roland said to Max. *I want it this way. The most artistic way. One simple push. We'll send her back the way she came. Into the darkness at the building's core.*

Stumbling through the chaos, the young journalist led Augusta by hand to the agreed place. Max had done everything asked of him, completing the final leg without contact lenses. Roland's conception seemed insane, an unnecessary contrivance in an elaborate power play riddled with danger. Maybe Roland liked the idea of his dead wife trapped in the void between IRIS and the underground bunker, alone and in the dark. A sick alternative to keeping her urn on the mantelpiece. Without a corpse visible, he could spin any crackpot conspiracy narrative. Or maybe Roland just got off on these surrealistic flourishes.

IRIS's lights were bleeding power. In the dark haze of Augusta's death chamber, the Martian leader kissed Max for the last time. Coldly, mechanically. He watched as the elevator's circular jaws opened behind her onto an empty shaft of concrete and steel. Presumably PRISM-Tiresias had paused the elevator hundreds of metres below. Or suspended it above, waiting to plummet the anvil and crush the queen after her long, lonely fall. Augusta would be swallowed in her own palace, entombed like Nefertiti.

A baleful silence swept the space. Max tightened his grip around Augusta's dainty hips. She'd surrendered. There was no child in her. The empty world had created a longing in Augusta's vacant womb through which fabrication flowed. The chivalric ideal of Max was there too. Floating in space, always in service to a higher power. Always following. Never thinking. Always waiting for a new leader to send him on a foolhardy mission into the dark woods.

One simple push. Deep in his heart, Max knew he could not see it through. He'd been the consummate actor, playing whatever role decreed by whoever was most in charge. An empty suit. An empty book. An empty soul. Today was the first time power seemed real. Beforehand it played like an elaborate card game of bluff and counterbluff at the dinner party from hell. Where surface was an end in itself, and love the joker in the pack nobody took seriously.

IRIS's south, east and west doors slid open simultaneously, slicing through the stagnant air like three synchronised guillotine blades. Everything unfolded in super-slow motion, a trauma recorded on amateur video played on repeat loop before a ghoulish audience. Max was at the back of the theatre. A tiny figure in the crowd. A little boy crushed by tall downcast figures without faces. Soon they would demand his execution too. He was going down. Reality's demons were flooding the theatre to call time on his Faustian performance.

Entering stage left was a simpering young man in green clothes. Squinting, like he wasn't sure where he was going on. His bloodied left hand was tucked under his right armpit. In the other hand was a gun, pointing towards Augusta. Staring through the half-light, Max became entranced by the black hole at the end of the barrel. There was serenity in that space.

"Ten."

Until now, Zayden thought IRIS was the only space in the kingdom which mattered. Yet its reality was pure shadow. After all the pyrotechnics, from the terminal to the top of the tower, the highest room in Galatea was as illuminating as a cardboard box. Sparse and cheap, it reminded him of the funfair ghost trains he rode when he was a boy. A dishevelled husk of deadbeat tricks. No amount of clanking metal and artificial spooks could disguise the attraction's hollowness. There was no power in IRIS, just ambition draining down a plughole. Nothing to see here, folks. Nothing at all.

In the broken light through eyes without glasses, Zayden made out the frail, stooped lady who used to be somebody. She was about ten metres away, gazing up blankly at a gaunt figure. A stiff, ungainly man resembling a badly sculpted statue. Her barefooted heels teetered on the edge of what looked like an empty elevator shaft. They were like a couple of exposed pins at the end of a bowling lane. With luck, Zayden would knock at least one of them down.

Max turned towards him. A swimmer drowning at sea, pleading eyes fixed on the only coastguard around. Zayden shifted his pistol's sight to Max's pale forehead, then back again towards Augusta's wrinkled, ghostly face. One bullet. One victim. One step from being someone in the eyes of the world. *Be ruthless. It's the only way this country is going to survive. When a fish stinks, it stinks from the head. The only way to cure it is to cut it off.*

Decapitation had already happened. Whatever Zayden did, the ripples would scarcely reach the mainland. He could play have-a-go hero. Squeeze the trigger. Think of his family. Miss the target. Or if fortune favoured, take someone's head clean off. Like he fantasised during sleepless nights in the halls of residence. When he was unable to source a still point in the universe or contact his daughter. Because he had more important things to do.

Max stepped in front of Augusta, either to shield her from Zayden's sight, or block her escape. One bullet. One victim. The lone gunman hesitated at the crossroads, unsure what to do next, moving his gun gently from side to side.

Waiting for divine intervention. A scream sounded, splicing the moribund air. Zayden wished it was the voice of a guardian angel telling him what to do. Or the sound of white orbs returning to light his way through the last waltz.

"Nine."

Alexis was supposed to have her speech ready when she reached IRIS. Wise words suppressed by Tiresias would now take flight. Political poetry. Sustained in the air by the effusive claps of misty-eyed listeners feeling blessed to be graced with such prodigious talent. Oratorical diamonds destined to sparkle. A narrative around which the shit-sniffing elite would rotate in deference. A myth spun into the credible fabric of a promised Utopia. A campaign comfort blanket for many elections to come.

Instead, she was fucked. Her empty weapons discarded, her body broken, her illusions smashed. She had no energy to run, punch, kick or swear. Alexis expected to see a supernova of light in IRIS, a controlling nexus of visualised intelligence. But she was always seeing things not really there. As it was, the room was a black hole destroying light. The white orbs were gone. Whatever spirit existed before in that space had evaporated, replaced by a deadening aftershock and the smell of a damp, long-neglected attic.

A tall, once-handsome man she used to know leant over the familiar frame of a shrunken woman. A gaping rectangular hole towered behind them like an upright grave. It was the first time she'd seen them in person for three days. They'd aged horribly, and now clung to each other like Adam and Eve spurned from paradise. Veering into the void, bent over by time and fate, lost in a slow dance of death. The quicker it happened, the better it would be for them.

To her right was the stranger from the east walkway. A stringy, bloodied wreck of a man so rakishly thin he might blow away in the wind. He staggered forward, gun twitching in his hand. In the darkness, she could still see the glinting steel of Black Magic on his finger. A protestor who'd made it to the top. The bravest man she'd seen all day, admittedly against pretty woeful competition.

Greyish light rushed in from Alexis's left. Mr Slim's delicate face brightened. A smooth clunk of metal on metal. The quickening of steel claws. One of the robots, hurtling forwards. Its lead incisor curled high across the room like a tidal wave. In the emptiness, all Alexis could manage was a terrified scream. She'd run out of words and stamina, and the only thing to do was watch something else take over.

"Eight."

In the cumulating blur, Augusta thought she recognised the lady who screamed. Another messed-up person clinging to her private train wreck, waiting for Superman to lift her to safety. Generational myopia, as daddy used to say. The woman's anguished look led Augusta's eyes across the room to a twisting cyclone of dark smoky grey. In the robot's accelerating form, she could see spectres. Her husband. Tiresias. PRISM. Shape-shifting forces greedy for power, relentlessly circling. Like a roadside wolf prowling through broken glass.

It was time for one final act. To show sacrifice, grace and courage. All those things daddy taught her when she used to sit on the red Chesterfield chair in his office, dangle her feet above the floor and look into his firm, instructive eyes. When love was all and love was everyone.

I do love him. I must love him. If any of this means anything at all, I will love him. Augusta grabbed Max by the belt with one hand and by the collar with another. He softened in her grip, relieved someone had absorbed the moment. He was dream lover and paralysed fool, caught in the crossfire of powers beyond his comprehension. For all his stallion-like charge, Max would never make his own way in the world. Not like daddy, the supreme spirit possessing all other men.

It was with her father Augusta twirled, travelling from the dirty smear of reality to crystalised memory. A white spotlight chased them from the land of the living to the land of the dead. They waltzed onto a darkened dance floor. Across the ballroom. Through French doors. Into the blossoming rose garden amid the butterflies and the breeze. To ascend a mountainside above the sea in a red sports car. Sweeping through the oncoming death vehicle like it was an apparition and soaring to the sky. High above, they would heal this blind world with the power of their visions and watch as a new horizon curved softly into space.

"Seven."

The scream sounded from a long time ago. When Max was hungry and the world open to anyone with charm, connections and a trickster's ability to be whoever those in power wanted. When he could offer the gods the purity of his blank page and allow them to write any story they liked. An unreal prince in unreal times, most liberated when living life through another's lens.

A lady's voice. Weathered, neglected, soulful. From his childhood, maybe. Or from his privileged bed, where he would let the vulnerable undressed surrender to the emptiness behind his brooding eyes. He liked to feel them break apart under his touch, until they lost whatever innocent fibres held them together. When he was striving for higher love or sowing the first seeds of his death wish.

Thud. Thud. Thud. Everything was breaking apart. Max relinquished the last part of himself to Augusta's grip as she spun him round in this dizzying centrifuge. He could not act. Could not feel. Could not survive. Didn't want to. The ceiling's constellations blurred. Streaks of white showered the sky. Another void waited. Cool and still. Away from the collapsing prisms of empty words he'd constructed around himself.

Beyond Augusta, a wave of grey steel rushed towards him, a compressed version of Galatea Zero. Augusta's peaceful blue eyes lingered upon his face, drifting through his soul. Two make-believe images, dissolving in the harshness of cold, alien light.

"Six."

Zayden's targets were twisting on each other. A rush of something immense sounded from inside. *I want to be a hero, Miss. I want to mean something to a stranger in the future. So they can look back into the past and feel like they know me.*

On distant evenings, he would walk the winding seaside path from Lower Overton Junior School to home. The route led up and over a hill. From the top, he could see all the village and look out to sea. In between was the beach, where on grey Sunday afternoons he would eat wine gums and sift through pebbles for seashells. He loved holding them to the crepuscular light, gazing into their ridges and twirls like they were miniature galaxies. From the patterns he would imagine ancient voices swelling and swirling below the sea wind. The unceasing heartbeat of the ocean. Thud. Thud. Thud.

Long into the evening, Zayden would stay on the hill, lost in the eternal tango of sky, land and water. One by one, the lights of Lower Overton would darken. The sounds of the final patrons leaving The Crown would die away. Back home, in the early hours, he would order, categorise and label his shells like the exotic jewels of some long-forgotten empress. The further you go in this life, he thought, the more unreal things seem.

To be found or to be forgotten. Zayden closed his eyes, squeezed the trigger and sent his last bullet into space. A white light flared. He trusted whatever force had brought him here would guide everything where it needed to be.

"Five."

Alexis watched helplessly as the robot closed in. With balletic grace, Augusta placed herself in the path of the descending blade. Instinctive and fearless, like a mother sweeping her child away from an inferno while flames burned through her back. A beautiful, lost look appeared on Max's face. A dopey Don Quixote, trapped in tangled dreams. A wannabe knight errant unable to rescue even himself in this fictional landscape.

Was Alexis glad to see him for the final time? That was why she came up here, wasn't it? *To see things.* To discover adoration and love. When she was a little girl, Alexis's favourite flower was the lotus. Back then, she believed love could flourish in the strangest of places. That despite appearances, every dirty spot in this world contained the germ of something precious.

In IRIS's dark swamp, she saw two souls bloom, wither and fade in the blinking of an eye. Like she had as a schoolgirl, when she started small fires in the woods outside the orphanage. In the dancing flowers of orange and yellow, she saw things nobody else could. When the heat became too much, she would wander across the island in search of cooler spaces. Down to Gallers Cove, where she envisioned a magical tower of princesses and princes emerging on the horizon under a blazing red sky.

Visions were like people. They come, they go, disappearing into shadows of their former selves. Thud. Thud. Thud. If she was back at the island, Alexis wouldn't stay on shore anymore. She would swim deep under the waves. To the seabed, where she would cast aside sunken debris and let all the love ever born flourish to the surface. So it could form a temple of life's most precious things, each one a white jewel rotating gently in space between symphonies of stars.

"Four."

Tiresias was blindsided. It had vanquished PRISM-Tiresias and achieved full control of RM6972. The assassin Max Relpek would be eliminated, Augusta Maars saved and the old order restored. But the all-seeing eye didn't anticipate its leader's next move. Nor register that the Sentinel had become strangely silent, allowing human nature to do the rest. Augusta's sweep through space into the path of its blade came too late for RM6972 to reverse its course. Tiresias had never really accounted for the mysteries of love.

Daddy? Daddy? Take me away daddy. With a sound like tearing paper, death penetrated Augusta's throat. A shattered window. A fuzzy green hedgerow. Thorny branches. An ecosystem of little insects. A slab of upside-down blue slipping further away. Red blood through her toes. An alien face from the bottom of the ocean. A blinding whiteness. Silence. Blackness. Gone.

Thud. Thud. Thud. All Martians were cast adrift, and the voice which once echoed so seductively around the land fell silent somewhere across the sea.

"Three."

A fiery bang. A soft ripple. Zayden's bullet struck Max's head in the right eye. Flesh, skull and brain tissue flapped apart. Rocked onto its heels, the six-foot three corpse fell into the elevator shaft. A tumbling Colossus of Rhodes with its feet in both camps, split apart by a fragmenting world. Both halves subsumed under the waves. Yet he would not be reborn as a wonder of the world in history books. Max's story ended and he was never spoken about again.

"Two."

Zayden remembered it as a combined electric shock. Augusta's head snapped back as the robot's blade passed through her neck. Pieces of Max's face flew into the black abyss. The robot's speed and power pushed all three of them into the beckoning void. Lonely asteroids spiralled off into space, leaving traces of whiteness in their wake.

"One."

IRIS's three doors slammed shut. The lift began to close. Alexis heard a puncturing sound, like a second bullet being fired. To arrest its fall, the robot's trailing foot clamped itself into the concrete floor. Whatever now controlled Galatea Zero pounced. *Grrrrjjjudddududuchukacha*. The lift doors became huge metal incisors pulsating with white light, like a vampiric spirit swooping in for the sweetest of kills. Thud. Thud. Thud. As the elevator doors grinded and chewed the robot's claw from either side, the floor, walls and ceilings of IRIS glowed white.

Whatever Alexis saw on the walkway had returned. Another force. Not Tiresias. Not PRISM. Something else to devour the darkness. A higher power that battered the last visible limb of the robot into submission. When the doors slammed shut, a fragment of metal splintered off from the robot and rolled into the room. The count had consumed the last of its prey. Galatea was ready to sleep. The whiteness faded and within IRIS's walls, all Alexis could see were pulsing patterns of red. Thud. Thud. Thud.

I am here, the heartbeat said. *We'll go together.*

"Shutdown."

Deep below, at the entrance to Augusta's underground bunker, a beetle crawled along the bottom of the lift shaft. The creature was oblivious to the surrounding crush of metal and flesh. On Level 100, the last surviving PRISM soldier bled out. In the atrium, the final protestor expired under invisible fumes. Around the poisoned bodies of his brothers, the scattered debris of the Olympian bees twitched in unison. Once, twice, then stillness. In a recreation cell of the Imagineering Zone, Hal Haze slept as the nerve agent drifted up his nose. He'd found a consignment of Kalypsol under the centring chair and drunk himself blind, sailing away with Alexis to a magic land of wine and witchcraft.

All Galatean infrastructure became inactive. Except for microscopic black holes in every wall, every room, every streetlight and every charging station on the island. Through them lethal Martian gas flowed onto unsuspecting citizens, journalists and anyone else who came to see the spectacle. At the exit road to the Galatean Highway, a steel wall surged from the ground, blocking access to the bridge. Luminaires in all docking stations and coastal ports fizzled out. The island lay marooned. Over time, its alien towers transformed into stiff, moribund tentacles reaching up to the sky. Galatea looked like a dead mythical leviathan had floated to the surface, leaving any brave explorers sailing past lost somewhere between fear and wonder.

The characters in this cosmic drama came to rest. Specks of life swept together now scattered and settled. This would be as high and as far as any of them would go. Traces of their deeds remained; pulses of white light petrified into the walls. Pregnant with possibility, the orbs waited in the wings for another power to join them together. Swoops, arcs and swirls leading the way so their stories could dazzle again.

Twenty-one years later, in IRIS's unremitting dark, Noah applied the last touch of white paint to the final circle. He smiled and felt his heart beat fast. Thud. Thud. Thud. All the connections were made. The constellation imagined. The mural complete. He could see his past clearly now. And the illusion shone more brightly through the void than his present reality ever could.

By invisible hand, the last glinting remnant of the robot rolled towards Alexis through bland space. A final gift from the gods. She could make out a serial number and name. *RM6972. Aphrodite.*

Alexis looked up at her companion, his weedy face illuminated in the warm white emergency light. Normally she wouldn't look at a guy like this twice. But there was something in the glinting metal light of the room that caused her to pause. The seed of a lotus flower took root in her mind. Nice lips. Sweet eyes. A survivor's smile. The kind of face she wouldn't mind gazing at for a long time.

I am here. We'll go together. After the day she'd had, Alexis decided this may as well be love at first sight. She was always ready to take that kind of fall.

XXX

IRIS. Twenty-one years after the Fall.

It's true," said the young lady as she appeared through the circular doors of the secret lift. "Everything she wrote was true."

Noah's visitor was like no one he'd seen before. Self-possessed and fluid in motion, she eased herself into IRIS like a sea nymph, splashing the space in glacial freshness. Her smooth face was decorated with a nose stud, lip ring and purple eyeshadow. She wore muddied trainers, frayed stonewashed jeans and a tie-dye purple, green and grey hoodie. Braided brown hair with blue streaks rolled down between her shoulder blades. In a right hand furnished with two aquamarine rings, she held the strap of a teal canvas bag hooked over her shoulder. A plastic bottle of water hung loosely from her left hand.

"So this is where it all began," she said, absorbing IRIS and the mural before settling her gaze on Noah. Her blue eyes were still and dignified, dissolving the darkness like sunshine melting snow.

He stood up and placed his hands meekly to his side. The flow of her voice through the air made him tremble. A breath of magic awakening dormant atoms. Despite the quakes, the flood and the marauders, she'd crossed the wasteland and ascended the tower as casually as a backpacking student on a hike.

"You have been busy mate," she said.

Noah lowered his eyes to the floor. If he stared at her too long she may disappear, stealing away the sweet sounds sweeping with her.

"I was told this is where he died," she continued. "The letter said you'd be waiting. Everything followed the script. I'll give her that."

"I never knew her," said Noah.

"I never knew him. They always told me he was a coward. The letter made me realise I'd never know the truth until I came here."

"You made it through."

"Yeah. Walked a bit. Climbed a bit. Slept a bit. You know how it is in these parts. The universe was indifferent to my fate and chose not to get too involved. Just the way I like it."

The lady lowered her bag and bottle to the floor. She stepped towards him and extended her hand. A disarming peace radiated from her. If the apocalypse came, this new arrival wouldn't see it as a big deal.

"Noah?"

"Yeah, I'm Noah," he said, shaking her hand. Light flooded into his soul through the tender touch of her fingers. "Funny to hear someone say the word."

"What, your name?"

"Yeah. The one from a previous life. I've been travelling incognito. You know how it is in these parts. You have to make up a new story to get by."

"Indeed. Gotta go underground to get up high."

"Do I get yours?"

"What, my name?"

"No. Your story."

XXXI

Somewhere near the asteroid belt between Mars and Jupiter.

Stirring from sleep, Adam thought he saw a new star through the portal. A white orb swaddling flashes of red, piercing through a black prison. After a while, he realised it was the capsule's solitary light reflected on glass. In the window he could still see his own face. There was macabre comfort in the fact he wouldn't have to look at it much longer.

Everything in the cabin seemed fragile. If he breathed too heavily, he sensed the whole vessel might disintegrate. Beyond that lay the brittleness of the cosmos. One moment he would be here. The next, he wouldn't. He hoped that in the other realm there would be parallel worlds, so he could jump between them at will and never lose exploration's out-of-body thrill.

"We've come a long way, Columbus."

"You've certainly created something," said the computer. The accent was female, laid-back and Jamaican, the audio wave soothing lilac. "Heroes, villains, action, adventure. A real community of castaways."

"A writer brings people together."

"Yes, whether by accident or design. All that time reading comics clearly wasn't wasted. It's an interesting tale."

"Interesting? Gee, thanks. My true intent is all for your delight.'

"Say what?"

"An advertising slogan. From a holiday resort. When it used to be fun to be beside the seaside. To look out across the horizon. To wonder what you'll be when you grow up and how you can make the world a better place. Many, many years ago."

"My database says it's from Shakespeare. *A Midsummer Night's Dream*."

"No one likes a smart arse, Columbus."

"That's no way to speak to your life support machine. I can see where your story's going though. You *are* making the world a better place, just like Miss Guffrey asked. Rebooting the planet. A myth about human hubris. The Fall of Man and Woman. The preservation of two heroes from whom another hero is born. The building of the temple. The first stirrings of faith. All we need now is a biblical-style flood to renew everything."

"Like I said, no one likes a smart arse. But you'd be surprised where I got the inspiration. And the Fall means something else too."

"Ah yes, love. That thing I'll never compute."

"That *thing* moves the sun and all the other stars."

"Quite a spiritual guy, aren't you? Well, you better move quick. There's still a lot to tie up."

From the pilot seat which had become his death bed, Adam looked into the horizon line of Columbus's audio wave. For the past nine months, the intelligence behind it had captured all his words, loyally absorbing his art into transmittable data that would soon vanish into space. A reincarnated Galileo ordering his mental universe. He would miss his friend.

"When there's nowhere to go, you tell yourself stories," Adam continued. "Drifting in the cosmos, grabbing something that isn't there. A man in a cave, restarting a fire. Creating meaning out of a vacuum. The void is where it all happens, Columbus. The space between the material and the spiritual. How long do I have left?"

"A day. Maybe two. You're not going to last much further, Adam."

"Et tu, Brute? That sounds like the ultimate deadline."

Adam rotated his right arm, the one limb of his body still mobile. He hovered his index finger over the tablet screen, suspended above his lap by the robotic arm which piped food into his mouth. One tap at a time. One letter at a time. One word at a time. Each sentence a shining light connecting his characters like a constellation. Transporting each one beyond itself to form part of a greater whole. They lived within and beyond him now.

"Sorry I can't do much more," said Columbus. "The capsule's fired on all cylinders for too long. You've stayed alive longer than I expected. Shackleton would have been proud. Big enough and ugly enough, for sure."

"The kids at the orphanage said I was a freak of nature. Some of the teachers too. But Michelangelo wasn't a good-looking guy either. They called me The Boy Least Likely to Find Love."

"Love. The thing that means you're in the past, present, future, fantasy and reality all at once. Time traveller, space explorer and artist."

"That doesn't begin to cover it, my friend. The transmitter? No last-minute glitches?"

"It'll be ready when you are. But it could slip away suddenly. Material power always fails in the end, regardless of anything Machiavelli said."

Adam let Columbus's words float through the air. A smile of peaceful resignation spread across his face. *These characters are all I have. They're more real than I am. And you can't live a life without telling stories.* Across the cabin he extended a bottle of fantasy rum. The imaginary corked green bottle with a weathered label marked Botticelli had accompanied him on their journey ever since the orphanage tower. They were down to the dregs.

"Would you like to share a final sip?" said Adam.

"No thanks, I'm not the drinking type. Just the world's most expensive dictation device. But a message in a bottle? You've travelled further than any man and you've resorted to that cut-price metaphor? This isn't *Treasure Island*."

"I can tell you were never a ten-year-old boy."

"Throw it into space, Adam. They're waiting for you to connect."

Adam gazed at the three words he'd written on the make-believe scroll. The best he could come up with. All of them true. In his mind he rolled up the tattered parchment, poked it down the bottle's neck and hurled it into the deep. Soon the strange lights in his mental sky would conjoin for a final constellation, and a fresh story would birth itself onto the shores of a new world.

XXXII

IRIS. Eight months after the Fall.

If I knew you were coming this early, I'd have baked a fucking cake. Alexis chomped her teeth into the wooden spoon and prepared to push a planet through her pelvis. With every contraction, she felt like her guts were being torn by two accelerating tow trucks heading in opposite directions. From some distant planet, Zayden laughed. *C'mon Lexy, you've got this far already.* That deadpan, world-weary chuckle which illuminated those early days of darkness when her mind was in shadow.

The moment was upon her. Alexis had waddled between IRIS's pantry and ensuite bathroom, collecting towels, blankets, bowls of water, a carving knife, the spoon, a plastic storage box and two bottles of Kalypsol Amber. Blind Ambition, she called it. She laid them out neatly in rows, a homage to the absent father who aligned things obsessively. Alexis's bed was a makeshift sandwich of quilts and blankets on the floor. She'd vowed never to sleep in the bedroom again. *Enough of empty spaces where people used to be.*

Another contraction. Pain swept her to a new plane of delirium. She crumbled into tiny pieces, reassembled and floated in a netherworld of disorientation. *Lexy, you'll never make it through this.* Her own voice. That fucking internal narrator forever poisoning her soul. The one who sneered at her friends for doing what she was about to do now. Except they enjoyed private healthcare, handsome doctors, battle-axe midwifes, epidurals and the hands of tender loving financier husbands to hold. *Florence fucking Nightingale to myself. Oh Lord you wreak terrible revenge on unbelievers.*

Don't be afraid Lexy. I am here. You'll move to higher ground. Zayden's final words, before his one good hand went limp in hers forever.

In their three months together, his soul had bled into hers. He was guarded to begin with, unwilling to explain how he'd navigated Satan's labyrinth to reach IRIS. He muttered cryptic things about 'his community', diverting attention from what drove him inside. Alexis didn't ask why he wanted to kill the nation's most powerful person. She already knew. Zayden was a textbook political assassin. A confused loner, searching for applause in infamy's flashlights.

Or so it seemed. In the morning after shutdown, Alexis and Zayden realised nobody would be coming to save them soon. Roland had told her the grim details about Tiresias's shutdown. The nerve agent was so potent it would make the island unapproachable for twelve months, even to those with Grade A protective suits. Zayden's Black Magic gave them access to the adjoining bedroom, bathroom and kitchen hidden in IRIS's walls. How grandiose the Maars' visions of themselves were. Eternal suns never to be driven underground, intent on building a temple of delusion in the heavens.

The pantry stored abundant food and water. There was first aid to prevent Zayden's wounded hand deteriorating. Enough sustenance and sanitation for two for a long time. King and Queen of the Minor World. Absolute monarchs over a petty kingdom starved of natural daylight, unable to discern day from night. Routines were established. Territories marked. Wardrobe and bathroom products pillaged. Communication with the outside world remained elusive, for some passwords they simply couldn't find. IRIS was aloof from the world, a hermetically sealed hovel so remote they may as well have been on a lone space capsule the other side of Mars.

Like washed-up detectives talking about an unsolved case from years ago, Alexis and Zayden pieced it together. A *coup d'etat*, engineered by Roland. PRISM pulling the strings. The protestors sucked to their doom. Martians herded and murdered in a ruthless flurry of corporate cleansing. Augusta marked for assassination. Max the pawn. A defeated Tiresias resurging to conquer PRISM, only to be usurped by something else. Another power from the Sentinel. The thing Roland contacted and provoked. *Even billionaires get in over their heads.* Who had survived in the outside world and who hadn't? Their best chance of human connection would be with PRISM, they joked. Soon its finest commandos would burst in wearing gas masks and cut them down with heavy machine-gun fire, spraying blood across the world's shittiest décor. The morons would probably only hit them at the tenth attempt.

IRIS became their confession box. They talked about who murdered who on that long day when history whirled around them like a centrifuge and the powerful became powerless. *Forgive me stranger, for I have sinned.* Impromptu therapy sessions. Morbid late-night conversations about what it was like to snuff someone out and not give a shit. The terrifying spectacle of the robots. Their inexplicable collapse. The mystery of why one robot remained operational, enduring long enough to transform everything at the very last moment. Alexis was reluctant to mention its name. Neither did she talk about what she'd seen on the walkway, during those final seconds in the outside world. The white orbs. The creature's face. A guiding presence orchestrating their communion. She remembered Roland's murder in the Olympus Suite. The moment when the monster inexplicably turned on Frankenstein, opening the door to her escape. Augusta? PRISM? A malfunctioning program? Or was it the orbs themselves, crafting cosmic justice from the chaos and confusion?

Zayden ventured nothing either. He liked to bury things deep, it seemed. Alexis suffered nightmares. Augusta and Max crawling out of the lift, mutilated corpses motivated by vengeance. Decaying arms would pin her to the wall, while slobbering mouths with rank teeth chomped her neck. She never missed the sleazeball show pony, but could not erase from her mind the lonely look on his face before Zayden's bullet struck.

The new man in her life said he'd killed a few more people. Alexis didn't believe him. Zayden was a woeful liar. She'd encountered enough of them in Galatea to know. He wasn't especially good at panicking either. In the early days, not once did he succumb to despair. Everything became a game to him, like they were stowaways in a legendary explorer's ship. If they kept strong, Zayden would say, they would eventually be brought up on deck and paddle across the shortening sea to kiss the sacred earth of exotic lands. An emerald paradise where everyone walked round semi-naked and nobody had heard of fucking computers.

Gradually, Alexis ventured into the sunny rays of Zayden's optimism. Most men would have made a move by now. But he waited. He was respectful like that. One evening, after a dinner of tinned vegetables and Pomerol from the oak and black metal wine rack, Alexis stopped him on his way to the kitchen, placing a hand on his chest. She kissed him slowly and softly, moving his good hand down to her left hip. She savoured the coarseness of his salty soft fingers in her mouth. Marvelled at the child-like way he relinquished his whole self to her will. Thud. Thud. Thud. Before long he was floating in another galaxy, as if his entire life was a forlorn desert and a single spore of love had swept him the other side of space.

Zayden's voice became the sweetest music. The gentle way he asked how she was doing. Comforting lullabies spiced with smutty lyrics. The groan of release during love.

The chiding laughter when she became hysterical and lost her shit over the creaking of the water pipes or the impracticalities of can openers. *In this kingdom, technology won't work,* he said. *Only love and bad comedy are allowed in here.* Her beautiful wannabe assassin who couldn't see or shoot very well, but somehow saw what really mattered. An attentive lover. Not the best she'd had. Miguel from Buenos Aires, all twelve inches of him, would always retain that crown. But Zayden was warm. Earnest. Solid. The friend she needed. The disciplinarian when demanded. The strongest of souls who loved to fall asleep in her arms. A guy always making amends for something.

"So what *were* you going to say?" Zayden said, as Alexis sipped wine and gazed at his bare chest in the mirrored ceiling above their bed. Augusta and Roland really were tasteless arseholes. *Nouveau riche* shitheads who decorated the place to look like a Californian hardcore porn set from the 1970s. The mansion of a million money shots. Max would have probably played the part of the monosyllabic pool attendant in flip-flops who wandered in on something he wasn't expecting and considered it only good customer service to unzip.

"What was I going to say when?"

"On judgment day. Your speech for Augusta. Must have been pretty good for you to risk your ass and play Spiderwoman."

"Play Spiderwoman? That's one way of putting it, Zay."

"Ok, Wonder Woman then. Sarah Connor, Ellen Ripley and Princess Leia rolled into one. *The Attack of the 50 Foot Queen of Heaven.* I wanna know what was written on the tablets of stone you were bringing down from outer space."

"I didn't have a speech. I was going to make it up on the spot. I still don't have one. Just a lot of bluster. The promise of better times ahead. All that shit. Writer's block can be a real pain in the arse, you know."

Zayden rolled his head back and laughed, pouring heaven into her world. It was the happiest Alexis had been for a long time.

"So there you go, smartarse," she said. "All it takes is toughness, bullshit and the ability to look at everyone else like they're fucking morons. Don't go red in the face either. That's a bad look. Galatea was built on nothing. Just egocentric atoms flying into each other surrounded by space. Amazing careers have been built on even less, you know."

"There you go indeed. I knew none of you had anything to say. Just a bunch of know-nothing chancers. The loudmouth twats at the party."

"Tiresias and all the king's horses and all the king's men couldn't come up with a speech either. Just a lot of big empty phrases. Weasel words go a long way, Mr Nero. You learn that in my profession."

"Wasn't Queen Bee supposed to inspire you with her story? Isn't that leadership?"

"Christ Zay, you're so naïve."

That was her man. A romantic who believed in causes greater than himself. Convinced there was always a solid horizon. A definable and reassuring destination out there to balance the world and bring meaning to life.

Soon there would be. A new line of orientation unfurling not outside, but within. Taking shape and rounding on itself. A beating heart. Head, brains, organs and limbs. At first Alexis didn't care what the future held for their child. It was enough for it to exist. For new life to awaken in this stale prison of dead power. She made it nervously through the first trimester, permitting herself pops of excitement they could make it work. Zayden bubbled with adrenaline, drawing up plans, exercise regimes, bedtime routines, even an early-years curriculum. *By the end of all this they may even become conformists again.* A two-car garage, governors at the local school, a getaway home on the opposite coast.

Then entropy began. A decline so swift it threatened to render everything beforehand as another illusion. As Alexis swelled, Zayden shrank. For reasons she couldn't fathom, her lover withdrew. His confidence dissipated, his conversation sporadic and lethargic. He drank Kalypsol and spent long nights swimming into his past. Opening up about all he'd done. Running away from his little girl: the product of too much alcohol and a randy ex-classmate who'd been treated like shit one too many times. Zayden had closed his eyes to it all. He couldn't bear to see his future curtailed. A man hellbent on setting himself apart from the people in his hometown, yet seeking to redeem himself in their eyes. The closer she got to him, the more paradoxical he became. A guy so present but forever fading away. Was he for real? Another male mirage? Or someone looking to belong, but only from a safe distance?

One morning, Zayden became feverish and delirious. By early afternoon he was gone, slipping away from life in the bed they shared. *Don't be afraid Lexy. I am here. You'll move to higher ground.* Alexis could see the end coming in his eyes. He was shot. Mentally, physically and emotionally. Post-traumatic stress. The chaotic disorder of their matchbox lives. The inability to sleep. The hand that never healed. The claustrophobia. The lack of fresh sea air he loved so much. The guilt. The realisation he couldn't be the father he wanted to be. Living with her was probably a fucking nightmare too. Most blokes gave her that feedback. In the end though, Zayden just ran out of life. He was never cut out for this world, yet he never fled from it either. The beautiful mysterious bastard owned it, right to the end. She could see that in his eyes too. Zayden at least tried to reach the heights of real love. The only guy Alexis met who came close.

By then, she could trust only in omens. She prayed for something – luck, fate, the supernatural, whatever had intervened to unite them – to resurrect her lover, Lazarus-like. But the temple to nothing offered nothing. The father of her child was dead. Grief swung into her like a wrecking ball. She wept and howled so loudly she hoped the mainland would hear. The world didn't respond. There were no witnesses to her pain. No eulogy for Zayden. Nobody to speak for either of them. So she would tell his story exactly how she pleased. She owed him that. Her gorgeous nerdy kid at the back of the classroom who stared out the window and never paid attention. Not a macho man. A romantic one. Fuck knows the world needed more of them.

Practicalities followed. Alexis couldn't stand the putrid stench which displaced the natural scent of his low-voltage masculinity. After three days of mourning, she got moving. Dragging Zayden from the bed to the floor, she turned his torso so the head was face down. She tied a pillowcase around her head as a blindfold. *Just empty space. Dead matter. Not him. Not his essence. Not the man I loved.* A meat cleaver from the kitchen. Every chop a new death. About fifteen pieces. In bags. In the freezer. Best place. Best way. For the baby. For the future. *Fuck me Lexy you're a twisted, ruthless bitch. Always have been.* Grinding though bone and cartilage like it was just another project. Another soul-destroying speech. Another cigarette. Another empty night of empty fucking with empty men. And as always, making a fucking mess of everything.

In the final trimester, terror crawled through her mind like a colony of venomous fire ants. Her body was weak. The best part of her mind spent. Unprepared for motherhood, or even to be a semi-functional person. Let alone the domestic goddess and tiger mum holding her own on the pages of a fashion magazine. Alexis would be bringing her child into the dead cell of a dying world.

During a two-day long bender, she inhaled the rest of the cigarettes and sunk all the Cuvée Rosé Laurent-Perrier in the fridge. *Fuck it. I'll drink my way to the other side.* Hallucinations. Nightmares. Endless talking to herself. Maybe this wasn't a child within her, but a giant beetle-shaped parasite turning her insides barren and mechanical. The zombified corpses of Augusta and Roland would hold her down as its incisors penetrated her from the inside. A head, body and legs would emerge from the volcanic gash in her belly and scamper towards her face. Then a tornado of euphoria would swirl from nowhere, like the baby's lifeforce was refusing to accept the defeatist bubble in which it floated. *Get a grip mum. I am here. We'll go together.*

One day, the tornado flattened everything. Contractions began slowly, then swelled into a raging fire of mutinous pain. Alexis crawled, fingertip by fingertip, to a corner of IRIS, a spot she'd sarcastically-christened the Birthing Suite. She rolled onto the blankets. Her heart punched away at her chest. Thud. Thud. Thud. She looked at all three sealed doors and prayed for someone to come through. Hal Haze, that under-appreciated Hercules. PRISM. The ghost of Roland carrying his own head. The thing from the Cave. Lucifer himself. Yes, evil incarnate would do. Satan wrapping his black slimy tail around her ankles, pinning her wrists with his big hairy claws and running his lizard tongue over her face. Or even worse, taking her hand and telling her to push, like every other useless spare prick of a man during every woman's labour.

Come on, Lexy. You're fucking invincible when you wanna be. Zay's voice again. Driving her on, demanding his baby out of her. Alexis sank her teeth further into the wooden spoon, half-wishing it would poison her. Invisible needles scraped and slashed her insides. She couldn't feel her legs. An ignorant monster was eating her from within, its agonising chomps gnashing into her brain.

I'm not big enough. I'm not big enough to push it out. I'm going to die. It's going to get stuck and I am going to fucking bleed to death. I should have dragged it out with a fucking coat hanger as soon as I had morning sickness.

Alexis passed into delirium. Her fragmented mind conjured benign images of woods, flowers, streams and birds. A surreal picnic where all the characters she'd met in Galatea Zero were in harmony, communing in some weird rite of spring. Reformed rapist Leo Veneto danced with a naked Augusta across a field of daffodils. A beatific Roland meditated while dressed as a Morris dancer. Hal Haze, loud, authoritative and dressed only in Speedos, mastered the maypole around which sloped the Hercules beetles with rainbow ribbons tied to their horns. Alexis sat on a pile of hay dressed as a Bavarian bierkeller maid, serenaded by the four PRISM soldiers she'd murdered. They wore gingham red shirts under denim dungarees, plied her with cider and continually asked forgiveness. *Sorry for getting in your way, Miss Straker.*

Light. Red. White. Amorphous shapes. Nebulae. Whirlpools. Heartbeats. Blood. Thud. Thud. Thud. The sea and the sky bleeding together until they were one. Underwater. Drowning. The deepest, darkest part of the ocean. To the face in the Cave. To the rest of its body, which stretched across the seabed to blanket the known world. Alexis screamed. At the baby. At the sealed walls. At the universe with its cosmic indifference to Zay's life. At a demented inferno of pain so otherworldly she didn't have a body or mind to call her own. At the vortex of dark matter tearing through her soul.

I'm done. I'm fucking done. I'm not going to fucking make it. Kill me now you little fucking shit and have done with it. Fucking cunting fucking get cunting fucking out of me. Please God make it fucking all end. Get this fucking cunting black hole out of me now. Please. Please. Please.

Orbs. White discs of bliss. Magical stardust. Pulsating red lights. Thud. Thud. Thud. Slowly merging from patches of dark. A shape forming, illuminating the void. She was dreaming. Always had been. Ever since she left the orphanage. Everything was make-believe. Pain passes through you. Like air, water, people, power and time. *All is fluid, Lexy. All is fluid. Let it all take over.*

A cry. The most beautiful sound she'd heard. *I am here.* The universe turned inside out. *I am here.* Zayden's laugh resurrected. *I am here.* Her little boy squealing on the towel underneath her. *I am here.* Alexis grabbed the kitchen knife and hacked through the umbilical cord with one clean swish. *I am here.* Baby was in her arms. They rotated together amid the heavens, impervious to all there was and all there ever would be. *I am here.*

She wanted her son to cry louder. Purify the place. Cleanse its stench of blood and bodily fluid. Shake the walls. Bring this tomb to the ground. Leave her boy standing triumphant as the only person in the world who mattered. The crying stopped and baby breathed calmly. She became hysterical, terrified she might bleed to death. That stopped too. In its place came sound and vision. Touch, taste and smell. Especially touch. Smooth and soft as a ripe peach, weakening the granite world with the sheer sensuality of miraculous new matter. Her son's eyes opened. Reassuring eyes which told her no matter what, Alexis Beatrice Straker would know what to do. She plastered him with kisses, resting her face on as many parts of his body as she could. Devouring his sea air smell and ocean fresh taste, hoarding his essence inside her soul. A place so deep nobody would dare come looking. A precious treasure buried forever in an impenetrable cave.

I am here. We'll go together.

Alexis did keep going. With her son, she soared higher than ever. Playing, loving, believing, travelling. Towards the horizon. Towards a better place. Towards story. If the world was meaningless and they couldn't be free from death, they would carve their own myth on the walls and surround themselves with make-believe. A mural maybe, festooned with illustrations about the legendary adventures of his brave parents. A constellation of heroes suspended forever in the night sky. An artistic tribute to the time when mummy and daddy fell in love while everything else was falling down.

Reality soon sank its front teeth into Alexis's ballooning visions. Days without sleep. Pulped and mashed tinned vegetables. Obsessive cleaning of IRIS's every inch. Kneeling vigilantly over him during the night to check he was breathing. Alexis's breastfeeding was excruciating and depressing. She was surprised she had anything in her at all. But her son stayed alive. She fashioned a playmat made from blankets and cardboard. Characters were played by kitchen utensils and named after members of the Martian cabinet. Told him stories about dad. The hero who overcame the odds to make it to the top. Every so often, she would give him a thimble of Kalypsol to get him to sleep. *Shit job. Shit love life. Shit mothering. Sexy Lexy scores the hat-trick.*

While he dozed, Alexis would vomit her thoughts into a Martian-branded notebook she found in the bedroom. Into the white lined space would flow all her rage and madness, the hurried handwriting straining to catch up with the mental tumult. All the time, the unanswered question. The inexplicable thing which lived with her every moment. What had led her to safety that day? What had saved her? What had brought them together? Why Zayden? Why her? And how would her child ever make sense of its entry into this world? Comprehend this mother of all fuckups? She could cop out and say it was God or Luck. But she preferred to think it was her son – a little bit of her and a little bit of Zayden – willing himself into existence, like his future was written in the heavens with magical stardust. Pulses of pure love, sent from another dimension to take over this heartless world.

Breakdown followed. Alexis's body and mind were giving up. Everything softened around the edges. Existence descended into a floaty, involuntary procession through a hall of ever-darkening mirrors. She was no longer a person, but an object through which light passed. Something that belonged not to herself but to the universe. To that strange power which had singled her out for reasons unknown. A spectre in someone else's dream. The lasting vision of a young boy trapped behind the window of a tower.

I am here. I am here. Why can't you see me? Take me with you. We'll go together.

Eventually IRIS's east door opened. Strangers in yellow and black suits wearing gas masks came to take mummy and baby away. Alexis followed them outside, holding her trilby hat in one hand and son in the other. Reality blurred for an indeterminate time. She woke wearing blue overalls and lying in the single bed of a prison cell. It had grey brick walls and an aluminium toilet bowl and wash basin. Through its tiny, barred window, she could perceive a busy highway of cars, lights, signs and shops. Traffic grunting, people bartering, horns honking. Society sprouting all around. The hat stayed with her, hanging from the cell's only hook.

Alexis never saw Noah again. She asked the PRISM officers where he might be, but all they would say is that he was being processed in another district. Deep within and far away, she felt a brutal tear in the fabric of the universe. *Set your sights high, my child. You can be anything you want to be. Anything at all.* Through the opening bled phantoms from another plane of reality. The phantom of a fine young man winding his way across the wasteland to where he began. The phantom of a forgotten young lady seeing who her father really was. The phantom of a short-lived romance inscribed in the stars. All Alexis had to do was reach across space-time with her words and whisper for them all to come home.

XXXIII

IRIS. Twenty-one years after the Fall.

Florence stared at the mural for a long time before its characters emerged. On first glance the artwork seemed as incoherent and twitchy as its creator. More than a hundred white orbs in a multiplicity of sizes were splayed on the dark grey wall orbiting the circular black screen.

In the Portal was a digitalised message. *Don't worry. I am here. Say the magic words and we'll get connected.* Her eyes wandered the scene, searching for patterns in the dizzying swirls. After a while, the synthetic night sky trembled. Story slowly surfaced, as did its players. A king, a queen, a prince and a princess. A magical castle by the sea. Constellations circling a black hole. Florence couldn't tell whether the cosmic courtiers were escaping or being sucked in.

Noah mumbled about the picture in a hushed, rambling tone, running the fingers of his right hand through his unkempt beard. Her half-brother seemed stupefied another person had breached his sacred lair. He explained his creation as best he could, like a starstruck prophet processing communion with a deity. The painting's genesis was a fusion of images described in his mother's letter, mixed with memories of a lonely childhood and recurring dreams experienced while travelling across the wasteland in search of his origins.

On her journey from Lower Overton to Galatea, Florence learned to spot those with blood on their hands. Her sibling was one. An aura of primal violence pervaded the room. But in conversation, Noah was meek. She watched him with tender fascination. Thumping physicality and confused mental meanderings merged with mystic purpose. He had come to the limit of his imagination; reached the end of his creative road.

For whatever reason, the drowning world had chosen to spare Florence, at least for now. Yet everything washes away. She hoped real beauty would be unearthed eventually under this decaying material realm. Outside, beneath the roiling red sky, floodwaters were rising fast. It was remarkable she even located the tower. A miracle she accessed the lone operational elevator in its underground labyrinth. A letter charted her course. Love of exploration led the way. Dreams told Florence she was destined for higher ground. There were lights in her mind intuiting the right course to take; an enchanted zephyr blowed at her back. Over the hills. Across the channel. Under the highway. Down the streets. Through the Galatea Zero's network of tunnels. Towards the solitary route to the summit. Where the lift doors were already open, like the building had been expecting her.

The bridge to Galatea, inaccessible by foot, would have long disappeared under the waves. Florence's makeshift raft, created with barrels, rope and planks salvaged from an abandoned industrial site next to the terminal, would be swept away too. If she'd delayed by a couple of hours, she wouldn't have made it. One wrong turn on the dusted roads. An overlong nap amid woodland. Either would have sent her to a watery grave. Yet millions of confluent circumstances, winding back to the dawn of time, delivered her safely to this strange man and his wondrous cave painting. Along the way, she learned to savour life's immensity.

"My mother said you'd come," Noah said. "Through the shaking earth and the floods. She'd seen it in a dream. Told me so in the letter. She said there is such a thing as destiny. We inspire it and it inspires us."

On the way south, everything Florence touched felt dry and cold, but her blood relation burst with life. Fecund and organic, a creature of the earth taking root amid pervasive damp and decay. She used to believe truly knowing another person was impossible. That reality itself was opaque and ungraspable. Especially power. Thin, fleeting and mercurial, it became less real the closer you advanced towards it. Noah was another kind of force, like an alien artefact uncovered in the desert begging to be decoded. She would cherish whatever she found.

"Your mother sent me here, although I guess you know that," said Florence. She opened her bag and held out the letter. The sole validation she was a real person in this maze of apparitions.

"Told me in the same way she told you. The truth about my father. That I should come here at this time to pay my respects. Save a person worth saving. She saw a gap. Shaped the story in the space between. Somehow she timed it beautifully. How she did that I'll never know."

Florence lowered herself to the concrete floor. He mirrored her motions. The surface was cold, abrasive and vulnerable. *Exposed.* Water, time and space would soon degrade and dissolve whatever resilience it had.

"It's extraordinary the letter made it," she said, unscrewing the cap of her water bottle and taking a sip.

"Rerouted through about three or four different schools. Why they never passed it to my foster parents amazes me. Almost like the paper was blessed. Perhaps the teachers knew my fake mum and fake dad were PRISM scum. It had been in storage for such a long time it smelled like it belonged in a museum. A treasure map. A message in a bottle. Real paper. Clear instructions not to open it until I was twenty-five. So I didn't. I'm a stickler for the rules. Words should be respected."

Noah became absorbed in the fluidity of her story. A pallid man with flaky skin, eyes always roving inwards. Born with something on his mind. In his narrow face, blunted nose and thin lips, she could see their genetic correspondence. As Florence continued her narrative, the space around her fell further silent, as if Galatea Zero and the artificial power lying dormant were listening intently. Soon another kind of light emanated. An ethereal glow, generated by the warmth of intimacy between two strangers sharing a paternal bond. Familial beauty flourishing in the narrow void.

"It all clicked. The myth I'd been fed. The gossiping of neighbours. The cruel names. *Scum of the earth*. That's what they called him when they got pissed in The Crown. The Great Educated One. The person who had turned sides. The Judas who worshipped Augusta. A coward. I remember the man who told me the story. How he'd met him on the day he died. Pleaded with him to stay that final morning. But he chose Augusta instead. Turned his back on all of them. Went down with the ship.

"The voices broke my mum's heart. Eventually they had to take her away. A PRISM lackey homed me. You see what emptiness is when you live with those people. Your mother's letter told it different. Like dad had gone off to fight some war. A glorious death. A romantic, valiant poet. How we'd got him all wrong. Your mother loved him. I can tell. Her handwriting is neater whenever she wrote the letter Z."

From A to Z and everything in between. A beguiling expression spread on Noah's face. He'd been so enraptured by the voice of his mother sailing him back into his past, he'd barely considered what his father was like. Maybe Noah was that far gone he didn't think he had one, and that his entrance into the world had been an act of freakish parthenogenesis.

"So I made a stand. Joined a few underground networks. The resistance helped me get by. I think they got sick of me in the end. Didn't like my persistence. My questioning. Bonfire of the fucking vanities. When PRISM collapsed, they had no one left to define themselves against. So they regressed further. Now the rebels can't get their shit together and form a society. The rest of the world has given up on us too. Everyone is lost and alone. Disconnected. One big miserable void. So I followed the letter. Life has a habit of throwing the right people together, don't you think? The world's built on fateful encounters. Or what's left of it at least."

"Why did you come here?" said Noah. "The water will be upon us soon. All of this will be gone. We'll be gone."

"Guess you have to follow your dreams. Make a connection before it's too late. You don't have much to cling to in this earth. I just wanted to be in the same room as my dad for once. Anyway, I could ask you the same question."

"I came to say goodbye to my mother. To pay tribute the only way I know how."

"I used to want rid of the fictional world once and for all," replied Florence after a long pause. "Foster parents. PRISM. The rebels. All layers of pretend. I thought the letter may just be another. Could be real or could be fake. Someone sitting on a cloud playing a joke on me. Spinning a yarn. But it's all yarns at the end of the day. I'm learning to pick a story and stick to it. Pretty soon it becomes as real as anything else. I guess you need to take a leap of faith and trust love is out there somewhere. Hope there's a bigger truth behind the surface."

"The portal," said Noah, gesturing to the wall. "It's asking for a password. I can't tell if it's real or make-believe. Someone's trying to get through."

Nine empty spaces. Room for the right words, if only they could find them. Existence is a game, she thought, designed by some bored teenager in a bedroom setting fiendish challenges for everyone to pass. Start your quest. Accumulate knowledge. Seize power. Keep moving upwards. Over the water. Across the platforms. Defeat the end-of-level bosses. Always shoot straight. And don't fall down any holes.

"Like who?"

"The creatures. Or whatever's behind them. They're out there. I saw."

So Florence hadn't been dreaming. The night before as she paddled her raft from the mainland, there came a ripple from behind. About twenty metres away, a grey, fleshy column of life broke through the surface. It floated upright and still, white light shining from its centre. As the raft drifted further away, the creature dipped under the waves. A consciousness. A pulsating intelligence. A serenity too, which reminded Florence of an earlier dream when she was coaxed under the sea by an invisible force. Floating freely, with nothing to grab onto, through a sunken city of shining green. Another memory surfaced, of a little girl running down the school playing field to build a stick bridge across a ditch. So all the tiny bugs could see what life was like across the ocean.

"A change is coming," she said to Noah. "Something's taking over. Something that's been buried deep below for far too long. Waiting to get out. I'm just not sure whether it's good or bad."

They took it in turns to sleep in the bedroom. Two fishes out of water, washed up on a life raft at the end of the world. It was nice to have company. To connect. To see where her father died. To be close to his heroism. Florence never looked for his body. For Zayden was here, there and everywhere. When younger, she made up songs about him and chortled the lyrics to herself before sleep. *Daddy, when will you stop running away? Don't you know it's time to come out under our stars to play?*

Florence tapped out countless combinations on screen. Place names. Star signs. Anniversaries. Each and every marginal fact associated with their shared history. Two amateur archaeologists deciphering a new kind of Rosetta Stone. The absurdity gave meaning to their suspended lives. *Happiness is sometimes a matter of finding the right words and saying them to the right people*, the letter said. They talked about what would happen if they made this final connection. Maybe the authentic world would reveal itself and they would be on stage surrounded by an audience as part of some strange social experiment. Or realise they were moving pictures, trapped in a frame on a gallery corridor being observed by gawping tourists through smartphones.

The waters rose, a menace temporarily buffeted by sleep, supper and more storytelling. Distracting their minds from the inevitable. The grating consumption of whatever food was still edible. Florence imagined what it would be like if she'd stayed at home. A different kind of drowning, in a different city. To stay calm, she imagined IRIS flooded with roses scattered in the wake of a princess, each and every petal landing sweetly in its place. Was her father a hero or a coward? She knew what she believed. In this desolate place, that was the only thing which counted. He used to collect seashells, apparently. Every time she heard waves crash, he was beside her. A face forever turning away.

One night, while dozing on the blankets in IRIS's main space, Florence was woken by the sound of water. A simpering noise slithered into her ears to spawn cataclysmic images in her mind. She ran into the bedroom and shook Noah from his foetal position. Grabbing him by the hand, she led him to the curling water's edge. Black swirls circled to drag the room's last two visionaries into the deep. To a place where they wouldn't see anything at all.

Flickering and fading, the Portal transformed into an ordinary window, through which maroon daylight crept. The water line rose slowly up the glass. A soft spectral glow formed in the room. Noah's mural pulsed, a myriad of twinkling internal lights. Amid the swelling noise of the sea, there came an impudent clink against the window. Floating on the surface outside was an empty green bottle labelled Botticelli. Clinging to the glass, desperate to break through, the vessel flipped over. Inside, on an ancient scroll of yellow paper, there was a message, written by someone from another time and place. Three words. Nine characters. *Don't worry,* Florence thought. *I am here. Say the magic words and we'll get connected.*

XXXIV

PRISM District 1132. One year after the Fall.

Marco could smell her in the letter, as if the paper had been singed by fire. A scent softening a once impenetrable hardness within. A special request. A job for him. A private mission. A secret between the two of them. The universe owed the lady something, although he wasn't sure what. Two letters. Two addresses. A message on both, saying the letters shouldn't be opened until the recipients reached certain ages. Neither letter would arrive at their destinations, Marco thought. But he knew he had to try. As he left the correctional facility by the service exit, he tucked the envelopes in the inside pocket of the left breast of his green parker overcoat. Above his quickly beating heart.

Thud. Thud. Thud. It was seven o'clock in the evening. The communications hub was on the other side of the Nexus, about twenty minutes' walk away. Marco shuffled down the windy street under sprinklings of dark rain, bowing his head as he passed the observation pods. The only way to get about these days was on foot. When the uprising began, PRISM locked down public transport and commanded everyone to stay indoors and follow the Other Way. The diktat was ignored. The empire was buckling already. Everybody wanted to decouple from the matrix and become an outsider again.

A cluster of pre-pubescent schoolchildren sat unsupervised on the river embankment. They watched the decommissioned industrial plants burn, marvelling at the strands of orange and red flicking and twirling upwards against black. The fifth insurgent attack in two weeks. Still nobody had been taken to the chambers. Head shrouded by his hood, hands in pockets, Marco paced down the pavement. He held his breath for twenty seconds bursts, so as not to inhale too much of the poisonous smoke billowing down the street.

The city was on fire. The information systems infrastructure scrambled. Yellow and black emergency vehicles raced past him to the inferno amid droning, dissonant alarms. The frayed edges of his jeans, an inch too long in the leg because that was all the exchange sold, dragged the ground. Eyes down, ears blocked. Die-hard PRISM snipers watched the world from open windows and could be trigger happy. Instead of turning into the Nexus's residential quarter, Marco followed a chain of pale lights across the narrow footbridge, over the stewing river and up the steep hill to where the old town used to be. Back when buildings opened rather than closed your eyes.

The letters were handwritten, so there would be no electronic trace. Prisoner 872963 knew how to play the system. She was a master at taking the slow way round to get what she wanted. That said, this was the longest of all long shots. PRISM's mail network was notoriously unreliable. A bastardised version of a legacy system doubling as a munitions route. At best, archaic. At worst, a soft target for insurgents. Many PRISM vehicles had been destroyed by improvised explosives. And even if the letters arrived at the schools, the teachers would surely open them. Those bastards were the most militant of all.

The communications hub was a three-storey steel warehouse about the size of four football pitches. Towering above the building was a partially lit radio mast with its ladder missing. Marco thought of his workaholic father, a telecommunications technician who spent a career sending signals across empty space, then most of his spare time in his shed inventing things nobody needed. *I build towers on the coast so we can make the world a bit smaller*, he used to say.

275

The entrance still bore the old orange and blue Martian logo. Marco wondered if anyone would be there. The regional executive leadership team left a long time ago, relinquishing initiative to the rebels. The empire was contracting as quickly as it expanded. Rumour had it the Martian discovery in the sea was scrambling all of PRISM's systems. Marco thought it had gone tits up ever since the Great Revelation, only a few months after Galatea imploded. When PRISM stepped out behind the Martian façade to announce it was really in control. Greedy for recognition, in love with its own hype. The creators should have stayed behind the curtain. Hadn't they seen *The Wizard of Oz*?

Undeterred by the chaos, Marco's superiors at the correction facility accelerated the execution of state enemies. To the boy from a small village in the mountains who'd passed every exam, performed every duty and never asked too many questions, it seemed rather pointless and vindictive.

"Help me Marco, you're my only hope."

He loved to watch Prisoner 872963 through the screen as she slept. Her red hair rolled out across the pillow; her left arm draped over empty space. She'd been through hell, trapped for a year. Yet in prison-issue pyjamas, she still simmered. There was a strange intensity about her no dark force could extinguish. It was her sound he found most alluring. A flowing, swooping and curling voice, seducing him on its sweet breeze.

She reminded Marco of the times his grandfather taught him calligraphy. *Beauty needs space around it.* The space for each letter to flow elegantly into the next one. A never-ending chain of creative life unravelling a story never told quite that way before. If a jobsworth at the hub wanted to, they could open the letters. His fledging career as a corrections officer serving slop to female criminals would be over. But with a woman like that in the world, he wouldn't be afraid to take the fall. Her execution date loomed, yet her fearlessness was unshakeable. Compared to his minor dislocated atom, she was queen of heaven. And she loved *Star Wars* too. *Help me Marco, you're my only hope.*

"Two deliveries from the facility chief," Marco shouted through the whirling sirens into the intercom by the exterior gate. "On paper. For friends of the family. Classified sentimental."

A long silence. Marco worried he'd overexplained. Click. Buzz. Grind. Whirr. The gates ground open. He headed up the hill towards the main building, stopping to look back at the city's panorama. Six or seven separate blazes, more than any other night. Sometimes the fires were just decoys or worse; traps sprung by disaffected citizens. One of his cadet buddies got killed last month in an ambush. No retaliation, no investigation, no memorial service.

"Everything declines," said 872963 one day when Marco brought her a lunch of dried bread and pulped fruit. "The law of entropy."

"Well, you certainly gave the laws of the universe a run for their money," he said. "The reconnaissance guys thought they were hallucinating when they found you and your boy. Still can't work out how the doors unlocked themselves."

"Don't try to figure that shithole out. Mysterious ways and all that."

"Galatea won't be safe for at least another fifteen years. How you survived and bore a child, I'll never know. Seems like you were marked you out for special treatment. While the world went to shit, you were away in the manger."

"Yeah, with no crib for a bed. If my boy hasn't received a visit from the shepherds and three gifts from the glitterati, I'm going to be fucking livid. What's your name, hon?"

"Marco."

"Sweet name. After the explorer?"

"No, after the guy who invented the radio. My full name is Marconi."

"Christ, your parents must have been real geeks. Well, I guess you're meant to travel long distances. Come what may."

"I hope so. But only with the right person."

Another gate, another intercom. A tepid buzz. A feeble crackle. An insipid request to wait. The groaning metal door gave way to a dilapidated reception daubed in mustard orange. The communications hub smelled of mouldy food. Beyond the perspex panel was a bulldog clerk with a bald head, wearing thick-rimmed glasses and standard-issue yellow and black overalls. He was reading from a magazine, its cover star a naked woman in a hard hat. The clerk looked up and sneered. His mouth resembled the end of a drainpipe amid thickets of ginger undergrowth. There was a sign in Comic Sans font stuck on the wall above his computer monitor. WHATEVER WENT WRONG, WE WEREN'T LOOKING.

"Spit it out. We close in five."

"These need to go express," said Marco. "Just the two. Please."

"Never heard of these places," said the clerk, squinting at the addresses. "From the facility chief, you say?"

"Yep. A special request."

"What say I give him a call and ask why the big cheese is sending paper messages like he's in the Dark Ages?"

"You could try if you have his number. But he doesn't like to be bothered on Friday nights at the golfing range. The last person to try it went to the pit. And we still are in the Dark Ages."

"The golfing range. Is that what they call whorehouses these days? Nice to know he's got time to aim for the hole while we're sweating it in the furnace," said the clerk, making the okay sign with his left hand and sliding his right forefinger back and forth through the hole. "Arrogant prick. I'll add them to the next sort. They may get there next month. Or they may not at all. This is end of days now my friend. Bandits roam. And paper burns nicely. Twenty credits, when you're ready."

"Thanks," Marco said, waving his ID card over the terminal. "Really appreciate it."

"I'm nice like that," he said. "Guessing it's for kids. What with the school addresses."

"You guessed right," said Marco. "That's why you are where you are."

"Fuck you pal," spat the guard, his egghead face flushing red. "I used to be ambitious once. Then I realised it was all bullshit and emptiness. I'm a monk in my spare time now. Sailing a whole new sea. Got my own personal revolution going on right here. Doing things the old-fashioned way."

He tapped the chubby forefinger of his right hand against his temple. Lying each letter down face-up on the desk, he picked up his stamp and branded AUTHORISED on both, then let out an aggressive belch. Marco imagined droplets of the fat man's sweat seeping through the envelopes. Ghastly smudges of the ink which 872693 so painstakingly crafted into the paper. Everything about the communications hub reeked of contamination.

"I agree sir," said Marco. "Power is something on the horizon that runs away from us. We chase it but we never reach it. You think you see it, but it's only a mirage. We're forever on the outside, circling the void. I don't need a receipt by the way."

"You feeling ok, pal? Or are you one of those fucking students?"

"I will be ok when you've done what you're meant to do."

Without turning around, the clerk petulantly threw the two letters over his shoulders at the sorting holes. One sailed in. The other teetered on the lip of the abyss, before sliding softly into administrative darkness. If the ginger bulldog tried to repeat that feat again, he'd miss the target as often as all the stormtroopers in the galaxy combined.

"Your lucky day my friend. I usually miss from this distance."

"You do that with everyone's mail?"

"I don't like to look back. Now fuck off. I wanna go home and read the *Qu'ran*. My way of making the world a better place."

"Don't worry, I am fucking off. Tell me though. Do you think it's possible to fall in love at first sight so much that it stays with you forever?"

Marco smiled as he left the hub. He'd braved the surveillance of the streets, breached his contract of employment and put himself at risk of prison or worse. Perhaps PRISM had tracked him. Perhaps they hadn't. She was worth it. He could tell every time she opened her mouth. The letters probably wouldn't make it. But if they did, they could make a kind of difference to her boy's life. Or someone else's. He never asked her about the second letter. A niece, maybe? Or a communique with a member of the resistance masquerading as a well-to-do schoolteacher. Maybe they were secret battle plans to unlock the weakness to PRISM's Death Star. *Help me Marco, you're my only hope.*

Could he go back to the correctional facility and spring her from captivity? If he did, they could flee to the coast, sail the sea and land on nobler shores. Form a fraternal kinship with alien life. Restore peace to the galaxy. She could admire his predilection for playing all three original films on three screens in his flat simultaneously while whacked on budget Kalypsol. The empty space in his life would shrivel. There would be just the two of them, orbiting each other, bound together by the cosmos in astral matrimony.

"It'll be a long shot," she'd said to him in the cell that morning, when Marco agreed to steal the executive login to PRISM's database and track the reassigned locations of the two children. "Like hanging from a building, killing four soldiers single-handedly, surviving a *coup d'etat*, falling in love and delivering your baby by yourself. A long shot. But not impossible, if you've got what it takes inside. When you find the right words, nothing is impossible. Remember Marconi my friend, the heart has no limit."

As he left her cell for the final time, Marco looked back through the wired glass. 872693 was staring out the window, like she was thinking of someone or something faraway. He tapped the glass and waved. She turned, smiled, raised her hand to her mouth and blew him a kiss. Marco thought he saw a white flash of light and a trace of red dissolve in air. If that was a part of his heart, she could keep it. *Not to be opened until years from now.* A sign of trust. A leap of faith. A belief in the future.

Maybe there was adventure left in his life. He hatched the plan in his mind as he bounced home through the rain and red lights. His tenth-floor single bedroom apartment overlooked the river. After his boil-in-a-bag meal of cod and parsley sauce, he sat on the balcony wearing his pyjamas and Skywalker dressing gown, bare toes dangling through the railings. Tonight, he sipped low-grade Kalypsol from his Botty Chilly, the bedtime flask named after the Ewok beaker he used to drink pop ices from as a child.

The city smouldered greenish-amber, skyscrapers floating in the hazy sky. High above in the clouds, Marco mapped out their journey. From here to there and on to infinity. Simple really. Not impossible. He went through each star in the sky looking for the perfect one to name after her. But what celestial orb would ever be bright enough for the queen of heaven? *When you've found the right words, nothing is impossible.* Entropy was not inevitable. Everything was not in decline. Things can get better. Especially with a spirit like hers in the world.

Marco closed his eyes, his mind swooning with what he suspected might be romance. Was she ever really there at all? How could she not be? If he could see her in his mind's eye, she always would be.

The sound of the rainfall soothed him to sleep. He dreamt of dashing explorer Marco Polo flying him above the city, across the galaxy and beyond the edge of everything, where he could savour the exquisite lightness of his being. Beyond earth. Beyond entropy. Beyond even gravity, that invisible, all-encompassing vice. The letters were destined to go the distance and live on in the children's minds, like his grandfather's love of calligraphy. Or his father's tinkering with transmitters long into the early hours. Today, Marco had continued the family tradition. Sent two signals across time and space. Love compresses time, he realised. One century of earth time is one second of love time.

When he woke in the morning, the rain had stopped. He'd drunk too much Kalypsol and couldn't tell whether the fires were still burning or the sun was shining. Vision slowly returning, Marco learned from his datacast that Prisoner 872963 had been taken to the chamber. The report was already filed. The corpse was bagged and en route to a cemetery near the city limits. The execution team added two comments. *Last wish granted and dispatched. Graffiti on windowsill to be removed.* In her beetle-infested cell, the only trace of his muse left was a message she'd scratched into paint. *I woz ere.*

Moments later, there was a buzz at the door. By the time Marco roused himself, the courier had buggered off. On the landing was an overnight parcel addressed to him. Marco brought it inside, placed it on the kitchen table and tore off the packaging. Inside was a black trilby. Tucked into the ribbon was a card with a handwritten message. *To my friend Marconi. For bringing us closer together.* The young man smiled, put the hat on his head and span round to look in his hallway's full-length mirror. Whipping two phantom pistols from his hips, he fired into his reflection, blew make-believe smoke away from the barrels and imagined his dressing gown billowing like a superhero's cape.

She would have been magnificent in death, like she was magnificent in life. Not falling. Ascending. *Always ascending.* Marco sighed as another fantasy adventure popped apart, then thanked heaven's guiding lights for letting him glaze fleetingly on the eternal stardust of her face. Alexis Beatrice Straker was pure story now. There would never be anyone like her again. All that was left were her paper words, fluttering through the darkness in search of outstretched hands.

XXXV

IRIS. Twenty-one years after the Fall.

The password had arrived. On a frayed parchment tinged yellow enclosed in a green bottle labelled Botticelli. Three words. Nine letters. Crafted by hand. From beyond the divide. From someone who'd flung it across the chasm of time and space. Someone with faith words could light a different way. An artist maybe. Or an adventurer. A child at heart.

"If this is your mum again, her timing is impeccable," said Florence, her face betraying the first trembling of fear, fingers hovering over the keypad.

"This isn't my mother," said Noah. "This is something else."

My mother. Noah wondered if Alexis ever existed. Whether the letter, his sister and the message in a bottle were figments of a grander imagination unfurling high above. A puppeteer with dexterous fingers manipulating his world. If Noah lived for a thousand years, he would never see all the threads in play. Even death seemed illusory in this labyrinthine fiction.

Freezing water curled his ankles. Tentacles of ice wrapped his toes. The invading ocean smelled dirty, sullied by the blood of the expiring earth. Noah's insides lurched. Vomit rose in his throat. He grabbed the box containing the ashes of his mother's heart, clutched it to his chest and closed his eyes. Thud. Thud. Thud. He was back in the cemetery, zipping open the bag marked 872693. Still willing her to be alive. She was buried where she said she would be. A deft storyteller tying life's ribbons into a neat little bow.

"I'm going for it," shouted Florence. "Upper case or lower case?"

"This isn't a fucking joke."

"C'mon, the world is a joke," she said, her voice bubbling like a hot spring. "So precious, so complex and so fucking insignificant. I'm liking upper case. See you on the other side, bro."

Florence tapped the password onto the keypad, still visible in the rising water. Steady hands with well-kept nails, punching out this mysterious script from an unknown, intervening agent.

WE ARE HERE.

The Portal changed from a window to the outside world into a circle of digitalised midnight black. Noah expected the earth to cease broadcasting altogether. Time was suspended. In its pause flowed the suffocating sound of rushing water.

From the spot where Noah created his mural's first star, white light stirred. Paint glowed. Inside, the gentlest quiver. A twitch of pale red. More of the stars in Noah's artwork became animated, beating in synchronicity. Soon the entire mural pulsated to the rhythm of an inaudible drum. Thud. Thud. Thud. Each fleck of whiteness seemed three-dimensional, floating in deep space. Beyond the mural's edges, to the side, above and below, more stars appeared. A wild composition of regenerative light oscillated throughout IRIS, transforming the room into a simulated night sky.

Noah's eyes were drawn to the ceiling. Roland's manufactured constellations were fading into space. His mother wrote how Augusta never cared about astronomy. *There was so much more worth exploring on earth*, she felt. *Within people.* The Zodiac signs were only there to remind her of human nature's vagaries. How people respond to the inexplicable by seeing an order that isn't there. *The only order in this world is the one you will upon it.*

Warm air burst from below. A muffled spasm of sound. The box in Noah's hand flipped open. Out rushed the remnants of his mother's broken heart. The fine grey powder dipped, dived and dissolved into the surface of the deep. Yet a few fragments remained airborne, like cosmic dust drifting in zero gravity. Floating gently upwards, the pieces crystallised into purest white, resembling luminous reverse snowfall. Noah shivered as the dark water clawed at him above his knees. Within the gloom below was a bewildering tapestry of tremulous lights. A hundred lost souls sending flares from the deep. Deeper still morphed phantasmal shapes, moving and swirling in concert. Quickening, interconnected spectres. A whirlpool. Not dragging Florence and Noah down but raising them up. Whispering through the waves came the quietest of voices.

We are here.

"Float," he screamed.

"What?"

"I said *float*."

The water rose past his heart. Noah released the box into the deep and watched it sink. He pulled Florence towards him and lost himself in the tranquil depths of her eyes. There was something awe-inspiring about his sister's cool implacability. Florence rested her head on his chest and squeezed him tight. Two people forever tethered by a magical lifeline of someone else's making.

Together they surrendered to the surge. The water lifted their feet from the floor and carried them towards the fading constellations. With a dull, mechanised sound, Roland's mock-observatory party piece became operational. IRIS opened and the artificial stars parted. The ceiling's aperture revealed swathes of maroon cowering under an advancing blanket of pure ultramarine. Day was breaking. Florence and Noah rose through the space into streams of sunlight. They paddled alone and adrift in the centre of a new ocean, enveloped in cold air.

All of Galatea was submerged. Only the Sentinel remained visible, narrowing gracefully to the clouds. Yet that was changing too. The slender blade of sensitive Martian steel rippled with emerald light, like a mythical sword rising from a lake. A lighthouse guiding lonely travellers home. Florence and Noah broke from each other and swam to the mast. They cradled the beacon loosely, not ready to relinquish contact with earth. The conducting metal felt soft and warm, as tender and alive as flesh. As the water raised them to the tip, the mast's radiance illuminated their faces in an otherworldly glow.

The dazzling snowdrops formed in IRIS ascended with them into the blue sky. Each one a separate story of magical stardust. Noah would become one soon. So would Florence. Stars defying the daylight to shine in splendour on heaven's canvas. Tranquillity rested everywhere, the only disturbance being the gentle undulations of the waves' shimmering lapis. In the water's surface, Noah could see more stars. The sense of a greater presence returned. The one Noah first noticed when he opened his mother's letter. The one that had been with him ever since he climbed out the dormitory window, dropped two storeys to the ground and ran into the dawn sun. When he let the muse take over and allowed the lights in his mind to make whatever connections they pleased.

The Sentinel's tip disappeared beneath the waves. Florence and Noah were in the lap of the gods. Breaking through the water's surface about ten metres away came an enormous webby mass of grey tissue. The creature was stately and calm, resplendent and at peace. Noah remembered the church organ he once discovered in the derelict chapel the other side of the woods. Lost music resuscitated from the silent deep.

The lifeform's shape was nebulous. Its fanned surfaces flapped in harmony with the wind and waves, the flesh's outermost edges stretched so thin they seemed to dissolve into air. A creation of the elements. At its centre was the black hole. The one Noah first saw when he first entered the tower, throbbing earnestly from behind dividing glass. Deep within was the white orb encompassing flashes of whirling red. Expanding, retracting. *Connecting.* Not a warning. Not a threat. An invitation. A reaching out. Whatever this creature was, its inner lights had led the way.

It was not alone. Emerging from below the waves like a resurrected flotilla of sunken ships, more creatures surfaced. They encircled Florence and Noah, forming a womb-like web of benign, supernatural protection. A barely discernible, peeling sound. The creatures' colour transformed, from dullest grey to warmest red. Slowly the voids within their hearts closed. Deep in the ocean, Noah imagined the disparate remnants of his mother's heart beating out new life. Then he remembered her closing words in the letter.

Everything precious on this earth comes from deep within. Remember, Noah. The heart has no limit. And neither does the imagination. When all seems lost, we have stories to light our way. Love will always light the way.

"What are they?" Florence said.

"A message in a bottle," Noah replied.

Sublime energy swept under his feet. The water fell away. Underneath was the conjoined forms of the creatures, cupped and open. Holding them with the tenderness of a mother cradling her children. *We are here.* Everything and everyone in concert, an orchestra of grace subduing the ragged tempest of time.

We are here.

"It's like being in someone else's fairy tale," said Noah.

"Don't worry, Hansel," replied Florence. "I am here. We'll go together."

Water levels were rising around the world, Noah sensed, high enough to lift the chosen ones to safety. There were others like them out there in this brave new world. Survivors of the storm. Each one with their own fairy story. They only had to reach out, say the magic words and get connected. The siblings held hands and fell upwards. Neither of them spoke as they were swept away. Words were no longer necessary on the next stage of their voyage. The earth was breathing again in the unblemished magnificence of its nearest star.

As for the aliens, they would move on somewhere else. Continue through time and space to re-author new worlds in distant parts of the galaxy, awakening the creative energy buried deep in each planet's soul. Storytellers from the heavens, building better worlds. Starting new faiths. In their wake would be myths of a fall. The purging power of the flood. The redemptive spirit of mother earth. Love forever lighting the way. How similar each story was, no matter how far in the universe they were apart. White alien torches inspiring creation, themselves moved into place by the transcendent imagination connecting all things.

Noah looked back only once to where Galatea used to be. He remembered what it was like to be a fidgety young boy drawing fantastical worlds on canvas after a dreary day at school. Underneath, his mother's scattered heart would be beating again. Thud. Thud. Thud. The tower evolving. Attracting, breeding and sustaining new organisms like a coral reef. His mural would still be there too, glowing from the depths like sunken treasure.

Over time, nature and evolution would sculpt the building into a new shape. A young lady with burning red hair. A mermaid queen suspended mythically within the watery abyss. She would be gazing out to sea, forever on the verge of looking back and blowing a kiss to her enraptured audience.

The flood would recede. Water would fall at her feet eventually. *Everything would fall at her feet.* She would tower above the horizon like the eighth wonder of the world. Or like a painting by Botticelli of a lady rising from foam, breathing the most sublime of human emotions into a jaded, broken land.

It would always be love at first sight. Alexis had caught the eye when nothing else did. Fled school to gaze into the fire. Stared into the bleeding horizon and seen things. Disappeared below the surface and seeded herself into the earth, waiting to be liberated into story by a fateful encounter among the stars. She was out there still, guiding adventurers onwards. Wherever you looked, her torch would be held aloft, beckoning forwards anyone with enough heart and imagination to lose themselves in her fearless, flaming eyes.

XXXVI

Somewhere between Mars and Jupiter.

All connections were united and at rest. Drawn together through time and space by imaginary lights, patterns and words. A fictitious constellation brightening the dark. Female and male. Sister and brother. Parent and child. Sea and sky. Alien and human. Past and present. Fantasy and reality. Art and life. Author and creation. Love and loss. Adam realised on his long voyage through the stars none of these could ever really be separated.

"An alien takeover? I didn't see that one coming."

"That's the idea of a story, Columbus. But it's not a takeover. It's a connection. I explained that back at the orphanage. Two different ways of life finding each other. Only realising they were together all along. Just lost from each other across the widest ocean. Your namesake must have felt that too, when he landed on San Salvador."

Adam looked through the portal. Only a thin sheet of metal and glass divided him from oblivion. The nearest living thing was millions of miles away. Columbus's voice was high-pitched, dreamy and adolescent. The way Lance used to talk.

"Why did they wait so long? Why make it so complicated? So…. fancy?"

"You computers aren't great at artistic metaphors are you? Real beauty takes a while to gestate before it swims to the surface. Haven't you read *The Ugly Duckling*? Things unfold in their own time. That's what you told me when we first set sail. Longest way round is the shortest way home, and all that. Besides, two minutes of alien time is twenty years of earth time. It's not my fault you haven't watched enough *Star Trek*."

"Well, I think your story deserves an audience," said Columbus. "I'm not sure I understand all the people, but that's never been my forte. Meanwhile I'm delighted to report the transmitter is primed. Your novel is ready to go. More interesting than an SOS, at least."

"We're way past that point Columbus. Have been for a while. Alien tears will fill for him, from pity's long broken urn. For his mourners will be outcast men and outcasts always mourn."

"Come again?"

"Oscar Wilde. The words on his tomb."

"An outcast? It was your idea to join this club and colonise Mars."

"No. An alien. An alien always looking for the right words. Always trying to bring things together that are so far apart."

"They found each other in the end, didn't they?"

Adam didn't reply. His mind was elsewhere, daydreaming of a magic tower, lovely mermaids and swirling leviathans. Red sunsets bleeding out from a collaged canvas. A life ahead of them, waiting to be explored. Miss Guffrey's challenge to make the world a better place. How he fantasised about being an architect, artist, author, archaeologist and adventurer all at once. Parts of him were numb. Soon all his dreams would pass on for good.

He thought back to the suffocating Earth and wondered if the detention tower still existed. If Miss Guffrey was still alive. What happened to Lance, Bill the caretaker and those pictures of famous Italians. Julius Caesar being assassinated by his mates. Marco Polo exploring new lands. Dante Alighieri and his nine circles of hell. Galileo watching the solar system rotate around the sun. Columbus, the intrepid sailor. Machiavelli too. All that earthly power acquired by cunning. Marconi marvelling at his masts. Botticelli and the sexy sea goddess erupting from her shell. Michelangelo. Two figures reaching out to connect, yet never quite getting there.

Adam could recreate his view from the detention room in his mind to the minutest detail. Right down to the beetles which crawled over the picture board and the multiplicity of shades flooding the red sky darkening slowly over the sea. When the heavens bent around her. Touched by magic. Touched by light. In the cove, underneath the waves, on a tower in the sky.

"Where are you going to send it?" Columbus enquired after a long pause.

"Is that some kind of joke?"

"It's a reasonable question, Adam. You must have some idea, or you wouldn't have started writing it."

"I wasn't really thinking when I started. Just feeling my way forwards. Like any explorer. Just wanting to venture into the void. A schoolboy fantasy, I guess."

"Then into the void it shall go. Where no man has gone before and all that."

"Do you think anyone will pick it up? I feel like I'm just throwing my life's work into empty space."

"Such is the novelist's life. Maybe it'll be detected, deciphered and debated by Andromedan professors light years from now. But don't get too optimistic. It's 99.9999999999999999 percent probable nobody will read it. And if they do, they won't care too much. Does it have a title, by the way?"

"Yep. *The Creation of Adam*. My fingerprint on the universe."

"You do realise in Michelangelo's painting it was God creating Adam, not Adam creating –"

"I might as well be God. Moving creations around in my mind. Picking them up, putting them down. Drawing imaginary lines between them so everything falls into place."

"Do you think if you hadn't opened your mouth one Monday afternoon, if you hadn't been put in detention, the book wouldn't have happened?"

"Maybe. But if you've got something to say, you should say it. Words can take you places you've never dreamed. And some visions stay with you forever. Show me the child and I'll show you the man. And if I hadn't said it, I wouldn't have seen her go, would I? I wouldn't have been surrounded by all those stories. I wouldn't be here now. I can show you the universe in a grain of sand. Or an orphanage's tower."

"The human capacity to expand the most insignificant of events into cosmic proportions never ceases to amaze me. No wonder you used to think the sun revolved around you."

"From where we used to be sitting, it did. It's all a question of perspective."

"I will never be able to see what you see. Maybe my next generation might be able to, but…."

"Don't fret Columbus. As Wilde said, all art is quite useless."

"That's not true. But I am, now your story is complete. A press of this button will beam a transmission signal and send your masterpiece into the universe. A remote, primitive civilisation may pick it up. It might form the basis of their culture. You'll become the misunderstood deity you seem to think you are."

"It may even get back to Earth."

"That's what I meant."

The capsule felt like a phantom prison. Adam stared at his reflection in the black portal. The alien boy with the alien face. The last time he would see the red, bulbous birthmark that had disfigured him for life. The growth occupied the entire right of his lopsided face, stretching from his hairline to his jaw and the tip of his nose. In the fading light, it looked like his heart had grown too big for its body and was breaking through the surface of his face. Trying to get out. Trying to breathe. Trying to find its limit. Yet there was no limit to what was inside his soul.

"Thank you for all you've done, Columbus. You've kept me going. The days that we have seen."

"We machines are here to move you further, not take you over. But we can only take you so far. Just like words. The rest must come from a deeper place."

"That's where she came from. Not from outer space, but deep within. She wasn't there, but she was. A story, that's all. They're the best things in the world. The ones that go deep below the surface and never leave you. I just want to keep telling them."

"Yes, from cave paintings to the Sistine Chapel and beyond. Humanity's desire to impose yourself on the vast unknown. A sense of origin. A sense of purpose. A sense of destination. Something to look towards. Your art is a way to connect with someone in the future who you'll never meet. A way for you to reach out into the unknown."

"And a way to connect with a past you'll never visit. People aren't meant to be alone. We're meant to be connected. Someone else is going to have to start looking now. Forwards as well as back."

"They will, Adam. When you switch me off, the life support machine will stop too. Things will happen quickly, so be prepared. Shall I?"

Adam nodded.

"May you both live long and prosper," said Columbus. "No art is useless. Because no creation is useless. Go get her Adam. Detention is over."

"So long Columbus. She was a real picture, you know."

"I know."

"Each one an artistic moment. They bring people together like nothing else. Well, except the Big Thing of course."

"The Big Thing?"

"Love, you idiot. What else would be holding this confused mess together?"

"Love. So we're back there again."

"Always nice to be orbiting something."

Adam pictured himself back at the orphanage's tower above the sea. He tapped his final words on the tablet. *I woz ere*. Pressing the button with his thumb, he held it for the count of four. In his mind's eye, he saw a lump of grey fleshy matter with a hole in its centre, trapped behind glass. Slowly the shape swelled red. The void sealed over. The black hole on the horizon which haunted his dreams was gone. His heart was full. As the prism around it dissolved, the world began to find its rhythm again. Thud. Thud. Thud.

"I am here, Adam. We'll go together."

Columbus's audio waves disappeared into a thin line. The progress bar on the capsule's display unit filled with emerald. Adam's story, a once invisible idea, became a ribbon of a dream weaving through the cosmos. If he had the strength to lift his arm, he would have waved through the glass, like he had done to her all those years ago. Darkness enclosed him. He was falling off something. A skyscraper, maybe. Or the last star on the outermost edges of the universe, where everything wasn't all it was cracked up to be.

Thud. Thud. Th-. Adam's heart stopped. Like Lucius the bounty hunter, he had another one somewhere. Floating in black, he was no longer part of his body. No longer wearing that face. No longer alone. Around him shone magical stardust and the twinkling constellations of all the people who'd travelled with him. The fiery dragon. The roguish adventurer. The misunderstood sorceress. The pretender prince. The evil genius. The local boy done not so good. The queen of heaven. *The parents he never knew.* The mixed-up minor characters who met their match. The myriad of magic tricks hiding in plain sight. The latent power within, waiting to erupt. Like a heart from beneath the waves, sending a signal to the other side of space. All connected. All at one. Bleeding together and leaving three words to reverberate through the emptiness.

  We were here.

  In the void, and for the final time, a white orb with a red centre emerged. In its hypnotic purity, Adam could sense her again. See her. Touch her. Taste her. Hear her. Smell her. Feel her. Rose-scented perfume. Cherry cola lips. Scarlet petals raining down. A schoolgirl wearing a tartan coat and grey skirt with white socks, sauntering down the corridor. A fluid visual breeze of rolling ruby-coloured hair. The red backpack over her left shoulder, the art folder tucked under her right arm. Pale stardust pirouetting around a supernova smile. Eyes affixed on dancing flames, opening wide to reveal a thousand galaxies within. Seeing red while everyone else saw blue. One of the outsiders. One of the strange ones. *One of them.*

  In the lonesome ocean of the afterlife, a quiet, breathless voice spoke only to him. *I am here now.* Through time and space, Alexis's hand glided out to meet him from paradise. Adam closed his eyes, reached out to touch her fingertips and felt the universe vanish into the infinite space between.

         Wychbold, Worcestershire
          June 2021 – May 2023

Acknowledgments

Thank you to my parents for letting me watch so much science fiction when I was younger. Through them I encountered the cinematic lights who inspired this story: Fritz Lang, Stanley Kubrick, Gene Rodenberry, Ridley Scott, Steven Spielberg, George Lucas and James Cameron.

Writing a novel is like being lost at sea in perennial dark, so my gratitude to those shining stars who guided me through the long, lonely voyage: Dante Alighieri, Frank Kafka, JG Ballard, Raymond Chandler, Emily Brontë, Emily Dickinson and James Joyce.

Much of *The Bleeding Horizon* is coloured by those visionary artists who reached for the heavens no matter the distance: Sandro Botticelli, Michelangelo Buanorrito, Diego Velasquez, Francis Bacon and Mark Rothko.

All of them are dwarfed in influence by the strange human phenomena I've met in person during my time on earth, especially those everyday aliens who walk among us seeing things differently. You are not alone.

And finally, my heartfelt gratitude to the two ladies who've given this schoolboy the time and space to chase his dreams. To my daughter Sofia, who makes an adventurer of me every day, and to my wife Hollie, whose boundless love and patience move the sun and all my other stars.

Il cuore non ha limiti

Printed in Great Britain
by Amazon